HOLMES

VOLUME 2

Six more short stories inspired by the works
of Sir Arthur Conan Doyle

MELVYN SMALL

Published in paperback in 2016 by Sixth Element Publishing
on behalf of Melvyn Small

First Edition

Sixth Element Publishing
Arthur Robinson House
13-14 The Green
Billingham TS23 1EU
Tel: 01642 360253
www.6epublishing.net

© Melvyn Small 2016

ISBN 978-1-908299-96-3

British Library Cataloguing in Publication Data. A catalogue record for this book is available
from the British Library.

Edited and proofread by:
David Forrest
Michael Richardson
Joe Middleton
Robert Myers
Trevor Smith
Michael Streets
Richard Walker

This work is entirely a work of fiction. The names, characters, organisations, places, events
and incidents portrayed are either products of the author's imagination or used in a fictitious
manner. Any resemblance to actual persons, living or dead, or actual events is purely
coincidental.

www.melsmall.com

For the woman x

VOLUME 2

THE BLUE DEBACLE

1

I've never particularly enjoyed early morning starts. My university days rarely saw me making the first of my lectures, with my preference being to plagiarise other, more scholarly students' notes over a pub lunch in the student union bar. That I graduated at all directly opposed the clever money of the back row gambling cabal.

Of late, breakfasts in the Baker Street Kitchen with Holmes had been tending towards brunch. However, on Mary's insistence, and much to the relief of my accountant, things had become somewhat more regimented recently. Consequently, I had "Doctor Spocks", or nine o'clock appointments scheduled on at least three mornings of the week.

Obviously this didn't include Fridays, or dress down Fridays as Holmes called them, when I would shun my usual uniform of suit, shirt and no tie, for a polo and chinos. Early morning starts on a Friday lacked feasibility, largely due to our proclivity to attend the open mic spot at the Irish bar on a Thursday evening.

As I eased myself slowly into the now typical early morning ritual, I flicked on the tablet computer I kept resting on the kitchen worktop and surfed to my usual destination of The Northern Echo website. The headline was dramatic: "Evil Hackers Ransack The

1

Bank". My first thought was this is Middlesbrough, not El Paso. There's more than one bank.

The article gripped me as I flicked on the kettle and threw bread in the toaster. I don't mind telling you it actually filled me with a perverse glee, it seemed to me the ideal case for Holmes and myself. A classic old-school crime caper for us to sink our combined teeth into. With the computing skills Holmes had to hand, we'd have it solved inside a day.

In my fantasy, the expectation was that Holmes and I would dissect the information, much of which was already provided by the Echo, apply some excellent deduction, negotiate a few twists and turns, solve the crime that had set the local press aghast, and celebrate our inevitable success with one over the eight pints of Engineer's Thumb in the Twisted Lip.

As I saw it, Holmes and I were teetering on the brink of becoming local legends. The extrapolation of my thought train led me to the scene of the unveiling of a blue plaque outside my surgery, accompanied by the gentle applause of both local dignitaries and minor celebrities. I envisaged a ceremony in which Mayor Raaz pulled a cord and delivered a gushing eulogy praising our unrivalled investigative brilliance. 'Doctor John Watson', read the sign. 'Psychologist, Author, Detective.' Follow up story in the Evening Gazette, Pulitzer Prize for me when the nationals get hold of it, freedom of the town, all good... That never happened...

As I scraped the last of the margarine across my toast, and contemplated tracking Holmes down ahead of our planned meet late that afternoon, there was a size-twelve knock at the front door.

I answered the door, still chewing on my toast, to be greeted by a vaguely recognisable, well-dressed petite lady, flanked by two burly and rather unnerving uniformed policemen.

"Doctor John Watson?" she enquired.

"Yes," I replied, spitting out some of the contents of my mouth in the process.

Then came a sequence of words I'd only previously witnessed on television. "Doctor John Watson, I'm arresting you on suspicion of being an accessory in the unauthorised access of, and the subsequent theft of funds from, the computer systems of the Panama Swiss Banking Group. You do not have to say anything, but it may harm your defence if you do not mention when questioned something which you later rely on in court. Anything you do say may be given in evidence."

With that, I was pulled out into a crisp September Teesside morning wearing nothing but my stripy pyjama bottoms and a faded University of Sheffield tee shirt. Even the Sweeney let you put your trousers on.

The backseat of a police car was something I was familiar with, however this was the first time I had experienced it as a suspected criminal. Indeed, it was the first time I'd been suspected of anything, since the commonly-held assumption that I fluked my first year anatomy and physiology viva.

I was dreading being seen. Odd really as I'd been in the rear of a police car several times, on the way to some investigation or other, and it had never crossed my mind that I would be thought a criminal. Perhaps it was my attire. Perhaps it was the look of terror seared across my face.

As I was guided into the police station, I demanded that the officer on the reception desk get me Superintendent Spaulding. With him unavailable, or at least that is what I was told, I was cosseted into an anteroom, off the corridor that ran beside the main desk. I was then seated in one of those cheap plastic chairs you find in community centres and subjected to the messy indignation of having my fingerprints taken. Where were they expecting to find my fingerprints? On their account, this was a digital malefaction.

Fingers inked, they then directed me from the anteroom to what I assumed would be a holding cell. En route I spotted Holmes being bundled into a room at the other end of the corridor, for what could only have been a replica procedure.

"Don't tell 'em anything, Doc," he called, "they'll be laughed out of court."

You would think a jail cell exists to serve one purpose: to physically detain a person in body. The imprisonment of the body is irrelevant however, when compared to the constraint it places on the mind. The pure starkness of the domain extends time, dragging it out in front of you. The place was crying out for that 30x fast forward function you use to skip past the adverts on Sky.

As I sat on a mattress not much thicker than the toast I'd been buttering not long since, I struggled to see how anyone could spend time in that box without leaving part of their mind permanently there.

The problem was the absence of a frame of reference. A passing cloud would have sufficed. I suppose it's like travelling at sea, and how a viewable horizon can prevent you from feeling seasick.

In my imagination I could see Holmes, lying on a bed similar to mine, his arms folded, his legs crossed, and his mind completely unfazed by the situation. Whereas my brain was jailed, his would be running free. He would already be working on a disentanglement of this bind we had both found ourselves in. I'm not embarrassed to tell you that the thought actually provided me with some comfort. I gained little solace from my innocence, but took mountains of it from my association with that incredible creature caged only a few feet away.

2

As my arresting officer made her way into the interview room, it dawned on me where I recognised her from. I'd seen her in this setting before, alongside Lestrade. She was the labelless interrogator Holmes had tagged "Razor Cheeks" during her and Lestrade's attempted ruination of Alec and Alice MacGregor, a quite innocent couple erroneously implicated in the series of killings I subsequently chronicled as 'The Case of the Fifty Orange Pills'.

This was the lady that Holmes had developed an intense dislike for, despite, to my knowledge, him never having spoken a word to her. By this point in our association, I trusted his reading of a person enough to feel concerned, even though he'd gathered much of his data on her through a glass wall.

In short, if the scenario wasn't daunting enough, I was facing an acerbic harpy who, to me, made Lestrade look about as terrifying as a Blue Peter presenter. Bad analogy, I'm sorry.

"Interview of Doctor John James Watson commencing at eleven minutes past eleven am, September the third. Detective Inspector Anne Bradstreet questioning with Police Constable George Hardwick in attendance." She sat alone in the seat opposite me, PC Hardwick remaining standing to one side. She didn't hang around. "Could you please explain your involvement in the robbery of the Panama Swiss Bank?"

"Yes," I replied, "none whatsoever. I wasn't involved. I don't believe Holmes was either."

"I never mentioned that we thought Sherlock Holmes may be implicated in this. Why do you say that?"

"Because I saw him in the corridor being manhandled into a room in a similar manner as I was." Given I was being strangled by my insides, I was happy with my retort.

"Doctor, a digital forensic analysis has uncovered a trail leading back to 22 Baker Street, Flat 1B. Your mobile phone records show that on seven out of the twelve times the bank's systems were accessed, you were in the general vicinity of that address."

"I'm not answering any further questions without my solicitor present."

"In the corridor, Holmes told you to keep quiet. Do you have something to hide, Doctor?"

"I don't know what he meant by that. I suspect he was playing with you."

"Playing, Doctor? The funds taken from the bank run into the millions. They're still trying to establish an exact figure. Playing with us, John? This is an extremely serious offence."

"My solicitor," I insisted.

Bradstreet stood up before exhaling audibly through her nostrils, her tightly pursed lips preventing any exhaust from her mouth. Flicking her hands from the resting place on her hips, she then sat back down, clicking off the tape machine as she landed. "Look, John," she said, "let's talk off the record. I don't know any more about this computer gubbins than you do. What I do know is I've spoken to Holmes and he isn't doing himself any favours. I can't get a sensible word out of him." She paused to suggest some empathy with my predicament. "I know he's your friend, but if he's done this job, for whatever reason, you need to tell me what you know. You don't want to go down with him."

I was both annoyed and insulted with her far too obvious interview strategy, divide and turn us against each other, plumb into the basic human instinct of self-preservation. From the outset, she'd completely misunderstood me. I would have given myself up for Holmes on any day.

"I don't know anything," I responded. Then, against my better judgement, I went into bat for Holmes. "You can't imagine Sherlock Holmes. He's like nothing you've ever seen. It's not in his psyche to commit a crime for personal gain."

"Maybe he was motivated by something else?" said Bradstreet. "The intellectual challenge. I'm told this was a massive undertaking that would have required months of planning and preparation. Maybe this was his masterpiece, his chef d'oeuvre."

"No," I retorted, "his monument won't be grandiose. Size doesn't matter. His interest lies in the simple, the atomic. He'd garner more satisfaction from predicting which way a fly walked across a beer tray than putting a man on Mars.

"His mind is singularly unique. At first I thought he had Asperger's but that's not it. His character and mood veer all over the place, he jumps in and out of this reality. I even thought he was bipolar, but there are more than two states of mind, three, four maybe, five even. Sometimes he chatters like an excited child, sometimes he drifts in silence around another realm. Then there are the dark ruinous moods, where his grip on the will to live seems so utterly tenuous.

"He won't place any consideration into how serious this is, it's just another puzzle to figure out. He won't vary his method on circumstance. He's toying with you, playing games. He'll already know more about you then you'll ever know about him."

"You say he's not motivated by money, but he has no apparent means of income," she commented.

"He's got investments or something. Martha mentioned them once. However much has gone missing, what would he spend it on? He wears the same clothes, he doesn't drive and I've only ever seen him eat cereal and toast. Oh yeah, and the odd parmo. He's like the Cynic of Sinope, living naked in a jar... Ah," I gasped, interrupting myself.

"What?" seized Bradstreet, I assumed in the hope that I'd recalled something to incriminate my friend.

"The Diogenes Club, Mycroft must have named it after him." Regardless of the circumstances I found myself in, I had to smile.

"What are you rambling on about? You're worse than him."

"His brother, Mycroft runs a club in Stockton, The Diogenes. He must have named it after Holmes. Diogenes of Sinope, the chap who shunned all possessions and made a virtue of poverty. Holmes is not your man."

I sat back, having said a lot more than I'd intended. Maybe Bradstreet's technique was more sophisticated than I'd given her credit for. Holmes wasn't involved in this. He had no reason to be. Not the Holmes I knew.

Ironically the most compelling fact, the fact that confirmed his innocence, was that he'd been caught. If Holmes had done it, they would never have tracked it back to him so easily.

Some insight into Holmes' computing talent would have confirmed this. There was many an example to demonstrate how he could have easily removed monies from whatever account he had wished to, with no suggestion of a trace. The problem was these examples would do nothing but incriminate him on other, if well-intentioned, not particularly legal activities.

3

Previous to this, I'd considered my solicitor somewhat of a freeloader. Someone more interested in invoicing than representing my interests. However, within moments of his arrival the following day and the first ten sentences exchanged with Detective Inspector Bradstreet, he had mentioned the phrase "wrongful arrest" seventeen times. If he'd have been as successful during my divorce negotiations, I may have got to keep the car and the barbeque, instead of them going to my non-driving, vegetarian ex-wife.

I exited the police station into quite a throng. This was more due to Holmes' notoriety than any reflected glory cast upon me. The crowd comprised both local journalists and members of the community, some of whom carried banners featuring slogans such as 'Free the Boro 2'.

"John, over here," shouted Mary from her car, parked a short distance away. Without even the courtesy of a "no comment", I pushed my way through the phalanx and jumped into the passenger seat. Mary looked at me; no words were required. It appeared my recently established innocence was short-lived. As she pulled away, several of the journalists took opportune snap shots through the car's windscreen.

Mary tried to speak to me several times on the short distance across town to Baker Street. Each time she looked at me, her eyes narrowed in disappointment. She was clearly annoyed with me, however with my admonishment not forthcoming, I decided to state my defence.

"Mary," I appealed, "neither Holmes nor I have done anything wrong."

"Sherlock has done nothing wrong?" she replied in sarcastic despair.

"Okay," I revised, "this thing with the bank has nothing to do with us."

"Then why did the police drag you both out of your beds this morning?"

"They got it wrong. Holmes and I aren't bank robbers, for goodness sake."

"I know," she conceded as she pulled up outside Hud Couture, "but I've still been worried to death. You go and get Martha to put the kettle on, I need to get back to the pub. There's only me on today, so I had to lock the door. I'll come and see you later and we can figure out what to do with this mess."

Martha's mood was in sharp contrast and lacking concern. "You're out then," she said dismissively, hardly diverted from her work. "What about Sherlock? Where's he?"

"I'm not sure," I replied, feeling I'd somehow deserted my friend.

Martha stopped busying herself to address me. "Don't worry, flower, he'll sort it. Sherlock Holmes isn't a bloody bank robber. Although when they all rocked up this morning, I thought they'd come for Al Capone. There was about twenty of 'em."

"What time was this?" I asked.

"I dunno," she replied, "about seven. He was giving them loads but then just seemed to give up and jump into one of the cars."

"It's not like he was going to win that argument," I commented.

"No," pondered Martha, "but it was odd the way he gave in like he did. He seemed to turn on a shilling."

I was as bewildered as Martha, however our combined deliberation was interrupted by a figure at the door.

"Mycro, you old geezer," shrieked Martha, "come and give Lil' Sis a big squeeze."

"Hey, Honey Bunny," smiled Mycroft, "it's been too long."

He broke off their hug to address her. "Have you thought any more about my proposal?"

"I never stop thinking about it, Darl, but I'm still a little bit married."

"Ah, Ma, what are you doing to me? Ditch him, he's a peckerhead."

Martha's response was vaguely muted. To her knowledge, her husband was dead, but this wasn't something she was about to share. Instead she just smiled and resumed their hug, this serving to obscure any emotion betrayed by her face.

"Ye-ah," said Mycroft, "some chick rocked up at the club yesterday, riffing a load of questions about our kid. Apparently he's been booked in at the Hotel Alcatraz again. I wonder how she tracked him back to me?"

"That won't have been that hard, my mate," said Martha. "I'm guessing she was some sort of detective, and you do have the same surname. It wouldn't have been hard, Sweetie."

"Was she a diminutive rather angular woman?" I asked.

Mycroft stared back at me confused.

"Was she a skinny little short-arse?" clarified Martha.

"Yeah," said Mycroft in drawn out confirmation.

"Actually I might be to blame for that," I said. "I kind of let it slip when I figured you'd named the club after Sherlock."

"What?" he replied, puzzled, Martha also interested in my assertion.

"Diogenes of Sinope, the Cynic, the guy who gave away all his stuff believing poverty a virtue."

Both Mycroft and Martha looked back at me blankly.

"You know," I continued, "he carried a torch in the day time claiming to be looking for an honest man. Sherlock has no possessions, except for all those books which I don't think he ever reads. I don't think I've met a more frugal bloke and he certainly doesn't believe anyone is particularly honest. Sherlock is Diogenes."

"Frugal?" queried Mycroft. "The little fucker's loaded."

"What?" I remarked.

"Yeah," said Martha, "he's got hundreds of thousands stacked up in bonds and investments and stuff."

"Really? He hardly spends a thing. So the club's not named after him?"

"No, man," replied Mycroft. "I just thought it was a cool name. I thought Diogenes played for Brazil."

"Has he not told you about the curse of dimensionality?" asked Martha, accentuating the last three words. "He's bored me to death with it."

"No."

"Yeah, it's some mathematical puzzle thing. He made a computer programme to solve it. That's what he uses for his investing. The little git's made thousands."

"It's just a few lines of code but it's real clever monkeys, man," added Mycroft.

"It wouldn't surprise me if he isn't a millionaire," said Martha.

I was flabbergasted. "A millionaire? I bet I've bought him hundreds of beers and I don't think he's returned the favour more than four times."

"Don't get me wrong," said Mycroft, "our kid's not tight, he'd give you the shirt off his back. He just can't be arsed to go to the bar. He thinks it's admin."

I was lost for words. Not two hours before I was using my insight into his character to reassure the police of his innocence, and it was transpiring that I hardly knew him at all.

"We need to get him out," blurted Mycroft. "Before Sunday. If our mam finds out, she'll go mental."

"He has a mother?"

"Of course, dude, he's not the man who fell to fucking earth."

"What about a father?"

"Nah. The old fella, God bless him, died a while back. That's why Sherl goes over every Sunday to take our mam out for dinner. To make sure the old girl's getting her veggies and that."

"Does he? I never knew that. I mean I never see him on a Sunday but I assumed he was just sleeping off Saturday night excess."

"Yeah, have you not noticed on Monday how he's always had a shave? He takes her up the Welly, or down the Kings maybe if it's raining. I try to get over too, but with the nippers and the club and everything it's not always easy. Does he still use your cab, Marth?"

"No, he bloody doesn't," she snapped.

"Filled it with petrol, did he? I knew he would. Fucking idiot."

"Hang on," I said, "he's been in prison before. Surely your mother is used to him spending a little time at Her Majesty's pleasure?"

"Ah yeah, no," responded Mycroft, "last time we told her he was on a kibbutz. That worked out quite well 'cos he came back really skinny. Our Ma was too busy feeding him back up to ask any questions. Although she still keeps asking when she's gonna see the photos."

4

The next day Mary and I visited Detective Inspector Lestrade in hospital. Following the explosion of his car on Baker Street, the poor chap was in some state. Despite Holmes' intervention, he had taken quite a blast and, to ease his recovery, the doctors had induced him into a coma.

We entered the room to find Constable Hardwick with a rather attractive lady, who turned out to be Lestrade's wife. Given Lestrade's appearance and manner, she was somewhat of a surprise. Disregarding Lestrade, she was someone who would undoubtedly turn heads.

"How is he?" asked Mary.

"We really don't know," responded a distressed Mrs Lestrade. "They're not telling us much. His breathing seems to be improving but I don't know how much of that is the machine."

In order to establish a more informed view, I left the room to hunt down the consultant. When I caught up with him, I learned little, and drew the conclusion that there was an unhealthy level of medical uncertainty clouding Lestrade's status.

On re-entering the room, I couldn't bring myself to sow any false hopes. My urge was to provide reassurance, but it seemed wrong to do so. "We've just got to wait and see," I told her. Her downtrodden look suggested she'd expected no more.

We sat there in relative silence, the only soundtrack provided by Lestrade's mechanically-aided breathing. An hour or so after we arrived, we made our excuses and left.

Hardwick caught up with us as we made our way down the corridor. "Can we have a word later?" he asked. "I'll see you in the Lip after I've dropped Catherine off. In a couple of hours maybe?"

"Okay," I agreed, surprised but interested by his request.

It was sad to see Lestrade in such a state. At a surface level, he wasn't the most likeable of chaps, but I always felt his intentions were good. He was just clumsy. I was sure Holmes would endorse my mood. He took every opportunity to goad and harass the inspector, but it was easy to assume there was a semblance of respect. Holmes, battered by the attentions of a certain Sebastian Moran had, after all, raced down Baker Street in an attempt to save the inspector's life, reaching him just as his car exploded. If Holmes had not made this intervention, perhaps Lestrade's brave fight for life would have already concluded.

I once queried Holmes on the antagonism he directed at Lestrade. His justification was that it was a strategy to unbalance him. He claimed that Lestrade had had it in for him ever since his conviction for a cyber-attack on a payday loans company called Wad Wappers. Thinking Holmes escaped lightly with a short custodial sentence, coupled with a series of addiction counselling sessions, actually directed by myself, there was unfinished business. If Holmes were to falter again, Lestrade was determined he would be the one to catch him. In fact, Holmes had meandered across the lines of legitimacy several times to my knowledge. It was doubtful whether Holmes' goading of Lestrade had anything to do with him remaining well outside the inspector's clutches, he was simply smarter than him.

Justification aside, it must be said that Holmes did apply a disproportionately high amount of zeal in his mockery. Holmes was a man of extremes. On more than one occasion, he told me how his preference was to view the world in binary.

Given the earlier revelations, which had opened up new facets of Holmes' character, I was starting to doubt my own opinions. Moments before Holmes had risked his own life in the rescue of Lestrade, he had been typically scathing in his assessment of the inspector. But even if the vitriol Holmes regularly flung at Lestrade was real, he couldn't despise him enough to allow him to walk to his death, surely? Then there was Holmes' response in the aftermath of the explosion and the way he nursed Lestrade until the arrival of the ambulance, urging him to cling on to what looked like the last threads of life.

Okay, I thought, how would Holmes approach this? What were the scenarios that fitted the available facts? If Holmes' disdain for Lestrade was manufactured, then his reaction to his injuries did make sense. It was no more than the concern you would expect one human being to show another.

What else? Maybe Holmes bore some responsibility for the explosion. Perhaps he had planted the bomb and had, at the last moment, thought better of it. It was fanciful but it would explain how he knew the bomb was there. How else would he have known unless he planted it, or at least was in league with those that did?

I relived the events running up to the explosion in my mind. If Holmes was aware of the bomb, then he was some actor. But then I'd seen that in him. He was an excellent actor. I'd seen him transform his personality directly in front of me. He used it as a disguise.

My train of thought took me to a darker and darker place. Was the man who had grown into my friend a perfect imposter?

5

Hardwick turned into the Twisted Lip around the time we'd agreed. With myself nursing the dregs of a pint, he asked me if I wanted a refill before joining me at my table.

I cautioned him as he sat. "Should we really be speaking? I'm both a suspect and a witness in a case you and your colleagues are investigating."

"Probably not," he said, "but Sherlock's a mate and he needs some help. You need to somehow get a word with him. Bradstreet has got him by the throat and he's just making it worse. He needs to stop pissing around."

Given my current tendency for suspicion, I was uncertain as to Hardwick's motives. " 'A mate?' " I queried. "You've never seemed particularly pally to me."

"Look," sighed Hardwick, "a while back my niece went missing. We feared the worst, but Holmes found her and had her back home within three hours. He left his dad's death bed to help. When he got back, the old fella had passed away. Helping us meant he never got to say goodbye." He looked at me with appeal in his eyes. "He never mentioned that once. I wouldn't have even known if Mycro hadn't let slip months later."

I relaxed back in my seat ready to listen.

"You really need to know Bradstreet," said Hardwick. "She's psychotic. The joke around the station is she went to officer training college in Auschwitz. Some of the lads call her 'Stalin's Darling'."

"Sherlock certainly saw something in her he didn't like," I interjected.

"She's determined to lay this at his door," he continued. "She's not bothered who actually did it. Who cares about a bank getting done over? This is not about justice, it's about her career. Sherlock Holmes would be a massive feather in her cap. She's after Lestrade's chair while the poor sod's laid up in hospital. Holmes just isn't taking this seriously enough. He just sits there taking the piss. The tapes of the interviews are circulating around the station. They're hilarious. Yesterday he asked her how she managed to sit down with that plum up her arse, then, when she was called away, he told the observing officer she had a meeting with the Royal Mail. Modelling for the next stamp." I just listened, as Holmes would have perhaps done. "When she told him the inspector was still in a coma, he told her that was his favourite Smiths song."

Hardwick explained how Bradstreet had reviewed the cases Holmes had been involved with and had formed the opinion that, given the information available, Holmes couldn't have drawn the conclusions he had done, unless he'd had some sort of inside information at his disposal.

"Mister Holmes," she had said, "if this is true, you are quite incredible, I'm in awe."

"You know what the problem here is, don't you?" Holmes had replied. "It's you. Yup, you should never meet your heroes."

DI Bradstreet had then rounded on the robbery of the Panama Swiss Bank. The techniques used to access the bank's systems bore all the hallmarks of the organic attack method pioneered by Holmes. The theft from the bank, she had postulated, was the real reason Holmes had created the technique in the first place. This was the opus he had worked towards over a number of years.

Holmes' only response to this accusation was to ask Bradstreet if she had any siblings. She had snapped at him, telling him she had a sister, and he had responded by asking if she wished she'd been an only child.

"You need to speak to him," said Hardwick. "He's walking himself straight into prison. He's even refused legal representation. Says he can defend himself."

"How can I?" I asked. "They think I'm involved with this. They won't let me anywhere near him."

"Ask the super. He must owe you a favour. He certainly owes Holmes one, after he saved Lestrade's arse. I'm sure he'll be able to wangle something."

In complete contradiction to my intuition, I found myself making the return journey to Middlesbrough police station, not particularly long after I'd been extricated from it. On reaching the desk, I requested an audience with Superintendent Spaulding. With him now available, I was ushered into his office to be greeted by him and Detective Inspector Bradstreet.

"Hello, John," he said, offering his hand. "You know I appreciate all the help yourself and Holmes have given us lately, but I need to play this straight down the line. That's why I have pulled DI Bradstreet into this chat as investigating officer."

Bradstreet stood silently to attention by his desk, clearly annoyed by my visit. She was just as frightening whilst mute and motionless. I explained my concerns to Spaulding, and how I was worried that Holmes was not taking his situation seriously enough. I convinced him that if I were given the chance to speak to Holmes, there was a chance I could get him to adjust his outlook and be more cooperative. Spaulding agreed and told me it was important to convince Holmes to accept legal representation.

"Sir," interrupted Bradstreet, "I'm not sure this is wise. Any collusion between Holmes and Watson could be detrimental to the investigation."

"What's important here, Inspector, is that we get to the truth," asserted the superintendent.

Bradstreet was visibly annoyed at the castigation but offered no response, other than that displayed by her body language.

DI Bradstreet and I filed into the interview suite to find Holmes already seated.

"Doc," said Holmes gleefully as he looked up at me. "Did you have to bring Laughing Gas with you?" he appended, directing a look of scorn at Bradstreet. "Missus Bradstreet, you've shaved," he smiled. "There's really no need to put yourself out for me."

Putting pleasantries aside, I got straight to the point. "Sherlock, you've got to stop messing around. This is serious."

"This is not serious, Doc, this is just money. Nobody dies," he interrupted.

"It is serious, they could put you in prison for a very long time. Ten, fifteen years maybe."

"Twenty," interjected DI Bradstreet.

Holmes was having none of it. "You know she really enjoys her work. She strip searches me every day. I think it's been a while since she, you know... I've grown to love the smell of latex in a morning."

"Sherlock," I bleated in frustration.

"Trust me, Doc," he said calmly, before sitting back in his chair.

On those few words, I was turned around. I was comforted by the thought that the clowning Holmes was not the dominant personality. I was sure he had a plan. I'd seen that face before.

He then snapped shut, reverting to the irrelevant. "Nice weather we're having," he said, "quite merry for this time of year."

It was an odd turn of phrase, that hardly sat with any of the characters I'd seen Holmes portray.

6

By all accounts, Holmes' appearance in front of the magistrates' court did not go well. A desperate outlook being cut worse by a previous altercation between Holmes and one of the presiding judges.

Not that Holmes was particularly concerned. He made no plea and offered no defence.

This was much to the frustration of the court. He was urged to engage but was not forthcoming. As he was led from the court past DI Bradstreet, he flinched as if she'd goosed him. Apparently his mockery did little to tarnish the shine from her victory.

I visited Holmes at the earliest opportunity. It was a new experience for me. In spite of the work I undertook counselling ex-convicts, I had to that date avoided a prison visit. On reaching HMP Holme House, I was taken to the visitors' area. It was a large room of neatly spaced tables, reminiscent of an examination hall.

I had hung my hopes on him walking out of the magistrates' court a free man. Reasoning that there was method in the particular madness of his approach, I'd expected him to deliver a perfectly reasoned defence.

My first concern was to his state of mind. "How are you coping?" I asked.

"I'm fine," he smiled. "I've only been here a few hours. I'm a bit pissed off they didn't give me me old room, but you can't have everything."

"Sherlock, this is not funny," I remarked.

"Don't worry, Doc," he replied, "it'll be fine. It didn't do Nelson Mandela any harm. Oh, maybe they'll do a charity record for me: 'Free-ee Sherlock Holmes,' aw if only John Lennon was still alive. He'd be all over this."

I interrupted his japery to ask him the crucial question. "Did you do it?"

Holmes shot a look at a nearby prison guard. The inference being that he couldn't speak freely enough to provide an accurate response. To me that didn't matter. It was about time he stopped clowning around and started answering some questions with responses other than jest. If I was to be his interrogator, then so be it.

"Of course not," smiled a confident Holmes, looking up to gauge the prison officer's response.

"There was a digital trail leading right to your door."

"Geez, Doc," he protested, "you're worse than Pigeon Thighs."

I didn't respond, wishing to reinforce the seriousness of the circumstances.

"Okay," he exhaled, "that's dead easy to do. Remember a while back when all those celebrity nudes got leaked? I fancied a squint so I piggybacked in on the IP address of Lestrade's works computer. I bet he still hasn't figured out why he keeps getting a nod and a wink from the IT guy."

There was a muffled chuckle from the prison guard.

"It's disappointing that the Five O have been so easily confused," he said. "I'm clever enough to rob the place, but daft enough not to cover my tracks. What am I? One or the other? I can't be both. The coin can't land on both sides."

"Could you prove that?" I asked. "Enough to convince Bradstreet?"

"You've got to be kidding. She's fucking biscuits."

I had to agree. Following the brief contact I'd had with her, I was left with the view that she saw the facts of the matter as no more than a minor inconvenience.

"How did you know the bomb was there, Sherlock?"

"Bloody hell, Doc, are you pinning that on me as well? I nearly had my head blown off saving that fat bastard. How is he anyway?"

"Not good actually. The doctors seem to be at a bit of a loss."

"He'll be alright," reassured Holmes, "he's a tough owld bugger."

"Sherlock, how did you know?"

"You're serious, aren't you? Shine a light in my eyes, why don't yer?"

Again I stayed silent, awaiting an answer.

"The wheel," he sighed. "The way it was turned away from the kerb. He couldn't have left it parked like that. Someone had to have been messing about with it."

"Who?"

"Dunno. No data."

"The Professor?"

His expression was that of a maybe.

"You'll never guess who's in here," he said, the pitch of his voice lifting a semitone.

"Half the BBC?"

My joke eluded him, prompting no more than a confused dismissal. "Sebastian Moran," he replied.

"Fancy Round Three, d'you?"

"I reckon I'd have him next time."

"I'm not sure you would, Sherlock. I think it's better if you stay well away."

Holmes raised his brow in quasi affront.

"What's the weather like out there?" he responded somewhat tangentially.

I left the visiting area, my mind a mélange of jostling thoughts and theories. That was the second time in two meetings that Holmes had referenced the weather. Other than an occasional gripe about the wind buffeting along Albert Road, I didn't recall a propensity for meteorology. I dismissed this as the narrowed fascination of a prisoner.

Perhaps the comment that stuck out was the one of Colonel Sebastian Moran. Holmes had played a major part in the arrest of Moran for the torture and murder of a local property landlord called

Davy Arrowsmith. Holmes' involvement had included two violent struggles with Moran, one which could be perhaps classified a draw, and another which was an unarguable loss for Holmes.

I rapidly formed the conclusion that Moran was key to the whole affair. The scenario formed before my eyes. The lack of a struggle displayed by Holmes on his passage to prison could be explained easily by him wanting to meet up with Moran again. I was concerned he was bent on revenge and the consequences might be dire.

Maybe Holmes had robbed the bank after all, not for monetary gain, but to get at Moran. Was it so outlandish? Despite his protestations, if he had done it, it made sense to leave the trail that led back to him. All the facts were slotting into place.

There was a possibility that it wasn't Holmes that did the robbery, but that he was taking advantage of circumstance to plot a route to Moran. I just couldn't see Holmes doing that. He never relied on chance. He didn't grasp at opportunities, he engineered them.

The more I racked my brain, the more I was distracted by something Holmes once told me: "This detection lark is a lot easier if you know something other people don't." What did I know that was unique? After the insight I'd recently gained into Holmes' background and character, I was beginning to wonder if I knew anything about him at all. He played characters. They were his disguise. Was the Holmes I knew nothing more than a charade?

I returned to Mary and the Twisted Lip to find Detective Inspector Bradstreet waiting for me.

"I believe you've been to see my friend Sherlock. How's he getting along?" she asked.

"He's doing just fine," I replied.

"Yes, but then this is not his first time, is it? I've been reading up on the Wad Wappers case. A very similar MO as the Americans might put it."

"It's entirely different. Holmes didn't take any personal gain from that," I said before quipping, "Except of course for the twelve weeks of free treatment he got from me."

"No monetary gain, no. Just the satisfaction of wronging a

right. Many people think the regulators let the Panama Swiss Bank off lightly following their involvement in that recent tax evasion scandal."

"Did they?" I queried, this not being something I was particularly aware of.

"Has Holmes ever spoken about the bank to you?"

"No, I think his only interest in the bank is the recept …" I was struck by a thought.

"Sorry, Doctor, you were saying?"

"Yeah sorry, I've just remembered I haven't paid my credit card bill. It's easy to forget when people keep dragging you off to jail." Not thinking she believed that, I quickly continued. "Holmes has never mentioned the bank. Other than that one time with Wad Wappers, which happened before I knew him, I've never seen him as someone who would go on some sort of crusade. He's just not that principled. At least I don't think he is. Besides, the tax evasion thing was about stealing from the tax man. Holmes' consternation with Wad Wappers was about their treatment of the normal hardworking people."

Bradstreet seemed to be frustrated by my view. "What about the bomb? How did he know about that?"

"How do you know we've even discussed that?" I asked.

"Walls have ears."

"As do prison guards," I retorted. "So you must already know."

"I'd rather hear it from you."

"Observation. Nothing escapes Holmes. Even the finest minutiae viewed in his periphery. He noticed the car wheel was at a strange angle and, in what, a second, he concluded that something was wrong, and the car had been interfered with." None of this was really what Bradstreet wanted to hear. "He didn't make a decision to save your colleague's life, there wasn't time. He acted on instinct. That tells you as much about Sherlock Holmes as you need to know."

"So who could have planted the bomb?"

"We don't know," I replied. "No data."

Bradstreet exhaled as she rose to her feet, offering her hand before leaving.

7

Merryweather, Merryweather! Holmes hadn't turned into a weather girl, he was trying to tell me something. A woman we once met at the bank, the bank that was robbed, was called Miss Merryweather. That's why he described the weather as "merry". The clue to this whole debacle must lay with her.

Following recently enhanced diligence, I had a full diary. As I worked through my appointments, I mulled over my approach to Miss Merryweather. With the excitement elsewhere, it was a long morning.

We'd met Miss Merryweather on two occasions, both times within the context of cases Holmes and I were investigating. The inescapable irony was that one of these meetings was during our investigation of 'The Case of the Goldfish Bowl', when we attempted to foil the robbery of the very bank that Holmes was now in prison for robbing. As it transpired, there appeared no robbery to foil. Indeed that whole case seemed less about goldfish and more about red herrings. In our defence, it was early in our detecting careers and we were still learning.

I'd like to tell you I threw myself into my work through that day, but in all honesty it was more of a stumble. I'm sure I was giving my patients the level of attention they deserved, but as I scanned down the paperwork it screamed, 'Dull, dull, dull'.

Only one name stood out, that of 'Ernie Radle'. This was a new one. Who on earth was called Ernie any more? The accompanying documentation didn't offer many clues.

As was the habit I'd fallen into over the years, I spoke to my next patient without looking up from my desk. "Hello, please take a seat."

"Hello, Doctor, would you like me to slip behind the screen and remove my clothes?" I looked up to see a familiar face. Irene Adler, the woman, the woman whose brief liaison had had such a profound effect on Holmes. "Well? On or off?"

"On, I think, Irene. The grip I have on my career is fragile enough as it is."

"Oh well, don't say I didn't offer," she said, flirting a mischievous smile.

"Ernie Radle?" I asked, as she took her seat.

"Anagrammatically, yes."

I nodded, not feeling that was a clue I should have unpicked.

"It seems we have a problem. My beloved has been incarcerated by those nasty policemen. What are we to do?"

"How do you even know that?" I asked. "You've come from another country. You have a slight tan. The tan of someone who lives in a hot country, not the type you get on holiday. News of Holmes' incarceration won't have travelled that far and wide."

"I dreamt he died," she replied, with a tone of pensivity. "The dream was so lucid I had to allay my fears. I checked the internet and the Northern Echo website told me he was alive, if not well, and residing at Her Majesty's pleasure."

"Indeed," I remarked. "But where have you been all this time? And you're married."

Irene raised her eyebrows, impressed, I hope, by my building deductive skills, and my noticing of the slightly lighter skin on her wedding ring finger. "Yes, I'm now Irene Norton," she said. "But I still tend to use my professional name when I'm on away days. I married the governor of Arkansas, three, four months ago. My husband, Frey, is talking about running for President."

"You could become the first lady? Perish the thought."

"Yes. Imagine the mischief that would allow."

"So what does your husband think of you dashing halfway across the world to the aid of another man?"

"You know, I'm not sure I mentioned it."

"It's a marriage based on trust then."

"Yes, of course. I trust him implicitly to do just as I expect him to. The only pity is he's not asked me to join in. Some of those interns are quite pretty, and what's good for the goose…"

The rest of Irene's sentence was cropped by a smile and I suspect the realisation that she was exposing more information than circumstances required.

I appraised Irene of the situation and she sat in silence for a while pondering the information I had imparted. "I need to see him," she said on my conclusion.

"I'm not sure that's a good idea, Irene. He's acting a bit odd at the minute and goodness knows what he'll make of 'Irene Norton'."

Irene registered the thought, but made no comment. "I'll not tell him," she said.

"If I can deduce that you're a married woman, Irene, I'm quite sure Sherlock Holmes will have no problem doing the same."

"I'll wear gloves."

"That'll not fool him."

"I think it will, Doctor. I have a talent. I can unbalance a man. Even the beautiful creature that is Sherlock Holmes. You shouldn't underestimate me."

"I wouldn't dare," I conceded.

"Right," she chirped, "so how are we going to get me to see him? Sherlock Holmes is not a bank robber. We need to sort this mess out, before the old man realises I'm missing."

Getting Irene to see Holmes wasn't going to be easy. The prison service doesn't let just anyone roll in off the street. It was a struggle for me to arrange my visit, my assumption being that my request had ultimately been sanctioned by Superintendent Spaulding.

Irene was dismissive. "Don't you understand the power of a lie, Doctor. Tell them I'm his long lost cousin from New Zealand or something."

"It doesn't seem very believable that you would fly halfway around the world just to visit someone on remand."

"Does it ask for air miles on the form? Besides, little inconsistencies add to the lie. Give it some validity. It doesn't have to ring true. It just has to ring. People believe what they want to."

In actual fact, our passage to the packed visitors' room was surprisingly easy. I assumed the quantity of paperwork involved reduced the chance of it ever being read. Irene, dressed in a figure-hugging knee-length black dress, with matching long gloves, and black stockings and shoes, had the whole room aghast. Apparently the sexy widow look was quite popular among the prison fraternity.

Holmes will have known we were coming, however he still appeared perturbed as Irene and I sat at his table.

"Are you okay, Sherlock?" asked Irene. "You look like you've seen a ghost."

"Must be the prison food," he replied, a dry nervousness in his voice. "Will you be staying long? We're having a football match against the guards later and I want to get me bets on."

"Don't be like that, Sherlock," purred Irene. "I haven't seen you in ages."

"I never expected to see you again," he murmured, pensively fading into the distance. "This prison had no walls until now."

The exuberance Irene entered with stuttered. "Do you hate me, Sherlock?" she asked with a soft seriousness.

Holmes smiled a whisky-wry smile under the briefest of nasal exhalations. "No, it's worse than that," he replied, nodding a glassy-eyed acceptance.

"Would you rather I hadn't come?"

"Yes."

"I couldn't leave you languishing, my love," she said quietly, before rescuing the mood with a snapping return to her ebullience. "Now who do I have to sleep with to get you out of here?"

The prison guards watching over us shuffled on their feet with fallacious anticipation.

"Don't you worry about me," said Holmes. "I'm fine. I'm just in here saving a bit of rent."

"No, you're not," I interjected, "Martha's still charging. By the way, she sends her love. It's a shame you're banged up in here," I continued, "the weather out there is lovely. Quite merry."

Holmes shot a look at the nearby prison guards who then moved out of earshot.

"That's quite a trick," commented Irene. "You must teach me that."

"I've been feeding them horse racing tips."

"Quid pro quo?" I remarked.

"I don't know what the stake is," he retorted, his gaze still glued to Irene.

"So, Sherlock," I whispered, "do you think Miss Merryweather is key to this whole caper?"

"No."

"So why the cryptic clue?"

"I just think she's worth talking to. Just a feeling really. Those two blokes we met. You might wanna ask her about them. Yeah, and I probably wouldn't mention it to Bradstreet."

"Detective Inspector Bradstreet has the working assumption that Sherlock is guilty," I explained to Irene. "She's too wrapped up in herself to care what has actually happened."

"Personality issues?" queried Irene. "Maybe that's something we can exploit."

"Possibly," I responded, "I also see signs of sexual repression."

"Yeah but who would?" said Holmes. "It would be like shagging an ironing board."

"That's not helpful, Sherlock," castigated Irene, "and profanity doesn't suit you. You should be directing your energies into getting yourself out of here. Prove that those unique skills I've read so much about are a bit more than tuppenny magic tricks."

Holmes' face dropped in dismay. He looked injured by a comment half founded in jest. "Logic is rare," he whispered through a dry throat.

I'm quite sure Irene hadn't expected her barb to embed as it did.

"I'm sorry," she said in bewildered response, "I haven't come here to upset you."

"If I didn't love you so much, you couldn't cut me so deep," muttered a vacant Holmes. It was an odd line, with a poignancy diminished by its delivery. I assumed it was stolen, probably from some song lyric or other.

Irene didn't respond. It struck me that she was fast discovering the extent of the debilitating effect she had on Holmes, and how

27

she could slay him with the most innocuous of comments. She was unaware of the singularly unique hold she had on him.

Holmes looked to me, thus diverting the moment. "Go with your instinct, John. You don't do enough of that. It's better to go up a dead end than nowhere at all. The learning comes from the journey not the destination."

I nodded, however my instinct was something I was rapidly losing faith in. It felt that, along with a few preconceptions, it had been shot to pieces.

"I've had a word with our mate," chirped Holmes, changing both the tack and the tone of the conversation.

"Sebastian Moran?" I presumed, checking Holmes' face to see if any of the previous damage had been reinstated.

"Yeah," he continued, "we're actually getting on quite well. Well, we're not at the point of dropping soap in the showers, but he is opening up to me."

"What's he got to say?" I asked.

"He's been talking a lot about this mysterious Professor bloke. Actually, he doesn't know a lot more than us, but he reckons he's a bit of a headline act. Saturday night, main stage."

"Involved in what?"

"Anything you want, mate. Anything from Scooby snacks to murder by numbers. Can you imagine if crime was like Woolco? You know, everything from pick 'n' mix to Dunlop radials. That's our Professor."

"What? D'you mean some sort of criminal odd job man?"

"A bit more than that, Doc. He's top drawer."

I turned to Irene who was listening quietly to our interchange. "You have an association with this chap. Remember that media file you were in possession of when we first met? We think that those two meat heads that grabbed you were only the foot soldiers. Lurking in the background there is someone we now know as 'the Professor'."

"Yeah, but it's more than just him and a couple of head the balls," continued Holmes. "He's got people all around the world."

Irene looked a lot calmer than I expected.

"Well, I've got nothing they want," she said.

"You know what was on that file," I pointed out.

Irene just smiled. She still wasn't about to reveal anything of the file's contents to us, and it was clear Holmes wasn't expecting Irene to be forthcoming.

"I've also been having a few chats about this bank job," said Holmes. "You know there's a bit of a criminal element in here. The word on the street, well the landing, is that it was an inside job. The general feeling is it's well outside the CV of any of the local villains."

"So where do we go now?" I asked.

"Wherever it takes you," he said. "This is one for you, Doc. There's not much more I can do from in here. It's time for you to get me out."

I felt sick with the weight of responsibility. "How?" I appealed.

"Follow your instinct."

"What if I can't do it? What if I can't get you out?"

"What's can't? There ain't no can'ts," smiled Holmes. "Follow your instincts."

As we set to leave, Irene took a diversion and walked over to one of the guards; without speaking, her nose less than two inches from his, she looked him square in the face. He stared back, his face a blend of uncertainty and nervousness. Irene pursed her lips, shook her head, and zipped up his fly.

The room, that, to a man and woman had tracked her progress, erupted in laughter.

Irene and I convened in the Irish bar on Bedford Street to plan our next steps. Clearly, the bank and Miss Merryweather were the obvious port of call, but how were we to approach her? Given there was an ongoing investigation into its robbery, and I was associated with the main suspect, an official approach seemed pointless. Had he not been laid in a coma, Lestrade might have been able to secure access, however Detective Inspector Bradstreet was not going to be so accommodating. Besides, Holmes had warned against her inclusion.

We were left with one option, an informal approach outside her work hours. Bargaining that Miss Merryweather was in work that day, Irene agreed to meet outside the bank at four o'clock.

Irene's egress from the bar was interrupted by Mycroft's entry. Her effect on Holmes' brother was instantaneous. "Mycroft Holmes, at your service," he said, almost bowing as he offered her his hand.

"Irene Adler," she responded with a tight-lipped smile.

"Mycroft is Sherlock's brother," I clarified. "Irene is a friend of Sherlock's."

"Surely not," remarked Mycroft.

"We've just come back from visiting Sherlock," I interrupted.

"Yeah, man," said Mycroft, "that's what I came about. How's he doing?"

"He's okay, I think. Seems to be making a few friends in there."

"Friends?"

"Well, acquaintances."

"Anyway," said Mycroft, rapidly distracted from the plight of his brother. "Are you new in town, Irene? Do you need anyone to show you around? You know, some food maybe, a few drinks down Southfield Road and back to your place for rampant sex."

"You're very presumptuous," smiled Irene.

"Okay," refined Mycroft, "let's just have sex then."

"Maybe I'll pass on that. Besides, what would your wife think?"

"How do you know I'm married?"

"Single men are rarely so bold," she replied, apologetic for seeing so clearly through him.

"Mycroft," I said, diverting his unwelcomed attentions, "do you have a theory on all this? Could Sherlock possibly have anything to do with this thing at the bank?"

"Yeah, man," he replied, "the little shit's far too clever for his own good. It wouldn't surprise me if he's just grown a bit too big for his trainees. He's been overdue a fall on his arse for years, and here it is, big style."

"You think he could have done it?"

"Yeah, why not? Nobody else could have. Not without his help anyway."

"Nobody else?"

"Well, not many."

Holmes' own brother thought his incarceration legitimate. But what was my view? Recent revelations had made me question my understanding of Holmes, a round-dodging millionaire who paid surreptitious Sunday visits to his mother. Hardly the most treacherous of non-disclosures. So what if he had a few investments tucked away, why would that be worthy of mention for a master logician? His logic and deductive skills were of far more value, and he rarely made reference to them, other than through example of their usage.

What did my instinct tell me? It told me to trust him. Forget instinct, there was no logic in it. Even if the robbery from the bank systems was some intellectual challenge, how did Bradstreet put it, his 'chef d'oeuvre', why do that one thing and risk ruin to everything else? The Holmes of late was on the right side of the law. He sometimes didn't always appreciate where the line was drawn, but the times he strayed over it tended to be with laudable intent.

That said, it wasn't long before this that he'd talked about giving up on his burgeoning detective career. The bank job could have been his last dance, his pension plan, or something in between. Whenever I settled on a thought, there was a contradiction not allowing it to sit quite straight. As Holmes might put it, I couldn't get my thoughts to compile.

Wherever the truth lay, Sherlock Holmes was facing a lengthy prison sentence and it appeared myself and Irene Adler represented his only chance of an alternative outcome. In the cases Holmes and I had investigated to that point, you couldn't count the erroneous conclusions I'd drawn personally, and yet I was his best hope. It affected me physically, my neck and shoulders stiffening as I thought it through. I can tell you, this was just too real.

8

At the agreed hour, I met Irene outside the Panama Swiss Bank. Miss Merryweather appeared a short time later dressed in a pinstriped suit jacket and matching skirt, the tightness of which challenged the bounds of business respectability.

We trailed her on her journey home until a point which felt like a safe distance from her workplace. As we turned into Corporation Road, I called out, causing her to turn and recognise me.

"Hello," she said. "You're Sherlock's friend, aren't you?"

"I am," I replied, "thank you for remembering me. This is another friend of Sherlock's, Irene Adler."

They both nodded to each other and shared a polite if strained smile. Shaking hands, they looked over each other in the process. Adler edged the contest in looks, perhaps due to her precise, understated style, with Merryweather coming back strongly with youth on her side. I interrupted their mutual assessment of each other to make a proposal. "Would you like to pop somewhere for a coffee? We'd like to talk over a few things with you."

"I'd prefer a proper drink," she replied.

I decided against walking into the Twisted Lip and facing Mary with two of the most beautiful women in Middlesbrough at that time. Clearly Mary wouldn't have had a problem with this, but I felt it preferable to avoid any consequential discussion.

Taking a looping route to a destination not far from where our trek had begun we, Irene and I at least, returned to the Irish bar to find it now perhaps a tenth full with the beginnings of the early evening crowd. Irene and Miss Merryweather's entrance didn't go unnoticed by the regulars.

I bought us all drinks and we moved to one of the booths. "Miss Merryweather," I began, "we'd like to ask you some questions about the recent robbery of the bank. I'll understand if you don't want to answer."

"Why?" she laughed. "I didn't do it."

"No," I clarified, "I mean if it would cause you problems at work."

"It should be fine," she responded, more puzzled than concerned.

"Do you know that Sherlock has been arrested for the robbery?" I asked.

"Really?" she shrieked. "It just goes to show, you never really know someone, do you?"

"He didn't do it," I responded. "The problem is the police are hell bent on pinning it on him."

Miss Merryweather adjusted her seating position, a look of concern resident on her brow. At the same time, Irene glanced at me to suggest she was yet to align with my working assumption of Holmes' innocence.

"So what can I do to help?" said Merryweather. "I really liked your friend. He came to see me after Ralphie died. A few times actually."

"Really, I never knew that."

"Yeah, he was sweet. He took me out a few times. Never let me pay for a thing. How can I help?"

"Can you remember the first time we met you? You arranged a meeting with two chaps from your head office. Can you remember their names?"

"No," she said, "there are so many people coming up and down. I can never keep track. I should be able to find out though." Delving into her oversized handbag, she pulled out a small laptop and flipped open the top. "I should still have the meeting invite in my diary. I hope I can find it," she said as the laptop cycled up its startup routines. "I was sad when he broke it off."

"Broke it off?" I questioned.

"Yeah, we were kind of an item for a few weeks."

"A few weeks," muttered Irene, "he's probably had longer relationships with curries."

In response, Miss Merryweather pointed a suspicious look at her. "Yeah," she continued, "I remember him telling me I was beautiful, eyes open and eyes closed."

"I've just done that sick-in-the-mouth thing," mumbled Irene.

"You know he once told me that whenever I was in a room, it was as if I was the only woman in it."

Irene looked away, searching for a retort she couldn't frame.

"Ah, here you go," said Miss Merryweather," it was a few months ago, wasn't it?" She tapped on the cursor keys. "That's odd," she said, "I can't find it. It should definitely be in there. I remember booking the room and adding those guys to the invite."

"Could the meeting record have been housekept away?"

"They aren't usually. Oooh, that reminds me, I spoke to one of them on Messenger. Let me check the history." Again she tapped up and down on the cursor keys without success. "Now that is weird. Usually you can look back about a year, but there's nothing." She looked across at us, a look of concern on her face. "I'm so sorry," she said.

"It's okay," I reassured. "It's not your fault."

"I'd better get off," she said, sipping the last of her white wine spritzer. "I'm really sorry I couldn't help. If there's anything else, just let me know."

"It's okay," I repeated. "Could you leave me a number? Just in case we have any further questions."

"Yeah, sure," she said, "no problem," before pulling an eyebrow pencil from her handbag and scribing her number up my forearm. "Does Sherlock have a number? You know, for when he gets out."

"No," snapped Irene, "the terms of his probation from the last time he was in prison don't allow him to have a phone."

"Oh, okay," said Miss Merryweather as she stood to leave.

As the door clipped shut on Miss Merryweather's exit, Irene grabbed my arm to examine. "She's done that before the little tart," she sneered, before casting it away. "She was pretty useless as well."

I just smiled to myself, choosing not to pick up on the unexpected jealousy that Miss Merryweather had encouraged. "Quite the contrary, Irene," I said, "I think we have our men."

Irene flashed me a confused look in order to elicit an explanation.

"All trace of them has vanished," I continued. "Their tracks have been covered. It's reverse thinking. Erm, no it's not. Anyway, why cover your tracks unless you have something to hide? Remember what Mycroft said? 'Not without his help'. When we met those chaps, we were investigating the possibility of the bank being robbed. Holmes had this long conversation with them about systems and ciphers and stuff. Most of which went right over my head."

"Most?" questioned Irene.

"Alright, that might have been closer to all. Anyway, we thought we were ensuring the bank was safe. What if they wanted that information to help them with a robbery?" I hypothesised.

"They probably didn't even work for the bank," said Irene. "Two guys that no one has ever seen before turn up from head office. Who's going to think twice? It wouldn't have been difficult to get themselves put on to the personnel system. The security safeguards they have on that kit won't be the same as they have on the banking systems. It could probably be arranged by slipping a few quid to some underpaid minion in some far away location. How come Holmes didn't twig that they weren't legit?"

"Most of the time he would," I replied, "but sometimes the logic takes over and he doesn't look up. His reading of people is phenomenal, but on rare occasions one slips by. Usually when he's tripping off something else. It happened with those chaps that grabbed you, Smith and Jones. It was a long time before he realised they weren't FBI. He's frighteningly good, but not perfect. Sometimes he's almost human. So what do we do now? Go to the police?"

"No," sighed Irene, "we need more. From what you've said the police don't appear to be particularly disposed to investigating other lines of enquiry. Can you not remember their names? They were probably false but it would be somewhere to start."

"No, sorry. Bill maybe. Bill? Nope, it was months ago. A lot of brain cells have been extinguished under the Engineer's Thumb since then. The amount Sherlock and I knock back it's all I can do to remember my PIN number."

Irene smiled. "I have an idea," she said. "Hypnosis."

"Hypnosis?" I queried.

"Yeah, I do it all the time. It's a tool of the trade."

"Your trade being?"

"I'm gonna say roving international business woman."

"And you can hypnotise me and make me remember the names of these chaps?"

"Of course, I do it all the time. I can regress you back to that meeting and it will be like you're still there. Well, you probably won't be able to remember all that techno babble, but a couple of names should be no problem. Don't you use it in your treatment?"

"No, it's not something I've even considered."

"My uncle taught me how to do it. Both my uncles could do it. Uncle Ray used it in medical practice. He helped me get over my sex addiction. Well, sort of. Uncle Peter, he was a bit of an embarrassment. He had a show in Ibiza. He used to make people walk like chickens and take their trousers off. He's now doing five years in the Zaragoza Hilton."

"You're not going to make me take my trousers off, are you?"

"I can't make any promises," she smiled.

"Okay," I agreed, "but we can't do it here. Let's nip round the corner to the Lip."

"Wouldn't my hotel room be better?"

"No, I've got an idea."

We made our way to the Twisted Lip to find it sparsely populated with the odd office worker.

"Mary, you couldn't close up, could you? There's something we want to try."

"First things first, John," she replied, stalling my clumsy fervour. "What is that number scrawled up your arm?"

"Ah, yes, that relates to a lead we've been following in our attempts to resolve Sherlock's current predicament."

Irene nodded in confirmation to encourage her acceptance.

"And this lady is?" continued Mary, gesturing to Irene.

"Ah yes, sorry, Mary, this is Irene Adler. Irene, this is my better half, Mary Morstan, owner and manageress of this fine hostelry."

"Irene Adler," exclaimed Mary. "I've heard a lot about you."

"None of it true, I expect," smirked Irene.

"Okay, ladies and gentlemen, we're closing," announced Mary to a grumbled response from patrons with various levels of libation occupying their glasses.

As Mary ushered the dissenters to the door, Irene and I took seats towards the rear of the establishment. "Mary, do you have a small vanity mirror?" Irene asked on Mary's return from locking the door.

"Yeah," said Mary, returning behind the bar to rummage in her handbag. On delivering the mirror to Irene, she suggested she would leave us to it and tidy up in the back, however I had a plan for Mary and her quite brilliant artistic talents. If this hypnosis thing worked and Irene could regress me back to the meeting at the bank, I wanted Mary to draw the protagonists. Just like I'd seen on countless television shows, I would describe the two gentlemen in order that Mary could sketch them out. Although Mary lacked confidence in the proposal, she was happy for the attempt. She retrieved her sketchpad and pencil from behind the bar and took a seat at the table.

Irene shined up the vanity mirror on her skirts and began to use it to flash light across my eyes. She spoke in a slow comforting voice, perhaps a semitone below her normal speaking voice. I was unsure whether this would work, but it wasn't long before I felt my eyes heavying and myself drifting into an involuntary sleep.

I woke into the most bizarre of experiences. It was like the most lucid of dreams. I was walking down a corridor, the periphery of which segued into a haze. Ahead of me, Miss Merryweather provided a lead for me to follow. It wasn't an accurate facsimile of the similar journey I'd taken through the actual bank during my visit there months before, Holmes wasn't with me for one, but my senses told me I was in the same place.

Miss Merryweather pushed through a door and into a meeting room. There sat the two gentlemen whose identities I was trying to establish. There was no sign of Holmes in the room either, however both Irene and Mary were present. Mary sat at the opposite end of the table from the rest of us, whilst Irene leant against a wall on the other side of the room to me, behind and to the side of the two men.

"Would you like to introduce yourself, Doctor?" said Irene.

"Yes, Doctor John Watson," I stuttered, instinctively holding out my hand.

"My name is Bill Morris," said the first chap, "and this is my colleague, Duncan Ross."

"Bill Morris and Duncan Ross," I echoed. "I'm very pleased to meet you." My hope was that the repetition would commit their names to my memory.

"We were expecting to meet Sherlock Holmes," said Ross.

"Yes," I responded, "he's been unexpectedly detained. I can speak on his behalf."

"Would it not be better to reschedule, Jim?" asked Ross of Morris.

Ross calling Bill Morris "Jim" dislodged a thought. He'd done that in the real meeting. At the time, I'd dismissed it as a slip of the tongue, however now it bore relevance. I looked to Irene, still in her standing position, who smiled to me.

As my view returned to Morris and Ross, the vignette drifted into the surreal. Without my noticing, Mary had moved from her seat at the end of the table to stand behind them. Drawing on a whiteboard I'd not noticed previously, she had started to sketch out the two men's likenesses.

"No, Mary," I corrected, "Bill's eyes are wider than that and his eyebrows are thinner. You need to narrow the nose. His hair is grey." And so I continued describing the men's features and requesting the necessary corrections. Morris and Ross sat silent and unperturbed by this peculiar action.

It wasn't long before Mary's illustrations were complete. Irene, who had been moving sylphlike around the room during the drafting, stopped to address me. "John, it's time for us to go now. I'm going to snap my fingers and you're going to wake up. You'll remember everything."

I pushed up from the table to leave the room, looking down as I did so. The table I was pushing up from was no longer the one from the bank's conference room, but rather the one in the bar.

"That was brilliant," I gasped. "Can I give you a call next time I can't find my phone?"

"That would be quite a trick," responded Irene dryly.

"You'll have to teach me how to do that," said Mary, pushing over her drawings. "It will be useful next time I want him to unload the dishwasher."

The sketchbook revealed two reasonable representations of the two men I'd just met through my semi-conscious sojourn. After a few directed amendments, the drawings were fantastically accurate.

"So there we go," I said, "Bill Morris and Duncan Ross. I still can't believe how well that worked."

"But those aren't their real names, are they?" said Irene. "You mentioned a 'Jim'."

"Yeah, Ross referred to Morris as Jim. He did that when we met for real. I remember it now. What next?"

"Well, the first thing is to find out if Bill Morris and Duncan Ross are real people, real bank employees. I'm not sure it will help, but I'm interested to know if their identities were stolen or created."

"Miss Merryweather should be able to help," I said, transferring her number from my arm to my phone. Mary flashed me a look of mock suspicion before rising to go and reopen the pub.

Receptive to my request, Miss Merryweather said she would log on and take a look on the bank intranet. She said she had good enough recollection of what they looked like, and now that she had names, she would be able to check these against the staff directory. She also said she would have a ring around to see if any of her friends at work had come across these chaps.

As we sat back in our chairs waiting for Miss Merryweather to call back, a thought struck me. Holmes would have remembered the names of Morris and Ross. Why on Earth didn't he mention this on either of my visits to him in prison? I relayed my confusion to Irene.

"He's training you, Sweetie," she smiled, whilst playing with her phone. "Maybe it's some sort of succession plan. Stars that shine that bright never shine long." Her statement trailed off into a thoughtful silence. I was left with the feeling that, contrary to my previous assumption, Sherlock had a hook or two in her also. My thought train was however derailed by her suggestion of Sherlock's untimely demise. Surely not? She couldn't know that. Maybe she was going to run away with him?

As my already confused mind tried to assimilate another thought, Irene pointed her phone at me to display the results of her quick search of the internet. "William Morris, Panama Swiss Bank. Look like our man?"

"Nothing like him," I responded.

"It looks like Mister Morris has had his identity stolen. I can't find this Ross chap, mind. Maybe he's not very social. Surprisingly not all IT nerds are."

She then used her phone to photograph Mary's sketches before leaving on the promise she would return soon. When I queried where she was going, she said that it wasn't only our Professor friend that had a worldwide network of associates, and she had "a few people to wake up".

Shortly after Irene left, Miss Merryweather returned my call to say she had checked the staff directory and although both Messrs Morris and Ross were listed, she didn't recognise them. Perhaps exceeding her brief, she called both of them at home to ask them if they ever remembered meeting with Sherlock Holmes. Not Sherlock Holmes and Doctor Watson, just Sherlock Holmes. Neither of them did.

Maybe an hour and a half later, Irene returned to the bar with news. No one she knew had ever come across Duncan Ross, however one of her associates had recognised Morris as a certain James Ryder. If her sources were to be believed, computer crime was his raison d'être, and although the job on the bank was a few levels above what he'd purportedly been involved in previously, it was certainly something that would slot well into his portfolio of offences.

"We need to tell the police," I exclaimed, "get them to get him picked up."

"Yep," replied Irene, "but they're gonna need a shovel. He's dead. A boating accident in the Caribbean. It appears he didn't waste any time spending his ill-gotten gains, but made the mistake of trying to save a few quid on a decent crew."

"We need to go to the police anyway. Surely we have enough to get Sherlock released?"

"It's probably best if you go on your own," said Irene. "I borrowed a police car from them a while back and, erm, parked it in the Tees."

I made my way alone to the police station to plead the case for the defence, piecing it together in my head as I went. I reasoned that Detective Inspector Bradstreet would pay me little heed, but I was sure Superintendent Spaulding would be more partisan, and open to the new evidence we had collected.

As I'd hoped, he allowed me straight through to his office, where I relayed the sequence of events we'd pieced together, from the original meeting in which we discussed the bank's system security, to our tracing of James Ryder and the location of his unfortunate demise. I managed to fluff past how we'd actually identified James Ryder, but offered Miss Merryweather as a witness willing to corroborate that the pictures of the deceased, shown on various news websites, were that of the man Holmes, myself and indeed Lestrade had met in the bank's offices all those months ago.

All through my story, Spaulding nodded. On the conclusion of my précis, he held his hand out for me to shake. "Leave it with me," he said, "I'll speak to DI Bradstreet and we'll take this to a judge."

9

I felt the discussion with Superintendent Spaulding had gone well. We had a credible story, enough uncertainty as to Holmes' accusation and a more viable candidate of a suspect, supported by a credible witness. The wheels only parted company on Spaulding's inclusion of Detective Inspector Bradstreet. It was difficult to see how she would pursue the conclusion of Holmes' incarceration with any great verve.

As I sat in the Twisted Lip, with the odd and only accompaniment of a pot of tea, Martha appeared. "Sherly's just rang," she said. "He wants you to pick him up. He's at some pub in Portrack."

"He's out?" I exclaimed.

"Looks like it," she responded matter-of-factly.

"Okay," I said, "I'll get a cab."

"Here," said Martha, throwing me a set of keys, "take mine. Bring him back in style. Unless of course he is on the run, in which case leave the bugger there."

As I pulled up outside the rather questionable establishment, Holmes stumbled out shoulder first. "Fuck you," he shouted to an unseen adversary.

"Prick," he mumbled as he jumped in the back. "Reckoned I'd slept with his wife."

"Had you?" I asked.

"I fucking hope not," he said. "He had a face like a pop welder's mat. Fuck knows what she must be like."

"I see your time in prison has been far from correctional," I commented, tongue in cheek.

"Yep, just another poor soul the prison service has failed to reintegrate back into society. Have the police managed to track down the real villains? Bill Morris and Duncan Ross?"

"Erm, not quite. You knew it was them?"

"Well yeah, I was in the meeting."

"Why didn't you tell me?"

"You were in the meeting."

"But I couldn't remember their names."

"Ah right, you shoulda said. That wasn't their real names anyway, was it?"

"Well no, we don't know who Duncan Ross was but Morris is actually called James Ryder."

"Yes, Jim. That's why Ross called him 'Jim'."

"What, you remembered that?"

"Yeah, but I got a bit distracted. Bob Mortimer sometimes calls

Vic Reeves Jim and my mind somehow flicked to that. I probably hadn't had enough to drink that day."

"What, so Bob Mortimer is to blame for the ransacking of the Panama Swiss Bank vaults?"

"Yep, pretty much. 'He wouldn't let it lie'."

"Never mind," I sighed. "To err is human I suppose."

"Aye," responded Holmes, "and to arr is pirate. Never go to prison, Doc. The jokes are shite."

I wasn't tempted to laugh.

"So, Doc, how come you ended up remembering?"

"Ah, yes. That was interesting. Irene hypnotised me."

"Really?" remarked Holmes. "How does that work then?"

"Well, she put me in this weird trance and it took me back in my mind to the meeting we had. It was kind of like a dream but more aligned to real events."

"Right," said Holmes. "So you can access any part of your mind and retrieve the information stored there. Wow, that is interesting."

"You know, Sherlock, I wouldn't have had to go through that if you'd just shared your thoughts on Morris and Ross. Then we might have had you out of there a lot sooner."

"It doesn't matter," dismissed Holmes. "I was in the semi-finals of the table tennis competition anyway. I would have won but some fucker had his own bat. He was good like. He must have been Desmond Douglas' cousin or something."

Holmes sighed, sitting forward in his chair. "The real thing in all this is why I didn't suss that Morris and Ross were snide."

"Sherlock, you can't deduce everything."

"Maybe not," he replied, the tone in his voice suggesting something of interest. "But the thing was there was nothing wrong with the deduction. Morris and Ross were perfect. They wore suits that hadn't seen a drycleaner in a while, over laundered shirts. Ross had a multi-coloured ink mark on his cuff, which looked like it had been picked up from cleaning down a whiteboard. He even looked uncomfortable in a tie. Like he wasn't used to wearing one."

"People who work in banks wear ties," I remarked.

"Not computer programmers," responded Holmes. "Not the

good ones at least. Yeah and there was his knuckle as well. He kept holding the knuckle of his left hand, as if he had the kind of strain injury that programmers often get." Holmes had that excitable air about him that he usually got when conclusions had been more of a challenge to draw. "The same went for Smith and Jones," he continued. "Other than the shoes, where clearly I dropped a bollock, everything was cock on. Those bloody shoes. I suspect whoever dressed them, didn't include those shoes in the outfit.

"Their suits were exactly as you would expect on the back of an FBI agent. Like they'd been flung on the back of a chair in a hotel room. It was like they'd been deliberately distressed to suggest the look of a G Man's suit. Jones especially, everything about him told the story you expected to be there. Except those bloody shoes, it was like some sort of method acting for twats."

Given that Holmes was sharing his failings, I thought it right to expose mine. "Sherlock," I said, "I need to make a confession."

"You're gay?" he quipped. "No, worse than that, you support Sunderland?"

"No," I said, circumnavigating his japery. "I thought you'd done it. I thought it was you who'd hacked into the bank's systems."

"Yeah, makes sense," came the unexpected response. "It was certainly a scenario. What was your reasoning?"

"I had several, but the one I favoured was that you'd deliberately got yourself locked up in order to get to Moran."

"Mmm, yeah, would have been a lot of work for that, though. If I wanted to spend some time in Holme House, I could have just slapped a rozzer or something. Actually, I could have just groped Bradstreet. Tried to get the plum out of her arse."

"You seemed to take advantage of the situation to learn more about the Professor. That just didn't seem like something you would normally do. You normally engineer an opening."

Holmes laughed. "Opportunities come in strange disguises." His tone eradicated any sentiment from the discussion. "Anyway, how's the Fat Controller getting along? The word inside is that he's struggling. Some bastards arranged a party. They called it a wake. I tell you what, I pissed in their punch."

"You didn't."

"Let's just say I added something from the workshop with a little known laxative effect."

"He's not doing well. His doctors certainly aren't bringing much confidence. I tell you what though, his wife's a bit of a looker."

"Really," he exclaimed. "So she's effectively on the market then? Kind of under offer subject to contract killing."

I glared at the inappropriateness of his comment through the rear view mirror.

"Have the Five O got any idea who did it?"

"I've not heard anything."

"Mmm, I doubt they'll get much joy there. Any evidence they might have stumbled over will have been blown to pieces. I tell you what, I'll have a look next week. Fancy it, Doc?"

"Yeah, why not. My patients are getting sick of the sight of me."

We chanced upon Detective Inspector Bradstreet as I pulled the cab up on Baker Street, just outside the Twisted Lip.

"You're investigating the explosion," said Holmes as she approached. "Or licking piss off a nettle. One of those."

"Yes," she confirmed. "The super's asked me to look into the attempt on Lestrade's life."

"Got anywhere?"

"No, not really. There's not a lot of evidence."

"Don't let that stop you," laughed Holmes.

"Do you have any thoughts, Mister Holmes?" sighed Bradstreet, her serious demeanour stagnating in dismissal.

"Yeah, millions," he said. "The first one being beer. Prison can sure be a thirsty place for an innocent man."

"You were only in for four days," she defended.

"I tell you what you could do," he responded. "Open your knees and feel the breeze occasionally. That might help. Anyway, catch you later."

As Holmes entered the Twisted Lip, it was apparent he'd assumed I would be funding his freedom celebrations.

"You can afford to get the first few in, can't you?" I asserted.

"Yeah, alright," he responded dejectedly. "Drinks for everyone, on my tab," he announced. The occupants of the bar were exactly Holmes, myself and Mary, who never drank while she was working.

10

Irene entered the Twisted Lip, tracked by Holmes through an underlook until she arrived at the table. With two options available, she took the chair nearest Holmes. It didn't take the deductive skills of Sherlock Holmes to understand she was dressed for travel. Holmes interrupted her before she had chance to speak. "Don't say goodbye."

Irene shone a broad smile, corrupted by a glassiness in her eyes. "I love you, you strange creature."

"Then stay."

"It's not practical, my sweet."

"Practicalities don't matter. We could be together."

"The practicalities are everything. I'm disappointed in you. You know logic is a dish that can't be peppered with passion. That you're not thinking like that, is something I'll treasure forever. I'm really flattered."

Holmes smiled a smile of concession, cut with a distant malaise.

"Sherlock, you're so sweet. You should take off those clothes. Be the person you really are." Holmes' look suggested it unlikely. "Did you manage to unlock your phone?"

"No," he replied, dragging the useless item which he had carried for months from his pocket. It was odd that he had kept it charged.

"5683," said Irene.

"Love," he whispered. "5 L, 6 O, 8 V and 3 is E. From the numbers on the keypad."

"Love," confirmed Irene. "It seems so cruel now. What did I say? 'Something you will never get'. I was trying to be funny."

"It was clever. So simple. I should have cracked it. I don't know about love."

I felt I was intruding and that I should make my excuses and leave, but didn't want to interrupt. Besides, I was captivated.

"I've upset you, haven't I?" said Irene.

"Nah," grinned Sherlock, tears brimming in his eyes.

"That I have affected Sherlock Holmes will be my medal," she said. "My ring. Always, my love. Always."

Irene stood, placed her hand on his shoulder and left. We would never see her again.

DEAD COLD CASES

1

After a hard day treating some of the fragile minds of Teesside, I was maybe three well-deserved sips into a fine beer when Holmes came billowing into the pub. "Doc, I need your eyes. Well, another set of eyes and I can't think of a better set of peepers than your baby blues."

He picked up my glass, took a large gulp and winced. Crashing the glass back down on the bar, he grabbed me by the arm and directed me towards the door. Before we reached it, he stopped. "Two seconds" he said, unhanding me to return and address the barman, "Stop recycling your flushing fluid, you cheap get." The scolded barman stared back unable to form a retort. There had been nothing wrong with the beer. It was beautiful.

We turned left out of the bar and looped round into Baker Street under the shadow of Church House, an ominous and derelict fifteen-storey office block that would perhaps be more suitably sited in Gotham City than Middlesbrough.

On reaching Flat 1B, I found that Holmes had pinned several photographs and newspaper cuttings to the wall. Red twine traced lines between some of the postings. Numerous coloured paper notes, several with profanities scribbled on them, littered both the wall and floorboards.

"Sherlock, what's all this about?" I queried. Whatever it was, it seemed a sizeable undertaking.

"Cold cases," he replied. "Dead cold cases. None of which the Boro Five O have come anywhere near solving."

"Why are you looking at them?" I queried. "Have they asked you to get involved?"

"Nope, but what else is there to do?" he returned, his stride unfaltered. "Five murders, none of them solved, and all occurring within about twelve months of each other. Teesside doesn't have five unsolved murders in a year. It just doesn't happen, Doc. Not five… and not with such a perfect lack of evidence and leads."

"Do they have anything in common?"

"Apart from the lack of evidence, no. Different methods, different murder weapons, different locations, different everything. You couldn't find a more disparate set of victims if you tried."

"Did they all have Nectar cards?" I japed glibly.

"No," he responded, not latching on to my inappropriate attempt at humour, "I've checked. They didn't even all buy the same brand of probiotic yogurt. I've done some of that big data gubbins and the lack of commonality is, well, uncommon. Never mind six degrees of separation, there's at least fifty." He paused. "Why won't this compile?" he snarled, spinning around to review the debris of his handy work.

"Maybe that's it. Maybe the thing they have in common is nothing," I postulated carelessly, as my mind strayed into the problem in hand.

"Doc, you're on fire. What does that mean?"

"I'm not really sure."

Holmes pointed a disappointed scowl at me.

"Maybe he's mixing it up to cover his tracks," I commented, attempting to recover my standing in the discussion.

"How do you know it's a he?"

"Or she," I corrected.

"This is actually starting to make sense," said Holmes, "but when the theme is that there isn't one, it's very difficult to narrow the field. Random won't rationalise."

"Maybe there's no connection. Five evidenceless murders in the area is unusual, but it may just be a statistical anomaly. An unfathomable hot spot. Are you sure you're not making something of this that isn't there?"

Holmes strode straight past my doubt. "This is a bit of a three-pint problem, Doc. Fancy a beer?"

"Surprisingly, yes," I responded.

2

It's probably worth noting that Holmes' feverish interest in these cases, abandoned to varying degrees by the local constabulary, occurred only six months after the same police force had dragged him out of his Baker Street lodgings and incarcerated him for a crime to which he was only tenuously linked. It would have been well within reason for him to leave the detection to the people who got more regularly paid for its undertaking.

Unfettered by this, Holmes' mind raced as would a steam train. It was "a puzzle within a puzzle" as he would later call it. He marched into the bar and ordered two pints of the Engineer's Thumb. I was about to protest that I would have preferred to select my own libation, however given he'd ordered what I had a mind for, I resisted comment.

"Of course, those cases all have something else in common," he said as he rested the beer in front of me. "That our mate Superintendent Spaulding and his merry men at Cleveland Constabulary are nowhere near getting to the bottom of any of them. Then again, that lot still struggle with the top on a Muller Corner."

Holmes slapped his left bicep a few times with the fingers of his right hand before continuing.

"Okay," he said, "first up is John Horner, shot dead in the head by a sniper's bullet, while jogging in Stewart Park with his wife Jennie a year ago on Boxing Day. The murderer holed up behind a big old oak tree and shot him in the side of the head as they ran past. It was a two-hundred yard shot, quite a skill, especially if the wind was up, which apparently it was."

"What did he do for a living?" I asked, wondering if his career could have generated a motive.

"He was a carpet fitter," replied Holmes. "Unless he carpeted over someone's gerbil, I can't imagine why he would have many enemies."

Holmes wet his lips with a brief sip of his drink.

"Then we have Emma Percy and Tom Armatage killed on the seafront at Seaton Carew. That was stupidly cruel. Someone snuck in the back seat of their car, while they were snogging in the front, and garrotted them both, apparently simultaneously, with some cheese wire. Whoever did this planned a contingency. The mechanisms of the car's front door locks were superglued up. I also suspect a cheese wire wasn't the only weapon. He had some balls too. It was done in the early evening when it was still light and there will have been plenty of people about. Nobody saw a thing until a copper looked in the car around midnight."

"That that level of evil can exist makes you question the existence of a god," I commented. "Two kids just starting out on life. What place has such evil in the universe?"

"I fell out with God a long time ago, Doc. I don't think he ever liked me," he responded, looking away as he spoke.

In my work as a psychologist, especially the cases sent my way by various judges and magistrates, I saw evil all the time. I thought it was something I would become hardened to. That I would eventually get used to. I never did, but then I never blamed the individual. I always saw psychosis as an error in nature. A broken connection between the mind and the soul. In some cases, medication and my intervention re-established a connection of sorts. In all too many situations, my efforts were futile.

"Three months later we have Harry Baker," voiced Holmes, "the lead singer of the death metal band Bastard Miserables. He was electrocuted by his microphone while performing at the Musiclounge on Yarm Road, Stockton."

"I read about that in the Gazette," I commented. "Wasn't that put down to an accident?"

"It was," replied Holmes. "Someone had been tinkering around with the wiring in the amp. None of the other members of the band claimed any responsibility for making repairs, so the Five O assumed Harry had done it himself. I've had a word with the lads in the band. Harry had never attempted any electrical repairs before. He'd always left that sort of stuff to his dad, who used to work as a tiffy at ICI and knew his way around a screwdriver."

"Okay," I said, prompting him to continue.

"Finally, we have a six month gap to the death of Robert Peterson in Yarm. That's annoying, there's nothing in September to keep this three month interval thing going. Clearly not as annoying as it is to poor old Bob who had a few starlings jammed in the chimney of his cottage. The place filled with smoke and he succumbed to the fumes. That would have been put down to an accident too, except for the fact that some of the roof slates were disturbed by the killer. To me, this is Murder Five. There's a fourth one out there somewhere. Someone, somewhere, is lying dead and undiscovered in a locked room. Murder Four will turn up. You mark my words."

With Holmes fizzing like a firework, we gulped down our beer and dashed along Baker Street to flag a cab on Linthorpe Road. He hesitated, staring at the taxi cab's council license plate before muttering, "Eleven eleven," and jumping in. Our first port of call was Stewart Park, scene of the John Horner killing. Just as Holmes had described, there was an aged and towering oak tree, around two-hundred yards from the path used by joggers of various builds and abilities.

"Two-hundred yards is further than you'd imagine, isn't it?" said Holmes as we stood by the tree, peering down to the spot where John Horner was killed. "The shooter could have easily hit his wife. Especially if she was running behind him or if the wind carried the bullet."

Holmes crouched on his haunches at the foot of the tree to run the backs of his fingers through the grass. "We needed to be here just after it happened," he sighed. "Then I could have made some smart-arsed crack about the killer sitting here smoking a Marlboro Light while he waited for the Horners to jog past."

He then sprang up to ghost around the site at a little over walking pace, his arms outstretched and angled slightly behind him, his head weaving from side to side on his neck. Then, quite suddenly, he stopped. "Right, I'm bored with this," he said. "Here's what happened. Yer man pulled up over there, hopped over the fence, and sat waiting for the Horners to jog past. Smoking a Marlboro Light. When he saw the poor sods approaching, he pulled the rifle out of his holdall and took the shot lying on his belly. One shot was all he needed. He lobbed the gun back in his bag, jumped back over the railings and was away."

"How did you deduce all that?" I asked.

"It was less about deduction and more to do with reading the story in the Northern Echo to be honest. I made the rest up. Unfortunately, old crime scenes don't give much away."

From Stewart Park, we took another taxi to the Horner family home, a modest semi-detached residence in Acklam. Jennie Horner answered the door clutching the hand of a small child who could not have been much more than three years old.

"Hello, Missus Horner," said Holmes. "My name is Sherlock Holmes and this is my associate Doctor John Watson."

"I recognise you from the papers," she responded. "Is this something to do with Jack?"

"It is. The police seem to have hit a bit of a wall so we're trying to bring a different perspective on things."

"The police have been bloody hopeless," she snapped.

"Indeed," replied Holmes. "Would you mind answering a few questions?"

"No, come in," she sighed, leading us down a hallway into a lounge strewn with the child's toys. On escaping her clutches, the little girl was immediately transfixed by Holmes, moving to stand a few feet away from him and engage him in a staring contest.

"Hello, Isabella," said Holmes. "Aren't you pretty?"

"Batman," said the child.

Holmes contorted his face in wonderment and smiled at her mother.

"Leave the man alone," said Mrs Horner. "Since her dad died, she seems fascinated whenever there's a man in the house. Not that there's that many. If my boiler didn't keep packing up, there wouldn't be any."

The child turned away only briefly before returning to hand Holmes some plastic building blocks.

Holmes flashed a generous smile. "Can I ask you the obvious question, Missus Horner?"

"Jenny," she corrected. "Yes."

"Jenny, was your husband in any sort of trouble? Did he have any enemies?"

"The police asked that," she replied. "I told them no at the time and I've racked my brains ever since. There's nothing. He was just a normal bloke who worked hard and loved his family."

"Did you often go jogging in Stewart Park?"

"It was the first time. The first time I'd been there in years. We both bought each other running shoes as presents and decided to give them a try by running off some of the food we'd been eating over Christmas."

"So why Stewart Park? There are closer places."

"I don't know. It was my suggestion. Our parents used to take us there when we were kids. I suppose I was just feeling sentimental." She shook her head, still not believing the drastic impact of such a casual turn of fate.

"It really is a dreadful thing," consoled Holmes. "We'll do our utmost to find whoever did this." With that, he rose from his chair.

"Is that it?" she asked. "Is there nothing else you need to know?"

"No, that's been very useful."

"Well, if there's anything else, erm, just come round. I hardly ever go anywhere."

Holmes returned a reassuring nod before offering his hand to shake. He then went to return the bricks back to Isabella before snatching away his hand. He presented the little girl his palm to show the bricks were gone only for them then to appear in his other hand.

"How did you know the child's name?" I asked as we left.

"A few things really," he replied. "Isabella was the most common girls' name around the time she was born, she had two books about characters called Isabella, a princess and a unicorn. Oh, and I read it in the Northern Echo."

"And what did we learn from that extensive round of questioning?"

"Something," replied Holmes enigmatically.

3

The following morning, we breakfasted at the Baker Street Kitchen before heading along the street to look in on Martha at the boutique. As was not unusual, Holmes had had little to say throughout breakfast, however it was clear there was an unrelenting dialogue going on in his head, with him humming and twitching through the course of the meal. As I began to cross the road to Martha's, Holmes carried on before stopping dead in his tracks. "This is it," he said. "Murder Four."

"Murder Four?" I queried. "Ah, Davy Arrowsmith you mean. Killed upstairs in the Twisted Lip."

"No," said Holmes. "Lestrade, and the bomb. Okay, as it stands it's only attempted murder, but it gives us our September date. Detective Inspector Barry Lestrade nips into the Lip for a natter with us, on the way home for sex and a sausage casserole, and boom."

"All these incidents have one thing in common," I remarked.

"What's that?" asked Holmes.

"They all occurred on Teesside."

"Actually, that's a good point. Maybe we should do that thing they do, where they find the centre point of all the crimes and violin! That's where the killer lives. I saw it on a documentary about Jack the Ripper. They call it geographic profiling or something."

Diverting from our intended destination, we left Martha to her own devices, and climbed the stairs to Flat 1B. On re-entering the improvised crime room of Holmes' lounge, Holmes scrabbled around behind a pile of books, to pull out a map. "It's a bit old," he said, "but it will do." He then laid the map out on the floor and drove map pins into the murder locations. Taking his ball of red twine he then connected up the five pins. His focused labour was only interrupted by the words, "Oooh, Ayresome Park," as he prodded the site of Middlesbrough FC's old stadium.

He stood up and snapped, "Brilliant."

"Where is it?" I asked.

"This flat," he replied, "or as close to it as this kind of thing would get you."

"Do you think someone is trying to frame you?"

"Wouldn't be the first time."

"You weren't framed, you were guilty."

"I was guilty but that doesn't mean I wasn't set up. Anyway, the point is you can't get done for geography. Living in the centre of a crime spree doesn't bang the criminal to rights, it just gives Plod somewhere to start looking."

"Sorry," I said, for causing the distraction.

"No, Doc, don't apologise. I'm starting to realise that thinking in straight lines is the last thing we need here. Keep 'em coming. We're making progress."

"The proximity of this flat to the centre of the crime zone must just be a coincidence," I remarked.

"I don't believe in coincidences."

"Neither do I."

"That's a coincidence."

"Could it be our friend the Professor?" I asked.

"I hope not."

"Why?"

"Because, if so, he's kippered at least five people and he flaming hates us."

"Let's hope it's not him then."

"Let's. It makes it too hard if he knows we're coming."

" 'We' Sherlock? I'm not sure if 'we', specifically me, should be getting into this."

"I understand," he replied. "This is not gonna be an easy one. We'd be risking our lives. I'm more than happy for you to sit this one out, but I'm dug into this now. If I'm right about these things being connected and there being a three-month interval, we don't have much time. If we don't crack this one, in what, a week and a half, another random, innocent person is killed. Three months after that another. There's no scope for larking about with this one, Doc." His face contorted with concern, as he tapped his flattened palm against the side of his head, as if to quell a cranial tension. "I hate working to deadlines."

"Fancy another pint?" I asked, hoping to provide respite from the challenge to more myself than he.

"I'm not sure," he replied thoughtfully. "Let's have one anyway."

Holmes' guardianship of the 'People's Republic' was yet another of the contradictions that defined him. However close you got to him through the comradeship of shared experience, there was always an underlying fragility in the shackles that tied. The relationships he maintained with myself and even Martha always felt momentary. "He would follow you to the ends of the earth," his brother Mycroft once commented, "and then leave you there."

However, when it came to the people of Teesside, his self-assigned obligation was unswerving, and indeed somewhat of a concern for those of us who sought to protect him. Personally, I was acutely unnerved by the path we were setting out on, but, as always, I couldn't let him walk into danger alone.

On entering the Twisted Lip, Holmes took a seat. His non-vocalised instruction being that I should get the drinks. I arrived at our usual table to find Holmes laid flat back in the chair, his eyes staring into the ceiling.

"Imagine the kudos we'd get for solving these crimes," I commented, attempting to paint some legitimacy around my forthcoming involvement. Holmes responded with curled-lip disdain-cum-confusion. "By 'kudos' I don't mean the aftershave," I clarified.

"Yeah, I know," he replied. "I don't want to smell nice, I want to solve the puzzle, oh yeah and nail the gadgie behind this."

"Doesn't it bother you that you've become a bit of a local hero?" I asked. "They named a pub after you."

"It gets in the way. I used to be able to move around like a ghost. I didn't even have any bar presence. Now the eyes are everywhere. Corrupting the data."

There was a faint tinge of sorrow in his tone. A longing for the time before. I felt a twinge of guilt at my enjoyment of the glory he reflected my way. We lived in an age that craved celebrity and yet Holmes saw it as an unwelcome hindrance.

The concern generated by my involvement in such a perilous endeavour had caused me to stumble into making a clumsy statement. I knew Holmes well enough to know he sought no recognition. However, it was to my eternal frustration that I couldn't expunge from my mind the possibility of cracking the shell that encased him, to reveal a few more human characteristics. Really, I suppose I envied him for his ignorance of the trinkets sought by the wider population. He lived in a ratty little flat, had no car, hardly any clothes and few friends, but, in his mind, he travelled the universe.

"So what have we got?" said Holmes, recapping from his laid back posture. "Five murders, one attempted murder. None of which the Boro Five O have managed to lay a glove on.

"John Horner a middle-aged carpet fitter, a couple of teenage sixth form students, a twenty-seven year old singer, who, when he's not destroying music, works in a factory that makes air filters or something, Detective Inspector Barry Lestrade, not really sure what he does, and old Bob Peterson, a retired school teacher.

"They were born, grew up and lived in different areas around Teesside, except for the singer who was born in Ramsgate. They don't share a birthday, a star sign, nothing. Not one single thing in common."

"Except they're all dead," I exhaled carelessly. "Well, except for Lestrade."

"He's dead to me," said Holmes. "Since he made me ruin me coat."

Holmes' intervention to save Lestrade from the bomb planted under his car had resulted in an unsung victim: Holmes' much prized leather-yoked donkey jacket having been shredded in the explosion.

"How is the old bugger?" asked Holmes. "I haven't heard anything in months."

"He's doing well, I think. I saw Constable Hardwick in town the other day. He said he might be out of hospital next week."

"What about his stand in? Vinegar Vera. Has she thawed out yet?"

"Vinegar Vera?"

"DI Bradstreet."

"He never mentioned her."

"I think she wants me, you know. All that pent up sexual frustration going to waste." He sighed. "Yeah, she definitely wants to... erm," he said, rounding off the sentence with a two syllable whistle.

"Why don't you then? Think of it as a public service."

"Sod that," came the response. "It would take a braver man than me."

4

After a morning engaged in my primary vocation of psychiatry, I returned to the Twisted Lip around lunchtime to find Holmes in our usual berth. Two pints of Engineer's Thumb sat on the table before him.

"How did you know I was coming?" I asked, sitting to take a sip.

"I heard Mary whispering sweet sod all on her phone. You were either coming or she was having an affair. Either way you needed a drink."

"Look," he said with a tone of urgency, "I can't be bothered going through all the rigmarole of how I got to this conclusion, but I have an idea. Something that explains why all these murders are so different. It's an exercise. The victims are not the thing, they can be selected at random. It's the method that's being varied and that's different on purpose. Do you see?"

"Not really."

"Okay," smiled Holmes, "imagine you were training footie skills. You'd start with passing maybe then tackling, dribbling, heading, positioning, movement... well unless you're English and passing and movement doesn't seem to flaming matter. With these murders, we have shooting, a close-quarter garrotting, an electrocution made to look like an accident and so on."

"So this is not a serial killer then?"

"No, it's more like contract killers pulling together a CV."

"You think there's more than one?"

"Difficult to tell. Not enough data."

He sat up in his seat, his head and eyes jerking wildly as if on independent tracts. "Actually, Doc," he said, inhaling through a mouth widened with realisation, "that makes more sense. Each murder seems to be more sophisticated than the previous one. I thought that was just a function of the training, but it may well be one killer trying to outdo another.

"These are not murders. They're assassinations. Each more daring and complex than the previous. Some bastard's using the People's Republic as a training ground."

"So we need to find them and stop them. How?" I asked.

"It's not the trainees we need to stop, it's the bloody trainer. The root cause. We don't have assassinations in the Boro. We have the odd angry murder but nothing like this. This is something new and we need stop it."

Again, I was in possession of the same portfolio of facts as Holmes, only for him to form a far different conclusion. Since Holmes first walked me through the murders, I'd fixed the thought that we were looking for a serial killer. In hindsight, that assumption was so obviously flawed given the broad range of techniques the killings had involved. Serial killers focus on the victims. There's no need to deviate from a tried and tested method of killing. Better to keep the same method and refine it as you go.

I swayed back in my chair, unable to corral my thoughts. "You know, Sherlock, I envy the way you see things differently."

"It's nothing to envy. You can't turn it off. You look at everything as something to be fully understood. The more you do, the more it takes you over, the more it wears you out. I've heard musicians say, you know real ones, that once you have written music you can never listen to it in the same way again. The enjoyment is taken from you; it becomes something you want to analyse. That's what I have, but with all six senses," he laughed. "Music is the only distraction I get." He raised his glass towards his lips before tilting it slightly in my direction. "Beer works too," he smiled before gulping down a sizeable volume. "Another?"

"Why not," I replied, as he stood, picking up our glasses for return to the bar. "Six senses? I thought there were only five."

"Yeah, sound, sight, touch, smell, taste and humour."

Holmes returned to the table with replenished drinks and a knowing grin. "We've got a visitor coming," he said as he retook his seat.

"You should have told me earlier, Sherlock, I would have tidied round a bit. Who is it?"

"Let's not spoil the surprise," he said.

"I do love surprises."

"No, you don't," he replied curtly.

Fifteen, maybe twenty minutes later, a familiar figure appeared.

"Here she is," said Holmes in mock joy as DI Bradstreet entered. "Miss Face-like-a-slapped-arse 1979."

"I'm not that old," retorted Bradstreet dryly. Apparently, there was some semblance of humour under her frosted exterior.

"What did you want to see me about?" she asked, her normal demeanour tersely resumed.

"Okay," said Holmes, "here's the thing. We've been looking into a few cases that were catching a bit of a cold. John Horner, Emma Percy…"

"Mister Holmes," interrupted Bradstreet, "Cleveland Police are quite capable of undertaking the work we are so poorly paid for."

"Clearly," barbed Holmes. "So you don't want to know what we've come up with then?" Bradstreet stared back in consideration of her response. "You must be interested, or you wouldn't be here?" he added. She was obviously torn. Her peaked interest jostling with her reticence to accept his help.

"Okay," she conceded, sitting down with her lip curled, "entertain me."

Holmes' look portrayed our shared thought that providing her with entertainment was a far from likely outcome. He then sketched out the hypothesis we'd just formed and his theory on how the murders were linked, before suggesting the likelihood that there were multiple killers.

"I find it difficult to believe there's a criminal overlord running a training centre for assassins in Middlesbrough," responded Bradstreet on Holmes' conclusion. "However, I am professionally obliged to discuss this with my colleagues back at the station."

"I think 'acerbic' is the word that best describes her," I commented as she exited.

Holmes smiled before rounding his lips and whistling the same two syllable self-censor he'd used earlier, appended with a suggestive nod.

"Sherlock," I enquired, "what purpose did that serve? I laud your transparency, but I'm confused by you wanting to share our thoughts at this stage. I thought you preferred to manage down the information you provide to the police."

"I want them to get more interested in this. To create some noise. A distraction for what we're about to do. Put the defence on the wrong foot if you like."

"And what are we about to do?"

"I don't know yet."

The road ahead was uncertain, but it wasn't the uncertainty driving my discomfort. It was clear the journey would be a treacherous one. Oddly, despite my discomfort, I felt a perverted interest in what was to happen next.

5

I wandered around Flat 1B staring myself blind at the scattered paraphernalia strewn everywhere until I was struck by a thought. To this day, I couldn't tell you where the thought came from. I'd almost fixated myself into a stupor, and there it was. I reacted like a child gifted an unsuspected Christmas.

Shaking Holmes from his face-down slumber on the settee, I was almost bouncing off my feet.

"Bloody hell, Doc," he said, as he emerged from his afternoon nap. "I was just about to have sex with a naked Russian acrobat. You should never wake a man from a horny dream. Oh, Olga, I'm so sorry. Will you ever forgive me?"

"Sherlock, get up! I think I've figured it out."

"Just give us a minute, will you?" he said, his eyes rolling into his forehead to focus on some imaginary scene.

I stared back at him puzzled and frustrated until I realised his predicament.

"Okay, what is it?" he asked as he rolled off the settee and on to the floor before clambering to his feet, adjusting his attire as he rose.

"Well," I blurted, "John Horner, running." I picked up a pad and one of the many pens scattered across the floor. "Can you write that down for for me?" I asked, handing him the pen and pad.

"Running," he repeated, as he scribbled down the word in uppercase letters, before looking back up to me.

"Okay," I continued, "next we have the courting couple, Emma and Tom. Can you write down 'heavy petting' for me?"

"Heavy petting," said Holmes, pronouncing each syllable as he wrote.

"Then we had whatshisname, Harry Baker, the singer in that death metal band. However, if you've ever heard death metal, it's more shouting that than singing."

"Too right," agreed Holmes. "They sound like they've been possessed by a tone-deaf wildebeest in the rutting season." He scrawled down the word 'shouting', smiling in dawning realisation as he did. On scratching out the G, he chose not to disturb my flow, but instead sat obediently, pen poised. "Oh, Doc, you shine like a sun. What's next?"

"Bombing, Lestrade, and finally smoking. The chap in Yarm, Bob Peterson, he died of smoke inhalation. And there we have it," I said, my enthusiasm petering out on the recalling that there was a lot more to this than a puzzle.

"Running, heavy petting, shouting, bombing, smoking," read out Holmes. "Very good, it's that sign they used to have at the baths. Except it's just 'petting'. 'Heavy petting' is a Bad Manners album. That's sick. I used to love that sign. Fancy spoiling something like that. I've seen that sign. They have it on sale in a furniture shop in Yarm. Cinnamon Sunset."

"Cinnamon Bay," I corrected.

"Yeah, something like that."

"What were you doing in there?"

"Trying to buy a magnifying glass."

"What for?"

"Well, I'm not getting any younger. However, with you hanging around the flat all the time, I do think my eyesight's improving."

After a short journey to Yarm, preceded by a longer discussion with Martha to borrow her cab, we returned to the flat with a replica metal 'Will Patrons Kindly Refrain From' sign. Positioning it on the mantelpiece, we both stood back, mouths pursed and hands on hips, attempting to spark some inspiration.

"It's a shame they're not in the right order," I commented, "then we'd have an idea of what the next murder attempt would be."

Holmes waved his finger in the air, tracing the order of the murders across their related icons on the sign.

"Oh, that's bad," he said, grabbing a felt tip pen from the floor and drawing a zero over the running icon in the top left corner of the poster.

I assume you remember the sign? It was a safety notice used at public swimming pools years ago, to warn against anti-social and hazardous behaviour. Nine instructions in all, arranged as comical little sketches in a three by three matrix under the heading 'Will Patrons Kindly Refrain From'. I can still remember it now. From left to right, top to bottom there was: running, pushing, acrobatics or gymnastics, shouting, ducking, petting, not heavy petting, bombing, swimming in the diving area, and smoking. The possibility of someone sneaking a crafty fag in the shallow end seems an unlikely scenario, even back in those days.

After the zero in the top left, Holmes then placed an X on the far right of the second row and then a zero on the left hand side at the same level. It was soon apparent what he was doing. He was tracing out a game of noughts and crosses. He placed an X in the bottom left over the bombing icon and a zero, or rather a nought, in the bottom right.

"The next move has got to be here," he said, pointing the pen tip at the 'ducking' symbol in the middle square. "It looks like the next murder will be a drowning."

He then moved to where the map plotting out the various murder locations was still laid on the floor. "If we've got two murderers," he mumbled, "a nought killer and a cross killer, then this becomes a different picture. It looks like Nought is operating in the South and Cross is doing his stuff north of here. It's difficult to know much about Cross however, with only Baker Street and Seaton Carew plotted." Holmes paced around stalking over the map. "Let's assume that these two fellas meet and it's about in the middle, so somewhere near Baker Street. Nought therefore lives south of here and Cross heads home northwards. So the next killing will be near where Cross lives in the North."

"There's a lot of water between here and Seaton Carew," I observed.

"Yes," agreed Holmes, "but I'm somehow drawn to here," he said, tapping the end of the pen on the map. "The nature reserve at Seal Sands."

"That's quite an area," I commented.

"Yes," confirmed Holmes solemnly. "And it's also quite secluded."

6

"Sherlock, can I say the unsayable?" I asked.

"Difficult, that's a bit like expecting the unexpected. I tried that once and my head nearly shot off."

"This root cause," I continued, "the trainer chap you referred to earlier. It's got to be our friend the Professor. He's got to be at the bottom of all this. There can't be two psychotic criminal geniuses operating on Teesside, surely?"

"Yes, there can," he replied. "There's no data to lead us to that conclusion, but there's just as much to lead us elsewhere."

"Elsewhere?" I queried. "Where do you have in mind?"

"Nowhere. I have nothing in mind. But I'm quite happy to give your thoughts a borrow. Whoever it is, he's Hovis."

"Hovis?" I asked.

"Brown bread. Dead."

"Sherlock, we're not killers. When, if, we find this chap, we turn him into the police."

"I agree, Doc. I just don't see that option being available to us. At some point, he's gonna train his sights on us."

"Us?"

"Yeah, at the minute he finds us entertaining. If we're going to catch him, we need to start annoying him. We need to unsettle him. Bring him down from his observation tower and into the streets."

"Let's not do that then. Let's find another way."

Holmes stayed silent. Pensive, as he searched for a non-existent scenario.

"He's gonna kill you first," he said, placing his glass on the table without imbibing.

"Me?" I replied, my neck weighing heavily.

"Yeah," he sighed, tilting his head and looking back at me apologetically. "He'd want to weaken me, remove you from my armoury, take away the perspective you bring. Where I go around corners, you cut across the grass."

To be complimented and frightened for your life in the same moment is a heady mix of emotions, I tell you.

"That's alright then," I remarked. "So you've drawn this conclusion and never thought to mention it at all?"

"I didn't want to worry you. Besides, he wants to kill me as well. I'm the star of the show. I reckon he's got something special in mind for me. I'm thinking a fatal fight at the top of High Force. I fall and swirl to my death, trapped in an inescapable eddy. I always dream I die in water. It's probably because I'm a Pisces."

"Okay, fine, it sounds like quite a do. I'll RSVP as soon as the invitation comes through, shall I? Except I won't be able to because me, and probably my plus one, will probably already be dead!"

"Not if we kill him first."

"I'm a doctor not a hit man."

"Okay, I'll kill him. You can just be the bait."

"How's that better?"

Holmes puffed his cheeks out and exhaled, his eyes flicking in their sockets.

Occasionally in life, if you're fortunate less than once, there are times when the most difficult path is the easiest one to take. I was staring right down mine and it was frightening. The general efficacy of Holmes' conjecture had me scared for my life.

7

Holmes paced around the living room of his billet in 22 Baker Street, deftly avoiding the clutter of pens and paper that littered the floor. His main focus was on the map still pinned with the locations of the killings. Dropping to his haunches, he prodded his finger at the expanse of water near Seal Sands. "That's handy," he said. "There's only one road in."

"He might come in by boat," I reasoned.

"He might," chimed Holmes. "Can you swim?"

"Of course," I confirmed. "Can you?"

"Nineteen lengths of the Forum," he replied.

"Couldn't you have made it twenty?"

"I didn't want to show off," he said, rising to his feet. "We need to get over there. But not dressed like this. Let's go and see what Marth can knock up for us."

We entered Hud Couture to find the proprietor in the back with the kettle boiling.

"Missus Hudson," called Holmes.

Martha appeared, looking vaguely annoyed by the interruption. "You can hear that kettle boiling at fifty yards. Two teas, is it?"

"No, I'm good," said Holmes to her surprise. "We need your help. Me and the Doc are going to a fancy dress party."

"Sherlock," she exclaimed, "this is a fashion boutique not a fancy dress shop. Do I look like Mister Benn the shopkeeper?"

"No, his moustache was quite nice and well-trimmed," retorted Holmes, tracing the shape of a small stamp on his upper lip. That didn't help. Arms crossed, Martha only needed a stare to reply. "Oh come on, Martha. You know you like seeing us in our undercrackers."

"Batman and Robin, is it?"

"No," recoiled Holmes. "We need to look like a couple of old fishermen. Salty seadogs who look like they've been kicking around the seaside their whole lives."

"Well, the Doc might take a bit of work, but I think you've got that boxed off already. Just stick a couple of sardines in your pocket. Actually, don't bother." Holmes shrugged a whatever. "Okay," agreed Martha, "I've got some stuff upstairs that might work. I was gonna take it to the church jumble, but it looks like the kids will have to do without their Sunday School biscuits."

After a short period of audible rummaging, Martha returned with a large cardboard box piled with old, thick, scratchy clothes. There was a horrible dark suit in a Prince of Wales check and two or three Aran wool pullovers.

"What have we got here?" asked Holmes, taking the heavy load from her. Placing the box on the floor, he worked his way through the pile, throwing items in my direction as he went.

Once we were dressed, Martha sat each of us on a chair in the middle of the shop floor and smeared Holmes' and then my face with makeup. A review of her work in the mirror proved impressive.

"We look ancient," I commented.

"I can't take all the credit for that," mocked Martha.

"She's always liked a dressing up box," smirked Holmes.

As I moved to change back into my jacket and trousers, Holmes interrupted me. "Leave it on, Doc, let's give it a test drive."

"What d'you mean?" I asked.

"Let's go and take a look at the crime scene."

"For which crime?"

"The one that hasn't happened yet over at Seal Sands."

"You're not using my cab dressed like that," interjected Martha.

"It's too conspicuous anyway. We'll get the train to Seaton Carew. It goes in twenty-five minutes. We've time for a cooking lager on the way to the station. I'm parched."

Moving around in a state of disguise is actually quite a liberating experience. We sat on the rattling local train to Seaton Carew Station with hardly a glance in our direction. It was as if I was in a bubble. If you can find someone with Martha's skill in transformation, I would strongly recommend it.

With our ultimate destination away from the station, we alighted the train with a reasonable distance to cover on foot, the heavy clothes causing a fair sweat. I thought myself quite fit, however I did find the trek arduous. Oddly Holmes, a man strange to exercise, seemed unaffected.

"I think he'll come from the other direction," he said as we walked.

"How do you know that?" I panted.

"I don't. I just think he's unlikely to come through a town full of people eating candyfloss and chips from a cone."

"It's a wide area," I said as we left the road to yomp across the fields and sand dunes.

On reaching the coast, Holmes came to standstill. Placing his hands in his pockets, he gazed across the watery expanse. With the wind quelled and the sun uninhibited by cloud, it was a refreshing vista. Oddly Holmes seemed more interested in the water than the landscape that bounded it, the latter only warranting the most casual of glances.

"We need to camp out," said Holmes, his view still fixed on the water.

"Camp out?" I questioned.

"Yeah, go and grab a tent and a camping stove."

I responded with a look of disdain, not relishing the idea of sleeping under canvas on the hard irregular ground.

"Have you not been camping before?" asked Holmes.

"No, never."

"Not even in your mam's back garden?"

"Nope."

"You haven't lived."

The next afternoon we trekked the same journey from the railway station, our progress hampered by large backpacks containing the camping gear that Holmes had hastily pulled together.

On reaching a fairly flat piece of ground between two mounds of dune, Holmes called a halt to our trudge. Climbing out of my charge, I let the pack thud to the ground. In response, Holmes flashed me a look of disdain, before mirroring my action.

His disappointment still evident, he unfastened the ties on the top of my pack to reveal two four packs of Carling Black Label. His brow still furrowed, he pulled a can from its pack and tapped its top before angling it away to mitigate any effects of its impact with the ground. The can popped open with the minimum of fuss and he handed it to me, before repeating the process with a second can for himself. "Let's rehydrate and we'll get the tent up," he said as he took a seat on the sand.

Sleeping in the tent wasn't actually as horrific as I had feared. Holmes had packed a pair of roll up foam mats, and once you had manoeuvred the sand into the rough terrain of your body, the combined effect provided a requisite amount of comfort. This, added to the soothing soundtrack provided by the ocean, allowed me a decent amount of sleep. I'm uncertain if it was the same for Holmes, who I never saw sleeping throughout.

I awoke reasonably refreshed the first morning to the sound and smell of sausages sizzling on a gas stove. As I peered my way out of the tent into the cool light of the morning, Holmes handed me sausage and brown sauce, sandwiched in a large bap and accompanied by one of the cans of lager that had escaped the previous night's consumption.

"Sleep well?" he enquired cheerfully.

I confirmed the adequacy of my slumber before tucking into the manna before me.

"I can smell rats," mumbled Holmes with an air of concern. Looking around, I reasoned he was smelling a rat in the metaphorical sense, however the phrase "little furry bastards" soon cleared that up. He then warned me against dropping any of the food in our camp area.

"If only a stray sausage could attract the vermin we're looking for," I commented to Holmes' nod of agreement.

Hot on the heels of my first experience of camping, came my introduction to another popular pastime that to that date I'd avoided. Holmes dug into the bottom of one of the backpacks to retrieve two fishing lines and a small tin of sardines in tomato sauce.

"That's not going to last very long," I remarked, pointing at the tin.

"This is just what we use to catch the small fish," he replied. "Then we use the small fish to catch the bigger fish." Given my inexperience in the domain, I conceded to his explanation.

We made our way over the dunes until we reached the shore. Staring out over the water, I was confused as to the mechanics of our fishing expedition. I couldn't figure how we would project our fishing lines far enough out into the water. The procedure became clear when I looked over my shoulder to see Holmes pulling on the bow of a battered old wooden rowing boat.

"That doesn't look particularly sea-worthy," I commented as he tugged it in fits and starts across the sand.

"It'll be fine," he replied.

Assisting him in his task, we coaxed the boat into the water, before rolling up our trouser legs to wade out to a reasonable depth for boarding. With Holmes at oar and me over the prow, we travelled out a fair distance from the coastline.

"That's probably about nineteen lengths of the Forum," I commented as we reached what seemed to me a more than adequate distance.

Holmes stowed the oars and removed two cans of lager from his plastic shopping bag. He passed a can to me and popped open one for himself, before lowering those remaining in the bag over the side suspended from the oar cleat. He then laid back to bask in the late morning sun.

"Are we gonna do any fishing?" I enquired.

"Of course," replied Holmes. "I knew there was something."

We bobbed up and down for over three hours in that dilapidated death trap without tweaking the interest of a single fish. At one point, I checked my line to find my bait gone, but with my interest for the hunt waned, I slung the line back overboard without replenishing it.

"Have you ever caught a fish using this technique?" I asked, as we made our way back to camp.

"I've never caught a fish," he replied.

By the evening of day two, with our provisions of sausages and lager running perilously low, Holmes set off into town for supplies. I was left to guard the camp. However as he disappeared across the dunes, I was struck with the vapidity of my instructions. What was I to do on the event of the killer appearing? Fortunately, that scenario wasn't exercised and inside an hour or so, Holmes returned with an emperor's banquet of pastry-encased processed meat. I fielded a sausage and bean bake thrown in my direction and observed the lighting up of his face as he unpacked two packs of Peroni from one of his shopping bags. "You've got to have a few Peronis when you're on yer holidays," he remarked.

For three unseasonably mild March days we camped, fished unsuccessfully and ate artery-clogging fare. As the time passed, the reason for us being there faded from the forefront of my consciousness. I was jolted back to task by a message received by Holmes on his smartphone.

"Looks like the game's kicked off," he said, peering into the screen of his phone, which he'd studiously kept charged throughout the duration of our stay, using a small solar panel. With me not having the same planning and foresight, my phone had long since given up. "A girl has gone missing in Saltburn. Helen Stoner didn't return home yesterday after a night out down the Boro," he said, biting thoughtfully on his left thumbnail.

"Are we in the wrong place?" I asked.

Holmes took some time to consider. "No, no, no," he muttered before looking across the landscape, his eyes narrowed.

"Should we get ourselves over to Saltburn?"

"No, let's stay here," he replied. His decision was unqualified and, to me, confusing.

Our routine of eating, sleeping and fishing was unaffected by the news from Saltburn, however that was where my thoughts lay. The next morning, Holmes was proved right.

"He's here," he whispered, moving to turn off the camping stove. "Did you hear something?"

"No, but the locals have. The plovers have stopped chirping."

We both stood to stare across the dunes as the light advanced on the morning. Holmes' eyes darted from side to side, but appeared to be serving only as direction finders for his hearing. Then, from the dune to our right, two figures rose from the sand. It was obvious from their silhouettes that they each carried firearms.

"Two," remarked Holmes with quiet surprise.

"Good morning," called one of the characters as he approached. "Please don't think about moving."

Neither Holmes nor I offered a response. As they got closer, it was apparent that their weaponry exhibited some sophistication.

8

Our two captors appeared to be in their mid-twenties, if that; barely youths. Dressed in military camouflage, they were of similar height and build, one dark-haired, the other fair.

"What's this about?" I asked.

"Our... mentor... has decided the entertainment you've been providing him with has diminished to the point where it's no longer interesting. He'd now rather you weren't getting in the way. It's bad for business having you meddling where you're not wanted."

"Yeah," remarked the other, "when you saved Lestrade you buggered up our little game."

Holmes stared blankly back at him.

"We need you to put these on," said the first, the one with the dark hair, presenting two pairs of steel handcuffs. He then passed his gun to the other before walking behind Holmes to cuff him.

"You know you're getting old when sadistic serial killers start looking as young as you two," I commented as he pulled my arms back.

"We're not serial killers," replied the other. "We're professional assassins."

"Tamado, tomato," I retorted.

"Either way you die," came the cold response from the dark-haired one as he cuffed me.

We were frog-marched down to the shore, our progress encouraged by the jab of a machine gun barrel between the shoulder blades, Holmes still yet to break his silence. When we reached the beach, the dark-haired assassin again handed his weapon to the blond one before retrieving some heavy-looking chains from his backpack, with which he proceeded to bind together our feet. He then dragged the wooden rowing boat from the location we'd left it earlier and pushed both Holmes and I into it.

As we lay in the hull of the boat, the two men piled timber and driftwood of various shapes and sizes on top of us.

"I always wanted a Viking burial," whispered Holmes, "but I was somehow expecting to be dead first."

"Sherlock, this is it. We're going to die."

"Keep calm, and still," he replied quietly through the crash of the wood being loaded above us.

Following the boat's filling with timber, came the terrifying sound of the kindling being lit at our feet. The wood started to crackle and within seconds, I could feel the heat of the flame boiling off the dampness my trouser legs had absorbed from the dew on our early morning march through the dunes. Then came the motion of the boat as the two men heaved it out into the water. Staring up through the wood at the sky, it was difficult to gauge how fast we were drifting, but it felt like we'd been caught by the tide and were moving with a reasonable speed. As the heat increased, I tried to escape it by walking myself up the bottom of the boat on my shoulder blades. It was difficult, with progress hampered by the weight of timber on top of us.

As the heat approached unbearable, I could do nothing but cry out. "Sherlock," I screamed.

"Right," he said, "with me. Rock the boat, baby." He swayed

from left to right, creating a lateral rocking motion. After three or four oscillations, I managed to synchronise with him, perhaps more than doubling the effect. It wasn't long before we were creating quite a sway, to the point where the seawater was starting to swill in over the sides of the boat, immediately reducing the heat.

Just as I became convinced by Holmes' solution to our predicament, a shot rang out. Our assailants had started shooting at us from their position on the shore, a second shot splintering through the side of the boat just near my left ear.

"Keep going," shouted Holmes.

There was then a cold, dulled silence, as the boat capsized and we were plunged into the freezing water. With the constraint of our metal bonds, I could do nothing but sink. I jack-knifed my body in an attempt to return to the surface, but it was useless.

Then through the watery gloom, I saw Holmes. He strapped a mask to my face and I could breathe. Gesticulating with his finger, he pointed downwards. I had little choice but to comply and sink to the seabed. It was difficult to see, but Holmes, who was wearing a mask similar to the one he'd given me, mimed an imaginary watch and signalled ten with his fingers.

He swam to my feet and worked on the chains until he had unlocked the padlock, before swimming behind me to work on the handcuffs. After a short while pulling at my wrists, he returned to view, shaking his head to communicate a lack of success.

He floated in front of me for a good few minutes, waving his free arms in the water to maintain station. He then pointed at his imaginary watch again and angled his head to tell me it was time to go. Hooking his arm under mine, he dragged me through the water, myself adding some locomotion with kicks of my feet.

It was a long swim and we were both breathless as he dragged us onto the beach.

"What happened?" I panted as I recovered my wind.

"We didn't die," he breathed back, from his position lying beside me.

"Yeah, I know that. Where did the masks come from?"

"I stashed them. A few days ago."

"You knew we were going to get dumped in the water?"

"I thought we might be," he said, regathering his breath. "I wasn't expecting them to set fire to us. That wasn't on the fucking poster. 'Will patrons kindly refrain from Viking burials.' "

"Why didn't you tell me?"

"I didn't want to worry you."

"You didn't want to worry me?" I protested in exasperation. "And how did you get the chains off?"

"I picked the locks."

"You picked the locks?"

"Yeah, I've been practising. Can you stop repeating me? It's really annoying."

"Sherlock," I exhaled.

"Stop whinging," he retorted. "I saved you, didn't I? Do you want me to throw you back in?"

"Sherlock, we could have frozen to death in that water. We still might if we don't get out of these wet clothes."

"Nah," replied Holmes, "Hartlepool Power Station keeps this water nice and warm. They pump it round the reactors to cool them. You weren't thinking of having kids, were you? If you do, they'll probably end up having super powers now. It'll be a bugger trying to get them to come in for their tea."

I rolled onto my stomach in order that Sherlock could work on the handcuffs. In under a couple of minutes, he had freed me. As I moved to right myself, he shushed me.

"Be quiet," he whispered.

Continuing my roll, I looked in the direction of his observation, fully expecting to see the outlines of our two assassin friends. Instead, in roughly the area we'd been set adrift, I identified a familiar figure. It was Detective Inspector Bradstreet accompanied by a number of armed police officers.

"It's okay," I said softly. "It's only Bradstreet."

"I know," confirmed Holmes. "Let's stay dead."

"What?"

"It gives us an edge. If everyone thinks we're dead, it will be easier to grab those two goons."

On his direction, we both crawled slowly out of view to lay with our backs behind the mound of a sand dune. We were perhaps only three-hundred yards from the site that was now being investigated as our murder scene.

"We can't do this, Sherlock. If Mary thinks I've been killed, she'll be distraught."

"Nah," he dismissed.

"Eh?" I queried in consternation, nearly unscrewing my neck to look at him.

"They won't let this out straight away. It helps them too. Trust me, Doc, opportunities come in strange disguises. Anyway, back in a minute."

As I lay shivering and trying to warm myself in the morning sun, Holmes ran across the dunes, stooped to ensure he stayed out of sight of the police contingent. He ducked out of my eye line before rising to run back. He returned to where I was laid with two black bin bags. "There you go," he said. "A towel and a change of clothes."

"You think of everything," I remarked.

"Except Viking burials apparently. Little gets."

9

We made our way back to civilisation on foot along the railway track. The trains were few and easily observed, affording us plenty of time to duck out of sight.

"Those two weren't from here," commented Holmes as we trudged in single file, him at point, me bringing up the rear. "Their accents weren't right."

"Neither of them had much of an accent," I recalled.

"Yeah," said Holmes, "the vowels weren't the right shape." We stumbled a bit further before he continued. "They were different, but also the same. They're from different places, but the way they both spoke was heading somewhere else."

"I haven't got a clue what you are talking about," I mumbled,

He turned to face me and grab my shoulders, his mouth wide in realisation. "University students," he exclaimed. "They had that moshed up accent some students get. The fickle, easily-led ones."

"I can't say I've ever noticed it," I said as he unhanded me to resume our trek.

"The map makes sense now," he said as he walked. "The centre point of the crimes wasn't the flat. It was the university. It's only a stone's throw away from Baker Street."

Without warning, he left the rail tracks to hop over the wooden rails of a farm fence.

"It's over here," he called back to me.

"What is?" I asked.

"Where we are going."

"Where are we going?"

"You'll see."

I was too tired to continue such a potentially fruitless debate. Instead I threw my hands in my pockets and stomped after him, head down to navigate the unevenness of the field. It wasn't long before the surroundings became familiar. We were at Wolviston. We walked down the lane by the church, between the Welly and the Ship Inn, before heading down the bank into Billingham. Half way down the bank, he turned into the drive of a large detached property.

"Where are you going?" I asked.

"In here," he replied.

I followed somewhat nervously, wondering if the residents were home, my concern mitigated slightly by confusion. On reaching the door, Holmes grabbed a large terracotta plant pot, containing not much more than soil and weedy grass, and rolled it from its standing position. From beneath it, he recovered a key which he then used to unlock the door. He entered and I wandered in behind, surveying the surroundings for a clue on who might live there. The obvious fact, hanging in the air, was that it had been vacant for at least a few weeks.

"It's alright, isn't it?" said Holmes.

"It's lovely," I replied. "Who owns it?"

"I do," said Holmes. "This is my other gaff."

"You never cease to amaze me, Sherlock."

"I will one day," he smiled. "Everything has an end. Do you fancy a beer? We could nip back up to the Welly."

"We could," I replied, "All that walking has worked up a bit of a thirst. But we're supposed to be dead, and given you're on the front of the Gazette every other week, I think you'll be spotted."

"Good point," he replied. "Never mind. I've got something upstairs that should sort that."

A short while later, we found ourselves in the Wellington Inn, adorned in the most unconvincing of false beards. We wouldn't have looked more ridiculous if we'd worn prosthetic penises for noses.

"Ah that's nice," said Holmes as he chugged down a craft beer, the brand of which I don't recall. "All that lager made me feel a bit gassy."

"I know, I was in the tent with you," I replied. "If you don't mind me asking, why do you own such a thing as these stupid beards?"

"They're not working, are they?" smiled Holmes. "Martha got them for a fancy dress party. I was going through a beardy stage at the time and we went as each other."

"What? You were dragged up as Martha?"

"Yeah, don't laugh. I nearly pulled."

"I'm not laughing. I'm wondering why on earth you bought two."

"I've actually got three. They were on offer… Oh shit," hissed Holmes looking over my shoulder.

I twisted around to see the headline ticking across the screen of the television on the wall: 'Sherlock Holmes Feared Dead'.

"Mary," I exhaled, putting my hand to my ridiculously-bearded face and spinning back around to flash him a look of disappointment.

"It doesn't mention you," he defended, as I shook my head in disbelief. "Sup up," he sighed. "We'll go down to the house and give her a ring. Actually we could use the phone behind the bar and have a few more beers."

"We'll go back to the house," I asserted. "I'm not ringing from a pub."

On re-entering Holmes' palatial abode, he picked up a phone and threw it in my direction. My call with Mary was fraught. She'd seen the news and was beside herself. After a long period of placating, during which she dismissed our endeavours as "stupid games", I managed to calm her down. This was largely achieved with the use of a white lie that the news story was mostly one of misunderstanding.

I made my way into the kitchen to find Holmes rounded over a laptop.

"Are you reading the news of your demise?" I commented glibly, exhausted by my previous discussion. Looking over his shoulder, I observed the laptop screen which was displaying a picture of a man's face as it appeared to morph from one person to another. Eyes would narrow, noses change length and ears dance up and down in an amusing wiggle.

"What's that?" I enquired.

"It's a facial search algorithm. I knocked it up a while back. You feed in some key features such as eye colour, face shape, haircut, etcetera, and it trawls the internet looking for a match. I developed it for the police, but when they threw me in prison I thought, 'fuck 'em'."

"That's amazing," I remarked.

"It is if it works," muttered Holmes. "I've never really tried it before." He tapped his fingers impatiently on the kitchen table. "The clock's ticking now. Those two clowns will soon realise we're not dead."

"Mary won't say anything," I appealed.

"No, but people seep data. It won't be long before we're the resurrection."

Holmes flicked a couple of keys to toggle the laptop to another view. "Recognise blondie?" he said. There on the screen was a picture of one of our erstwhile captors. "Paul Roylott," he said, before flicking back to the previous view to find the animation settled on the picture of a young Chinese chap. "Mmm," he hummed, "the software still needs some work." He percussed a few keys and restarted the search, standing up to pace up and down the kitchen. Periodically he glanced at the laptop screen in an almost furtive manner. "Viola," he exclaimed when the picture settled on bandit number two, 'Michael Grimesby'.

"What now?" I asked,

"We kill them."

"Sherlock," I protested.

"I'm kidding," he responded. "Get on the phone to Chisel Chin, give her these fellas' names, and tell her to get over to the university with some armed rozzers. We'll meet her over there."

"What? You think after murdering us they'll have gone back to take in a few lectures?"

"No, but there's a good chance they'll report back to…"

Holmes tailed off before the end of the sentence. He closed his eyes and held his arms out in front of him, his hands in a grasping shape. His shoulders snaked from side to side, taking his neck and head with them. Occasionally he shuffled his feet to provide a slight reorientation. All through, his eyes darted behind closed eyelids. He then opened them and looked at me. "No," he said, "it would be carnage. People would be killed."

Holmes had stepped through the scenario we were heading to and drawn the conclusion that Grimesby and Roylott could not be taken without a fight. Given their proclivity for firearms, there was a severe risk of members of the public being caught in the crossfire.

"Grimesby lives over in Fairfield," he continued. "I'm gonna go over there and wait for him to shuffle on home."

"I'm coming with you."

"It's okay, Doc, it's a one-man job. You go an' see Mary."

On my insistence that I stay with him, we headed out of the house and turned down the driveway. Holmes selected the fob on a keyring he'd retrieved from an empty fruit bowl in the hall, and activated the large garage door that rose to reveal a beautiful vintage Porsche.

"Nice," I commented.

"Ye-ah," whooped Holmes in two syllables.

We climbed in and Holmes turned over the engine. It screamed but was never going to start. "When was the last time you drove it?" I asked.

"A few years ago."

"The petrol's gone off."

"Really?"

"Yeah, the same happened with my old lawn mower. That's why I wasn't too bothered when the wife got it in the divorce settlement. Even though she went to live in a second floor flat."

A short while later we were standing at the bus stop on the roundabout opposite the Kings Arms, our faces again obscured by obviously false beards. "Our dad was bar skittles champion of the Kings," said Holmes, nodding in the direction of the pub.

"Right," I remarked, not knowing what to do with the statement.

"Yup," he replied, "he had a method. The Holmes spiralling technique ended up getting banned. Shame really, it could have been the new Fosbury Flop."

The bus ride was uncomfortable, largely due to the attention grabbed by our worthless disguises. Travelling to somewhere in Stockton, we alighted the bus to complete the remaining mile or so of the journey on foot.

We snuck up to the house, taking care not to be exposed by the view from the windows. On reaching the front door, Holmes tried the handle to find it unlocked, before slowly swinging open the door. As quietly as we could, we crept in, our destination guided by the electronic sounds of a videogame emanating from the lounge. Before entering, Holmes looked back at me. He flashed me a look, void of concern, and turned into the door.

Grimesby, who was lying along the couch playing the video game, sprang to his feet. Adopting a martial arts type posture, he squared off to Holmes, taking care to keep a bead on me. As I moved sideways to broaden our attack, Holmes barrelled in. Showing scant regard to an inadequate defence, he whipped a hooked punch into the side of Grimesby's face causing him to crash to the carpet. Feinting to finish the job with a kick to the ribs, he resisted and turned away.

"Right, Doc," he said, "give us a hand."

Between us, we manhandled Grimesby up the staircase to dump his groaning body in the bathtub. Holmes turned on the tap to send the water thundering into his face. Between bursts, I expected an interrogation but there was none. That said it didn't appear any information would be forthcoming, with Grimesby laying there steadfast.

"We won't get anything out of him or his mate," said Holmes as he dragged him dripping from the bath. "They're too well trained," he murmured.

"So why the waterboarding?"

"I was just tapping the barometer," he said dismissively.

As Holmes reached the top of the stairs, he released the struggling carcass of his prisoner, letting him crash down the stairs. Skipping down the steps in pursuit, he hauled Grimesby back to his feet to direct him back into the living room. Retrieving a chair from the kitchen and Grimesby's own handcuffs from his pocket, he bound him to the chair, finishing the job with some locally-acquired packing tape applied to both ankles and mouth.

Holmes then picked up Grimesby's phone from the sofa. He angled it, allowing the light from window to scan across the screen, as I'd seen him do many times before. He then unlocked the phone on the first attempt. There was a short exchange of text messages before Holmes looked up to address me.

"Righteo," he sang. "Matey is on his way."

Holmes returned to the kitchen to fetch another chair. I watched with curiosity as he placed it back to back with the one occupied by Grimesby, the second chair facing on to the window.

"Doc, fancy sitting here?" he enquired, pointing to the chair. His plan was apparent. The scene he was setting was one in which Grimesby played the part of a captured Holmes, whereas myself, somewhat typecast, filled in as myself.

It wasn't long after I'd been taped into position that I observed the figure of Roylott, making his way gingerly towards the front door through the window. Calling "hallo" on entry, he came straight to the lounge. As he swung open the door, there was a thud and he skidded dead-like across my feet.

"Two nil," asserted Holmes from behind my plane of view.

Holmes freed me from my bonds and between us we substituted Roylott into my position. As we waited for "Vinegar Vera" et al to respond, Holmes made his way into the kitchen to return with some very small bottles of beers. "He's only got this French cooking," he said, handing myself two of the four bottles, before picking up the games controller vacated on our arrival by Grimesby. "Fancy a game of Mario Karts while we wait?"

To Bradstreet's protest but on Superintendent Spaulding's insistence, Holmes was included in the initial interrogation. Oddly, Bradstreet chose to interview both men at the same time.

The men, dressed in dark blue overalls with their hands cuffed behind their backs, sat stony-faced and still as Detective Inspector Bradstreet rotated through some quite typical questions.

Her approach was more accusational than investigative, the strategy focusing on the exaggerated consequences of their crimes, should they choose not to speak. I suspect there wasn't actually an approach that would shake them from their silence. Holmes was right. They were well-prepared for this eventuality.

Holmes sat next to her to the large part mirroring the still persona of the two assassins. As Bradstreet concluded and Holmes and her stood to exit, Holmes appended a final question. "Are you expecting your professor friend to drag you out of this mess?"

The query prompted Roylott to flick his eyes to meet those of Holmes. This was the most activity the session had solicited from either of them.

10

Although Holmes was not one prone to retrospection, his preference to move on, he was always happy to celebrate the conclusion of our numerous episodes. Probably because this invariably involved copious amounts of alcohol. I found myself staggered by the turnaround we'd achieved. With scant evidence, and the local police force floundering, we had put two dangerous killers behind bars. Holmes' focus was now on the Engineer's Thumb, which he considered to be pouring half a degree on the cold side.

Also worthy of recognition was the story of Helen Stoner. Fortunately, the apparent abduction of the Saltburn girl turned out to be a falsehood. She'd simply had a heavy night out in Middlesbrough, lost her phone and her house keys, and took a few days to steel the courage to confess her dalliances to her parents. In the end, it worked out well. Her parents were relieved to see her and they soon forgave her waywardness.

As we sat in the Twisted Lip, the sporadic dialogue was saved by the entrance of Constable Hardwick. Dressed for the street, he congratulated us on our success and expressed his relief at the spurious nature of the news of our recent demises.

Holmes provided little recognition to either point, instead repointing the conversation to the subject of Detective Inspector Lestrade. Hardwick informed us that the news was good, and the inspector had left care to begin the final stages of his recuperation at home.

"Good," nodded Holmes. "He's still a dick though."

"Sherlock," I admonished.

"Okay, he's been in the wars and I'm sorry about that, but if it looks like a dick and talks like a dick; it's a dick."

"You mean duck," I corrected.

"You think Lestrade's a duck? You'd need a few gallon of hoisin sauce to get through all that."

I shook my head in exhausted desperation.

"Lestrade is so stupid that he couldn't find his arse with a satnav," continued Holmes, with childish mockery.

"Lestrade is so stupid that he still thinks the Hokey Cokey is what it's all about," added Hardwick.

"Lestrade is so stupid that he can't count past ten with his socks on," returned Holmes.

"Lestrade is so stupid that he failed a blood test," replied Hardwick.

"Lestrade is so stupid that he put a stamp on an email." Holmes.

"Lestrade is so stupid that he sits in the back of the car, because he thinks he gets a longer ride." Hardwick.

"Lestrade is so stupid that he applied for a b…"

At this point, you need to remember that Holmes only ever misses somewhere between very little and nothing at all. As Holmes and Hardwick's tirade continued, in walked Lestrade. The big lumbering policeman, in his size ten shoes, had stomped up unnoticed.

"Constable Hardwick," he boomed.

"Ah, Inspector Lestrade. I never saw you there," said Holmes.

There was a silence, broken by Lestrade on the introduction of his wife. "Our Lass," he said.

"Catherine," said Mrs Lestrade, offering her hand.

"I love your wheels," replied Holmes, much to her bewilderment.

Lestrade threw a bag from Psyche Attire in Holmes' direction. "That's for you," he grunted. "It's a thank you."

"Cheers," replied Holmes, looking in the bag and taking from it a leather-yoked donkey jacket. It was a replica of the one shredded by the bomb that, had it not been for Holmes, would have rendered Lestrade dead.

Holmes stood to try on the jacket, dry-faced but eyes smiling.

"How did you know my size, or did you just go for twenty sizes below yours?" Lestrade stayed stone-faced.

"Aw, Baz, you shouldn't have," said Holmes, offering Lestrade his hand.

Lestrade shook. "Don't mention it," he replied.

"Yeah, we don't want those gay rumours rearing their ugly heads again, do we?" japed Holmes. "I don't wanna have to start picking out curtains with yer," he added, before flashing a glance at a confused Mrs Lestrade.

THE NEW YARM STRANGLER

1

It was one of those typical mornings where Holmes was offering little in the way of dialogue. Feeling a little out of sorts, following some excessive consumption in the Irish Bar the previous evening, I was happy to just sit and watch Holmes as he employed his usual tactic of meticulously dividing his toast into precise soldiers. Through the course of the many times I'd observed this ritual, I'd grown to pity the poor irregular soldiers taken from the edge of the slice, who were eaten first and thus denied the glory of a dunking into his soft-boiled egg. To them, all chance of valour refused.

As the final conformant soldier set out on his solitary mission to Holmes' second boiled egg, the familiar spectre of Detective Inspector Lestrade appeared in the doorway. Without invite he joined us, sitting in one of the two vacant positions. "There's hell on up in Norton," he said, with obvious urgency in his voice.

Holmes carefully completed the consumption of his yolk-sodden soldier before repositioning his attention to Lestrade and acknowledging the bewildered detective with an "okay".

"Three murders," said Lestrade. "All strangled. The bodies all discovered within an hour of each other. We've got the whole village on lockdown. There's a bloody serial killer on the loose."

"What and you're asking for our help finding this fella? Have you had a knock on the head or something?"

"Yes. I have. I was blown halfway along Baker Street by a bomb. I suffered severe head injuries and ended up in a medically-induced coma for six weeks."

"Oh yeah, I remember that now. I was really worried. Fortunately, they managed to fix the footpath."

"I was almost killed!"

"Yeah, but I use that path to get to the pub."

"Look, Sherlock. Are you coming?"

"Fancy it, Doc?"

I just nodded. Not seriously considering my opinion to be a contributing factor to the decision. It wasn't a valid question. We were always going. Holmes just couldn't forgo the opportunity to toy with Lestrade. I'm quite sure he missed Lestrade through those months the Inspector was in hospital and, following that, the time he spent in various establishments recuperating. That he made it back to active duty was, to me, a surprise and somewhat of a testament to the man's animal-like tenacity.

"Howay then," exhaled Holmes, "let's go an' have a shufti."

2

As Lestrade and I walked across the grassed area near the duck pond to inspect the body of the first victim, we turned to see that Holmes had stopped some distance behind us. Standing perhaps twenty-five to thirty yards away from where the body was lain, his demeanour was that of someone waiting for a bus. He surveyed the scene in a slow and apparently disinterested manner, hardly glancing at the victim. Gone was the light-weight mood that earlier facilitated the jocular goading of Lestrade. In its place, a coin-opposite.

Eric Breckinridge was a retired engineer. A widower, he lived alone on the Crooksbarn estate. I'm no pathologist but the cause of death seemed easy to confirm, the bruising encircling his neck suggesting strongly that he'd been strangled. On also noticing the odd rock and a number of half wall bricks in the general vicinity of the body, I paid careful attention to the victim's head. There was no sign of trauma to the skull, or for that matter elsewhere on the body. To my mind, strangulation was the definite cause of Breckinridge's expiry.

I approached one of the scene of crime officers to ask what possessions they had recovered from the body. The only thing of note was that of his mobile phone, which had run short of charge. This didn't seem of great significance to me, the absence of both house keys and a wallet being the overriding point of interest.

"Doctor Pondicherry reckons he's been dead around six hours," said Lestrade, as Holmes approached. Oddly Holmes seemed hesitant, as if perturbed by the sight of the dead body.

"Where is Ray?" asked Holmes, using the nickname for pathologist Shreya Pondicherry, by which only he called her.

"At the second murder scene," replied Lestrade.

"Do you know it was second?" asked Holmes. "After this one?"

"Well, no," Lestrade corrected. "Pondicherry called earlier to say that victim died at a very similar time."

Holmes nodded. "What else is there?"

"Not much," I replied, "just a dead mobile phone. The damp must have got into it."

"No wallet?" queried Holmes.

"No, the killer must have taken it," responded Lestrade.

"Must have," chimed Holmes.

"That's odd," I interjected. "It was raining this morning but the body's no more than damp."

"He must have been killed somewhere else and dumped here," conjectured Lestrade.

"Must have," repeated Holmes via a mumble, before resuming his survey of the surrounding area. Without explanation, he set off away from us and across the grass, to scale a brick wall on the periphery of the area. From out of sight, and after just moments, a large blue thick plastic sheet was propelled over the top of the wall. Holmes followed it shortly afterwards.

He ambled back over to us, still maintaining his air of disinterest. "That would have kept a body dry," he said on his return, "and those bricks and shit would have weighed it down, until the wind got under it.

Then, for the briefest of moments, he focused on the body. He angled his head one way and then the other, before asking me to unbutton the victim's shirt. I did so to reveal a tattoo of a butterfly that filled most of his chest.

"Papillon," commented Holmes.

"Sorry?" I asked.

"That old film with Steve McQueen and Justin Hoffman."

"Dustin Hoffman."

"Yeah, that's him. Raymond."

"Rain Man."

"Alright, Barry fucking Took. You know what I mean."

"Barry Norman."

Holmes snorted, stifling a laugh with a grimace. At last I'd provoked some go in him.

"Papillon had a butterfly tattoo like that," he said, taking out his mobile phone to take a picture of the artwork. Lestrade flashed back the disappointed look of a wronged schoolteacher. It was a violation of Holmes' parole conditions to own a computing device of any sort. I myself was surprised at the abandon Holmes showed in flaunting the device in front of the police officer, who was well aware of the restrictions Holmes had had placed upon him by the courts.

On Holmes' insistence, we walked along the High Street to the site of the second murder. Again, he showed little interest in the body, laid part on the grass verge across a short metal fence flattened under impact. His enthusiasm in anything seemed faint, with the vigour I had provoked with my earlier antagonism proving to be short-lived. After some child-like scraping of his feet across the pavement, he approached one of the SOCOs for a summary. Oliver Oakshott, a local bricklayer, had also been strangled. Unlike the first victim, Oakshott was still in possession of his wallet and house keys, however some remarkable parity remained, in that his mobile phone was also flat of charge.

The third victim was Wendy Gate, an anaesthetist who also lived locally. We arrived at the scene to find Doctor Pondicherry midway through her examination. Ms Gate's possessions were laid neatly on a tray beside the body. Again, it was clear that strangulation had been the cause of her expiration.

"That's the third mobile of three that has lost its charge for one reason or another," I commented.

"Have you noticed something else?" added Holmes. "All the phones are the same make." Holding his hand up to scrape the stubble on his chin, he muttered, "Same operating system," without further elaboration.

"Can you unbutton her blouse?" he asked the doctor.

A little confused by the request, Pondicherry complied to reveal a small butterfly tattooed to the inside of her left breast. Holmes flashed a look of knowing in my direction, before turning to address Lestrade. "I've seen enough," he said despondently. "I'll have a ponder and get back to you."

"Back to the office?" I asked Holmes, feeling more familiar surroundings of the Twisted Lip might shake him from his funk.

"Nah, let's have a few round here," he replied. "It's supposed to be good. They've been calling it New Yarm."

Our entrance into the Highland Laddie prompted memories of Alastair Bruce and 'The Case of the Fifty Orange Pills'. This location had been significant in our apprehension of the crazy scientist who had poisoned half a dozen people with his experimental drugs.

It's worthy of admission that the Highland Laddie provides a different experience to that of our usual haunts, however it was still one I appreciated. Making a mental note to bring Mary here one evening, I began my review of the case. Lestrade's hypothesis that we were facing a serial killer seemed to have legs. The consistency in the murderer's attack suggested a single protagonist, however Doctor Pondicherry's conclusion that all three victims had been killed at around the same time presented logistical doubts. That said, a synchronised attack by three killers, all using the same murder method, seemed incredible.

The butterfly tattoos on two of the three victims were also worthy of note, especially as this was one of the things that seemed to draw out Holmes' interest. Reverting back to my mental notebook, I put an asterisk against this feature of the case.

Next on the list was the coincidence of the three dead mobile phones. If this was more than coincidence, which I suspected it was, what sort of a clue did it offer? Given the technical nature of the puzzle, it was more something for Holmes to ponder, however despite my expert summarisation, I was struggling with his engagement levels.

Certain that Holmes had heard little of my narrative, I enquired after his well-being.

"I'm fine," he assured. "Just feeling a little washed out."

"Do you have any thoughts?"

"Yeah, I like it in here."

"I mean on the case."

"No need, Doc, you're doing fine. You seem to be seeing doubts everywhere. Which is good."

"Shall we get out there and see if we can pick up any more clues?"

"Nah," he replied disinterestedly. "Let the police chase down the obvious avenues. It's not until the ripples settle that you get a clear reflection."

3

That afternoon we made that horrible journey to the mortuary, entering to find Doctor Pondicherry engaged in the examination of the second victim. Pondicherry's dress was akin to what a surgeon might wear, however Oliver Oakshott wasn't about to be saved on the table. "This is all pretty standard stuff," she commented on our approach. "He's telling me nothing more than we concluded in situ. He was strangled, with some brute force. Can you pop some gloves on, John? There is something of interest."

Despondent at being selected for this morbid task, I helped the doctor manoeuvre the naked body onto its side. The aspect of interest she was referring to was a large butterfly tattoo covering the majority of his back. That completed the set of three. It was now difficult to dismiss this as coincidence. But why would a particular design of body art make a victim of someone?

On our return to Baker Street, Holmes looked into the Dr Jekyll and Mr Hyde Tattoo Studio. He ducked behind the curtain to where the proprietor was applying a tattoo of a red heraldic lion to a young lady's bottom. Neither the tattooist nor his subject seemed fazed by our intrusion.

Holmes flicked through the photographs on his phone with the tattooist asking him if he recognised any of the work. "That's Joey Whatshisface from Inklings over in Stockton," he said on review of Wendy Gate's tattoo. "He loves a thick black line." With respect to the adornment of Breckinridge's chest, he wasn't so sure. "That looks old man," he said after much consideration, "and it's not an English pen. Far East somewhere, I reckon. He'll have picked that up in the army."

The sight of Oakshott's tattoo stuttered him. "I know that work," he said pensively, "it's mine. That's Oli, isn't it? We spent about six weeks on that. Is he dead?"

"If he's not," replied Holmes, "he's gonna wake up with one hell of a headache. When we left him the pathologist was sawing the top of his skull off."

Holmes' tasteless skit washed over the poor tattooist who was clearly unsettled by the knowledge of Oakshott's death.

"Did you know Oliver well?" I asked, in a tone apologetic for Holmes' transgression.

"Not really," he replied. "He just wandered in off the street wanting a tattoo. We chatted a bit while I was working, but just small talk. I couldn't tell you if he was married, where he worked or anything. Nice lad, though."

"Why a butterfly?" queried Holmes.

"It's just what he asked for."

"Did he have a particular design in mind?"

"Nah, he just left that up to me."

At last, Holmes was showing some interest.

We traversed the short distance along Baker Street to the Twisted Lip to find Detective Inspector Lestrade sitting in wait for us.

"What's this all about?" he asked us as we sat to join him.

"You're the detective," replied Holmes, signalling to Mary to furnish us with our usuals.

"Look," he replied, "Bradstreet's all over this. She's been sniffing around Spaulding all the time I was laid up. Trying to get him to send the big cases her way."

"Sounds like she's so far up Spaulding's arse, she can see your feet," japed Holmes.

"I'm sure Superintendent Spaulding knows when he's being manipulated," I reassured, as Mary set our drinks down heavily, clearly not enamoured by her recent inclusion of delivery in her job description.

Holmes sighed wearily, his reticence to engage resumed. "Okay," he conceded, "the multiple killings are key to this. In spite what you think Jumpin' Jack Flash, it's not a serial killer. Not in the usual sense. It was a coordinated attack. This is a war."

"What? You think there's a war going on in Norton?" queried Lestrade.

"Yeah," he said. "And it's not even a bank holiday weekend." He sat back, rubbing his mouth, a thought clearly welling in his mind. "The strangulation," he continued, "that's a bit old school, a bit gruesome. It's shock and awe. 'We can hit you hard and we can hit you fast and you won't even see us coming.' "

Lestrade looked baffled and frightened by the prospect.

"The butterflies," concluded Holmes, "they're a uniform, a symbol of allegiance."

"So what?" I asked. "Some sort of secret organisation?"

"I reckon so," he replied, "something like that. It's interesting that Oakshott wasn't that arsed about the design of a tattoo that covered the length of his back. He wasn't getting that for himself.

He wanted to join the club and show how committed he was to the cause. Hence the size of the thing."

"What cause?" asked Lestrade, drawn into Holmes' explanation.

"Dunno," said Holmes.

"So what do we do?"

"Well," he exhaled, "we're not gonna find the killer. Not unless your boys and girls turn up some DNA shit. Good luck with that by the way."

"You think it's only one killer?"

"Yeah… or more. We need to find the butterfly club and see what it's all about."

"How do we do that?" I asked.

"I'm not sure," said Holmes. "I need time to process the data. Another beer?"

"Not for me," responded Lestrade. "I better get back to the station and make sure Bradstreet isn't talking her way into my job. Let's catch up tomorrow when you've had time to do your processing."

"What is it?" I asked as Lestrade left. "You just don't seem interested in this."

"Doc," he said, as he stood to collect the empty glasses between his fingers. "I nearly got you killed last time out. I don't want to drag you through a war zone. You've got options. You don't need this shit."

"No, Sherlock. This is where I want to be."

"You daft get," he laughed whilst shaking his head, before angling a pensive look at Mary, at her duties behind the bar.

With Holmes' reticence, at least for the moment allayed, we headed on over to Norton to investigate the home of Eric Breckinridge. Given that the killer had apparently stolen Breckinridge's keys in the attack, it seemed logical to assume that they had interest in the contents of his house.

Breckinridge lived in a tidy semi-detached place, central in an aging but well-presented housing estate. We approached the front door to find it unlocked, my assumption being that the killer had left it that way.

We stepped into the lounge to find it stacked with military memorabilia. It was reminiscent of Isaac Wilson's place in Sheffield, which we'd visited during our search for Martha's estranged husband Paul. The various items on display were however from an altogether different era.

"Don't soldiers like their jobs?" remarked Holmes. "I bet your place isn't cluttered with pictures of your patients and stuff."

"Only you, Sherlock," I joked.

Holmes snorted before beginning his familiar reconnaissance routine, standing stationary with hands in pockets, his head and eyes flitting in a seemingly random progress, sometimes with his eyes not even open.

"There's nothing missing," he concluded.

"How do you know?"

"There's no gaps."

"What about the other rooms?"

"I'll go and check," he sighed, skulking out of the room, his hands still buried in his pockets.

While Holmes was away, I performed my own survey. The item that drew most of my attention amongst the numerous medals, pendants and frames, was one of the many photographs of uniformed soldiers. Nestled on an expensive-looking sideboard was the picture of two soldiers, one of whom was clearly Breckinridge. It seemed to take pride of position. Using my handkerchief to avoid leaving any fingerprints, I carefully removed the picture through the back of the frame. Under some newspaper, written in blue ink on the back of the photograph were the words 'Sandy Stark and Eric Breckinridge, 1960'.

I presented my find to Holmes on his return. His response was a shake of head and shoulders with uncertainty of the relevance.

"Did you find anything?" I asked.

"Nowt," he replied sharply.

"Has the killer been here?" I asked.

"It doesn't look like it," he replied.

"So who left the door open?"

"Probably the police. A couple of hours ago. Can you not smell Bradstreet's perfume?"

"Where did they get a key?"

"I dunno. A neighbour?"

"So why steal a key and then not bother using it?"

"Dunno. A change of mind. Some better advice."

As Holmes breezed out of the room, something caught my eye. Sandwiched between the sofa and the door was a wall socket with a phone charger plugged in and switched on. I laid the back of my hand across it. It was on the hot side of warm. The abandoned state of the charger seemed out of kilter with the unrelenting order elsewhere. I flicked off the switch and banked the observation for consideration later.

4

The next morning, we set off on the bus back to Norton, our plan to assess the feasibility of each of the three murders being the work of a single killer. Starting off at the duck pond, we chased along the High Street to the site of the second murder. From there, we ran to the third location, pausing only briefly to consider ducking into the Highland Laddie.

"We could stop the watch?" reasoned Holmes, before the look I returned convinced him to continue. Yomping through the streets of Norton was an embarrassing experience, the sight of two middle-aged men, jogging in hardly sporting attire, drawing some attention.

"Twenty-three minutes and five seconds," I panted as we reached the site of Wendy Gate's demise.

"Add a couple of minutes for the actual killings," appended a more well-for-wear Holmes. "It's doable, well within the tolerance of Ray's time of death estimates."

"But only if you know exactly where you are going," I added.

"Indeed," said Holmes. "And how could the killer, or killers, know that all three victims would be out and about on the same night?"

"They must have been meeting up somewhere," I reasoned.

"Yeah," breathed a thoughtful Holmes. "Well done, Doc. You're getting good at this malarkey."

We adjourned to our new favourite table in the Highland Laddie.

"Okay," said Holmes, "the duck pond's here, here's the High Street." He drew imaginary lines on the table. Grabbing some ketchup sachets from a pot ramekin on a nearby table, he placed one by the duck pond, one on the High Street, and one in the approximate location of the Wendy Gate killing. He then fished out some packets of salad cream. "Breckinridge lives here, Oakshott here and Gate here." He planted a salad cream at each site. "So where are they all coming from?"

He leaned back in his chair to point his eyes at the ceiling before snapping them shut. As I'd seen before, his eyelids undulated in a manner similar to the rapid eye movement induced during dream sleep. He maintained this state for a time best measured in minutes rather than seconds, before rocking forward as if jolted from a nap.

"Finish your beer," he said. "There's something we need to have a look at."

On leaving the Highland Laddie, we weaved purposefully through the housed streets, with Holmes apparently certain of his destination.

"Do you know what, Doc?" he laughed. "As we're going through all this, I can almost see your story for the Gazette being written. 'The Case of the Butterfly Murders'. I might have a go at writing down some of the stuff I got up to before we met, and start a rival column in the Northern Echo."

"I'm not sure about that as a title," I remarked.

"Sod yer then," he replied, affronted by my rejection of his creative input. "I'll definitely do it now."

"Go for it," I encouraged. "It's really not that difficult."

"I will," he snapped. "I've a great story about how I captured a big cat that was terrorising the hikers in Hamsterley Forest."

"Using logic and deduction?"

"No. A massive ball of wool."

At the end of a short trek, we reached a large old house. Mansion-like, it was dark and gloomy, and looked unused, its windows thick with dirt.

"This is it," said Holmes, "this is where they all were shortly before they were killed."

"You know that for definite?" I queried. It seemed too much of a feat to extrapolate such accuracy from a few scattered condiment packets.

"Geography will judge me," he replied mock-ominously. "There's no fun in definite, nothing is absolute, but it does look dodgy though, doesn't it? Howay." He skipped off up the driveway to head around the side of the building. Thinking it more prudent to stick with him, rather than stand exposed in the street, I followed, rounding the corner to the rear of the property to see Holmes heaving on the heavy wooden sash windows. He worked his way across, trying each one in turn only to find them locked. Stepping back, his face contorted, lips pursed, he returned to work on the penultimate window in the row. Using a small penknife retrieved from his pocket, he soon had the latch unclipped and the window open. Without turning to address me, he disappeared inside.

After a brief pause to wrestle with internal conflict, I followed him to find myself in an area of oak and opulence. The room, which appeared to be some sort of library, presented a stark contrast to the exterior of the building. The light was dim, however the smell of old leather and polish reeked grandeur.

"Over here," whispered Holmes, appearing from behind a heavy wooden door.

"Okay," I whispered back.

"Doc?"

"What?"

"Why are we whispering? There's nobody here."

"It just adds to the tension," I replied, dismissing his observation with a curled lip and a shake of the head.

We wound along an oak-panelled corridor, past walls adorned with expensive-looking artwork, to the foot of a large staircase. Creaking our way up the stairs, hollowed with use, we encountered a pair of wooden doors, larger and more impressive than any of those we'd seen en route.

Holmes tried the handles to find both doors locked. I was worried about him leaving fingerprints, but he appeared not to share my concern.

"The whole house leads to here," he remarked through an air of despondency.

"Can't you pick the lock?" I asked.

"Nah, I've only learned handcuffs and padlocks," he said in low voice, glancing at the penknife he had still in hand with a look of disappointed dismissal. "They'll be back later. We'll see what this is all about then."

"They might not meet every night."

"They'll be back tonight," he asserted. "They're on a war footing. They need to get themselves lined up. Plan a response. They'll be back, around midnight I reckon.

"They might have moved their base," I postulated. "Gone to ground."

"Mmmm," agreed Holmes begrudgingly.

"Shall we stay here and wait for them? Hide somewhere?"

"Sod that, I'd be bored stiff. Let's go to the pub."

5

We entered the George and Dragon through a wall of noise. A group of beautiful people with terrible singing voices were shouting their way through a rendition of Adam and the Ants' 'Kings of the Wild Frontier', their only accompaniment being the innovative pounding of their feet on the floorboards to emulate the Ants' twin drummers.

Electing not to join them in the 'Pool Room', which appeared void of a pool table, we turned the other way and into the bar.

"Let's go up the road after this, and see if Laura's about," said Holmes as we commenced our pints of 'cooking lager'. We were, after all, on duty.

"Laura?" I queried.

"Yeah, Laura Merryweather from the bank. Her and her mates go in Canteen and Cocktails. Oooh," he whooped in a high treble key, "let's have a mojito."

"Sherlock, we're drinking sub-premium lager in order to keep our wits about us. I don't think cocktails are the way forward."

"I hate it when you first name me," he replied, duly castigated. "Especially when it involves alcohol."

"Do you still see Ms Merryweather then?"

"Nah, not really."

"That's a shame, she was nice."

"And very accommodating," he appended, double clicking a wink.

I whistled, mimicking the suggestive two-syllable tweet that he often used.

"Doc, a gentleman never tells. Especially not after mad crazy sex like that."

Canteen and Cocktails was in sharp contrast to the George. In my mind, I penned it to the list of venues I would be taking Mary to.

"A pint of Lottery Winner," said Holmes, directing me towards the Peroni and contorting his mouth into a flat wide grin, our attempt at alcoholic restraint long since abandoned.

I turned from the bar to find Holmes in cheerful conversation with Ms Merryweather. She had transgressed well inside his personal space and had her lithe-athletic body planted to his side. There was no denying her beauty when she was in her workwear, however her evening attire moved her up to another level. One at which she would possibly usurp she who should not be mentioned, Mrs Irene Norton nee Adler, the woman.

"Would you like a drink?" I asked Ms Merryweather, handing Holmes his Peroni.

"No," she declined, "I have a mojito over there." She then returned her attention to Holmes. "They let you out of prison then?"

"That was just some big misunderstanding," he explained.

"I hope they didn't get you in the showers."

"Nah," he smiled.

"I would have," she said, smacking a ruby red kiss on his cheek.

Holmes was lavished in her attentions, for reasons that were a bigger mystery to me than the one we were engaged upon. Glamorous and not without wit, she could have had her pick of any man in the room, single or married. Instead, she sought out the company of a barely-shaved ruffian. I can tell you, the workings of a woman's mind are something I've long since given up on. A pity really given my other profession.

"Do you fancy some food?" asked Holmes, as we bade our farewells and left the bar. On my confirmation that I was feeling a little peckish, he suggested we visit a local kebab shop.

"I'm not that hungry," said Holmes as we stood in the queue. "I'll just have some of yours."

"A small donner kebab," I ordered on reaching the front of the queue.

"Make that a large one, mate," revised Holmes. "Plenty of onions," he added directing the man with his finger, before pointing at three differently-coloured plastic bottles behind the counter. "Are these different strengths of chilli sauce?"

"Yeah," replied the man, annoyed at Holmes' interventions, "hot, really fucking hot and napalm."

"Napalm," selected Holmes with a nod of encouragement.

"Sherlock," I protested, "I have irritable bowel syndrome."

"We both will after this."

6

"Well, this isn't at all suspicious," I remarked as we stood huddled by a lamppost. "Two grown men sharing a kebab in perhaps the lightest spot on the street."

"It's not. It would be suspicious if we were hiding in the shadows, you know, like stranglers do. I tell you what, this chilli sauce is a bit warm."

"Warm," I remarked. "I've gone blind in one eye."

" 'The Case of the Butterfly's Lair'," announced Holmes with dramatic climax.

"That's worse than this kebab," I replied dismissively.

It wasn't long before Holmes' earlier prediction was proven correct. As we stood there, several characters, disguised against a distant view, appeared from each end of the street. In groups of two, three, occasionally four, they filed their way into the house, hardly speaking to each other as they did.

Holmes watched intently without comment, his forehead furrowed. On the procession's evaporation, he flicked me a knowing glance and we made our way over to the house, ghosting down its side to the access point we'd used earlier, to find the window he'd unlocked still unsprung. Holmes manhandled it open and snuck inside. As I followed him through, I caught my trouser leg on the window catch. In my attempt to extract myself, I stumbled, landing with a thump on the floor inside.

"That's the way, Doc," whispered Holmes. "Don't let them know we're coming."

On the recovery of both my feet and my composure, we travelled along the oak-lined corridors, before making our way up the stairs towards the ominous wooden doors that had barred our way a few hours before. This time the creak in each step seemed treble the volume of our previous ascent. On reaching the top, Holmes grabbed the handle of the right hand door, turning it slowly to create a minimum of noise. He then gradually pushed open the door. I was fully expecting the door hinges to squeal protest into the dark night air. However at the velocity employed by Holmes, they stayed silent. We slipped inside to see a congregation, all of whom were fortuitously facing away from us. On Holmes' pointed direction, we slipped behind a long hanging curtain and out of view.

Having only had the briefest of moments to recce the room, I managed to absorb a fair amount of its detail. Curtains similar to the ones we were hiding behind, purple in colour, encased the whole room. Hanging from ceiling to floor, they swathed the space in a cathedral of fabric.

Up front, at the end of the room to which all were facing, was a long low altar. Constructed from a dark foreboding stone, its surface was empty, excepting the framed photographs of three individuals. We were too far away to recognise the pictures in the mounts, however my assumption, which was to be proved correct later, was that they were of the three strangulation victims.

Behind the altar, high up on the wall, hung three symbols, all in what appeared to be silver. To the left a crescent moon, to the right a crucifix, and to the centre a large butterfly, remarkable in that in each quarter was an engraved eye looking out from the wing.

The only other furnishings to the room were the numerous, perhaps six feet high, candlesticks which stood in front of the curtains, encircling the area to provide the only illumination.

All the people we'd watched troop in earlier appeared to be there. Clad in robes of the same purple-coloured material which adorned the walls, they lined up standing in rows, excepting one individual who stood ahead, closest to the altar. On everyone's back was a butterfly of the same design to that which hung from the wall. The only other accessory being the silver belts that grasped their waists.

Holmes and I peered through self-made gaps in the curtains to sneak a look at the proceedings, just as the figure at the head of the group called out. "I am Paparatti," he announced.

"I am Paparatti," the others repeated.

Holmes looked in my direction to give the look that he normally accompanied with a, "What the fuck?"

"We Paparatti," said the lead.

"We Paparatti," they all echoed.

Now Sherlock Holmes was not a man without humour. I grant you his humour tended towards the gin-dry variety, but it was there, very much so. In my experience, intelligence and humour are close bedfellows and Holmes had both in abundance.

I say this so when I now say he was someone not prone to laughter, it does not portray the wrong impression. He did laugh on occasion, but this was almost invariably stifled by a nasal throttling. He certainly wasn't one for a hearty belly laugh.

As we hid behind those curtains watching the ritual unfold, Holmes started to bubble. Both circumstance and scenario made it perhaps the most inappropriate time in which to succumb to a fit of mirth, however I looked to Holmes to see him with his lips rolled in and him juddering with stifled laughter. I rapidly shook my head, silently pleading with him to be quiet, however that just exacerbated matters, with him then rolling off his feet and on to his side, tears streaming from his eyes.

I had no option but to escalate my intervention. I jumped on top of him, pressing my palm across his mouth. From close quarters, I stared into his eyes, urging him to snap out of it. If anything, I made the situation worse. I was sure we would be discovered. Then he stopped, angling his head to look past mine. I rolled off him and onto my back to see the Paparatti, every man and woman of them, standing over us.

"Evening," said Holmes as they pulled us to our feet and pushed us into the centre of the room. One of the group dragged some wooden chairs from behind the curtains and we were unceremoniously dumped into them, our hands tied behind our backs with what felt like those nylon ties that gardeners use.

"This is the third time I've been tied to a chair this year," I sniped sideways at Holmes, through the corner of my mouth.

"His lass is a bit kinky," he explained to our captors.

"And who might you be?" asked the older of the group, a man I recognised as Sandy Stark from the photograph I'd seen previously in Eric Breckinridge's living room. He was a lot older, but it was most certainly him.

"You know the Geneva Convention as well as I do, Colonel," jibed Holmes. "We don't have to talk."

"You have to tell us your name, rank and serial number," replied Stark, playing along.

"Serial number?" pondered Holmes. "You couldn't get me Miles video card from me wallet could yer?"

"Or we could shoot you as spies," Stark added. "You're not in uniform."

"At least we're not dressed up like the Pointer Sisters," retorted Holmes. "Even the women look weird. If strangely alluring." He turned to one of the females. "Have you got anything on under that clobber?"

"Mister Hartherley," snarled Stark, "this little shit is starting to grind on me. Could you please apply some manipulation?"

At that, a younger man stepped from the crowd.

"I'm not gonna be scared by some gadgie in a dress," said Holmes defiantly, before the man withdrew a curved knife from a sheath on his belt. "Yep, that works," he responded, nodding his head to one side, his mouth shaped in agreement.

"I recognise him," said Hatherley. "He's in the papers all the time. Some sort of private detective."

"Consulting detective," corrected Holmes.

"I'm not sure who his mate is," added Hatherley, glancing dismissively in my direction.

"This is the esteemed Doctor John Watson, mender of minds, chronicler of the most perplexing crimes of the modern era, and the invaluable associate of the great Sherlock Holmes. That's me by the way."

I was aghast at his response in both content and conveyance. My only reaction was to stare back in his direction open-mouthed across angled shoulders.

"Well, Mister Sherlock Holmes," said Stark. "What have we done to warrant this most unwelcome of intrusions?"

"I'm not telling you," replied Holmes. "Not while we're tied up like this."

"Victor," sighed Stark, "cut them loose."

We were released and taken by Stark alone to another room in the building. It appeared to be some sort of office of which Stark was clearly the resident. A copy of the photograph of him and Breckinridge was propped on a large wall-to-wall bookcase, behind an important-looking desk. Stark started the discussion whilst moving around the room in the process of disrobing from his garb.

"Do you mind not doing that?" said Holmes.

"Doing what?" asked Stark.

"Pissing around while we're trying to talk to you. You're up and down like a Port Clarence stripper. In fact, you look a bit like one of 'em."

Stark, who had no hair, complied, sitting at the other side of the desk, his fingers mingled. "Look gentlemen," he exhaled, "although secret, this organisation is in no way criminal. We're just a group of normal, like-minded individuals who have come together in the protection of our neighbours and the community around us."

"As normal and like-minded as cross-dressing vigilante freaks get," nodded Holmes.

"But you're not secret, are you?" I pointed out. "Someone knows all about this place and has killed three of you."

"Indeed," replied Stark mournfully. "The Paparatti are not about revenge and reprisals, but we need to find these people and prevent any recurrence."

"How far have you got?" asked Holmes.

"Not very," grimaced Stark. "We don't know who we're facing. At present it's about maintaining a defence until we have a better understanding of our enemy."

"Any vigilantism recently, that might have upset someone?"

"Not really," said Stark. "We chased some counterfeiters out of town a few weeks back, but this is far and above what they would have been capable of."

"Tell me more about that," said Holmes.

"Well, a short while ago a couple of local business owners

111

started getting passed a lot of fake ten pound notes. You know, they normally get the odd one, but they were seeing a fair few more than is usually the case. The notes were also very good quality. The chaps are quite good at detecting dodgy tenners, however some were managing to sneak into their tills.

"Consequently we mobilised the Paparatti. We hung around incognito in the various bars and restaurants in the village, and it wasn't long before we identified the two culprits. Victor applied a small amount of pressure and they told us the whole story. They had a press in a barn of some disused farm out in the sticks, and were merrily printing away millions of pounds worth of counterfeit currency. They really weren't very bright. The notes we were finding were ones they'd skimmed off the top for gratuities and expenses. We kicked them in the bum, smashed up their press, and warned them against ever operating in the area again."

"Could you take us to this place out in the sticks?" asked Holmes.

"We could, but I don't know how much use that would be. After we smashed up the press, we burnt the barn to the ground. We didn't want them having a change of mind and returning."

"That sounds a bit criminal to me."

"We do bend the rules. But never to anyone's detriment."

"I'm not sure they're that bendy."

Stark responded with no more than a shrug. He clearly thought the actions of him and his group justifiable.

"So where is it?" asked Holmes.

"Where's what?"

"The counterfeit welly you took from that barn. The reason Eric's killer took his keys from him, which I assume included a key to this place."

Stark recoiled at Holmes' casual and yet lightning deduction. "It's locked away in a strong box in the attic."

"You see, Mister Stark, Colonel, the two guys you rumbled were only the labourers. If they're dumb enough to palm off damp tenners on a night in the Top House, they're not smart enough to produce pictures of Her Majesty that nine times out of ten slip under the radar. Your two mates were part of a much bigger outfit. An outfit that responded to your interference with a show of extreme force. You trashed their operation and stole all their product. They now have some sort of commitment to fulfil and no way of fulfilling it. Consequently, they want their dosh back."

"So what should we do?"

"Well, unless you want to lose any more butterflies, I would suggest you make a very public showing of you no longer having what they want. Get rid of the cash. Show them you don't want to carry on a fight you can't possibly win."

"How?" asked Stark.

"I'll leave that up to you. You clearly don't lack imagination."

"How unreal was all that," I commented, as we left the building.

"Yep," agreed Holmes. "We can't tell the Five O about that crowd."

"You think we should preserve their anonymity?"

"No, they'd lock us up. They'd think we were bonkers."

7

The next morning, I sat in the Baker Street Kitchen awaiting Holmes' arrival. After the various exertions of the night before, I was expecting him to be late and he didn't disappoint. He eventually entered to find me most of the way down an enormous pot of tea, examining a ten pound note I had received in my change the night before.

"What's up?" he asked as he joined me at our usual table.

"Nothing," I replied, "I'm just trying to decide if this tenner I picked up last night is real or not."

"Let's have a look." Taking it from me, he did all but the obvious. Most people when examining a ten pound note will hold it up to the light and examine the watermark etcetera. Holmes did everything but. He smelt it, felt it by rubbing it across the inside of his forearm, and even listened to it by dragging it across the ridges of his thumbprint. "Yup, it's dodgy," he said before slipping it into the top pocket of his polo shirt.

"Okay," I conceded, "then you'll have to pay for breakfast. Without that, I can't cover it."

"Ah, right," replied Holmes before handing it back to me.

"It's legitimate?" I queried.

"Looks like," he responded.

As Holmes ordered his usual fare, I received a text message.

"What's a matter?" asked Holmes.

"Nothing," I replied. "It's Mary. She is just reminding me I promised to do some heavy lifting for her in the Lip today."

"Is that a euphemism?"

"No."

Holmes snapped on a grin. "Then why did you look so frustrated when you checked your phone? If there's a lot to do, I can help."

"No, it's not that. It's this new phone. I forgot to charge it when we got in last night and it's nearly dead. It's a nightmare, it barely lasts half a day."

"Was it time for an upgrade?"

"No, I was careless enough to have my old one in my pocket when I went for a dip off Seaton Carew a few weeks ago."

"Really?" exclaimed Holmes. "You should be more careful. Let me have a look."

Holmes took the phone from me to tap in my PIN and start an intense furrowed-brow examination. "That's your problem," he said. "You've got every app known to man running in the background. Next time you charge it, you wanna give Selby Power Station a call and ask them to lob another log on the fire." On ending the sentence, his face dropped. "Oh," he exhaled, "that's it. I've just had one of those TV detective moments."

"What d'you mean?

"You know. When some tiny and unrelated fact, like a car door slamming or an answerphone machine flicking on, makes the whole case drop into place. It happens to Jonathan Creek and Adrian Monk all the time. Not so much the great Columbo."

"I don't have the wildest clue what you're talking about. It's a bit early for me, plus I had a late night last night."

"Okay," said Holmes. "The three victims all had dead mobile phones. What if the reason for them all running out of charge was they'd been hacked and had a particularly chatty and power sapping app added to them? An application that allowed someone to track their whereabouts remotely. It would explain how the killer could get between the victims so quickly."

"I get you. At least I think I do," I said, as Holmes' toast and eggs, soft-boiled to two minutes and forty-five seconds, arrived.

After breakfast, we made our way to Middlesbrough Police Station, where we were shepherded to an incident room packed with both uniformed and plain-clothed police officers.

"Have those phones been charged up yet?" asked Holmes on entry.

"No, not yet," said Lestrade. "We need a judge to grant permission for that."

"Ah, well, there isn't one here. Permission granted. Does anyone have a phone like this?"

"I do," volunteered Constable Hardwick, "but you're not touching it."

"Aw, come on, George, I won't touch it, well I'll touch it but, you know, I won't touch it."

Hardwick begrudgingly handed over his phone to watch Holmes weigh it in one hand against the victim's phone in his other. "Feel that," he said, handing the phones to Lestrade. "That one's a bit lighter. It's got a virus and that makes them lose weight."

"I think I can feel it," commented Lestrade. "Is that true?"

"Is it bollocks," he replied, shaking his head and sighing to the rumblings of the general assembly. "George, what I really need is your charging cable. Have you got it on you?"

"What are you doing?" asked a disgruntled Lestrade as Holmes took a seat at his desk.

"Well," said Holmes, "I was gonna take the cabley thing and plug it into the computery thing and the phoney thing, in order that

I can have a look at what's on the phoney thing to see if there's anything that might have got those gadgies and girl killed."

"You can't do that. A judge would deem any evidence inadmissible," protested Lestrade.

"Don't tell one then," sneered Holmes, holding out his hand to receive the cable from Hardwick. "I can't believe you need a warrant to look at a victim's phone. You wonder how you fellas catch any criminals at all. Oh yeah, you don't, do you? That's usually down to me and the Doc."

"Alright," conceded Lestrade, to the officers around him. "We could argue we were trying to prevent any further killings. At the very least, it will shut that twat up."

"Righteo," said Holmes, "I'll tell you what I'm going to find and then I'll have a dig and find it. But when I do, you'll have to trust me because you won't understand it." Holmes glanced up at Lestrade for acceptance. "In order for our killer to know where each of the victims were, someone, probably not him, planted an app, a kind of virus if you like, on each of their phones."

"You think two people were involved?" asked one of the uniformed officers.

"Yeah, at least. Writing shit like this and being able to strangle people with your bare hands are not skills you normally find in the same person. So," he continued, "now with the apps planted, he can track victims. Getting around them all in under half an hour then becomes a bit of a doddle. However, he still thinks that half an hour is enough time for the first victim to be discovered and the balloon to go up. If the news gets to the third target, then it becomes a different game of dominos. Consequently, he covers the first victim in that blue tarpaulin in an attempt to delay the body's discovery. Why he didn't just lob the body over that wall I'll never know, but then the strangler is not the brains in this outfit.

"What he should have done is took the mobile phones and covered his tracks. The thing is the back room boy has himself down as a bit of a smart arse. Instead, he writes something into the app to make it delete itself. Any subsequent examination of the phones will then take them right off the menu. The problem is this app is a thirsty little beggar, and before it gets to the point of deleting itself, the phone battery goes flat. Or at least that's what I'm assuming. I reckon whoever wrote the code wasn't someone who normally programmed for a mobile platform. That shouldn't have stopped him testing it though. Knob head.

"It's a good job you didn't plug them in, 'cos then we would have been buggered. If you didn't have a clusterfuck of magistrates stopping you scratch your arse, then we'd never 'ave known."

"Do you want me to log you in?" asked Lestrade as Holmes connected up the phone in preparation for his work.

"No." Holmes logged straight into the inspector's account. "Oooh," he quipped, "look at the inspector's web history. The mucky pup. I didn't even know that was possible." He angled his head to one side whilst contorting his face in disgust.

All those present craned to try and catch a look at the screen. I could see it and all it displayed was a blank desktop featuring the force's insignia.

"Sherlock, if you dick around with my computer, I'll get Newport Bridge raised especially so I can drop it back down on your head," said Lestrade.

Holmes ignored him, his focus narrowing in on the task in hand. "Okay boys and girls," he said, "we have a bit of a race against the clock here. If I can't find what I am looking for before the app deletes itself, then we're fucked."

He held his hands in the air to flex his fingers, his eyes fixed dead on the computer screen. "And they're off," he cried in an impersonation approximating the horse racing commentator Sir Peter O'Sullevan. "Hacking Bastard is off well but the favourite Sherlock has the making of him and is pinned to his shoulder."

The whole room looked around at each other, fearing him demented. I was somewhat perturbed at the bizarreness of the spectacle myself.

"Hacking Bastard, Hacking Bastard," he continued, tapping maniacally on the keys. "Sherlock had an injury to fetlock earlier in the season, but is showing no signs of it as they round the first bend."

He then broke off. His face washed with worry. "The code's been obfuscated," he said in his normal speaking voice.

"What does that mean?" I asked.

"The computer code has been jumbled up to make it unintelligible to the human eye," replied one of the female uniformed officers.

"Yup," confirmed Holmes, pointing a look of surprise at her. "But not to mine though," he grinned before his fingers slammed back down on the keyboard, if anything, rattling more furiously than before. "Sherlock is definitely flagging as they hit the back straight," he continued, his mimic now segueing more towards the frenetic style of legendary Formula One commentator Murray Walker. "Hacking Bastard has lengthened his stride and is leaving the whole field in his wake. Where's Sherlock? Where's Sherlock? Third, fourth, fifth. The favourite will need some performance to win from here. And what's this? Deadline is approaching from behind? As they hit the bend, it's Hacking Bastard followed by Deadline with a gap of ten to twelve lengths between them and the field. It's hard to see anyone outside the two front runners winning it from here.

"But what's this? Sherlock is gaining, Sherlock is gaining ground. Eight lengths, six lengths, four, three, two. They're neck and neck as they hit the home straight. It's Sherlock, it's Hacking Bastard, it's Sherlock, and don't rule out Deadline who isn't out of it yet.

"As they approach the line, it's Hacking Bastard, no, it's Sherlock, no, yes, no, it's Sherlock, Sherlock, Sherlock takes the tape, Hacking Bastard second and Deadline coming in a close third. Sherlock wins the Derby sponsored by the Europa Restaurant. Europa Parmos, better than your mam makes."

He rocked back in the chair. "I was right," he said, his persona calm and diametrically opposed to that of just a few seconds previous. "Get one of the other phones to your techie gadgies and ask them to look for the method signature 'destroy' and break the implementation. They'll know what that means."

"Can we use one of the other phones to trace our way back to the killer?" asked Lestrade.

"No," replied Holmes. "The app performs a handshake when

it's installed. When the routine runs, it broadcasts a 'hello'. This prompts the tracking application to call back and say 'over here mate'. The phone app then pings a confirmation and the tracker flicks into stealth mode. It's only during that second step that the tracker is exposed. It's a one-time deal. The tracker won't speak to the same phone twice."

"Couldn't we stick the app on another phone? Hardwick's, maybe?"

"Sorry," sighed Holmes. "The hacker will have harvested the phone's MAC address when he planted the app. The tracker will only speak to the phones it knows about." Holmes stood up, bouncing the chair backwards as he rose. "We've solved the mystery," he said, somewhat apologetically.

"Well, we know what happened," responded Lestrade. "But we don't know who or why."

Holmes rounded in his lips and gave a defeated shrug of the shoulders.

"Sherlock," I enquired, as we exited, "why do you think this programmer chappie went to the trouble of... what did you call it, obs...?"

"Obfuscation."

"Yeah that, the app was supposed to delete itself anyway. Why bother?"

"Habit maybe. Good practice. It could have just been a setting on his IDE."

"IDE?"

"Integrated development environment. It's what he used to write the code with. Actually, Doc, people do tend to adopt a style when they code. A way of formatting, naming conventions, stuff like that. The obfuscation blitzes it all. They could have been trying to disguise their work."

"You make it sound like computer programmers are like some sort of renaissance artists, with unique brushstrokes, and tendencies to use a particular palette of colour."

Holmes snorted. "I suppose it's a bit like that."

"Would you have been able to identify the programmer from what you saw, if it weren't for the obfuscation?"

"I'm not sure. I write more code than I read. Copying other people's stuff is cheating. It's a good idea though. It's a bit like the analysis of someone's handwriting. I might have a look at that."

"So are we done then?" I asked. "The mystery's solved. If the Paparatti get rid of all that counterfeit cash, then their adversaries will lose interest and return from whence they came. We'll never find them."

"I think we will," replied Holmes, confused at my dismissal. "We just need to get ourselves over to the Cabbage."

"The Cabbage?"

"The place where butterflies hang out. You get over to the Lip to give Mary that lift with her stuff, and I'll see you in there at last orders. Don't wear yourself out."

Holmes rolled into the Twisted Lip around ten forty-five carrying what I can only describe as a leather man bag.

"What's in your handbag?" I asked.

"Tools of the trade," he replied without further elaboration.

I grabbed my jacket from the hook and dressed to leave.

"Easy, Doc," remarked Holmes. "There's time for one for the road. While you're up, I'll have a pint of Digit please."

Four rounds later, we left for Norton in a taxi cab.

"Do you feel like providing me with any enlightenment yet?" I asked.

"Wait until we get there," replied Holmes. "I'll tell everyone together." He fixed his view to the cab window and the intermittent activity of late evening Middlesbrough.

On reaching Norton, Holmes directed the cab driver to drop us in Norton High Street close to the site of the Highland Laddie.

Against my expectation, the temptation to nip into the Laddie for a top up was resisted.

We made our way through the streets to the 'Cabbage', to get there just as the Paparatti themselves were arriving.

"They must do this every night," I remarked as we followed them in.

Not picking up on my comment Holmes just nodded "Evening" to various individuals with no response. We made our way up the main staircase and into the meeting hall with all the paraphernalia we'd seen previously. Holmes acquired a couple of chairs from behind one of the purple curtains and we sat down to wait for their entrance.

As they filed in, dressed in their purple robes, to take a formation similar to that we had observed on our first visit, I noticed something I'd not seen before. Two gaps in the ranks. Gaps, I presume, once filled by Oliver Oakshott and Wendy Gate.

Colonel Sandy Stark, in matching regalia, entered to take his position front and slightly off-centre. "Mister Holmes," he commented, "you really don't stand on invite, do you?"

"I've never been to anything that involves an invitation," replied Holmes. "Not even our kid's wedding."

"Court summonses?" I quipped, to cause a disappointed scowl to be fired in my direction.

"How can we be of assistance?" asked Stark.

"Do you mind if I speak to your mates?" he asked, gesticulating towards the ranks of Paparatti.

"Be my guest," replied Stark with an open hand.

"Okay, my little butterflies," announced Holmes. "I have a theory that might lead us closer to the killer of your comrades. If you don't mind, I'd like to take a look at your mobile phones."

The Paparatti stood motionless.

"Do you not have pockets in them dresses?"

On Stark's nod, they filed out, to return a few minutes later, phones in hand. Holmes milled around them as they entered. "Not that one, not that one, nope, nope, yep," he said, before relieving a middle-aged gentleman of his phone. "Nope, nope, nope," he continued, before stopping to address a young female. "Yep, that one. Where's your butterfly tattooed?" he asked, his eyes glinting.

"That would be telling," she replied.

"So, it's on your arse then," he retorted before resuming his search.

"Inner thigh," she remarked from behind him.

By the time he'd surveyed the whole group, he had half a dozen phones in his possession. He returned to the chair he'd been sitting on earlier to recover his bag stored beneath it. Taking out a laptop and a cable, he sat on the chair with the laptop balanced on his knees. One by one, he plugged in the phones. Each time after a period of around ten minutes, he silently shook his head and handed the phone back, remembering each one's owner.

As he plugged in the final phone, our quest looked to be yielding a fruitless return. Then as the ten-minute period felt due to expire, he sat up in his chair. "Got the get," he muttered, tapping intermittently on the laptop's keyboard. He looked up to the young girl he'd had the exchange with earlier. "You're a lucky bunny. You slipped through the snare."

"Would you care to elaborate?" interjected Stark.

"I would," said Holmes. "The mobile phones of your dead colleagues had an app planted on them, a kind of virus. That's what the killer used to track their movements. The phone of Miss Inner Thigh here has the same virus. Lucky for her, it failed to install. If I reinstall it, it could lead us right to them."

"There'll be a trail?"

"Assuming the tracker's still switched on and they still have it with them, yep. Wider than Stockton High Street."

"Make it so," ordered Stark.

"I think that's maybe a job for tomorrow," replied Holmes. "We don't want to be dicking around with this crowd in the middle of the night."

"We shouldn't be getting involved at all," I intervened. "I think we should hand it over to the police from here."

"Nah," dismissed Holmes. "Let me have a look first. It might be a dead end."

"You're not going without me." I replied.

"Victor and I will come too," added Stark.

Holmes' response was to contort his face into a frown. "I'm not going on a hop with two gadgies dragged up like Pepsi and Shirley."

"We'll be dressed for the occasion," responded Stark.

"That worries me even more."

"Do we need both of you? Can't Pepsi have a day off?"

"Hatherley's a good man, ex-Royal Engineers. If this turns into a scrap, I want him around."

"A good man in what way? He took well to being trained as a killer, or he used to polish Mother Teresa's flip flops?"

"See you at dawn," insisted Stark.

"Can you leave it a bit later? The Doc here likes a lie in. What time is dawn these days?"

"About five thirty."

"Fuck that," exclaimed Holmes. "We'll see you back here about nine."

9

The next morning, my attention was diverted away from my morning routine by the beeping of a car horn. I peered through the curtains and into the street below, to see the face of Holmes, grinning at me through the driver side window of Hansom, Martha's London taxi.

"I'm surprised you got this," I commented, as I climbed in the rear.

"Not as surprised as Martha will be," he replied.

"Do I need to be worried about this?" I asked as we made our way up the A19 to Norton.

"Nah," said Holmes, "I'm not really expecting to find anything. The clever money will be on them having buggered off by now. I certainly can't see them sat there with the tracker on, playing doms and eating a crisp sandwich. I just want to make sure."

"Bloody hell, it's Bravo Two Zero," exclaimed Holmes as we pulled up outside the Paparatti building to find Stark and Victor Hatherley dressed in camouflage combat gear.

Pulling up to the kerb, he jumped down from the driver's seat to make his way to the boot of the cab to retrieve his laptop. It was left to me to alight and greet Stark and Hatherley.

"We've picked a fine morning for it," commented Stark as I shook their hands. By now, Holmes had positioned his laptop in the footwell of the cab's passenger compartment and was squatting on the kerb to operate it.

"Right ladies," he remarked, as he plugged in the phone. "Prepare to be astonished and amazed. It's time for some white man's magic." I'm not sure how that comment sat with Hatherly, who was of African descent, but thought it prudent not to draw any further attention by interceding an apology for what could have been construed as a racist remark.

As Holmes craned his forearm to shadow the laptop's screen against the glare of the mid-morning sun, Stark, Hatherley and myself watched over his shoulder for any indicators of success.

To me, and probably them, the contents of the screen looked unfathomable. Holmes seemed to suck up every byte of information, his eyes locked to the screen.

Then there was something we could all understand as the strange words and figures were replaced by a map drawn in green on a black background. Two cross hairs running edge to edge tracked up and down and side to side before steadying themselves over a particular location. "Looks like a farm. Near Blakeston."

"That's not that far from here," commented Hatherley. "I went to school near there."

We all jumped in the cab to have Holmes drive us to the general locale of our quarry. Parking the cab by the side of a farm track, we travelled the remaining distance on foot. As Holmes had speculated, the destination of our journey was an old, apparently disused, farm consisting of a stone cottage and a number of barns and other outbuildings.

"Why do they keep picking farms to hide out in?" I queried as we trudged up the lane.

"There's a lot of flat ground around them," responded Stark. "It makes it easier to spot people approaching."

"And yet we're just bobbing on up there," I appended.

Holmes stopped us a short distance out. His eyes scanned the scene, darting to and fro between each building. "Let's try that little shed thing there," he said, pointing to a wooden hut, slightly divorced from the other constructions. As we reached it, Holmes placed the palm of his hand on the side of the hut's wall, before pressing his ear to the back of the same hand. "No one home," he commented.

We moved round to the doorway to find the door open. Holmes stepped in to stand dead still. His mouth rounded in a breathless whistle. "It's a trap," he whispered.

A scattering of furniture occupied the single room of the building. Central to the piece was a thick-topped wooden table. Atop it a collection of electrical equipment, including a laptop computer, not unlike the one Holmes had been using earlier.

"What d'you mean? A bomb?" I queried, less than a second before a projectile tore through one wall of the building to exit via the other. Wood splintered everywhere to the point where I could feel fragments striking against my back and neck.

I dropped to the floor for cover.

"No, not a bomb," replied Holmes with ridiculous calmness.

With the comparative difference in the light levels inside and outside the building, the bullet left a laser trail of light tracing its path across the room.

"Secure the area," screamed Stark, flipping over the table to slide against a wall. Hatherly followed orders from his now kneeling position, dragging a chest of drawers and some other items around us to form a small encampment within the room.

As I made to join their makeshift refuge, I looked up to see Holmes still standing bolt upright.

"Get down," I shrieked as bullets two and three shot across the room, passing either side of him. It was as if he was oblivious to the carnage ensuing around him. Hands in pockets, he had engaged his familiar survey routine, his eyes and neck flitting in a staccato twitch as he absorbed the detail of the space around him. His only concession to the ensuing mayhem, a wide-eyed urgency in his manner.

I couldn't bear it. I was sure the next shot would strike him through the chest. I crawled over to him and reached up to drag him to the floor just as the next bullet hit the building.

"Cheers, Doc," said Holmes from his position now laid beside me. "Is this still where you want to be?"

"I'll have to get back to you on that one," I responded as another set of light traces were drilled above us.

"Who the fuck's out there? The Bolivian army?"

"Hard to tell," I replied, my nerves making light of an horrendous situation. "No data."

You may think my retort flippant in the circumstances. Brave even. It was neither. I was petrified for my life. Extreme stress is a thing most bizarre. It cleaves out such oddity. Holmes' response was to snort a laugh as three or four more bullets hit, lower this time, their progress curtailed by the walls of our camp.

"You know, I've always wanted to be in a situation like this. It's just like the westerns me and our kid used to watch on a Saturday afternoon. I bet it's much more fun if you have a gun and can shoot back. We're not quite getting it right, are we? You know: Viking burials, western shootouts… Have you got a gun, Colonel?" called Holmes.

"I'm afraid not," replied Stark, agitated, but not to the point you might expect.

"Okay. I was just wondering," he said, as another shot rang out, raining more wood dust and splinters upon us. He then whispered to me, "He's a shit soldier, isn't he?"

"Why don't they just come in and shoot us point blank?" called Stark.

"They don't know we're not armed. Given you're at war with

these gadgies, there's a chance you might have come packing a catapult or two," spoke Holmes matter-of-factly.

"Indeed, bit of a mess this," replied Stark.

"Nah," said Holmes, "this is not messy. It's no-drain tuna."

"Is that right?" remarked Stark, with an air of disbelief.

"Far side of the room," called Holmes. "The flooring is loose. We need to crawl over there and get under the floor. And then stay still, perfectly still."

"Understood," replied Stark, "I can't see there's a better plan."

"Hang on a bit," said Holmes, before scurrying out of the camp and across the floor to the adjacent wall on his knees. He waited motionless, seemingly listening for something. As the next volley of rounds banged out, he drove his heel into the wall dislodging a large section. A section large enough for us to crawl out of.

Then, as Holmes had suggested, we sniped over to the far side of the room to find the last section of the floor loose to the hand. Prising away the remaining purchase, we slid between the floor joists, replacing the floorboards as best we could to mask our egress.

It didn't seem long before the scene fell silent. There was then a crash as our assailants bundled through the door, to fan out to different sectors of the room above us.

Through the slight gaps in the floorboards, I could just make out the outlines of the three men as they paced slowly around. The floor creaked with added drama on each step. At one point, a standing foot rested directly above my face, just a few inches from my nose, the floorboard bowing under its weight. I fought my breathing, resisting its urge to quicken and create noise.

"Did you not see them exit?" snarled one man, who transpired to be in command.

"No, sir, sorry," replied one.

"No," added the other, both of them sounding younger in years than their commander.

"Professor," said the first subordinate, "Armed Response should be here in three minutes."

"Come on then," he growled in frustration before marching out of the building. "What a piece of work this man is."

10

"Three minutes, my arse," remarked Holmes as we drew breaths I never thought I'd draw. The world had never looked so beautiful. I could have stood marvelling that landscape for a month, a year.

My daydream was interrupted by Stark. "Gentlemen, we're going to go. I see no point us being here when the police arrive. Are you coming?"

"Nah," said Holmes, himself taking in the view. "We'll wait for a lift."

Stark held out his hand. After a pause slight but long enough for uncertainty, Holmes accepted his handshake.

"I expect we'll meet again, Doctor," remarked Stark, turning to press my hand. I just smiled in response, not really imagining why we would.

"Sherlock," I remarked, as we watched the two men disappear into the distance.

"Doc."

"We don't need a lift. We have Martha's cab with us, and if we get it back now she might not notice it's gone."

"Oh yeah, nice one, Doc. I forgot about that."

"You're not intending to follow them, are you?" I asked. "The Professor, I mean."

"Bollocks to that," responded Holmes. "They've got guns. Besides, I don't think there's any need."

"I was so hoping you were gonna say that."

"Do you think the Professor killed those people to get to us?"

"No, but he seemed to get more involved after we did. He's certainly getting more hands on than he has been so far."

"Is that a good or a bad thing?

"I'm not sure."

"No data?"

"No, there's plenty of data alright."

THE ORB OF IRONOPOLIS

1

It was one of those tasteless Teesside days, on a morning fallen into the latter part of September. As the wind rattled raindrops off the window of the Baker Street Kitchen, we sat cosseted against the hoi pilloi and humdrum of honest work, enjoying a late but particularly well-prepared breakfast.

With my burgeoning careers of aspiring author and consulting detective running alongside the commitments of my medical practice, I had reduced my patient time to a four day a week maximum. This freed up Fridays for perhaps more enjoyable endeavours. It turned out, for the large part, that said endeavours involved unrushed breakfasts and liquid lunches.

This is not to say I didn't find my work as a psychologist fulfilling, there were times when I took great pride in the achievement, however the heady cocktail of danger and excitement generated by the pursuit of some nefarious miscreant was something I would struggle to describe to you. Couple this with the artistry I felt I was now managing to apply to my literary recollections of our various escapades, and I was living through one of life's golden periods.

Then there was Sherlock Holmes. He was one of those people it's hard to not enjoy being around. Even his dark moods apportioned no great hardship to those scattered around him, in that he internalised these episodes to a stone silence. As both his friend and, with gathering momentum his psychologist, I was interested to know where he retreated to during these periods of stark isolation.

But you never did quite know where Holmes was in mind. No

more than you could predict where he would go in body. For all his almost religious steadfastness in method and his consistency of approach, Holmes would think nothing of wrong footing you with a beautiful turn of capriciousness.

As our breakfast ebbed to its conclusion, Martha passed the window of the Kitchen, a coat above her head in a vain attempt to shield herself from the rain. She stepped through the door and came to sit at our table, proceeding to hand Holmes an envelope.

Holmes took the envelope, his face scrunched in suspicion. As was his way, he chose not to simply open it, but rather examine it for clues to its content.

"Well, open it," ordered Martha. "It's from the town hall."

"I can see that," replied Holmes. "What does the town hall want from me?"

"How will we ever find out?" came her typically sarcastic response. "Open it, you dick."

"It's an invitation," said Holmes, flexing the item between his fingers, before throwing it on the table. "I don't do invitations."

"It will be for the Orb Ball," remarked Martha excitedly. "Can I be your plus one? They're supposed to be brilliant."

"Sod that," sighed Holmes.

"Who else you gonna take, Norman No Mates?"

"No one. I don't do invitations. You're expected to have a good time. I'm more of an impromptu kinda guy."

" 'An impromptu kinda guy' who sits in the same pub, at the same table, drinking the same drink every day," I interjected.

"You're an impromptu kinda knob if you don't go," snapped Martha. "It's the event of the year."

"You've at least got to open the envelope," I said. "It would be so funny if it was just a council tax bill."

Holmes shook his head before expelling a sigh of inevitability and tearing open the item of contention. "It's an invite to this year's orb ball."

"No shit, Sherlock," whooped Martha.

He glanced warily up at her before reading out the invite:

"Dear Mr Holmes,

"The Mayor of Middlesbrough cordially invites you and a guest to attend the Forty-seventh Orb of Ironopolis Ball. Reception at seven o'clock. Dinner at eight o'clock. Thursday the eleventh of November. Middlesbrough Town Hall. Formal attire."

"For 'a guest' read 'Martha Hudson'," amended Martha as he finished.

"Sorry, Marth, I'm not going. It'll be full of Haverton Hillbillies and dodgy bastards who've ran the Great North Run dressed as a twat to earn two-hundred quid for some charity you've never even heard of."

"Sherley, I've already picked out my dress," said Martha, the force of her response escalating yet further.

"Actually," I interrupted. "Where's my invite? I've done as much for the community as you have."

"They probably didn't post it to 22 Baker Street," Holmes pointed out. "Cos you don't live there."

"Good point."

"Don't worry about a suit," continued Martha, "I'll sort that out. I don't want my date for the ball looking like he's just slept the night in the bus station."

"I'm not going," retorted Holmes steadfastly.

"You bloody well are!" replied Martha, leaving the cafe with the discussion at stalemate, if perhaps not in her mind.

The Orb of Ironopolis Ball is an annual event, hosted by the incumbent mayor of Middlesbrough in order to pay thanks to all those who have made a significant contribution to the community in the previous year. Generally, invites are bestowed to those who've made significant charitable contributions, or public servants, such as nurses and firemen. It's an acknowledgement to those who have gone beyond the call of duty in some way, shape or form. In addition to this, there's a fair splattering of the more well-heeled, such as local business owners and the like. The ball is held under the auspices of it being a charitable affair, therefore to include those with a little cash on hip allowing a reduced or gratis ticket price for those such as Florence, an out-of-work cleaner from Brambles Farm who walked coast to coast in a pair of carpet slippers to earn two-thousand pounds for the Butterwick Hospice.

The ball gets its name, not surprisingly, from the Orb of Ironopolis, the centrepiece of Middlesbrough's crown jewels, an icon of equal standing to that of the Transporter Bridge. About the size of a grapefruit, it is platinum in construction, with two heavily jewel-encrusted bands running circumferentially through its poles to divide it into quadrants. Pride of place on the top of the orb sits a spectacular red carbuncle known as the Eye of Middlesbrough, a brilliant ruby the size of a small hen's egg.

The orb, which gets rolled out, figuratively not physically, on official occasions such as the installation of a new mayor or the granting of freedom of the town, is steeped in superstition. Some say that if the orb ever went missing then the town would crumble and fall into the River Tees, to be washed out into the blackness of the North Sea. Others have it that the town's football team play in red to align with the colour of the ruby that sits atop the orb, and if anything should ever happen to it, then catastrophe would fall upon the team. That said, given the form of Middlesbrough Football Club through certain periods, if the orb was not lost, it must have been well hidden.

Following the impasse of the Baker Street Kitchen, I returned home to find my own invite to the ball sitting on the doormat, obscured by four pizza menus and the third charity request of the week asking me to bag up and donate my old clothes. This created a dilemma. If Holmes was dead set on not attending, then should I go? Conversely, if Mary was as keen on attending as Martha, would I not have to go? Then again if I did go and Martha missed out due to Holmes' decline, how would that make Martha feel? It was quite the pickle.

My solution to this was to consider all the potential outcomes, rule out the undesirable scenarios, and whatever remained, no matter how unlikely, would be the eventuality I would encourage.

I could go with Mary, I could take Martha (hmmm) or I could go alone. I ruled out the unpalatable and was left with absolutely nothing. Holmes would have to go. It was the only way of not upsetting one or more of the ladies of Baker Street. Sorry, that makes them sound like prostitutes. Let's just call them the ladies.

Shortly after lunch, I made my way to the Twisted Lip to find Holmes reading the previous night's Evening Gazette and sipping on the unusual imbibement of a cup of tea.

"Tea, in the Twisted Lip?" I remarked, as I stood over him.

"Yeah, well, Martha's just thrown me out of the boutique. Somebody must have upset her."

"Oh right, I wonder who that could be? You know, Sherlock, you're going to have to go."

"Go where?"

"The Orb Ball."

"Sod that."

"I've got an invitation too. I can't go without you."

"Why not?"

"We're Sherlock Holmes and Doctor Watson, self-appointed guardians of Middlesbrough. I can't go without you."

"Yeah, you can. We're not Eric and Ern."

"Why are you so against it?"

"Doc, it will be mind-numbing. All small talk and canapés. It would kill me."

"If I go without you, the only topic of conversation I'll be engaged in all night will be 'Where's Sherlock?' "

Holmes just shot me a dismissive glance as he slurped his next intake of tea. I sighed, deciding to change tack I took a seat at his table, scraping my chair across the floor as I sat.

"Look at poor Mary," I replied, nodding in her direction. "She works hard every evening, it's such a shame she'll miss out on this little diversion to her humdrum existence. Never mind, perhaps she can while away the evening serving you beer, like she does nearly every night."

"Poor cow," retorted Holmes. "Her old man sounds like a right get. He should take her out more."

"I take her to some of the finest establishments in Teesside," I protested.

"Then take her to this Orb Ball bollocks then."

"Okay then I will. Good luck with Martha, when she finds out Mary's going and she's not."

Holmes looked across at me with a long stare. Finally he acquiesced. "Sod it, I'll go. But I won't be responsible for my actions."

"You never are," I grinned, springing from my seat. "It'll be fine. We'll have a few beers, a bit to eat, nod at a few people and skedaddle early."

"Will we?" questioned Holmes ominously.

As I made my way back along Baker Street, I stuck my head around the door of Hud Couture. "Oy Cinderella," I called to the proprietor. "I've talked him into it. You shall go to the ball."

"Get in," whooped Martha, whilst repeatedly punching the air in a low rib-level action reminiscent of a footballer celebrating a goal.

2

During the time of which I write, Holmes had developed a fanatical and frankly unhealthy interest in dreams. He saw them as a clue to the unlocking of the mysteries of the mind. He was convinced if he could understand dreaming, he could open up a whole new realm of cognition and recollection.

Everything has a purpose, he said: eyebrows stop sweat from your forehead draining into your eyes, the lump on a beer glass stops it slipping through your fingers, so what was the purpose of dreams? He was convinced if you could understand dreams, you would unlock the mysteries of the mind. The ferocity in which he pursued this theory was a cause for concern. The mind isn't something to be tinkered with.

This wasn't the first time Holmes had given mention to what he termed collectively as "dream mechanics". It escapes me which, but during one of our many investigations, he explained to me how the mind has a tendency to try and understand a collection of facts by stitching them together in the order that makes the most sense. By doing so, it delivers the most compelling story.

"Facts are not as useful as you might expect," he said. "On their own, they have no meaning. We apply the meaning and then string all the facts together into some sort of story. If you return to the facts you can often apply different meanings and construct an altogether different scenario, just as plausible as the first."

More than once he used the example of a dream, and how a jumble of events occurring in a dream are interpreted by the mind on waking. The brain's instinct is to make sense and order of the world. It naturally finds a way to sew the facts together, but it may not be the only, or indeed correct, one.

The theory Holmes went on to develop on dreams was founded on the conjecture that the brain was arranged in a hierarchy similar to that of a personal computer, with faster access to the more volatile memory, backed up by slower but more stable storage. In his hypothesis, these represented everyday thoughts and long-term memories respectively. I'm not sure I picked up anything tangible on the mechanics of the brain during his exposition, however I did learn a bit about computer architecture.

Holmes postulated that each night, as you doze off to sleep, the thoughts and experiences of the day seep back into your deeper memory. Conversely, when you wake the next morning the reverse happens and some, if not all, of the memories from the previous day are pulled forward in your consciousness, the readily accessible area of your brain. This toing and froing of thoughts ran alongside a process he called 'refragmentation'. The idea was that this was more than a simple lift and shift of memories from one area of the mind to another, and some processing was involved to reorder and package your thoughts in a way that made them easier to recall. In doing so, some deeper memories, perhaps once forgotten, were dislodged and were consequently remembered.

The brain's attempts to process both recent and dislodged

memories resulted in dreams, the subconscious manifestation of Holmes' refragmentation. He thought that the pathways in the brain used for the storing away of memories, were the same as those used by the conscious, waking mind. Dreams were a window into refragmentation, a sneak preview of a forming picture.

Put simply, the brain has no way of knowing if it is processing data in a conscious or unconscious state, so it just does the best it can with it. One of the consequences of this is those times we all have when dreams and reality become confused. Those times when you can't tell if you are dreaming or not, and those memories that seem real but turn out to be an imagined fiction.

There was actually some level of consistency between Holmes' view and more conventional wisdom. Rapid eye movement sleep for example, which has been shown to bookend periods of deeper sleep when dreaming is thought not to be so prevalent, would perhaps correlate to the times at which Holmes suggested this memory management and refragmentation was taking place.

The problem with Holmes' theory was that it had no foundation in research. It was pure conjecture based upon a mental exercise confined to the singular, if not insignificant, mind of Mr Sherlock Holmes.

To my knowledge, Holmes' view on dreams was quite original and therefore somewhat contradictory to popular works of eminent psychologists such as Carl Jung and Sigmund Freud. There was certainly nothing in any of the papers I'd studied that came close to mentioning Holmes' theories on the storage of long term memory or, indeed, refragmentation.

During his more excitable tutorials on the subject, Holmes eulogised on boundless possibilities, such as freeing his mind from the confines of his body to allow it to travel in space and time. He thought he could train his mind to the point where he could invoke an out of body experience at will. I'm not sure exactly where he got to with this, but I assume he settled on the more realistic possibility that he would be able to gain greater access to the backwaters of the brain. In achieving this, he would be able to access every fact he'd ever acquired, and in doing so he would become the perfect deduction machine. In this citadel of the mind, there would be no mystery he couldn't figure.

3

As fate would have it, poor Martha woke up on the morning of the Orb Ball with a stinking cold, bad enough, despite her heroic dismissal, to exclude her from the event. With Holmes' refusing to "leave a man behind" it appeared that our little excursion was to be kiboshed, however, on all the insistence Martha could muster, she compelled us to go without her.

Begrudgingly, Holmes donned the glad rags Martha had selected for him, and we met at our prearranged rendezvous point of the Mink Tattoo Coffee Bar on Corporation Road for a "few stiffeners" before we went in.

Holmes in a dinner suit was something to behold. To be fair, he looked very smart, however, given his normal attire of donkey jacket and jeans, the contrast was something we struggled to acclimatise to, as we smirked our way through our aperitifs.

"Look," protested Holmes, "if you two don't stop grinning like knobs, I'm gonna do one. There's no reason for me to be here anyway."

"Sorry," said Mary and I in unison, attempting to expunge the looks from our faces.

On finishing our drinks, Holmes having consumed as much as Mary and I combined, we made our way down Albert Road to the venue. We passed through the bowels of Middlesbrough Town Hall, through stained-oak rooms with high ceilings, the opulence appearing far greater than I'd idly expected.

As we entered the reception area, a venue with decor sympathetic to the rest of the building, Holmes stopped still in his tracks. Hands in his trouser pockets, his eyes chased around the room.

"Let's just talk among ourselves for a while," I remarked to Mary as Holmes continued his survey.

After a few minutes, Holmes completed his analysis and returned his attention to us, snapping on a rather disingenuous smile that indicated we'd left his universe for a moment.

"Oh, you're back are you?" I japed. "Did you spot anything interesting?"

"There's ninety-three women in this room. Seventy-seven of them are showing visible signs of marriage."

"A ring, you mean?" suggested Mary.

"Among other things, yes. Statistically, twenty-three of them are unhappily married. So that's forty-one women in here effectively on the market. I would have sex with twenty-two of them. Three more pints and that number rises to thirty-one."

"So you're feeling lucky, are you?" she asked.

"Nah, but let's have the beers anyway."

Holmes made short work of the complementary bar in the early evening, accelerating his intake to match Mary and I, three for our one.

"Steady on, Sherlock," I commented, on his fourth or fifth replenishment within the space of thirty minutes.

"What?" he hicked.

"If you carry on at that rate, you'll end up drunk, face down in the soup."

"I never get drunk," he murmured. "My alcohol intake is regulated perfectly."

It was perhaps the speed of Holmes' consumption that drew the attention of one of the town's infamous luminaries, who sought to introduce himself following yet another one of Holmes' orbits past the bar. Somewhat worse for wear himself, he apparently saw Holmes as a kindred spirit, or perhaps more accurately someone to obscure his own abuse of the hospitality.

Simon Lord, or Sir Simon Lord to give him his full title, was a disgraced peer of the realm. A year, perhaps eighteen months previously, there'd been a minor scandal regarding the allowances claimed from the parliamentary seat he'd inherited from his late father. I wasn't the only one that thought him an arrogant sleazy individual, the common joke being that he thought the House of Lords was named in his honour. Given that the number of his visits to the upper chamber could be counted on the fingers of one hand, and he had not once troubled himself to vote, it did seem fair that his net contribution was questioned vehemently across the printed press.

To some slight credit, he did look to turn his reputation around. He resigned his seat, albeit under duress, and directed his attention to more laudable endeavours by becoming the figurehead of several local charities. But there was always something not quite right. You can move a stool around, looking for a level section of flooring, but sometimes it's not the floor but the stool that is crooked.

Sir Simon never stopped loving a trinket, especially if the said item was beyond the reach of others. These objects gave him the delusion of being special in some way. He hadn't reformed. He'd just swapped a section of plush benching in the House of Lords for a charitable trust he could lord it over. It's difficult to validate the reform of a man who turns up to a charity gala in a white Lamborghini driven by his supermodel girlfriend.

"So what's your story?" asked Holmes, seemingly unaware of Sir Simon's notoriety.

"You disappoint me, Sherlock. I've read all about you in the local papers. I thought you'd be able to tell all there is to know about me by the turn of my cuff and the scratches on my shoe leather. Where's this deductive reasoning I've heard so much about?"

"That's all bollocks," responded Holmes blankly, his attention already focusing on his next drink. "Besides I'm on a night off."

"A night off?" boomed Sir Simon. "I'm sure if there were some dastardly murder here tonight you'd spring to your heels. Nail the ne'er-do-well with a few acutely reasoned observations. Perhaps the orb will get stolen. Wouldn't that be a wheeze?"

"Yeah, fucking hilarious," retorted Holmes, already growing bored of the unwelcome attention.

"I'm a successful businessman and the patron of a number of successful charities."

"Really?" replied Holmes, confused by the remark.

"You asked me what my 'story' was."

"Success isn't always a good thing. Just ask the sperm that impregnated your mother."

"You know, I don't appreciate your manner. I didn't come here to be abused by some scrubbed up oik."

"Fuck off then, you pointless cock-sucking shuffle monkey," sneered Holmes, turning his attention towards the bar.

Sir Simon stood for a moment, unsure how to react. I cringed, fully expecting the exchange to escalate to something more physical in nature. As it was, the only violence came in the ferocity of Sir Simon's head shake as he withdrew. "Such felicity of expression," he sighed.

"I think I understand why you don't accept invitations now," I commented, my observation supported by a look from Mary, disapproving of both his petulance and turn of phrase. "You might want to turn it down a bit."

Holmes' glanced at us to suggest a level of concession.

"Do you know his dad used to be the seventh richest man in England?" I remarked, to butter down the tension.

"Yeah," replied Holmes, "and that was back when rich was a lot of money."

It was at that point a long, slender woman in a black jumpsuit introduced herself. "Katrina Spring," she said, offering her hand to Holmes, Mary and myself. "Nice work putting Sir Slime in his place."

"Sherlock Holmes at your service," replied Holmes with the slightest of nods.

"What other services do you supply?" she asked.

"Consulting detective work, computer hacking, taxi driving," I interjected, in an attempt not to be elbowed from the conversation.

"What can you detect about me?" she continued, with hardly a glance in Mary's nor my direction.

Holmes stepped back to look her up and down, before directing his eyes to flit about unfocused in the middle distance.

"You're married with two children, your husband works in the legal profession, and, for your sins," he paused, "you work for the local authority in some sort of media or public relations capacity. You arrived here from Durham, on the eighteen twenty-seven train. You sat on the right-hand side of the carriage facing forwards."

"No, I'm a school teacher, I'm unmarried, have no children, and I drove up here from Nunthorpe."

"You drive a Mercedes."

"I drive a Jaguar."

"You're a fan of David Bowie."

"Everyone's a fan of David Bowie."

Holmes returned a grin contaminated with the suggestion of achievement in his eyes.

"You're not very good at this, are you, Mister Holmes?" remarked Katrina.

"I now know where you live, what you do, what you drive, and that you're on the market," responded Holmes. "Not bad for forty seconds work."

Katrina smiled. Rocking her head to one side whilst biting her thumbnail, she conceded to some brief laughter. My dawning realisation was that of a seduction unravelling in front of me. It was, however, difficult to tell who was seducing who.

"What's it like being a school teacher?" asked Holmes. "That's the one job I've thought of doing."

"I enjoy it. I'd rather there was more discipline, but I find other ways of maintaining control."

"You can discipline me if you want. I've forgotten me PE kit, Miss."

"Then you'll have to do it in your vest and pants, then."

"I don't wear a vest, Miss."

"Just your pants, then," she purred.

"I don't wear pants either."

Katrina laughed, her mirth recoiled by disdain. Holmes was quick to redirect the conversation. "No husband? Divorced then?"

"I'm afraid that position has always remained vacant."

"Why's that? Someone in your past? Is it a tattoo or a torch you carry?"

"No," she smiled, "neither."

"No one? Long lost along the passage of time?"

"No," she said, her smile still fixed. "There's no one."

"Then you are blessed. And probably unique. So why is there nobody? Either then or now."

"No man has ever fulfilled my exacting requirements."

"A woman then?"

"Interesting, but unfortunately not."

"Why don't you give it a go? She looks nice," he said, gesticulating to a particularly glamorous blonde in the vicinity.

"No, that's really not my thing."

"You don't mind if I imagine that scenario, do you?"

"Why don't you go and talk to her, or is there someone else in here you like?"

"I can't see past you," replied Holmes, a mischievous smirk narrowing his upper lip.

Katrina flashed a tethered smile. "Mister Holmes, it's been a pleasure. But I'd better go mingle now."

"Well, that confirms it. Definitely a lesbian," I mocked on her retreat, to elicit a stealthy dig in the ribs from Mary.

"Nah, she's a horny pony if ever I saw one," whispered Holmes from the side of his mouth as he tracked her departure across the hall. "Drinks?" he enquired, turning to retrace his well-beaten passage to the bar.

"Prosecco," replied Mary.

"I'll have a…" I attempted to add before Holmes snapped in an interruption.

"I'm not buying that American piss."

"It's a free bar."

"I'm still not getting you any," responded Holmes. "Choose something else."

"As I was going to say," I asserted, "I'll have a Birra Moretti, please, Sherlock."

"Better," said Holmes.

4

At eight o'clock, a small gong was sounded and we trooped into the banqueting hall, to take our seats along a single long table, cluttered with all manner of ornamental paraphernalia, to the point where it was difficult to see where the food could be placed. The guests with the misfortune to be seated near to us were an eclectic bunch, none of whom appeared to be of particularly noble stock.

"Okay," said Holmes on sitting, "if anyone's not hungry could you order the lobster? I fancy trying a bit of surf and turf."

Any further discussion on the food order was cut short by another strike on the dinner gong and an announcement by a member of the mayor's staff. "My lords, ladies and gentlemen, please be upstanding for the Mayor of Middlesbrough."

Councillor Raaz, the mayor, was an odd little chap. There was no questioning his contribution as a public official, however there was an atypical level of comedy in the way he conducted his official duties. I assumed this was intentional, however with his deadpan delivery, it was difficult to be certain.

"Ladies and gentlemen," he announced, from his elevated position on a stage to the far end of the table. "I'm not sure there are any lords here. If there are, the sneaky beggars have nicked in because there were none on the invite list.

"Anyway, welcome to the Orb of Ironopolis Ball, or as I like to call it: 'A night on the Raaz,'" he called out, shaking his clenced fists either side of his face. "You know, this year I think the invite list we have put together is quite an interesting one. We have liars, fraudsters, thieves… and that's just my fellow council members.

"Seriously, you may look at the person sitting next to you and think what the hell is he or she doing here? There are certainly people here with some very chequered histories. But this event is not about ancient history, it's about what you have contributed to the town over the last year. In my view, which I know is not a view that is shared everywhere, it's what you do that is important, not what you have done. At least that's what I tell Missus Raaz when I've eaten all the Hobnobs.

"Hell, there's a lot of you here who have been to prison. I'm not worried though. I had a shower before I came out. I didn't want to be dropping any soap in front of you guys.

"Seriously, tonight is a thank you from the town to yourselves, for all you have contributed over this last year in business, in sport, or in the community in general. All you have to do is eat, drink and enjoy yourselves.

"Seriously though, take it easy at the bar, I don't want to have to put up the community charge... No, I mean it," he added as the audience laughed. "And don't make too much mess. I'm paying the mayoress minimum wages to clear up after you lot in the morning.

"And now ladies and gentlemen, without further ado, I give you this piece of scrap. Sorry, no, no, no. Ladies and gentlemen, I give you the Orb of Ironopolis."

At that, two uniformed men, dressed in red frock coats with silver braiding, footmen I suppose you'd call them, entered the stage to the applause of the assembly. They carried with them a large glass box which they set on an ornate platform. Inside the box, nestled on red velvet, was the orb. It was more impressive than I'd imagined. The platinum shone and the jewels sparkled to the point of captivation. Our fellow guests gazed back at it open-mouthed in awe. All except Holmes who flashed it the briefest of glances.

"Doctor John Watson," I said, introducing myself to our adjacent diners. "This is my better half, Mary Morstan, and this my friend and colleague, Mister Sherlock Holmes."

"I thought it was Batman," replied a rotund ruddy-faced gentlemen before introducing himself as, "Frank Moulton, local businessman."

"Batman?" queried the overweight woman to his right.

"It's just a careless joke that the local newspapers seized upon," I explained, pausing and raising my eyebrows in prompt.

"Flo Miller," she said.

"And what gets you here Missus Miller?" I asked, noticing her wedding ring.

"Charity work," she replied. "I did a sponsored walk for the Butterwick Hospice."

I then turned my attention to the blonde sitting to the left of the group, the same blonde woman whom Holmes had directed Katrina Spring towards earlier. "Hatty Durian," she said, "I'm here to represent my husband, Kevin Durian, he plays for Middlesbrough. He has a big match at the weekend, so couldn't come."

"Do you think he'll be playing?" asked Moulton. "His form hasn't been brilliant lately. I have a box at the Riverside." He looked around to gauge our respective responses.

"We don't talk about work," replied Hatty curtly.

"What was it the Norwich City fans were singing a few matches ago?" he continued before singing to the tune of Duran Duran's 'Rio'. "His name is Kevin and he kicks it in the stand, we can't believe that you still pay him fifty grand."

"As I said," responded an annoyed Hatty, "we don't talk about work."

"What line of work are you in?" I asked, trying to reorientate the passage of the conversation in the direction of something more conducive to good humour.

"Well, I just look after the house and stuff really."

"Aren't you a model as well?" queried Mary.

"I was, but since we got married I just look after Kevin now."

"Don't you have a staff of five people to do that?" said Moulton.

"Yes, but they need managing."

"Well," he sighed, "I don't know what you're doing to him but his form's been dire since you two got hitched. I suppose it's true what they say about it tiring the legs."

"Sex isn't his problem," interjected Holmes, not looking up from his puzzled analysis of the cutlery array. "It's the lack of it, and, of course, him finding out he's married a lesbian."

"A lesbian?" whooped Moulton, almost choking on his wine.

"If I'm a lesbian," protested Hatty, "how come I'm married to a male footballer?"

"Because women footballers don't earn as much?" reasoned Holmes with a thoughtful purse of the lips.

Hatty huffed in response, not knowing how to respond.

"Earlier in that room," continued Holmes. "The only people you took any real notice of were women. In particular, four very attractive women."

"I was just comparing myself against them," she said dismissively. "That's what women do."

"No," said Holmes. "It was more than that. There was a twitch in your lips, a dryness in your mouth causing you to take short sips of your drink. You angled your hand suggestively towards your crotch, but turned your knees away from any man that approached you."

Hatty, who was growing more and more annoyed, stood up sharply. "I'm not listening to this," she snapped, before storming away from the table.

"Sherlock," sighed Mary, shaking her head.

"She's in a bit of a rush," remarked Holmes, seemingly oblivious to his castigation. "Oh well, those rugs don't munch themselves."

"Is there any need for such homophobic remarks?" commented Mary.

"Homophobic?" replied Holmes, with elevated offence. "I'm not homophobic. You'd never find a bigger fan of Karma Chameleon than me. Ah, she wouldn't have eaten much anyway. Anyone mind if I have her pudding?"

"Such a shame for Martha, that we're never going to get invited back," I remarked.

So there we had it: Hatty Durian, who, if Holmes was to be believed, was a gold-digger who had betrayed her sexuality in the pursuit of wealth; Flo Miller, a retired cleaner who turned to charity work before finding herself bankrupt; and an award-winning local businessman called Frank Moulton, whose awards dried up just around the time he was convicted for fraud. It was hard to see how these were the best Middlesbrough had to offer.

"So what can you tell about me?" asked Flo as the dust settled.

"You eat too much and don't exercise enough. Go easy on them spuds, will yer?"

Flo recoiled in upset and disdain, her face contorted into a sneer.

"Sherlock," remarked Mary, in a tone that betrayed the desperation of her failure to regulate his output.

"You're struggling financially," continued Holmes. "That dress you're wearing is old. You can't afford to get it dry cleaned, so you've tried hand-washing it yourself. You're not happy about this, and are looking up your nose at the others in the room with designer dresses that they're wearing first time on."

"I'm unemployed," she responded. "I can't afford to buy a brand new dress for just one night. I haven't worked since I gave up my job to do my charity walk. My employer wouldn't give me the time off I needed."

"Oh, how was that?" asked Mary. "The walk, I mean."

"Yes," I said. "I read all about you. Walking coast to coast in a pair of carpet slippers is quite some feat."

"It's hard on the feet," she replied, clearly more warmed to Mary and I than she was to Holmes.

"How much did you raise?" asked Holmes.

"Two-thousand pounds."

"That's not a lot, is it? Hardly enough to leave your job for. You were a cleaner at the museum, weren't you?"

"There's nothing wrong with that."

"Nothing at all. You left just around the time that painting got stolen from the vault. The vault you used to clean."

"I never stole it."

"I never said you did. But someone thought you did. They couldn't prove anything, but suspected you strongly enough to ask you to go quietly. And not create any fuss."

"I never stole anything," she exhaled, tears welling in her eyes. As Hatty had done before her, she got up and rushed out of the room.

"This is going better than expected," I remarked on her departure, bellowing breath out of my cheeks.

"Well, she did ask," appealed Holmes. "She'll be back for her sticky toffee pudding," he added dismissively.

"I don't suppose we need Mister Holmes to do his party trick on me," said Moulton. "You all know all about me from those bastards in the newspapers."

147

"Trick?" spiked Holmes, his brow dropped with disdain.

"It sounds like you feel hard done by Mister Moulton," I interjected. "You did plead guilty at the fraud trial?"

"Yeah," growled Moulton, "but I've done my time, my wife's left me, the kids won't speak to me, and that's not enough for some people. How did the mayor put it? It's not what you've done, but what you are doing that's important. I've been helping reform ex-prisoners since I got out myself, finding them little jobs, giving them some direction in their lives. I'm doing as good a job now as I was when I was winning all those businessman of the year awards, but all I get is criticism. From here, there and every bloody where. It makes my blood boil."

"Have you seen the Colosseum in Rome?" asked Holmes, at somewhat of a tangent.

"Yeah, I was over there a few years back. Have you been to Rome, Mister Holmes?" replied Moulton

"No, I've never left England."

"He's never been out of the North of England," I qualified.

"I've been to Sheffield," protested Holmes.

"That's in the North," I replied. "At least it was last time I looked."

"Really?" remarked Holmes before continuing. "I was looking at it on those 4k tellies at Teesside Park the other day. They were showing the Colosseum."

"You're getting a television?"

Holmes sighed at my further interruption. "No, I was just looking at them. They have computers in them so I'm barred from having one anyway." He shot a look at me to show he wasn't valuing my antagonism. "My point is, do you think something like the Colosseum would have been possible without the odd backhander here and there?"

"Probably not," I conceded.

"Not if their planning department was anything like our lot," joked Moulton.

"There's fraud and dishonest behaviour of one form or another everywhere, in councils, in governments, in banks. It's only some of it that's seen as illegal, and if anything, the illegal stuff is what gets things done. They should have no problem with you, Mister Moulton. I read all about your case in the papers. From what I could see, you were just greasing the wheels. Let them whisper, but don't let them get to you."

Shortly before the official conclusion of the festivities, we made our way out into the cool November evening, myself and Mary glad with wine, Holmes devastated to the full extent of the drinks menu.

"Remember that I never get drunk crack?" he said. "The thing I mentioned earlier? I think I'm gonna have to change that to hardly ever." He raised his hand in goodbye and wobbled off up Albert Road.

Mary looked at me with concern. "He'll be alright," I said. "It's not far."

"I've never seen him drunk before," remarked Mary. "Nothing like that anyway."

"It's the worst I've ever seen him," I confirmed, "except for that one night he spent with Irene Adler."

5

I caught up with Holmes in the Twisted Lip at lunchtime the next day, to find him enjoying the hair of the dog. He looked a bit sprightlier than I expected, in that it appeared as if he'd only been run over by three freight trains.

"How's Martha?" I enquired as I took my seat.

"Still annoyed."

"I meant, is she over her flu?"

"Nah, that just makes it worse."

The transit of our discussion into the mundane was interrupted by the urgent entrance of Mayor Raaz.

"Mister Holmes, Doctor Watson," he said, "thank the heavens I've found you. Last night, somebody nicked the bloody orb."

"Well, it wasn't us," said Holmes. "I could hardly stand up."

"Of course not, of course not. I need your help to recover it, Mister Holmes."

"It sounds like a job for the police," I remarked.

"Oh no, Doctor Watson, if this gets out, I'm fucked. It's the mayor's job to look after that bloody thing. We need to keep this on the quiet."

"Okay," said Holmes, "sit down and tell us all about it. Everything you know. Omit nothing, no matter how trivial it seems. Would you like a drink to calm your nerves?"

"Alcohol, Mister Holmes? I'm a Muslim. Better make it a half."

"Doctor, could you do the honours?" asked Holmes, nodding in the direction of the bar.

"And a packet of pork scratchings," the mayor called after me, before appending, "Only kidding."

I returned to the table to catch the majority of the mayor's story. It was a simple one. After rising late, the mayor had been on his way to his office in the town hall when he'd noticed the door to the room that housed the orb was slightly ajar. He poked the door open the rest of the way to find the orb missing from its glass container.

"Well, that's not much to go on," commented Holmes. "Was the door definitely locked the night before?"

"Yes, I spoke with my men. They assure me they locked the door after returning the orb following last night's do."

"And where's the key kept?"

"It's locked away in the safe in my office."

"Is it still there?"

"Yes, Mister Holmes, yes."

"Is the CCTV all working okay?"

"Yes, perfectly. The first thing we did was to review the tapes and there was nothing."

"They can be hacked. What about security? Isn't the town hall guarded around the clock?"

"It is. We had extra men on last night, but with the party and everything I directed them to keep their eyes on the guests. You know there were some rum sorts around."

"The security team. Any new starters recently?"

"No, most of them have been with us for years."

"Most of them?"

"All have them have been there since before my time. I trust them all implicitly."

"Trust," murmured Holmes, "trust. Okay, Mayor, I think we need to have a look at this room of yours."

"Yes, Mister Holmes, I will take you there now."

"No, Mayor. If we're seen waltzing over to the town hall together, it's gonna look a bit suss. It's better if you get yourself back and we trail along later."

"Good point, Mister Holmes, you think of everything."

"We think of everything," corrected Holmes. "We'll not get your orb back without the invaluable assistance of my colleague Doctor Watson." He opened his hand in my direction.

"Understood. Mister Holmes, Doctor Watson," he nodded, as he took his leave.

As the mayor passed the window, Holmes shot a smile at me. The game was afoot.

After giving the mayor around a fifteen minute start, we made our way on foot along Baker Street before turning down Albert Road. On our arrival at the town hall reception, we were promptly ushered along to the scene of the crime, where we were greeted by the mayor and several of his staff.

The room that stored the orb was an ostentatious mix of a treasure store and an armoury, with various bejewelled objets d'art interspersed with ornamental swords, spears, flags, pendants and even a suit of armour.

"It's quite a little museum you have here," I commented on entry.

"It is indeed," replied the mayor. "These are the crown jewels of Middlesbrough. At least they were until some sneaky bastard nicked the main one. There are swords that saw action at the Charge of the Light Brigade, spears brought back from the Battle of Rorke's

Drift. All donated by Teessiders involved in those actions. Some of these swords are worth as much as the orb."

"I thought it was the Welsh that fought at Rorke's Drift?" I queried.

"It can't have been. Michael Caine isn't very Welsh, is he?"

I looked around to see Holmes yet to enter. Instead he was kneeling by the door, undertaking a hands-free examination of the lock, his nose almost but not quite touching it as his neck snaked from side to side. "Do you have the key?" he asked.

"Eustace, could you get the key from the safe, please," requested the mayor, before asking Holmes if he thought the lock had been picked. In return, Holmes flashed a noncommittal look.

A short while later, Eustace returned with the key. Taking it from him, Holmes turned it in the lock, turning his head to one side to examine the action of the mechanism, the odd thing being that the turning of the key didn't extend the latch bolt.

"That's strange," I remarked.

"Yeah," replied Holmes. "It looks like someone has been dicking around with it."

"Why?" questioned the mayor.

"I don't know," said Holmes. "But it hasn't been picked. It was never locked." He then moved into the room and began his typical staccato examination of the scene.

"Ah, cool," exclaimed the mayor. "Just like in your stories, Doctor Watson."

After a shorter than usual period, a silent Holmes concluded his survey and took a seat on a short wooden stool with an integral leather cushion pinned with brass tacks. He furled out his legs in front of him, and crossed his ankles and then his arms, before closing his eyes.

"Nap time, is it?" commented the mayor.

In response, I just shrugged, not having seen this element of his investigation previously. I reasoned that it may have been for effect. After as long as fifteen minutes, Holmes opened his eyes and rose to his feet, walking over to the suit of armour propped in the corner. He looked it dead in the eye for a few seconds and then shaped his mouth into a knowing grin. Slowly he eased the helmet off the shoulders of the metal figure to reveal the Orb of Ironopolis.

"That makes no sense," gasped the mayor.

"It makes perfect sense," responded Holmes. "It seems our thief has a sense of humour, and a return ticket. They saw it as too risky to smuggle the orb out last night. You had men on the doors searching people on the in and the out. It was easier to hide the orb away and come and retrieve it later. Tonight probably. They've had that lock apart in order that they could get a key made, but someone must have disturbed them, because they didn't put it back together properly. The chances are they don't realise their mistake."

"That's amazing, Mister Holmes. A thousand thank yous. I'll get you the keys to the town for this."

"It doesn't look like keys are an awful lot of use round here," replied Holmes glibly.

"Seriously, Mister Holmes, you're a genius."

"No, I'm really not," dismissed Holmes. "It's not like I've invented a new colour or something."

"Eustace," commanded the mayor. "I need that lock changing and a man posted outside this door twenty-four seven. When this scallywag returns, I want him battered over the head. Several times. And then several times more."

"I have a better idea," said Holmes.

"What, something that won't lead to charges of grievous bodily harm?" I asked.

"Yeah. I reckon we should leave the orb where it is and let them come for it."

"Are you crazy, Mister Holmes? I've only just got the bloody thing back."

"You have, but someone's still trying to steal it. If this attempt fails, the chances are they'll try again. They've already shown they can make short work of your security procedures. If we catch 'em, the problem goes away permanently."

"What do you suggest?"

"When you lock up tonight, the Doc and me will sneak back

in and camp out in this room. Matey shows up to grab the orb, but instead we grab them in the act. Twat, bang, wallop, problem solved."

" 'Twat, bang, wallop.' I like it," exclaimed the mayor. "Let's nail this son of a bitch."

With the plan agreed, Holmes and I said our goodbyes to the mayor and his staff, and agreed to reconvene at the Twisted Lip around four o'clock.

I remembered that I had a meeting that afternoon with an independent publishing company at their offices just off Billingham Green. They'd seen some of my Holmes articles in the Gazette and were keen to get the ill-fitting cobbles of my prose into the local bookshops for Christmas. All I had to do was sex up the some of the stories I'd already written, they'd design a cover and format my words into a paperback, and I could have a bestseller on my hands. Albeit a bestseller confined to Middlesbrough and the surrounding area.

It was really exciting. Even if I only sold half a dozen copies, I would still be a bona fide published author. Of course the fantasist in me had grander ideas, which included a long running television series and the occasional Hollywood blockbuster. I wondered who would play me, and what actor in their right mind would take on the role of Holmes. Given the random variation in his character, it seemed more like a three-man job.

I arrived at the Twisted Lip at around half past the hour to find Holmes in discussion with Mary.

"John," she protested, "he won't tell me who's trying to steal the orb. If you don't get him to spill the beans, I'm going to wipe that enigmatic grin around the other side of his face."

"He shouldn't have even told you an attempt had been made. The mayor swore us to secrecy."

"John, I was stood just over there when you were discussing it."

"Barmaids," remarked Holmes, "they see and hear everything."

"I'm the manager," she scolded. "Now tell me who did it or you're barred."

"That's a bit of a disproportionate response," said Holmes. "Besides, you were there too last night. Why don't you tell me who did it?"

Mary stepped back from her onslaught, narrowing her eyes and contorting her lips into intrigue. "Simon Lord," she blurted.

"Why d'you think that?" asked Holmes.

"I just don't like him."

"Women's intuition is a powerful thing. You've tried and convicted a gadgie quicker than I can tie up me trainees."

"Look," retorted Mary, "I don't for one minute believe all that charity work nonsense is anything more than a sham. He's a horrible, arrogant man, who's certainly not past grabbing anything that takes his fancy."

"He also mentioned it being stolen," I added. "That seems strangely prophetic, given that, as far as I'm aware, no one has tried stealing the orb before."

"I'm not sure," said Holmes. "He's all about being flash, he wouldn't steal something if he couldn't then brag about it. When he was skimming all that money off the taxpayer, he never failed to mention who was picking up the bill for all the antique cognac he was glugging. Is he your favourite too, Doc?"

"Actually no, I'm leaning towards Frank Moulton. I know he appears to be turning his life around, and I can't applaud him enough for working with ex-prisoners, but you heard him, he thinks the whole town has it in for him. What better way of sticking it up everyone than stealing the town's prime jewel? I think another key point is the ease in which the thief got around the CCTV."

"CCTV?" queried Mary. "I never knew about that."

"Yeah," I replied, "whoever got into the room where the orb was kept needed to pass several CCTV cameras on the way. Sherlock thinks these could have been hacked, but obviously that requires a certain level of skill. To my mind, Moulton could have easily found a cohort from within the group of prisoners he's been working with."

"I'm changing my mind," said Mary

"Ah," exclaimed Holmes, "a woman's intuition overruled by her prerogative to change her mind on a ten-bob bit."

"Hatty Durian," offered Mary. "If Sherlock is right and she has a marriage of convenience and riches, then what better way to extract herself than with a priceless piece of treasure?"

"With all due respect, do you think she has the skills to get around the CCTV cameras?" I queried.

"No, but I think she has all the attributes to get some slavering man to organise that for her."

"Is the orb really that valuable?" I queried. "It's only worth something if you can find a buyer, and it's not like you can advertise."

"It could be broken up," said Holmes. "The platinum could be melted down and the stones sold off separately."

"I'm not convinced," I said. "I think Flo Miller is a stronger possibility, given she was previously suspected of stealing a piece of artwork."

"But only 'suspected'," sighed Holmes.

"Well, yes," I replied, "but all of this is no more than speculation."

"There's no smoke without fire," added Mary.

"There's someone we haven't thought about," said Holmes. "Katrina Spring."

Both Mary and I were nonplussed.

"Maybe," I postulated, "but we don't know much more about her than we do the other two-hundred people that we never spoke to."

"Other than she's immune to Sherlock's pathetic attempts at seduction," grinned Mary.

"Who do you think it is then, Sherlock?" I asked.

"I'm not telling you," he said with feigned injury, before flashing a mischievous smile, "but I'm sure it's someone we spoke to last night. Let's play. We'll all write down who we think it is. Seal our answers in an envelope, and once we've found out who it is definitely, we'll open the envelopes and see who was right."

Mary and I looked at each other and smiled. It was going to be fun.

7

We arrived back at the town hall and entered against the tide of council staff leaving for the evening. Given that knowledge of the orb incident had been confined to just the mayor and a few of his security staff, we drew no significant attention.

The mayor greeted us with hearty handshakes. "Mister Holmes, I've been talking to my security staff and we think it would be better if a couple of them stayed with you tonight."

"You mean the same people who were looking after it when it went missing?" replied Holmes.

"Seriously though, you have spent time at her Majesty's pleasure yourself. You must understand my concerns."

Holmes flashed him a stern look. "You either trust me and Doctor Watson to sort this for you or you don't. The coin can't land on both sides. We're a team, we act as one. Anyone else will just get in the way."

Did we? Holmes had clearly seen an aspect of our collaboration that I had not realised. At the times previously when push had come to shove, it was Holmes who had reciprocated with the lion's share of both the pushing and the shoving.

"For your men," continued Holmes, "it needs to look as much like business as usual as possible. Whatever happens, they need to stay well away."

As Holmes and I sat in the town hall treasure room, in near perfect darkness, the steady silence of our barely-lit surroundings was broken by the pop of a drinks can being opened.

"Cooking lager?" asked Holmes, pushing a can in my direction.

"Why not?" I replied, as Holmes popped another for his own benefit.

"Doc, are you afraid of the dark?"

"No, I used to be."

"What happened?"

"I grew up. Are you afraid of the dark, Sherlock?"

"No, I quite like it. It's not as noisy."

"I've been meaning to ask, Sherlock, are you okay? You seem preoccupied. Like your mind is elsewhere."

"I'm fine."

"Where do you go? In those quiet times."

"Nowhere. Nowhere and everywhere."

"What does that mean?"

"I don't know. I can't describe it. But it makes me so tired."

"What does?"

"Searching for a way to explain."

"Explain what?"

"The unexplainable. I could paint it, but I don't have the brush and I don't know how to paint."

"I don't understand you, Sherlock. You're taking me round in circles."

"I thought you were a psychologist."

"I am but I'm still learning. I've only been doing it for twenty years. I do think you need a rest though. After this, let's take some time off."

"Go camping?"

"No," I laughed. "Not camping."

"Shame. I do like coffee from a flask."

"All we drank last time was lager. I'll have a think, and remember to factor in some stale coffee."

"Cool, Doc, I'll leave it with you. We hardly ever get paid for this shit anyway."

We settled back into our beers and waited for whatever was about to transpire, our backs against the wall containing the only door to the room.

At around midnight, I was awoken from a shallow slumber by a sharp knuckle in my flank.

"I wasn't asleep," I protested in a whisper.

"Bollocks," returned Holmes at low volume. Behind us we could hear the sound of a key being scraped against the metal of the lock in search of the keyhole. The key found the lock and turned before the door swung open gently. As we sat in silence, out of the light cast by the doorway, the silhouette of a slim-figured woman entered the room.

"Cooee," called Holmes from his sitting position.

"Cooee?" I remarked.

"Yeah, not sure where that came from," he said, as he sprang to his feet and flicked on the light. "Anyway, you're banged to rights, flower."

The woman, who was dressed top to bottom in a tight-fitting catsuit, including a mask to cover her face, turned towards us. Standing on the balls of her feet, her arms moved in low slow circles as she considered her options. "Am I?" she replied in a familiar voice I was struggling to place.

"Yeah," said Holmes, "there's two of us so come quietly or we'll jump on you, wrestle you to the ground, and probably cop a feel in the process."

"I won't be doing that last bit," I clarified.

She dropped to the floor, rolled over on her shoulders and sprang up near the adjacent wall, grabbing one of the ornamental swords from its wall mounting.

"You won't be doing any of that." she replied, shepherding any progress from Holmes or me with the sword's tip. "Move and I'll cut off anything that sticks out."

Holmes exhaled a resigned sigh. "That's just an ornament. You won't be able to do any damage with that."

In response, she skipped forward whipping the sword across his chest without any apparent contact. Holmes dropped his chin to inspect his tee shirt. There was a perfect slice across its width. "That was new," he protested. "George at Asda."

Alternating the pointing of the sword between myself and

Holmes, she edged slowly towards the suit of armour in the corner.

"The orb's not there," said Holmes. "We found your little hiding place."

Unperturbed, she reached the suit and lifted off the helmet with her free hand to reveal the orb.

"Didn't you tell the mayor to hide that away?" asked Holmes.

"No," I replied. "Didn't you?"

"Yeah, I did. That's just a Kitkat wrapper." He then whipped the chair out from behind him, directing its legs towards the woman. "We're gonna need it back anyway," he told her. "We're collecting them and we need that one for a set of cricket gear."

The woman made no response other than to remove the orb from its seat and push it into a lycra pocket to the rear of her waist. Holmes lunged forward with the chair to prompt a swing of her sword which clipped off a chair leg.

"Right, that's enough foreplay for now," said Holmes, examining the damage. "Give me back the orb and we'll say no more about it."

"Get out of my way, Holmes," snarled the woman.

Holmes contorted his mouth to one side in consideration and then hurled the remainder of the chair in her direction. In defence, she punched the chair out of the air with the sword's handguard, before rotating to re-orientate herself to Holmes' revised position. She spun around to see Holmes had also armed himself with a sword from the wall. You could see her smile through the material of the mask. I imagined she was confident in her swordsmanship.

Sparing no more time to assess her enemy, she lunged forward slashing the tip of her sword downwards with a flick of the wrist, to see Holmes parry with an unexpected amount of flair. She gave a quick flick of her head to the right, mirroring my own surprise.

They sized each other up for a short while, each presenting slight feints to prompt the other into action. Holmes struck first to provoke an elegant parry and riposte which transferred into a conversation of flashing blades. Backed up in the majority of the exchanges, Holmes found himself in the corridor outside the room. She was some competitor, agility verging on acrobatic. In the half light of the dimly lit hallway, sparks jumped from the blades as they clashed.

Although the perilous nature of the exchange had me concerned for the welfare of Holmes, I couldn't help but marvel at the elegance of her technique. She moved with such grace it was as if a ballet. That said, Holmes' more industrial style was not without its effectiveness. On one strike of her sword towards the base of his, he grappled briefly before using his strength to heave her back down the corridor. It was the first time he had earned any ground in the contest. Capitalising, he lashed out with increased fervour, backing her up slowly as she concentrated on a rear guard of defensive parries.

Just as Holmes had seized the initiative… disaster. On a blocked cross swipe, his blade broke, clanging to the floor. He stood defenceless, her blade just inches from his chest. I slowly eased back, my intention to duck back into the room for a replacement sword. Rather than take advantage, the woman continued her reverse transit along the corridor. Fending a warning to Holmes with her sword, her intended destination was soon obvious. At the far end of the corridor was a window. Now open, it was clearly her point of entry. On reaching the window she offered Holmes a salute of her sword, before driving its tip into the floor at her feet. As it oscillated in front of her, she stepped out of the window and into the night.

"Are you not going to go after her?" I asked.

Holmes glanced back towards the open window. "Nah," he responded.

"Are you scared of heights?" I queried.

"It's the same height in here as it is out there."

"You are. You're scared of heights."

"No, I'm not. I'm just not a massive fan of falling and hitting the ground really fast."

"Right," I realised. "I thought you fearless."

"No, lots of things concern me. Heights, rats, tax," he glanced at me to gauge my reaction, "spirit levels."

"Seriously," I said, diverting the discussion, "Mayor Raaz is not going to be too chuffed when we tell him we've lost the orb."

"The daft arse should never have agreed to that plan in the first place. We should have locked the orb in the safe."

"That would have been a better idea," I conceded.

Holmes glanced down at the remnants of the antique sword in his hand which now only boasted around three inches of blade. "He's not gonna be too happy about this either. Have you got any Brasso on yer?"

"Where did you learn how to do that?" I asked, laughing. "To swordfight, I mean."

"I'm not sure really. It was probably me and our kid jumping round the garden with bamboo sticks from our dad's greenhouse." He flashed the remainder of the sword through the air, mimicking the sound it would have made with a dry whistle.

"Sherlock," I suggested, "if I'm not mistaken that was that woman from last night. If not, it was someone of exactly the same height and build."

"It was also someone wearing the same perfume and deodorant. In pretty much the same proportions. But that doesn't mean it was definitely her."

"So it wasn't her?"

"Of course it was," said Holmes with a wide smile. "If you're going to disguise yourself you need to consider all the senses: sight, sound, definitely smell, erm, maybe not taste, oh yeah and I'm not sure about touch. But humour, yeah you need to consider that."

"Sherlock, you do know humour is not a sense?"

"Yes it is. 'Sense of humour'."

"Yeah, but on that basis the list would be endless. You could add 'sense of decency', 'sense of duty', 'sense of direction'…"

"Oh right, I see what you mean. But still if you want to disguise yourself, it helps if you don't tell the same jokes."

"Probably," I conceded.

"Okay," said Holmes. "We need to leave a note. Tell Mayor Raaz not to worry about the orb. If he brings the Five O in now we'll be buggered. Let's tell him we've gone deep undercover."

"What are we actually gonna do?" I asked.

"Go to the pub."

We returned back to the Twisted Lip, to both nurse the wounds to our dignity and put some distance between ourselves and Mayor Raaz. It was the early hours of the morning, however Mary, keen to learn of the mystery's unravelling, met us there to open up. She delivered us each a pint and handed us back the envelopes we'd sealed and signed earlier.

"Okay then," I said, deferring to Mary. "Ladies first."

Mary delicately unsealed the envelope to reveal the words 'Flo Miller'.

"Sorry, darling," I said. "I'm pretty sure the character we saw tonight wasn't her. I must admit however, that the same thought had crossed my mind, given she did seem envious of some of the wealth around her. A jewel like that could go a long way to redressing that imbalance."

Holmes rounded his lips, happy to allow the discussion to flow unabated.

"That was my thought," replied Mary. "She certainly needed the money, and that business at the museum didn't get cleaned up clearly enough to my mind. She may well have got a taste for it." A still silent Holmes grimaced in response. "What did you have, Sweetie?"

"She means me," I said, playing to Holmes, who, in response, had scraped forward in his chair. "Well, I'm afraid I used the tactic that tends to serve me well in many a pub quiz. I went for my first thought 'Frank Moulton'. I assumed the motive behind stealing the orb wasn't a financial one. There must be more profitable crimes than stealing something that would be as hard to find a buyer for as the orb. I assumed he was angry at the town and what better way to get back at it than stealing its crown jewel? So there was the motive, and the opportunity could have come at some point during the night when he slipped away to powder his nose, and means-wise I was looking at the cohorts he's come to know through his work with all those ex-prisoners. There must be an eclectic range of skills in that crowd."

Still Holmes stayed silent. He reached for the envelope sat on the table in front of him with the very tips of his fingers. He carefully parted the seals, adding to the tension with his absence of urgency.

"Hatty Durian," I announced as he revealed his answer. 'Katrina Spring', read the envelope.

"Katrina Spring?" I exclaimed. "I wasn't even considering her. So that woman we encountered tonight was Katrina Spring? I was sure it was Hatty."

"They are very similar in build," said Holmes, "but Hatty's boobs are slightly bigger."

"See, I wouldn't have noticed that," I said, nodding to Mary. "But, Sherlock, you came to that decision before our little escapade tonight. How on earth did you deduce that?"

"First," said Holmes, "can I agree with you, John? I don't think the crime was motivated by money either. The orb could be broken up and sold off in bits, but that's far too much hassle. You'd be better off nicking a fancy car."

"But, Sherlock," I interjected, "Katrina must have been the most unremarkable person we saw that night. What motive could she possibly have? What was she? A school teacher?"

"That's the point. She was unremarkable. At least that's how she wanted to come across. That makes her remarkable. Why was she there? And who drives to a do when there's a free bar? The other thing is that this gig was done by someone operating alone. All the people we met couldn't have done this without help. Especially Lord. He's a waste of a skin. If you were working with a mate, you would have just dropped the orb out of the window for them to catch and scarper. Finally, we have her name, 'Spring'. There's Jeff Winter, Donna Summer. I've never heard of anyone called 'Spring'. That must be made up."

Mary and I looked at each other and thought the same. There was little chance we would have drawn the same conclusion.

9

"So how are we going to locate her?" I asked Holmes. "If she's operating under a pseudonym, she won't be easy to track down."

Holmes just pointed a look of confused derision in my direction. "I'll see you here tomorrow, after tea," he replied, before rising to his feet and finishing the dregs of his drink in the same action.

An ebullient Holmes rolled into the Twisted Lip shortly after six-thirty. It appeared he was looking forward to meeting the woman who the previous night had almost run him through with an antique sword. If I didn't know better, I'd have thought he'd done something with his hair.

"Do you know where to find her?" I asked as we enjoyed an Engineer's Thumb at the bar.

"Yup," came the unqualified response.

"So where is it?"

"Somewhere in Marton. We can get the bus."

"Okay," I said, realising I was involved in a reasonably fruitless conversation. For once, it wasn't his distant morosity decelerating the flow of information, but his apparent shepherding of some future surprise.

The journey on the bus was just as quiet. As I'd experienced a couple of dozen times before, Holmes sat near the window, transfixed by its presentation of the evening that passed by it. In an attempt to understand the fascination he gleaned from this bizarre pastime, I skipped to the seat behind us and adopted a similar position to him. A couple of miles of scenery garnered no interest that I could identify. Perplexed by the activity, I almost didn't notice when Holmes stood to alight the bus at our stop.

The home of Katrina Spring was impressive for that of a schoolteacher. On three levels, it was new in construction, detached with a large, double garage. Holmes sidled on up to the door, passed the Jaguar parked on the drive, and rang the bell.

Katrina opened the door. "Sherlock Holmes and Doctor Watson, to what do I owe this intrusion?"

"You've won the postcode lottery," replied Holmes.

Katrina's lips straightened, her head nodding at the quip. "This is all very entertaining, gentlemen, but is there a point to it?"

"Yeah," said Holmes. "Can we have the orb back, please?"

"The orb? The Orb of Ironopolis. Why would you think I have that?"

"Because we were there when you took it. Where did you learn to fence like that?"

For a moment, Katrina's composure cracked, her eyes flicking slightly at Holmes' assertion. "I'm sorry, but I really don't know what you are talking about, and if you don't get off my doorstep I will have to introduce you to some mace."

By mace, I assumed she meant the self-defence spray. I admit the prospect of being gassed unnerved me somewhat. She then drew her hand into view from behind the door to reveal a rod capped with a spiked metal ball. If she'd have swung it at either of us, she would have murdered us both. As we considered our limited options, Katrina smiled a seductive smirk of victory. Oddly for Holmes, he mirrored her action, his response only skewed by a resigned deference. He gave a just noticeable nod of the head, before glancing at the mace and turning to leave the scene.

"That went well," I remarked, as we walked away.

"I was just tapping the barometer," he replied, his mind already working on the next encounter.

"Were you expecting her to just hand the orb over?"

"Nope."

"So why such a direct approach?"

"I wanted her to know we had her card marked. I was trying to get her to move the orb, but make her feel it's her decision."

"Move it? So you know where it is?"

"I didn't, but I do now. It's in her garage. Probably locked away in a tool box or something."

"How do you know that?"

"She kept glancing in that direction. Ever so slightly. It's definitely there."

"So why are we walking away? Surely we should stay and watch. She might be moving it as we speak."

"No, she's clever. She's someone who plans. She won't be moving anything anywhere until she has a safe place to move it to. We need to influence that."

"How do we do that?"

"I'm not sure."

We walked a while further in silence. There was no obvious destination, however from the expression on Holmes' face, it appeared that the motion was driving his thoughts. This was unusual for him as he normally adopted a more sedentary approach to his pondering. Also strange was a frustrated urgency in his stride. Something that I hardly recognised. His whole persona was unlike anything I'd seen since the time of the woman, Ms Irene Adler.

"You know," said Holmes, "when our dad used to come home from the pub he would always turn the telly over. It was his right to decide what channel was on. He paid for the bugger. Me and our kid used to switch over as soon as we heard the door. Nine times out of ten he'd turn it back to what we were watching."

"It's a great story, Sherlock, but how does it help?"

"I don't know. I'm still wondering how to get her to move the orb, but make her think it's her idea."

"Why don't we use the same technique we used to smoke Irene, sorry, the woman, out? Spray some of that stuff that smells of gas into her house. She thinks it's a gas leak, grabs the orb, runs out of the house, and we grab her."

"Mercaptan," clarified Holmes. "No, doing the same thing twice would be boring. Besides, think of your readers," he continued through a tone of annoyance, I suspected due to my mention of the woman. "Although, I wouldn't mind grabbing her. She's well fit."

167

"She is," I agreed. "And well out of your league."

"Maybe I'll meet her in the cup."

Whether it was by fate or design, our walk through the houses led us to the Southern Cross. We entered the pub to find, much to Holmes' glee, a pub quiz about to start.

"You get a couple of beers," he said, "and I'll get us an answer sheet."

We sat at a vacant table and he scribbled 'The Doyles' on the top of the paper. On this unilateral definition of our team name, he sat back, poised before the challenge ahead. It seemed as if the do with Katrina Spring had been suspended in his consciousness.

The quizmaster declared the commencement of proceedings and informed the packed pub that the theme of this week's quiz would be numbers.

"Great," said Holmes. "I'm good at maths."

"Round one, literature," announced our host. "How many novels did Emily Brontë write?"

Holmes looked at me baffled. "I've never even heard of her?"

"You've never heard of Emily Brontë?"

"Nope."

"Wuthering Heights?"

"I've heard the Kate Bush version. Didn't think it was a cover."

We struggled through the first round. With me not being a big reader, my knowledge of literature was scant and Holmes' was something close to a vacuum. In all, we collected about three points and on the round's conclusion we were well off the pace of the leaders, a team called the 'Southern Crossdressers'.

The next round concerned space and astrology. Given the subject was science rather than art, I was hoping for a better return. If Holmes' knowledge of literature was meagre, his understanding of the solar system was, well, confusing.

"Name the fifth planet from the sun," asked the quizmaster.

"From the sun?" pondered Holmes.

"Jupiter," I said, urging him to write down the answer.

"Jupiter?" he queried.

"Yes, Mercury, Venus, Earth, Mars, Jupiter."

"What about the moon?"

"The moon's not a planet."

"What is it then?"

"It's a moon. A satellite."

"The moon's a moon? That's a bit redundant. So it's Planet Earth and Moon Moon. Actually that explains that Duran Duran song and the bit about a 'lonely satellite'."

"Do you really not know that the moon isn't a planet?"

"Nah," he replied wistfully. "I've just never got round to checking it out. I'll look into that later. I've got a book on the moon somewhere, back at the flat."

"What about school? Did your teachers never mention it?"

"I never spent a lot of time at school. I had what they now call 'attention deficit disorder'. It wasn't called that at the time. The teachers just thought I was a twat. They kept banning me. It really pissed them off when I got ten O-levels."

"Sherlock," I exclaimed. "You really are the strangest of creatures."

"Cheers," he replied, a little confused.

Our saviour from embarrassment came in the form of a round on sport. By this point, we were still lagging behind, with team a called 'Quizteam Aguilera' the new leaders. As we wound our way through questions on boxing, football, athletics, etcetera, Holmes hardly looked from the answer sheet to consult. Instead, he scribbled the answers in isolation. It was hard however for me to protest. He got every answer right.

Next up was chemistry. With my schoolboy knowledge of the subject stretched with time, I feared the success of the previous round to be dulled. Not so. Again Holmes' one-man effort produced a perfect score.

As we entered the final round, the quizmaster announced the standings. "In third place, Quizly Adams, second Uvavu ..."

"Eranu," called the swell of the pub in unison.

"... and in third the Sausage Cottagers."

"What about us?" called Holmes.

169

"And you are?" asked the quizmaster.

"It's Batman," called someone from the crowd to reap some low-level laughter.

"The Doyles," said Holmes.

"The Doyles," replied the quizmaster. "You're fourth."

Holmes nodded. He clearly thought the contest was still live.

The subject of the final round was popular music. "Okay," called the quizmaster. "Name David Bowie's five UK number one singles. A point for each."

"David Bowie has only had five number ones?" I remarked.

"No," said Holmes, "he's only had three. He must be including the duets with Queen and Jagger. Space Oddity, Ashes to Ashes, Under Pressure, Let's Dance and Dancing in the Street," he continued in an asserted whisper as he wrote.

Holmes navigated the rest of the questions with aplomb, dropping only one point on a question concerning some contemporary dance track. He dismissed this as not real music. When the final standings were read, we were tied for the lead with the Sausage Cottagers.

My overriding memory of that night in the pub was of the binary nature of Holmes' knowledge. He had either an encyclopaedic recollection of a subject, or he would shudder to a halt. It was rare that his grasp of a subject was sporadic.

"Okay," said the quizmaster, "tiebreak time. Can I have a representative from both the Doyles and the Sausage Cottagers, please?"

To Holmes' interest, his adversary was greeted by the quizmaster in a manner that suggested they knew each other. "Now then, Mick."

"Alright, pal," replied Mick, nodding to the quizmaster before offering his hand to Holmes. After a noticeable pause, a concerned Holmes shook on the contest.

"Right," said the quizmaster, "whoever answers first, with the correct answer, wins the quiz and a gallon of beer. The Beatles had seventeen UK number one singles. Name one of the ones with a woman's name in the title."

"Hey Jude," called Mick.

"Lady Madonna," said Holmes, shortly after.

"The Sausage Cottagers win," announced the quizmaster, reaching to shake Mick's hand.

"No, they don't," appealed Holmes. " 'Jude' is a man's name. The song was written for Julian Lennon."

"I'm sorry, mate," replied the quizmaster. " 'Jude' is a woman's name and I'm afraid my word is final."

Mick offered a consoling handshake, which was roundly ignored by Holmes, who maintained his glare on the quizmaster. "Your final words will be 'ow that hurt' if you dick with me," said Holmes, as he turned and stomped from the pub.

I gave an apologetic nod to both the quizmaster and Mick before following in his trail.

By that point during our association, Holmes had been beaten to a pulp, set on fire, nearly drowned, and shot at with automatic firearms. None of these managed to generate the consternation that losing that pub quiz did.

"Where are you going, Sherlock?" I called, struggling to catch up to him as he strode down the road in the direction we'd previously come from.

"To burgle a house," he snapped. "Get that tin pineapple back."

"Sherlock!" I protested. "I'm a member of the medical profession. I can't be an accessory to this."

"Go back to the pub then. Finish yer beer."

"Sherlock," I pleaded.

"You know what the problem was, don't you?"

"What problem?"

"With that quiz. I never did any research. We went in unprepared."

"How on earth would you research a quiz? It's general knowledge. Anything could be asked."

"You don't research the questions," he replied sharply. "You research the gadgie asking them. See what he's into."

It made sense.

By the time we got to Katrina's place, his mood had quelled from

171

rage to determination. He skidded to a halt a short distance from the house to survey the scene.

"We go in through the roof," he said.

"We?" I queried.

"You're still here, aren't you? I assume you're gonna give me a bunk up."

"I thought you were scared of heights?"

"Just high ones."

We made our way carefully up to the house. Disguising our progress as best we could in the available shadow, we snuck down the side of the garage until we reached a wooden gate blocking our path. Holmes scaled the gate until the point where he was waist-level with the guttering of the sloping garage roof. After a cold scraping noise, he whispered, " 'ere, cop that," before handing me a roof tile. It wasn't long before I had a pile of seven or eight tiles at my feet. I looked up to see Holmes lowering himself into the hole he had made.

"Are you coming?" he asked, before dropping with a thud and a groan.

I clambered up the gate, doing the best I could to protect my suit. Climbing past the void in the roof, I lowered myself into it to the point where I was suspended by my elbows. I then dropped into the darkness with my knees bent in the hope they would serve to cushion my blind impact with the floor. My technique actually worked quite well, well enough that I managed to stay on my feet.

"Nice one," said Holmes, without turning to face me. Instead, he examined the contents of the garage with a small penlight. From what I could see in the spot of the light, it was a treasure trove of art and antiquity. As we surveyed the scene through open-mouthed awe, there was the flick of a light switch and the room was illuminated. We both spun around to see the figure of Katrina Spring. Dressed in a short, black silk nightdress, her only accessory was an ornamental sword similar to the one she'd wielded with such poise the previous evening.

"Good evening," said Holmes.

"Good evening," replied Katrina.

"You know, I don't think another sword fight will serve either of our purposes."

"You don't have a sword."

"I could find something," said Holmes, looking around the walls of the garage, which had the look of an armoury.

"So?" said Katrina.

"So," chimed Holmes, before moving to pull at a dust sheet which was obscuring something mounted on the wall.

"Is that the Dice Players?" I asked as the sheet dropped to the floor. "Georges de la Tour."

"It is," confirmed Katrina apologetically. "I kind of liberated it while on a school trip to Preston Park a few years back. The one I left in its place is a very good replica."

Holmes stalked round the room examining the various artefacts before stopping at a tea chest to pick up a book laid upon it. "EW Hornung. First edition. Is that where you got the idea? Raffles?"

"No," she replied, "I just like shiny things."

"You've got to give it back, Kitty Kat. There's no other way this ends. Unless you intend running me and the Doc through with that sword, it's the only way to stay classy."

Katrina held the sword in front of her to suggest she was considering the option. "What, all of it?"

"No, just the orb," he smiled. "Although that painting would look good in my flat. You should pop over sometime. I'm in on Wednesdays."

Katrina smiled. She whipped the sword a few times in front of her in what I took to be a concession, and laid it on a nearby shelf. She then moved to a small antique trunk, which she opened to remove a dark cloth bag, drawn together at the top with a string. She worked open the bag to reveal the orb. With the orb still cradled in the cloth, she handed it to Holmes.

Glancing down at it, his look was one of dismissal. I suspect he saw no value in such a trinket. He rewrapped it in its bag and then shaped to throw it in my direction.

"On yer head, Doc," he joked.

Katrina led us through the house and to the front door. As we stepped into the night, we turned to address her.

"You're dangerous," said Holmes to Katrina. "That's why I like you. It's also why …" The flow of Holmes' building seduction was dammed, as his attention was captured briefly by something in the hallway behind her. His rhetoric shuddered to a halt and the familiar look of cheek-riddled charm washed from his face. "Anyway," he continued, "as I said, stay classy."

In response, she narrowed her brow in confusion, before nodding and stepping back to close the door.

10

At lunchtime the next day, we sat in the Twisted Lip, awaiting the arrival of Mayor Raaz and his men to retrieve the orb. We sat on one table, accompanied by a couple of pints of Engineer's Thumb, whilst the orb sat on an adjacent table, balanced precariously on an old ashtray Mary had recovered from the storeroom.

"Sherlock," I remarked, "we've recovered the orb, but we don't have a thief to serve up to Mayor Raaz. He's not gonna be happy about that."

"No," said Holmes, "but Kitty will be useful in the future. She'd be no use to you in prison."

"Use to me?"

"Sorry, use to us."

"The mayor will look on this as a failure. After all, we had the orb at the beginning of the caper."

"Don't worry about failure," commented Holmes. "It's just destiny that never was."

"You know," I lamented, "it's not all doom and gloom. It's rather nice to have a case that involves neither a murder nor the shadow of a nefarious professor lurking like some unchecked disease."

"Yup," agreed Holmes, "but we haven't seen the back of our mate, the Professor."

"You never know," I postulated. "Maybe he'll just fade away."

"Maybe," he said, "but I do hope not. The mystery would kill me."

ELEVEN ELEVEN

1

It's a sad thing to watch the decline of a man into madness. In my line of work, you see too much of it. You try to develop a certain detachment, but never become completely annealed to watching the dereliction of a body to an empty container. Sometimes in the face of outrageous circumstance, you can do nothing but succumb. To watch the descent of a friend, your best friend, is beyond description.

I always thought Holmes a tortured genius. That was before I knew what tortured was. Great artists often lead tragic lives. Is it the art that leads them to tragedy or the tragedy that inspires their art? I saw Holmes as an artist. He couldn't wield a paintbrush or write a concerto, at least not to my knowledge, but he could chisel out a scenario like Michelangelo could fashion the smoothest sculpture. There wasn't one time with Holmes, not one of our escapades, where I didn't feel the best was yet to come. Until it was over, and there was nothing.

It had been months since Holmes and I had been involved in anything of interest, our last adventure involving the recovery of the Orb of Ironopolis. Holmes had been called upon to assist in the finding of several cats and a Nissan Juke, but all of these requests had been declined without any semblance of civility. It might have been for this reason that the time I was spending with Holmes was diminishing.

The consequence of this was that the amount of attention I could afford my patients was taking the opposite trajectory, and my partner in practice, Doctor Anstruther, who often covered my excursions, was seeing a little more of his beautiful young wife.

Then one day, I was nearing the end of my morning sessions, when I took a call from Mary. Her voice tinged with both concern and urgency, she provided a pragmatic précis of the situation. Suffice to say I needed to get to the Twisted Lip fast. I rushed through my consultation, cancelled the appointments I couldn't offload to Anstruther, and made my way over to Baker Street.

I entered the pub to find Holmes sitting bolt upright with his back to the window.

"Drugs or drink?" I asked Mary.

"Well, it's not drink," she replied. "He's had that pint sat in front of him for an hour and not touched a drop. He's lost it, John."

Holmes peered up at us as if we were strangers, his look a longing concoction of curiosity and confusion. "All this suffering and pain," he said. "Why is there a place in the universe for this? The people. What purpose does the violence serve?"

My concern escalated and it was apparent that Mary shared my worries. How do you answer that?

"He's precious, John," she said. "You need to look after him."

Holmes didn't even acknowledge that we were communicating. "We have to break out of this cycle of murder and misery," he said. "We can't carry on and expect something different to happen, the wheel will keep spinning. Can't you see that? Spinning like scratched vinyl stuck in a looping grove."

"Come on, Sherlock," I replied. "I think it's best if we get you back to the flat."

"Yes," he replied, almost childlike in nature. "Can you take me home, please?"

As we exited the Twisted Lip, Holmes stopped dead in his tracks to stare up at the sky. It was one of those strange, clear days where the moon is still visible in the daytime. "A troubadour moon," he said at low volume. "A messenger. But what's the message?"

Seeking to distract, I led him by the elbow in the direction of Flat 1B.

"The universe knows," he mumbled. "The universe knows."

I guided him up the stairs and into the living room to be greeted by a maelstrom of chaos. The semi-detached order of his usual living arrangement had been scattered into a total mess. His over-sized collection of books and old newspapers were strewn everywhere to form a foot-thick floor covering and the walls were scribbled with graffiti in thick black ink. With most of the scrawl illegible, the only word I could make out was that of 'Professor'. Other than that, there was the initials 'IN' and perhaps hundreds of depictions of a time, '11:11'.

"What is this?" I asked. "What is 'eleven eleven'?"

He looked back at me with eyes that looked at a perfect stranger. "I don't know," he said. "But I see it everywhere. On clocks, in telephone numbers, the licence number of a minicab. Everywhere I look, I'm being spoken to."

"It's nothing, Sherlock. It's just one of those things. Just coincidence. It's like imagining a face in the clouds."

"No, the universe knows. It has perfect order. I've been stealing from it and now it wants me to pay up."

"Pay what?"

"I don't know."

"Come on, Sherlock," I said, desperately searching for a way to provide him some respite. "It might be an idea for you to get your head down. Get some sleep."

"Yes," he said, "my eyes are tired."

I helped Holmes out of his jacket and laid him on his bed, laying the jacket over him as a blanket. There was no way I could leave him in that state. Moving back into the living room, I cleared some debris from the settee and settled into my vigil. With little to keep my mind active other than Holmes' expansive collection of years old newspapers and text books, by mid-evening I must have drifted off to sleep. I was woken around midnight by the sensation of someone watching me. As my eyes acclimatised to what light was available, I could make out the figure of Holmes standing dead centre in the room.

"She's been here, John. A vision in pink. We danced. Just for a little while. She smiled at me, that certain little smile. But then someone took her away. She never even said goodbye. That's the end. The very end."

"You were dreaming, Sherlock."

"No," he replied, "we danced. We did. She was holding me. It made me feel warm, unhollow. We danced." Tears welled in his eyes as he urged me to believe him. The look on his face was something I'd not seen before. Stoicism fractured by a quivering self-pity. He bravely defended, but his eyes and a tremble in his lips betrayed him. I wanted to hold him, but thought it better to provide distraction.

"Sherlock, this is quite normal. You know, my friend, it's never the one you haven't met. It's always the one you can't forget." I smiled, trying to offer some reassurance.

He looked back at me, holding a wide-eyed stare as he processed the statement.

"Come on, Sherlock," I said, "let's see if you can get back to sleep."

"Perchance to dream?" he muttered.

"No... I think you've done enough dreaming for one night."

I called Anstruther the next morning. With Holmes the way he was, and myself a little too close to provide a dispassionate analysis, I needed a second opinion. Anstruther arrived to find Holmes huddled on the floor under the window of the lounge.

"Hello, Sherlock, my name is Doctor Anstruther. I work with John. How are you feeling today? John tells me you've not been too well."

Holmes stared up at him suspiciously, from his position on the floor.

"Can you answer some questions for me?" continued Anstruther.

"Am I under arrest?"

"No, of course not, I'm here to help you."

"Then no."

"John tells me you've been having some quite lucid dreams. Dreams are something I'm really interested in. Could you tell me about those?"

"I never dream," snapped Holmes, descending further and further into himself.

Anstruther looked to me with a short shake of his head. He shepherded me into the kitchen to share his assessment, the conclusion of which was that Holmes should be admitted to hospital. My urge was to look after him myself, however it was difficult to argue with my colleague's opinion that Holmes needed round the clock attention. Anstruther was excellent, offering to complete the necessary paperwork for Holmes' admission. He even organised a minicab to take us there. I packed a few random articles from Holmes' scant yet consistent wardrobe into a bag for life and led him to the taxi cab.

My descending mood was actually buoyed by that taxi ride. Watching Holmes glued to the car window as he observed the world fly by, afforded me a glimpse of a Holmes I recognised. On our arrival, I stayed with him through his admission, before leaving him in the care of the staff of Roseberry Park Hospital. I expected some resistance, but saw none, with Holmes staring blankly at the various medical personnel and obediently allowing them to lead him through the process.

That evening, I returned to Roseberry Park. The Holmes I encountered was the diametric opposite to the one of just a few hours earlier. On first appearances, it appeared we may have overreacted. I entered his room to find him sitting on a chair, looking out of the window, his knees drawn into his chest.

"Hi, Doc," he said cheerfully, pulling his chair around to face me, "I wasn't expecting to see you."

"Why not?" I enquired. "You're in hospital, of course I'm going to come and see how you're getting along."

"I didn't think they allowed visitors."

"Even prisons allow visitors, Sherlock," I replied, taking a seat on his bed.

"Do they?"

"I visited you in prison. Earlier this year during that debacle with the PSB."

"Did you? I don't remember that." Although effusive in mood, it did appear he was having issues with his memory.

"How are you feeling, Sherlock?"

"I feel fine. Tickety-fucking-boo."

"Do you remember much about how you were feeling before I brought you here?"

"No, not much. Just feelings," he said pensively. "Feelings that I shouldn't be here. That this is not my island. That I shouldn't be here, but there's nowhere to swim to. It's hard…"

"What is?"

"To be the cuckoo of the whole world. Sometimes it gets so black, I'm frightened to death. That's what the drugs were all about. I just needed some time off."

"You've never spoken to me about drugs before," I remarked.

"Haven't I?" said Holmes dreamily.

"Not recently, anyway," I said, disturbed but trying to direct the discussion from the morose. "I like your outfit. Very Arthur Dent."

Holmes was dressed in striped blue pyjamas covered by a red almost velvet-looking dressing gown with the letters 'SH' embroidered to the chest pocket in gold.

"Yeah, some woman brought it in. Margaret or something. She thought I should know her. She was quite upset when I didn't. Who's Arthur Dent? Doesn't he work in Barnacles?"

"No, at least not to my knowledge. He's chap in Hitchhiker's Guide to the Galaxy. Forty-two, the answer to life, the universe and everything."

"I thought forty-two was the minimum amount of time it takes to lose an FA Cup final."

"So you remember some things?"

"I remember lots of things," smiled Holmes, "not necessarily in the right order."

"Do you mind if I try something?" I asked.

"As long as it doesn't involve a latex glove."

"No," I smiled. "It's just a game. Word association. I say a word and you tell me the first thing that comes into your head."

"Fire away," said Holmes, sitting back in his chair.

"Baker Street."

"Candlestickmaker Street," he replied.

"Martha."

"…and the Muffins"

"Professor."

"Yaffle."

"The Twisted Lip."

"Engineer's Thumb."

"The woman."

"Does this go on forever?" he sighed with a cold boredom.

I paused to blow air out of my cheeks and wonder where else to go. "It appears you have some gaps in your memory, Sherlock."

"What can you do about that?"

"You just need some rest. You've been through some trauma and your mind is catching up with you." I stood, placed my hand on his shoulder and left.

"See you later, my mate," I heard him call cheerfully.

2

I didn't see Holmes the next day. I called the hospital and they said he'd had a comfortable night and had spent most of the day sleeping, waking only occasionally to take small bites to eat. With rest perhaps the best medicine available to him, I agreed with the ward nurse that it would be better if I stayed away that day.

In the morning, I made my way over to Baker Street both to see Mary and, primarily, to provide Martha with an update on Holmes' condition. It was Martha who had delivered Holmes' pyjamas and dressing gown, they were Christmas presents from his mother, he'd never actually made use of. That Holmes didn't recognise her troubled her acutely. I did my utmost to calm her, but there was little I had to offer in the way of comfort, other than to tell her he'd seemed a lot better when I'd seen him previously.

Martha's concern was worrying. She'd known him longer than almost anyone and generally dismissed the various scrapes he got himself into, having seen it all before. This episode was unlike anything she'd seen previously and it unnerved her.

Leaving Martha with a consoling hug, I made my way along Baker Street to reiterate what scant reassurance I had to Mary. As we sat nursing a drink each, she reminded me of the invite we had to the grand opening of an establishment in Norton. Cathryn, who'd served us many a fine brunch in the Baker Street Kitchen, had left to become a partner in a micropub-cum-restaurant called The Hambletonian. It was fortunate that Cathryn's leaving the Kitchen was yet another block of data that Holmes was struggling to retrieve. Her culinary skills were renowned, but it was her ability to prepare Holmes' toast to an exact shade on the Dulux colour chart that was perhaps her successor's greatest challenge.

Mary and I arrived at the Hambletonian early to be welcomed with a warm greeting and a chilled glass of prosecco. We were impressed, the ambience of the place pulling you in like a warm blanket. We took a seat at one of the tables and, at points between her duties, we were joined by Cathryn who enquired after Holmes' wellbeing.

After a short while, in which I'd enjoyed a couple of craft ales and Mary had made a good job of a bottle of Pinot Grigio, we were joined by a girl I recognised, but was struggling to place. She asked after Holmes and sighed, slumping back in her chair, when I told her he was dealing with a few medical issues. With me still unable to place her, and Mary beckoning an introduction, I had to apologise. The girl laughed. "I'm Jo Vernon, PC Jo Vernon. We've bumped into each other at a few crime scenes."

"Ah, of course," I replied. "I didn't recognise you out of uniform." In my defence, other than a stray acknowledgement, I'd not really spoken to her before. "Why were you looking for Sherlock?" I enquired.

"When I'm not being a police officer, I work at a stables. A couple of days ago, one of the horses I look after went missing. I was hoping Sherlock could take a look. It's an important racehorse, entered in a major race. We expected him to go off favourite."

"What's the horse called?" asked Mary.

"Red Herring," she replied, expecting some disbelief.

"Anyone would think this was a wind up," I smiled.

"I can assure you it's not, Doctor," replied Jo. "He's a lovely horse. I'm at my wit's end that he's disappeared. I've been training him for over two years. I feel like I've lost a friend." Her comment resonated.

"What race was he to run in?" I asked.

"The Beryl Coronet, they call it the Derby of the North."

"I can't say I've heard of it," I said, "but then I'm not a big horseracing fan. A pound each way on the Grand National is usually the extent of my involvement. Could this be to do with someone else in the race, one of Red Herring's competitors?"

"Well," said Jo, "that thought crossed my mind too. There's a colt called Prosperous that might run him close, and it's a big race, with lots of prestige, but the prize money doesn't justify stealing a horse. There are other races and who's to say your horse will perform well on the day."

"Prestige is a currency too," I remarked.

"Yes," said Jo, "but there is a code of conduct in the horseracing fraternity and messing with someone else's horse is a big no no."

"When is the Beryl Coronet run?" asked Mary.

"About four weeks from now."

"Actually, in my experience, it's better to start close to home. Is there anyone at the yard you suspect?" I asked.

"No, I can't imagine anyone. We're like a family."

"Yes," I said, "but it's usually the one stood closest who can't see the full picture. Maybe I could have a look for you."

"You?" exclaimed Mary.

"I've seen enough of Holmes' method. I should be able to shed at least some light on this."

Jo looked as sceptical as Mary, but as the throng in The Hambletonian started to swell, she accepted my offer of help and we arranged to meet the next day.

Early the following morning, Jo picked me up in her VW Beetle and we travelled to the farm in Stokesley from where Red Herring had gone missing. When we arrived, Jo led me through the yard to the barn where the horse was once stabled. On our way there, we passed various members of the yard employees going about their early morning duties, none of whom afforded us much in the way of notice.

I entered the barn and walked into an unremarkable scene of whitewashed brick walls and an earth floor, spread with straw. I scoured the area for clues, but there were none. There was no lock on the door, therefore no need to break in and consequently no resulting clues.

"Could the stable door have been left open?" I asked Jo.

"Possibly," she said, "but I stabled him that night and I'm sure I put the bolt across. Besides, when he was discovered missing the next day, the stable door was bolted. He was a clever horse, but he couldn't bolt a door."

"It's not what you'd call top security, is it? A padlock wouldn't have gone amiss."

"There's electronic security to the external gates and closed-circuit TV cameras trained on the perimeter fence. Out of hours, the only access is via the intercom on the main entrance."

"Has the CCTV been checked?"

"Yes, I went through it with the yard owner. Other than her son stumbling in after a night out, there was nothing."

"What are the police doing?" I asked.

"We are looking at it," she said. "But we're a bit stretched for resources at the minute."

"I'm a man down myself," I replied. "How valuable is Red Herring?"

"To us, he could be priceless. If he wins a few big races, which we expect him to, and goes to stud, you could be talking millions."

"How valuable would he be to someone else?"

"He wouldn't be. You couldn't run him under another name, there's too much paperwork involved. You can't magic up a racehorse from nowhere. Without a few big wins under his belt, he has no value at stud. Even if someone did try to run or breed with him, we have all the DNA of all our best horses on record. If a three-year-old resembling him showed up somewhere, we'd soon get to know about it, and identifying him would be easy."

"So if he wasn't stolen, then what?" I wondered aloud.

"I don't know," replied Jo. "I'm at a complete loss."

I put my hands in my jacket pockets and tried to recreate Holmes' crime scene analysis technique. I scanned the area, sometimes with my eyes open, sometimes with them closed, trying to imagine the scenario in which the horse disappeared. It was useless. I could imagine the horse being led away by some shadowy, unrecognisable silhouette, but that was about it. Even that was pure imagination, there was nothing tangible to trigger that thought. I ended the charade and shook my head in the direction of Jo.

As we exited the stable, Jo bolted the door. The automated way in which she performed the task convinced me that she'd done exactly the same the night Red Herring went missing. We stepped across the yard to encounter a middle-aged woman, bounding towards us. Dressed in jodhpurs, riding boots and a plaid shirt too small for her frame, she was hanging on precariously to the last vestiges of her youth. As she approached, I could smell the unmistakable aroma of stale alcohol on her breath. It was perhaps the drinking that had ravaged her looks.

"Good morning, Jo," she called. "Who's our visitor?"

"Hi Xandra, this is Doctor John Watson, he works with the detective Sherlock Holmes. I asked him over to see if he could shed any light on Red Herring's disappearance."

"Doctor Watson," said the woman, offering me her hand, "Xandra Holder."

"Missus Holder owns the yard," added Jo.

"Missus Holder," I nodded.

"Please," she said, "Xandra. We're far too busy around here to be standing on ceremony."

"John," I replied.

"Well, John, have you any thoughts regarding our little mystery?"

"Not as yet, I'm afraid. There's not an awful lot to go on. If you don't mind, could you tell me if Red Herring was insured?"

"Yes, he was, but insurance money doesn't begin to compensate us for the years of early mornings and effort we've put in to get him up to par."

"And it's you who holds the policy?"

"Well, that would be Holder and Stevenson Holdings, but as I hold the majority stake, I would be the main beneficiary. Does that make me your prime suspect?"

"It's a bit early for suspects," I smiled, "but if you think of anyone else who would benefit from this, could you please let me know?"

"Certainly, Doctor, no one would like to see Red Herring back more than me. Besides, I wasn't going to make a claim. Lord knows what it would do to the premiums."

"Do you mind if I have a look around, speak to some of your staff?"

"Of course not, but stick with Jo. I don't want to see you trampled on. I can spot a horsey person from a mile away, and that certainly isn't you, Doctor." With that, she said her goodbyes and went about her morning activity.

"Is there a Mister Holder?" I asked Jo after Xandra had left.

"There was," she said, "but he left a few years ago. Xandra likes a drink and they used to fight a lot. I think it got too much for him in the end. It's a shame really, he was a nice lad."

"And he had no claim on the yard?"

"Nick's the Stevenson in Holder and Stevenson Holdings, but it's only a minority stake she gifted him as a wedding present. Xandra inherited the farm from her late father and built it up as a racehorse stables herself. It's all hers really, and the prenup she had drawn up before her marriage with Nick made sure it stayed that way. It didn't bother him anyway. There was no real fuss when they split up. He just got up one day and left. It was four or five days before she even told us he'd gone."

"Has she been romantically involved since?"

"There's been a few rumours concerning some of the young stable boys, but nothing she's ever gone public with."

We made our way across the yard, and Jo stopped us to introduce me to a stable girl who was leading a horse. In her twenties, she was Xandra's daughter, Mary Holder. I asked her a few questions regarding where she'd been on the night Red Herring went missing, but she couldn't furnish us with any useful information. She'd not been at the yard on the night of the disappearance, and had stayed with a friend in Guisborough. I thanked her for her help and we made our way into the house for coffee.

The kitchen was a spacious affair that needed to be, in that it served as a canteen to the yard's employees. From the general tidiness of the place, it was clear that Ms Holder was effective in promoting order. We entered to find Arthur Holder, Xandra's son and Mary's twin brother, finishing off what looked and smelled to be a full English breakfast.

"Good afternoon," mocked Jo.

"Heavy night," he grumbled.

Jo introduced us and flicked on the kettle.

Sitting on the bench opposite him, I asked him if he'd been out the previous evening.

"Yeah," he replied, not looking up from his plate. "I nipped into Stokesley for a few games of pool and things got out of hand."

"Did you lose all your money again?" asked Jo, with a tone of disappointment.

"No," he parried, "not all of it."

As he sat up to slurp the remaining contents of an over-large cup of tea, I enquired into his whereabouts on the night of disappearance. His recollection was variable, but he remembered going to bed quite late and not hearing anything until the alarm was raised the following morning.

"Do you have any pictures of Red Herring?" I asked Jo.

"I can do better than that," she said. "His twin brother, Red Faction, lives here too. I'll show you him after we've finished this coffee. They're the absolutely spit of each other, except for the flash Red Herring has on his forehead. It's in the shape of a fish, that's how come he gets his name."

After the coffee, we made our way over to Red Faction's stable.

He was a beautiful animal, perhaps a little smaller than I imagined a racehorse would be, with a shiny chestnut coat.

"Hello," cooed Jo, holding him by his cheeks to plant a kiss on the top of his nose. "Oooh, he's excited today. You like getting visitors, don't you?" She stepped around the enlivened animal as it flitted around the stable to pat it firmly on the back. "He's beautiful, isn't he, Doctor?"

"Yes, he is," I replied, maintaining a careful distance. "Does he race too?"

"No, we sometimes run him with the other horses, but he doesn't have the talent of his brother."

We left Red Faction and, on my request, we made our way on foot to the farm's entrance. The gate was open, but it and the fence that encircled the site looked well-maintained and secure. If the farm was locked up during the night, it was difficult to see how anyone could have removed something as big and excitable as a racehorse.

"Is the gate left open during the day?" I asked Jo.

"Yes," she replied. "We're back and forth to the gallop all day, so it would be impractical to not leave it open. It's locked every night at six and the cameras are switched on. It isn't unlocked until six the next morning."

"Does the whole family drink heavily?" I asked, as we made our way around the fence.

"No, Mary doesn't. She's teetotal. Takes after her father. She's our little starling."

"Starling?"

"Yeah," smiled Jo, "all shiny and friendly."

"Never trust someone who doesn't drink," I breathed.

"Sorry?" said Jo.

"It's nothing. Just something Holmes sometimes says. She should be okay, she hasn't got a moustache."

Deciding against a further attempt at imitating Holmes' technique, I kicked around the circumference of the farm looking for any obvious signs of intrusion. To my eye, the fence looked perfectly secure. If it had been secured properly, and there was no reason to believe it hadn't, it presented a formidable barrier.

With time wearing on, we made our way back into Middlesbrough to take brunch at the Baker Street Kitchen. My overriding thought was had the police started to make any progress with the investigation? Jo informed me that Lestrade had had a look, but wasn't placing a missing horse, even one of Red Herring's pedigree, high up on his list of priorities.

So what did we have in the way of suspects? Xandra Holder seemed the only one who would benefit financially. The insurance payout on a racehorse of Red Herring's quality must have been substantial and, although the farm seemed to be in good order, there was no explicit confirmation that its financial standing mirrored this. I queried this with Jo and she thought it unlikely Xander was experiencing money troubles. Given how well-maintained her place appeared, I was inclined to agree.

In a more incredible theory, I imagined Xandra's son, Arthur, might be involved. He could have perhaps lost the horse in a game of pool. More realistically, he could have run up some gambling debts, with no way to pay them. Jo laughed and scotched this theory. Arthur, she said, didn't have the wherewithal to pull off such a caper. It did seem this wasn't a train of thought worth pursuing with much energy, given Red Herring's lack of value on the open market.

Then we had Mary, the darling of the yard. There was nothing to suggest that she did anything but work hard and get on with everyone, however she had been conveniently absent on the night of the disappearance and, by Jo's account, was her father's daughter. Could the removal from her mother of the glory garnered by winning the Beryl Coronet exact a revenge pending from the exile of her father? Again, Jo thought not.

The one person that Jo couldn't provide a character reference for was herself. At this early stage, I couldn't rule her out, but what did she have in the way of motive? She clearly loved the animals. Maybe Red Herring was being mistreated, trained too hard by an overly-competitive Xandra Holder, and she had stepped in to supply some relief. The problem with this theory was that it was perfect speculation, with not an iota of fact to support it. It was obvious I would struggle to replicate the techniques of Sherlock Holmes, but it was wrong to abandon them so completely. Data, data, data, I needed data. All said, it was perhaps unrealistic to expect the villain of the piece to call in Sherlock Holmes to investigate. Given the reputation he had gained through the course of our acquaintance, it would be hard to imagine a criminal with that level of hubris. Remember at the start of this caper, it was Holmes that Jo was looking to engage.

With no one ruled either in or out, my mind turned to motive and perhaps our only other obvious line of investigation. If the motive was not financial, as it appeared not, then what else was there? The obvious thing was the prestige relating to the winning of the Beryl Coronet. On Jo's account, Red Herring's biggest barrier to glory was a horse called Prosperous. If this were the case then the converse would be true, with Red Herring's absence significantly benefitting Prosperous' chances. With Prosperous stabled at a place over in Wynyard, and me having a couple of patients to see that afternoon before going to see Holmes in the evening, we agreed to pick up the next day.

Given the circumstances, I'm ashamed to tell you this, but, I was lapping up this investigation. Not having Holmes there to lean on meant I was using muscles I would not normally use, and although I was experiencing the odd twinge, I was finding it thoroughly enjoyable.

3

That evening, on my way to pick up Mary, I ducked into a newsagent to pick up a copy of the Evening Gazette. Emblazoned across the front page, together with a picture of a concerned-looking Xandra, was news of Red Herring's disappearance. It was my implicit understanding that the story was to be kept low key, however it appeared Mrs Holder had formed other ideas.

Thoughts of this twist in the events were wiped from my mind as I entered Holmes' room at the hospital.

"John, Mary," beamed Holmes, "I was hoping you'd come. I have so much to tell you."

The Holmes I'd encountered on my previous visit was a stranger to the one we had just walked in on.

"How are you feeling today?" I enquired.

"I'm fine, I'm fine," he relied, impatiently. "I have found an answer to the problem of island living."

"Island living?" queried Mary.

I shook my head, encouraging Mary not to press.

"Yes," barked Holmes, as if the concept of the island and his exile upon it should be part of the national curriculum. "You see, I can't leave the island in body, but anything can be imagined in the corridors of the mind. Imagine, imagine what could be imagined."

"Sherlock," I intervened, "I'm not sure this is healthy at the minute."

"What minute? How will you know what's on the other side of the door if you don't open it?"

"You need to leave the door closed. At least until you're feeling a bit better."

" 'Feeling a bit better'? Are you saying there's something wrong with me?"

"Sherlock, you're in hospital. You had, well, an episode. The other day you couldn't remember who Martha was. You need to rest. Let's leave the corridors of the mind for another time."

"Ah," he exhaled, pulling his fingers through his hair. "That explains it. She looked well pissed off with me earlier. I thought I'd forgotten her birthday or something. And that bloke who lives next door. He's completely biscuits."

"He's ill. Like you are."

"Yeah, but he reckons he's a Viking who drove over on a longboat."

"You're not well yourself," I pleaded.

"Maybe, but if I was claiming to be a Viking, I'd make sure I could speak Norwegian first. That fella's three seals short of a clubbing."

Our frenetic discussion was interrupted by the arrival of Holmes' dinner. As the healthcare assistant rattled the trolley through the door, his vigour evaporated.

"Ah, Mister Holmes," she said in a thick East European accent, "you have visitors, I see. I hope you're going to behave yourself for me today."

Heaven knows how the dynamic had developed between the two, but she spoke to him as if he were a child.

Holmes looked askance at her, his darkened eyes tracking her suspiciously as she went about her duties.

"What's on the menu tonight?" I asked, attempting to mollify his mood.

"Chops," he replied curtly, his fixation on her unaffected.

"Come on," she said, "put your telly on. That keeps you quiet." She used the remote control to turn on the screen, suspended on an arm above his bed, and swung it around to face the room. The screen showed a familiar face, that of Xandra Holder.

"I was speaking to her earlier today," I remarked, somewhat surprised at the pace the story of Red Herring's disappearance was gathering. All four of us stood transfixed to the screen, the nurse turning up the volume in order that we could hear Xandra's pleas for the horse's safe return.

"Don't worry, Mary," said Holmes, "there's nothing going on there, she's minging."

"I think her looks have been impacted by her drinking," I conceded.

"What's she been drinking?" replied Holmes. "Plutonium?"

"Sherley," admonished Mary, with a sigh.

I was actually pleased by the comment, in that it echoed the Holmes of previous times.

"It's the most perplexing of cases," I said. "I've been helping out with it, but I'm not sure I'm doing any good. I can't seem to round upon a strong enough motive. I was on it all morning, and it feels like I'm getting nowhere."

"John," said Holmes, with a pensive almost paternal air. "Life wasn't meant to be run. Give yourself a break, it takes time for the ideas to ferment." Even in his stupefied state, he had moments of unique clarity.

As our East European friend backed out of the room, returning only to replace the television remote, Holmes' character reverted to what we'd seen on our arrival. "Doc, if you could leave your body and go anywhere, to any place at any time, where would you go?"

"I'm not sure," I replied. "It's not something I've ever thought about."

Holmes looked disappointed. "See, the laws of the universe don't apply to the soul. How could they?"

"Sherlock, are you talking about dying?"

"No, I would come back."

"Come back from where?"

"From anywhere."

"Where do you mean?"

"Anywhere."

"And how would you get there?"

"I don't know that yet."

"Sherlock, are we friends?" I asked, feeling the discussion unhealthy in the prevailing circumstances.

"Of course, Doc. You're my best friend."

"Well, as your friend, will you do something for me? Will you stop messing about with your mind? Close the doors, stay out of the corridors. Just until you've had a rest and are feeling more up to it."

I stepped the short distance across the room and grabbed his upper arms, to look him in the eye. There was a long pause as he considered my request.

"Yes, okay," he replied.

We left Holmes to his dinner and television and I looked in on the consultant who was treating him. There had been a couple of things that had been troubling me since this whole episode with Holmes began, and I was keen to share my thoughts.

Holmes' consultant was a chap called Fairbank, who I'd come across in a professional capacity previously. Fairbank was receptive to my feedback. My first concern related to an adventure that Holmes and I had become embroiled in a while previously. In 'The Case of the Fifty Orange Pills' we had faced a race against time to get some mind-bending drugs off the streets of Teesside. In order to fully understand what we were up against, Holmes had taken the rather reckless approach of sampling one of the pills. My thought was that his current mental state may be a legacy of him consuming this drug.

Fairbank remembered the incident, it was difficult not to given the media circus it had generated and that he was also an acquaintance of one of the drug's victims, a registrar at James Cook Hospital called Simone Merivale. Holmes had actually saved Merivale's life, using the unusual antidote of a bottle of tequila. Fairbank didn't dismiss the idea, but thought it unlikely given the elapsed time between Holmes taking the drug and the symptoms occurring. He'd also been in contact with Merivale within the last few weeks and said she appeared perfectly normal. He did however think it wise to get in touch with both Merivale and the other of the drug's surviving victims, Joanne Simpson, in order that he could undertake a detailed examination.

My other matter of concern was Holmes' experiments into what he called "dream mechanics" and "refragmentation". He had a theory about how the mind stored away information and was using mental exercises to try and tap into dormant and hidden memories. With Fairbank having an interest in oneirology, the study of dreams, he was fascinated by the concept, but conceded that in the thirty odd years he had been practising medicine, he'd not come across anyone who had been able to achieve the mastery of the mind that Holmes was attempting. Although it was impossible to definitely attribute this as the cause of Holmes' troubles, he was open to the idea that it might be a possibility. The analogy he used was that of overextending a limb past its normal stretching point and this resulting in a strain, however, given how unusual this was, there was no obvious treatment other than to encourage Holmes to rest and place his mind experiments on hiatus. His most poignant point was a recollection he drew from an interest he had in Greek mythology. A eulogy that told how dreams were the brothers of Hypnos, sleep, and Thanatos, death.

4

The story of Red Herring's disappearance quite literally became an overnight phenomenon, with the local media seeing it as Teesside's very own version of the Shergar kidnapping. It was difficult to open a newspaper without seeing the solemn face of Alexandra Holder looking back at you. I lost count of the number of times she appeared on the local television news. Papers being what they are, they also grabbed every flimsy excuse to feature a picture of the younger and much more attractive Mary Holder.

In the midst of the furore, Jo and I made our way to the Wynyard home of Sir George Burnwell, the owner of the racehorse Prosperous. The Burnwell residence was impressive. Set in a sizable chunk of the Wynyard estate, it comprised a gate lodge, various outbuildings and annexes, a paddock, and a couple of stable yards.

After Jo had talked us in through the intercom, we wound our way up the long drive to be greeted by Burnwell.

"Hello, Sir George, Jo Vernon. We met at Sedgefield Races a few years ago," she said, offering a handshake.

"Ah, yes," he replied, "we edged out one of your fillies for a win that day. I don't recognise your friend, though."

"John Watson," I said, holding out my hand.

"Not Doctor John Watson?" he remarked.

"Yes," I smiled.

"Excellent," he bellowed, "I'm an avid reader of your stories in the Gazette. Is Sherlock not with you?"

"No, I'm afraid Sherlock's not well at the minute."

"Oh, that's such a shame, I do like him. There's no better man than a straight-talker in my opinion. I hope he's up and back at 'em soon. So what's all this about?"

"We'd like to ask you a few questions if you don't mind. Regarding the disappearance of Red Herring. I'm afraid you are one of the very few people with a motive, so we'd like to rule you out."

"A motive? Me? What motive would I have?" he replied, both amused and perplexed.

"The Beryl Coronet," I explained. "With Red Herring out of the way, the prospects of your horse, Prosperous, improve significantly."

"I see," replied Burnwell. "That's an interesting theory, but it's not really my style to try and fiddle a race. However, I'm happy to provide you with any reassurances I can. How do I go about clearing my good name?"

"As I said," I replied. "We're not accusing you, it's more about ruling you out."

"Then rule away," he beamed. "This is all very exciting. I hope I make it into one of your stories, Doctor."

"Do you mind telling me where you were last Sunday night?"

"Sunday? Actually I was down in the smoke. I had some business meetings down there, so I took the missus and we made a weekend of it. I'll think twice about doing that again, the old girl spent a fortune."

"There you go," I replied. "You already have an alibi. Do you mind if we have a look around?"

"Be my guest, but if I'd stolen a horse, I would be foolish to stable it here."

Jo and I worked our way around the yard looking for any sign that Red Herring might have been there, halting at the billet of Prosperous. He was an impressive animal, almost black in colour and significantly larger than Red Herring if his brother Red Faction was to be used as a measure. If I was to wager, I would be placing my money on Prosperous.

Sir George really did have a wonderful stable of horses. Each one twitching and snorting as if it were ready to take on Pegasus himself. Other than our pause to admire Prosperous, the only other aspect of interest was the one empty stable. With its potential to have been a temporary holding place for Red Herring, we gave it a thorough examination. The problem was there wasn't that much to see. It was scrubbed to the point of it being sterile, and who knew if its cleanliness was a result of evidence removal or just a feature of a well-kept yard. From what we'd seen on our trip round the place, the latter seemed a reasonable assumption.

With our survey trending towards futile, I had one more thing to look at. I walked over to where Burnwell's horseboxes were parked and used my phone to take pictures of the tyre treads.

With the remaining threads of our enquiry safe in my pocket, Jo drove us across Teesside to the Holder place. We scoured the driveway and the area around the perimeter fence for tyre tracks but none we found matched the photos I'd taken. Indeed, of the few we did find, none appeared suspicious and were attributable to the general comings and goings of the farm. To make certain, I took some more photographs in order that we could match them against the Holder vehicles. Detective work was actually a lot harder than Holmes made it look. He would cleave something out of the minutiae, whereas we seemed to be stumbling around in pitch darkness. As our enthusiasm wrestled with despondency, we adjourned to the farm kitchen for a cup of tea.

The kitchen, which had previously been in perfect order, was strewn with newspapers, some of which had sections cut from them.

"There'll be hell on when Xandra sees this mess," said Jo to Arthur.

"It's her mess," replied Arthur, hardly looking up from his lunch.

On closer inspection, it was apparent that a theme ran through the litter, namely Xandra's new found notoriety.

"She's gone nuts," Arthur added. "I'm half expecting Trevor McDonald to pitch up."

As we settled down to our tea, the woman of the moment made an appearance. Hurriedly, she tidied up the paper and clippings, apologising for the mess as she went, before joining us at the table.

"Have you had any luck in figuring out what happened to my horse?" she asked.

"No," sighed Jo.

"Have you had any thoughts?" I asked. "I'm afraid the only thing that makes sense is that someone who works here was involved. If it had been an outsider, then there would be signs of a break in. Jo and I have been round that fence and there's nothing. Not even a trampled section of grass."

"Maybe the gate was left open and it was an opportunistic theft?" replied Xandra.

"But it wasn't," said Jo. "We reviewed the CCTV footage and when Arthur came back from the pub he tried the gate, before using the intercom to get you to buzz him in. We thought the recordings might have been tampered with, but if they had been, we wouldn't have seen Arthur."

"Arthur staggering back from the pub and getting me to buzz him in is a pretty regular event," remarked Xandra. "What we looked at could have been the CCTV from any one of a number of nights. The machine stores the recordings for fifty days. Whoever took the horse could have fiddled with them."

Jo shook her head. "Yeah, they could, but Arthur had his Boro shirt on. He'd been down the pub to watch the match and made a day of it. Middlesbrough have only been on television once this season."

"That sounds about right," sneered Arthur.

"So where does that leave us?" asked Xandra. "If it was one of my staff they still had to get Red Herring out of here. And from what you are saying, that's impossible."

"Indeed," I replied, my mind racing for a plausible scenario until my deliberations were interrupted by a phone call. It was the hospital. Holmes had gone missing.

We raced to the hospital and crashed our way through the doors to the consultant's office. Fairbank was both apologetic and embarrassed. More than anything, he was dumbfounded as to how Holmes could have got up and walked out of the hospital without anyone noticing. The next mystery was where he had got to, dressed in only pyjamas, dressing gown and hospital-issue slippers? The grounds of the hospital had been searched so he'd apparently put some distance between him and his cell. However, given he had no money, he had no means of paying for either a bus fare or a taxi ride. Not that many bus or taxi drivers would have given a lift to a man in a dressing gown.

As we walked back out and into the grounds, Holmes' mode of transport was immediately apparent. I asked Fairbank how he'd got into work that morning. When he told me he'd driven, the lack of a vehicle in his parking space afforded us an obvious clue. Jo rang the Middlesbrough police station and asked her colleagues, who had already been informed of Holmes' disappearance by the hospital, to look out for Fairbank's silver Mercedes SLE.

"Maybe he'll turn up on that bloody horse," joked Jo wryly, as we pulled out of the hospital to supplement the search. We worked our way around Middlesbrough looking in all of Holmes' usual haunts, before heading over to Wolviston to see if he'd gone to the house he had there. Jo was amazed that he owned such a mansion and yet lived in "that scruffy little flat" on Baker Street. My next thought was that he may have gone to his mother's, but given I didn't know where on Wolviston Court estate her house was exactly, we could do little but drive aimlessly around looking for some sort of clue. After a short while, I had the idea that it might be better if we asked Holmes' brother Mycroft to look down that particular avenue, so we headed over to the Diogenes Club in Stockton.

En route I took a call from Robert Nichols, editor of the Middlesbrough FC fanzine, Fly Me to The Moon. He'd been making his way to the Riverside Stadium to do a feature on some of the Middlesbrough footballers when he'd come across Holmes, sat on a fence in his dressing gown and slippers staring up at Temenos, the imposing sculpture by Anish Kapoor and Cecil Balmond that jets out over the river. Robert had attempted to communicate with Holmes, but hadn't managed to raise a response. He said Holmes had just stared back at him, as if he were talking a foreign language. I thanked Robert and we made our way to the stadium.

"I tried to give him my coat but he was having none of it," said Robert as we approached.

"Don't worry," I replied. "Sherlock hasn't been feeling himself lately. I'll see he's okay." I shook his hand, patting him on the shoulder as I relieved him of his guardianship of Holmes.

"Are you okay, Sherlock?" I asked. "You must be freezing."

"Yeah, fine. Just had a bad dream. I dreamt Sunderland had won the cup."

"Seriously, Sherlock, I'm worried about you. You need to be in hospital."

"I'm fine, Doc," he said with a listless distance. "I'm just a bit bent out of shape, that's all."

"What are you doing here?"

"I needed to see the sculpture. I think it's a portal." With its two enormous metal circles, knitted together with wire rope, he had a point.

"It's just pieces of metal," I said. "It's not gonna take you anywhere, and besides, you should be staying where you are at the moment. Let's stay on the island for now."

"Yeah," he sighed, "I just needed to see it. I've never really looked at it before."

"Come on, Sherlock, we need to get you back to hospital and into the warm." I slung my jacket over his shoulders, and led him back to Jo's car.

On the advice of Fairbank, Holmes was sectioned under the Mental Health Act. I'm not sure how necessary this was, given that Holmes wasn't resisting treatment, but it did mean he could be legally kept under lock and key to prevent any further escape attempts. I was actually listed as one of the three people involved in the assessment that was a prerequisite of the sectioning. It seemed appropriate, given I was the medical professional who knew him the most. However, that's not to say it wasn't a dreadful activity to be involved in.

I left Holmes in the care of Fairbank and reassured Holmes that I would be back later that day. Holmes seemed vacant and unconcerned. Jo dropped me at my office and I tried to busy myself with various admin tasks. With Holmes in the state he was, it was difficult to focus. I returned to the hospital a few hours later, travelling corridors swathed in dreadful trepidation of what I might find at their conclusion. The Holmes I did find was captivated in a melancholic daze. Sitting in his chair by the window, his knees pulled up to his chest, I thought he hadn't noticed my arrival until he spoke. "Thank you for distracting me from my solitude, John. Logic is a cold, lonely place."

"Sherlock, being alone and being lonely are two completely different things. You'll never be lonely. There's me, Martha, Mary. Friends for life."

He looked confused at my comment. "Do you think death more frightening than life?"

"Sherlock," I interrupted, "these thoughts aren't particularly healthy."

"I saw it again this morning."

"Saw what?"

"Eleven eleven. That's why I needed to see the portal."

"Seeing random numbers on clocks doesn't mean anything. You're seeing omens and harbingers where there aren't any."

"The universe knows," he replied quietly. "I always thought my death would be more exciting than this. I never thought I'd fade away in a hospital bed."

"You're not dying," I replied, encouraging the point with a smile. "You're just ill. Those experiments you've been doing with memory mechanics and refragmentation have popped a fuse. They've not been good for you. I think you've dislodged something. You need some rest."

"You know, those stories you write are really good. You should keep on with those. You're a natural. It's like poetry sometimes, and all those big words. I can't even spell them when I speak."

Again I snorted a laugh. "Sherlock, you're talking like we are at the end of something. This is a temporary thing. We'll get you back to being yourself. We can fix whatever's broken. I'm sure of that."

He turned to address me eye to eye, but with a vacancy that

stared past me into another realm. It was if he had no awareness of his surroundings.

"Take care of Martha for me," he muttered.

5

I sat with Holmes for three or four hours that evening, him curled into a ball asleep on his bed. Afraid of what I might return to, I didn't want to leave him. In the end, one of the nurses convinced me to go home and get some rest. As I wandered outside, the pending gloom of the night seemed to envelop me. Hungry but too tired to eat, I winced at the prospect of the mundanity. On my return home, I made a vain attempt, searching the cupboards in my kitchen for something to excite me, but gave up and slumped into bed.

I was jolted from my slumber by a phone call. Although I was in my own bed, it took me a few seconds to appreciate where I was, the illuminated numbers on my alarm clock finally allowing me to locate myself. By some bizarre coincidence, it was eleven minutes past eleven, the numbers that so captivated Holmes.

Phone calls in the middle of the night never bring good news. This one was no different. It was the hospital. One of the nurses had looked in on him to give him some medication and had been unable to rouse him. There was no medical reason for it, but he had slipped into a coma.

I arrived at the hospital a short while later to be greeted by the solemn faces of the medical staff. You would have thought they'd be resistant to circumstances such as this, but it appeared that Holmes, even in his mixed-up state, had formed some bonds.

Fairbank greeted me with a handshake before leading me into his office. He was at a loss as to explain the change in Holmes' condition. The only time he'd seen anything similar was what he'd sometimes found with old married couples, where one dies and the other gives up the will to live. Holmes was slipping from existence.

Seeing Holmes in the intensive care unit was terrible. With him wired up to all manner of machines, it looked beyond hopeless. I took a seat beside him and sat in silence, hoping that whatever he retained of his mind would let him know I was there. My eyes shot with tears, I afforded myself the briefest of smiles. Being sat in the company of a stone-silent Holmes was something I had a lot of experience of.

"You should speak to him," said the nurse. "He'll be able to hear you."

"What should I say?"

"Anything. Some people read."

The irony was that I'd had many a one-sided conversation with Holmes. In taxis or over breakfast in the Baker Street Kitchen, there'd been numerous discussions in which Holmes had barely taken part. Now when he couldn't reply, I was struggling to find anything to say. I blurted a few sentences in his direction and, after watching his monitors for a few hours, I made my way home.

Although Flat 1A was packed with books, few, if any, were appropriate for bedside reading. Consequently, the next day I gathered up copies of the stories of our adventures to date, along with several local newspapers, and headed back to the hospital. For the next few days, an unconscious Holmes was treated to such tales as 'The Case of the Valley Drive Mystery', 'The Case of the Darlington Substitution', and 'The Case of the Orb of Ironopolis'. When I'd worked my way through my canon, I read the newspapers cover to cover. When I'd exhausted the newspapers, I read our stories again. Having not read them for a while, there were elements of the stories worthy of minor edits. By the third or fourth run through I'd started to mark them up, polling Holmes' silent opinion on verbiage as I went.

By the middle of the next week, Holmes' condition had worsened, with him fading into a seemingly irreversible torpor, his brain activity at a level that was barely registering. Fairbank was at a loss, his only offering being that of palliative care to keep him as comfortable as possible. As far as we could establish, he'd given up the fight.

I looked down at that day's reading material in despair, my gloom marred by a picture of Xandra Holder looking up at me from one of the newspapers. I laughed, bewildered by what I saw. It was hard to believe that she'd managed to keep the story running for so long.

After a long day at the hospital, that stretched well into the evening, I returned home to find Mary in my bed. It was such a welcome surprise. I nestled in beside her and drifted straight to sleep.

In the early hours of the next morning, I had the strangest of experiences. I was woken by the feeling that someone was standing over me. As my eyes adjusted themselves to the low light, I saw what I would have sworn was the figure of Holmes. He put his fingers over his lips and glanced at Mary.

"Don't give up," he whispered. "Someone always gets pulled from the rubble."

He then melted into the shadows, as if he was never there. It must have been a dream, my brain grasping for hope that appeared incredible.

6

The next day I entered the hospital with the now habitual feeling of trepidation heightened. I didn't seriously imagine I'd seen the spirit of Holmes the previous evening, however I did carry the worry that my subconscious mind had pieced together the available information and drawn a fatal conclusion.

To my relief, his condition had actually improved slightly, his brain activity having taken an upturn.

"No reading material today?" commented the nurse as I took my seat by his bed. "Thank goodness. I used to enjoy those stories, but after fifty reads they become a bit, erm, I'm gonna say predictable."

"Thank you."

"Well you did ask."

"No, I didn't." I looked down at my friend lying there. "So what are we going talk about today, old chap? I know, how about 'The Case of the Red Herring'?"

"Oooh, yes," said the nurse, as she went about her duties. "I've not heard that one. Not a great title though, is it? It sounds like a box of fish."

"So, Sherlock, we have a racehorse that's gone missing. It's got no real value to anyone, except perhaps its owner, who is set to cop for the insurance, but doesn't really need the money. The mystery is how did the horse get past the seemingly impassable security fence, and if it did, how come there isn't a jot of evidence to prove this? What did you used to tell me? 'Exclude the impossible, whatever remains, however improbable, must be the truth.' What's impossible? Getting a horse over that fence, that's what's impossible. Under it maybe? No… That's it," I exclaimed. "It's still there. The horse is hidden on the farm somewhere. And I think I know where. Anyway, don't go anywhere. Entertain yourself for a bit. I've just got to pop out."

I rang Jo who picked me up outside the hospital and we made our way over to the farm. Much to Jo's annoyance, I saved my theory for a demonstration later. We got to the farm and made our way to the stable of Red Faction. Asking Jo to hold the animal still, I used my handkerchief and some hand cleanser I'd borrowed from the hospital to wash the horse's face. In doing so I confirmed my suspicions as the white fish-shaped flash of Red Herring slowly became apparent on the horse's forehead.

"Wow," said Jo. "So if this is Red Herring, where is Red Faction?"

"Somewhere else," I replied. "See the clever bit here is not what was done, but rather the order in which it was done. You put the horse to bed and the next morning it was found missing. Everyone, including me, assumed that between those two events the horse had been taken. But it hadn't. The horse, or rather a horse, had been taken earlier that day. When the gates are wide open and the closed circuit television is switched off. It was Red Faction that was taken. It's then a simple task for someone, in the middle of the night, to move Red Herring into his stable. They apply some gravy browning, or whatever that is, to his one distinguishing feature, and there we go. 'Viola' as Holmes would say."

"But who, and why?" queried Jo.

"Again, we have another assumption that was slightly awry. We've been wracking our brains in search of someone who stood to make a financial gain, but we were closer to home when we were considering Sir George Burnwell. The perpetrator was after a much different currency. Not fortune but fame."

"Xandra," said Jo. "She's become a media darling since all this kicked off."

"Indeed, but at the outset I don't think that was her plan. I think she has esteem issues. The Beryl Coronet was her chance of some time in the limelight, but she was worried that Prosperous had the beating of Red Herring, and couldn't bear to come second. Frightened by what she saw as humiliation, she found a way to take him out of the race. The media interest that followed was an unintended, but welcome side-effect that she grabbed with both hands. If the story hadn't gained the momentum it did, she would have probably made the switch back and stumbled on Red Herring grazing in a field somewhere. When the limelight she'd initially sought shone from a slightly different direction, she decided to bask in it for a while. The problem was she came to like it too much and didn't want it to end."

"It makes sense," said Jo, "but it's all speculation. We have no real proof it was Xandra."

"No, we don't. The proof comes by finding Red Faction. Have you any ideas where you could hide a racehorse round here?"

"There are plenty of fields and abandoned farms. He could be anywhere. We need to follow her when she rides out tomorrow. Can you ride a horse?"

"Nope. Donkey rides on Redcar beach are about my limit."

"Okay, I'll have to give you a croggy then."

A thought struck me on our journey home. I'd tried to look at this case through Holmes' eyes, to replicate the techniques he uses. If I'd only made use of my own skills and knowledge, I may well have rounded on a conclusion much sooner. With me being a trained and experienced psychologist, I should have approached this little puzzle, not from the physical world, but rather that of the mind and the behaviour it drives.

Okay, there would perhaps have still been a Holmesian catalyst at play, the reordering of facts to present an alternative scenario, being a staple of his method. However, this is not to say a greater consideration of human behaviour would not have hastened my journey to the solving of the case. At the same time, I was both exhilarated and depressed. I had identified a possible vocation for myself, that of psychological profiler, however it was clear that Holmes, without any of my training, could fulfil this role as equally well as me. I smiled on the realisation, causing Jo to cast me a curious glance from her position in the driving seat beside me.

Early next morning we travelled to the farm, with me concealed under a blanket on the back seats of Jo's VW. On our arrival, Jo went about her morning duties. After around half an hour, I could hear the snorting of a horse and the scuffing of hooves outside the car. I peered from my hiding place to see Jo astride a large bay stallion, offering me a riding hat.

"Come on," she said. "She's getting away."

"Did you have to pick such a big horse?" I asked as I climbed from the car.

"Well, he's got to carry two of us."

"How do I get up there?"

Jo exhaled and jumped down to give me a bunk up. After some struggle, she coaxed me into the saddle. With the horse still stationary, I wasn't enjoying the experience.

"Shuffle back then," she said. "Where am I supposed to sit?"

I edged back onto the beast's hindquarters and Jo hopped up into the driving seat. If it was unnerving when we were parked up, it was terrifying once she got going, the horse seeming to move in several directions at the same time. I've always thought horses to be such graceful animals, however the grace must be in the eye of the beholder, and not the poor soul hanging on for dear life.

We raced through the countryside, down tracks and across fields, with me convinced I was about to part company with my conveyance. I was half hoping for it, if it brought this ride of terror to an end. After a journey of a few miles, which I may well be exaggerating, we slowed down and entered a small copse.

"Over there," said Jo.

I didn't reply, my arms tight around her waist and the side of my head locked into the middle of her back. Jo prised herself free and dismounted, looking back up at me with a grimace of disdain. In an attempt to redeem myself, I manoeuvred myself off the horse and jumped down, staggering backwards slightly as I hit the ground.

We looked across the field to see Xandra tending to a horse that looked very much like Red Faction.

"Let's go and have a word then," I said, setting off towards Xandra.

She noticed us a third of the way across the field, freezing in her tracks before dropping her head.

"Good morning," I called as we got closer.

"Hello," she replied with a sigh.

"We've found your horse. He's living in this chap's stable."

"Yeah, I know. I put him there."

"We thought so."

"You see, Doctor, I needed something to happen in my life. It felt like I was drifting aimlessly across a millpond. I needed to chop things up a bit, for good or bad. I was hoping that was going to be the Beryl Coronet, but after seeing Prosperous, I didn't think we had a chance. I couldn't bear to lose."

"Don't worry," I consoled. "You haven't broken any laws."

"Well, there is wasting police time," said Jo. "But given we didn't spend a lot of time on it, I'll put in a word for you."

"No," I agreed. "All we've got to do is come up with a way to get this fella back home, that tells a story your adoring public will believe. Any thoughts on that?"

7

After I'd walked back to the farm, Jo gave me a lift back to the hospital. With me smelling of horse, it was a little embarrassing, but buoyed by my investigative success I wasn't overly bothered. I was stopped in the corridor of dread by one of the nurses who told me that Fairbank had asked to see me.

He stood to greet me as I entered his office. "Doctor Watson, John, there's been a change in Sherlock's condition."

"What a change for the better or worse?"

"We don't know. His brain activity has increased, but it's gone off the scale. It's more than we see in waking people undertaking complex tasks. We've never seen anything like it. We can't understand why he's not woken up."

"I can," I replied. "He's not ready yet. But he'll be back. I'm sure of it."

We moved into the care unit and the monitors that were limping along just hours earlier were buzzing.

"It looks like he's having some fun in there," I remarked.

"Yes," replied Fairbank. "But what damage is he doing? We've never seen anything close to this. At first, we thought the kit was on the blink."

"Mister Fairbank," I said, "it's a capital mistake to judge Sherlock Holmes against a benchmark you've taken from others."

"Well said, Doc," said Holmes.

Everyone in the room was astounded. Our eyes snapped on him, each of us assuming we'd imagined it. With gaping mouths, we looked at each other for confirmation.

"Sherlock," I asked, "are you awake?"

" 'Are you awake?' Do we ever really know?"

"How do you feel?"

"My head hurts a bit. What have they been putting in the drip? Absinthe?" His eyes opened and squinted shut as they acclimated to the light. "I need to sit up. I think I'm gonna puke."

Myself and the nurse rushed to help, easing him up into a seating position.

"Hello," he said, smiling at the nurse as he became aware of how pretty she was. "Nurse, I need you to write something in those notes you've been keeping. '22 Baker Street, Flat 1B. Free most Wednesdays. Bring a bottle'."

The nurse shook her head, narrowed her lips and rolled her eyes into her head. It was clear a rest had done nothing to dull his seductive charm.

"What time is it, Doc?" he asked. "Exactly."

"Eleven minutes past eleven," I sighed.

"Right," he replied, thoughtfully. "Sometimes the universe knows. Most of the time it's full of shit. Time to stretch my legs." He jumped down from the bed and collapsed, his legs weakened by days of inactivity. "I bet that happens all the time, does it?" he said, looking up from a crumpled mess on the floor.

"Nope," replied the nurse, shaking her head. "Never."

We helped him back up onto his bed and I sat with him a while. I was desperate to understand what had been happening inside his head during the days I'd sat by his bedside.

The electrical activity in his brain had ebbed to a point where a patient could feasibly have died, however Holmes was dismissive.

"I just needed a reboot," he said. "I got in a bit of a tangle."

Then there was the frenetic activity that followed. What was that all about? Holmes was equally as forthcoming. He was "thinking a few things through". My prompting did nothing but elicit a tired but enigmatic grin. Wherever he'd been on that journey, he wasn't sending out postcards. As I faded into exasperation, he reached towards me and grabbed my arm.

"Don't worry, Doc," he said. "I wasn't going anywhere. The republic needs its heroes. We've still got some work to do."

That evening felt golden. I thought I'd lost him. Getting him back felt like I'd turned a corner and happened across a long lost friend. A best friend who'd not changed in any way since I'd last seen him. Over that week or so, my mind had strayed into fantasy.

I'd imagined a life without him. In my head, I'd half written the eulogy I would deliver at his funeral.

As I sat alone at our table in the Twisted Lip, perfectly comfortable in my own company, I don't think I'd ever enjoyed such a common activity. I smiled to myself, recollecting an earlier conversation, in which Holmes had congratulated me on finding Red Herring.

"You're better than me," he'd remarked. "I might have to up your wages."

8

Although his mind seemed to recover in an instant, it took a short while for Holmes' physical recovery. It wasn't long however before we slipped back into our usual routine of breakfasts in the Baker Street Kitchen, libations in the Twisted Lip and the occasional parmo in O'Connells Irish bar.

In terms of adventure and intrigue, a lull followed. It seemed like "the universe" was offering Holmes a rest. This was something I welcomed, feeling like I'd been through the wringer myself.

A while later, on my way to stay at Mary's after a long and arduous day at my practice, I ducked into O'Connells for a night cap. It must have been a Thursday, as it was open mic night. Standing at the far end of the bar, I couldn't see the singer and, although the lyric was familiar, I was struggling to place the song. No one else in the bar appeared to be taking much notice, instead focusing on their respective conversations. A couple of sips into my beer, I recognised the song. It was Amy Winehouse's 'Love is a Losing Game'. Maybe it was its delivery in a male voice that had thrown me.

I worked my way along to the bar to get a view of the singer and was stopped in my tracks. It was Holmes sitting on a barstool with the guitar I'd only ever seen propped against the wall in Flat 1B. Although few of the pub's patrons appeared to be aware he was even there, he was really good, offering a delicate and considered performance, the words "gambling man" somehow seeming to resonate. All I could do was shake my head. It felt like there would never be an end to discovering new things about him. That there would always be something to uncover. Before I had chance to approach him, he finished the song, stood up, looked across the unresponsive audience, stepped off the stage and left.

I followed him into the street, but could see no sign of him in either direction. Like a ghost, he'd disappeared into the night, raising a doubt within me that I'd even seen him.

As I climbed into bed with Mary that night, I relayed the story of the earlier experience with my strange polymath of a friend. Mary interpreted my amazement as envy of his perpetually emerging talent.

"You've got a lovely singing voice, darling," she said, as she snuggled into my chest. "I've heard you in the shower. It's just the key you sing in hasn't been invented yet."

THE SONG OF THE SWAN

I don't know how to write this. You might say, "You don't know how to write". Whatever. You're probably right, but either way, this is the hardest thing I've ever had to do. If I drift at times, I'm sorry. It will be impossible not to.

1

I had not seen Holmes in some time. The last time may well have been the occasion I caught him performing at the open mic night in the Irish bar, O'Connells. It was an experience I'd many times since assumed I'd imagined. I occasionally ducked my head around the door of the Baker Street Kitchen of a morning, or, later on in the day, in one of the micro pubs down the road, but he was never to be seen. The student of the human condition, and its propensity to follow patterns, had apparently abandoned his own habitual instinct.

With Holmes, you had to let him dictate the time in which you were in his presence. However, with him being just the other side of a serious mental health episode, and after a few weeks of absence, perhaps a month, my curiosity had welled to the point where I was concerned for his welfare.

It wasn't unusual for Holmes to go missing for a month, or even longer periods, and I had no tangible reasons to worry, with Holmes appearing to be close to his old self. There was perhaps a slight darkening to his character, in that, less and less his barbed ripostes were returned with a grin. However, there was every chance I was imagining this, my perception tainted by those dark times just a few months previously. What was more evident was a detachment. A stepping back or a loosening of his interface with the world around him. It was as if he rattled around inside a shell too large for the kernel it encompassed. Other than that, his condition betrayed description, it was something you really needed to see first-hand. On more than one occasion, I wondered if I would ever see him again. It was at the same time fantastic and highly possible.

To this point, I'd avoided including others in my concerns, having no desire to share a worry that I may have imagined, but as I began to agonise to the point of distraction, I decided to seek the counsel of others. First on the list was Martha, perhaps his oldest and best friend. With a two-hour gap in my diary that Wednesday afternoon, I skipped out of the surgery and made my way to Baker Street. I wandered into her boutique, Hud Couture, to find her straightening the clothes on the shelves.

"Hi, Martha," I greeted on entry, "have you seen Sherlock recently?"

"No," she replied, without turning from her task.

"Okay, it's just I haven't seen him in about a month and was starting to get a little worried."

"Don't be. He's always going 404."

"What does that mean?"

"I'm not sure," she said, finally turning to me. "It's Sherley's word. I think it means he's nobbed off somewhere and there's no point looking for him. He'll show up when he wants to. He's still using the flat. At least it looks like his bed is being slept in."

"How can you tell? He never makes it," I replied. "Anyway, if he shows up, tell him I was asking after him."

"Will do, flower," she responded, before resuming her perpetual shelf straightening activity.

Martha's nonchalance at Holmes' disappearance did go some way to quell my concerns, however, any void created was soon backfilled with curiosity. Given I had a little time on my hands, I formed myself into a one-man search party, and made my way into town. I stalked up and down the shopping areas, in and out of the Cleveland Centre, and made a few laps of MIMA and the town hall. I barely recognised any of the faces I encountered.

If I'm honest, I felt a little put out. It was Holmes' prerogative to engage on whatever devices he saw fit, however, I was a little disconcerted that he had not sought to include me. It was not like he showed any reticence in striding across my threshold, should he require my accompaniment in some adventure or other, so it seemed a little unilateral to his favour, that he had excluded me from whatever he was engaged upon. In mitigation, I had no way of knowing whether his absence was caper-related. He may well have been involved in one of a number of pastimes, in which I would have struggled to contribute.

As my verve for the search began to wane, I happened upon Bradley. I knew Bradley from previous encounters, dating right back to the time when Holmes and I first fell in league together. Bradley was one of the hoodie-wearing youthful demographic of the town, whose nefarious activity required regulation by Holmes on the odd occasion. He wasn't a bad chap, and he had been known to lend a hand, once his instinctive resistance had been overcome. Uncharacteristically, he greeted me with a cry of camaraderie.

"Doctor Watson. The Man. How's it going, my mate?" he asked, offering me a knuckle which I tentatively jabbed at.

"I'm well, Bradley. How are you?"

"No point in grumbling, Doctor," he replied with volume.

"Indeed, it never seems to solve anything. Have you seen Sherlock around lately?"

"I've not seen him, but the jungle drums tell me he's gone native with all those student types up at the university."

"Gone native?"

"He's gone back to school and is doing classes and stuff with all da freaks and da geeks."

"Lectures, you mean?"

"Yeah, man. That's what they call them."

"Do you know what he's up to?"

"No, man, I ain't gonna go predicting Sherlock Holmes."

"Thank you for your help," I said, offering a handshake.

"No problemo, Doctorman," he replied, shaking my hand with the same level of trepidation I'd experienced when engaged in his fist bump.

As I shaped to leave, I turned back to address the youth. "Bradley, why are you speaking like that?"

"Like what?"

"Like you're Jamaican or something? Are you trying to work your way into one of my stories?"

"Yes," he replied sheepishly. "The girls seem to like it and you haven't mentioned me in ages."

Going back to school did seem the most harmless of endeavours for Holmes to be involved in. It was also perhaps the most curious and least expected. What on earth could he be studying? Holmes did indeed have gaps in his knowledge, but these coincided completely with a perfect lack of interest in the subject. If information wasn't of immediate, or at least regular, use to him, he saw no value in it. If it were not for his love of a pub quiz, the range of subjects he had to draw upon would have narrowed yet further, freeing up more "storage" in the amazing processing engine that was his brain.

Thinking I might chance upon Holmes, I made my way up to the university. I mooched around the pedestrianised area of Southfield Road, gleaning nothing but the occasional peculiar look from the students moving about their business.

After around half an hour, inspiration struck. What was I doing, searching for Holmes in open terrain? Surely, the most likely hunting ground would be within the sanctuary of a public house. My strategy revised, I made my way to the Southfield pub, where I ordered a pint and sat in wait. Two pints later, I extended my search area to the Star and two pints after that I checked out the Dickens Inn. I forget the quantity of my consumption in the Dickens Inn, but as I made my way across to the Camel's Hump, it was clear my investigation was nearing a natural adjournment.

I stumbled into the bar to see the familiar figure of Colin the Barbarian. Choosing not to engage with him, a local criminal of some disrepute, I took a seat a distance away. Half way down my pint, I decided to draw a close to proceedings. I had the odd feeling that Holmes was just a few feet away from me, and a little more persistence might deliver my quarry, however the alcohol-induced maelstrom developing in my head was denying me further pursuit. I felt like I was searching for a ghost. Now where had I heard that?

With my head in tatters, I walked in late to work the next day. I was too late for my first appointment, but fortunately Doctor Anstruther, the chap with whom I shared the building, had graciously stepped in and covered for me. It was us psychologists that were supposed to be discovering multiple personalities within the patients, not the other way around.

As I settled into a strong black coffee, Violet, our long-suffering receptionist, popped her head around my door. "Doctor, there's a gentleman to see you. He doesn't have an appointment, however you do seem to have an unexpected window in your diary."

"Does this gentleman have a name?"

"Yes. He does. It's Mister Munroe."

Violet ducked back around the door and soon after, a youngish chap, his persona nerdy and slightly awkward, appeared in her place.

"Hello, Doctor Watson," he said, offering his hand with a nervous lunge. "My name's Spencer, Spencer Munroe."

"How can I help you, Mister Munroe?" I enquired.

"I work for a company called the Westerway Agency. We have been awarded a commission by a large organisation and would like to secure the services of Mister Sherlock Holmes. He'll be adequately compensated, of course. Would you happen to know how we can contact him?"

"I'm afraid not," I replied. I was unforthcoming for two reasons; firstly, I didn't actually know where Holmes could be found, and secondly, I was struck by the thought that there were striking similarities between this encounter and a much earlier visit to my office, take away two nefarious agents called Smith and Jones, and add this queer little fellow. This was where it all started, and the previous visitors had turned out to have a much different character from that which they'd presented.

"But I understood you to be an associate of his?" queried Munroe.

"I am indeed, but unfortunately Sherlock Holmes seems to have disappeared off the face of the earth. I searched for him all day yesterday, with absolutely no luck." I chose not to mention his bed had been slept in.

"Now that is unfortunate," remarked Munroe.

"If you don't mind me asking, what exactly is it that you want Holmes to help you with, and what is the large organisation you are working for?"

"I'm afraid that there is a degree of commercial sensitivity involved, and I will only be able to disclose the details when Mister Holmes has signed a nondisclosure agreement."

"Well, as I said, I haven't a clue where Mister Holmes is." If he was going to farm the information he had, I wasn't going to be forthcoming with the little I knew.

"Doesn't he have a house in a place called Wolviston?" asked Munroe.

"He does," I confirmed, "but he's rarely there. There's no harm in you checking, but I wouldn't hold out much hope."

Munroe returned a look of irritated confusion, before standing to shake my hand. "Thank you for your help, Doctor," he said, before turning to leave. "Oh, sorry," he stammered, fishing around in his jacket pocket, "my business card. If you do bump into Mister Holmes, could you let him know I was enquiring after him?"

2

The day that followed my search for Sherlock Holmes was a long one, the main culprit being my one-man pub crawl along Southfield Road. I saw two, perhaps three, patients and by the time I was squaring up for an early exit, the visit of Spencer Munroe had been all but expunged from my mind. I rolled my chair under my desk and began my usual close down ritual. As I grabbed my mouse, a black window popped up on my monitor screen:

"X:\> Shush!"

" 'Shush' ?" I muttered.

"X:\> Don't read this out loud."

" 'Don't read this out loud'," I whispered, slayed by confusion.

"X:\> FFS Doc."

"X:\> Your room is bugged. Do as you're told or we'll be buggered."

By now, it was obvious that my mystery messenger was none other than the elusive Mr Sherlock Holmes.

"X:\> It's me, Sherlock."

"X:\> I need you to come and see me. I'm at the Swan Pub in Billingham. See you there in ten mins."

With that, the box closed, and with it any chance of me not having to trail halfway across Teesside.

I drove up to the Swan to see Holmes sitting to the front of the pub watching the traffic go by. Martha had graciously given me the use of her London taxi, which I parked to the rear of the building, making sure to position it as far from any other vehicles as I could. The last thing I wanted was the introduction of a dent from someone's careless opening of a car door. Damage to her prized possession, 'Hansom', would render my life worthless.

Returning to the front of the building, I found Holmes sitting sideways along one of the benches, his feet up, his knees angled in. On his knees rested his wrists, his fingertips pressed together. He made no acknowledgement of my arrival.

"Hello, Sherlock," I announced from behind him.

"Hiya, Doc," he replied wistfully, with a slight flick of his neck in my direction.

"Would you like another drink?" I asked.

Holmes glanced to his right at the damp circle marked on the table of the bench, the absence of a glass seeming to confuse him. "Yeah, Doc, cooking, please."

I returned to the table to find him seated right ways on the bench, tracing the mark left by his previous libation with the tip of his finger.

"Cheers, Doc," he said, as I placed the lager in front of him.

"Are you okay, Sherlock? In your mind, I mean?"

"As clear as a bell," he smiled. "A bell yet to chime."

"I hear you've gone back to school."

"School?"

"Yes. Apparently you've been hanging around the university until all hours. Martha tells me she's seen less of you than I have."

"Yeah, I tell you what some of the woman who go to those pubs on Southfield Road are amazing."

"Sherlock, most of them are undergrads. You're old enough to be their father."

"No, I'm not," he protested.

"What's the rule? Divide your age by two and add seven."

"Alright," he grumbled. "I'll avoid the maths students."

"But you're right, there are some sights. I was there last night. If only I was four years younger," I joked.

"You were there last night? So was I. I never saw you. What were you doing there?"

"I was looking for you. You've been off the map for over a month. I was starting to get worried."

"Aw, Doc, that's so sweet. But I'm a big boy now. I can look after myself."

"Yeah, of course you can. What on earth are you doing attending university lectures? And what subjects are you studying?"

"I'm not studying any subjects. I'm not even sure what they are. I'm studying the teacher."

"The teacher?"

"Well, you know, the lecturer."

"I don't understand. Oh, yes I do. The Professor," I exhaled past a dawning realisation.

"Yep," he popped, "or to give him his full name: Professor James Moriarty."

"Moriarty? I know that name. I worked on a court case he was involved in once. He's some sort of criminology guru. It was his expert witness testimony that got the chap off. In hindsight, that was probably one of his cohorts."

"I doubt he would do anything but give them up. At the very best, he was playing with it. The man has no soul."

"No soul? I didn't think you were religious, Sherlock?"

"I'm not sure I am. But I can see inside people, and he's as hollow as a drum."

"Are you sure it's him? The fellow who's been toying with us all these months?"

"It's him. His turn of phrase, the orchestration of his online presence, his shoes…"

"His shoes?"

"His shoes," he confirmed, accentuating his response with a sharp nod. "When he gives his lectures, he addresses the whole class but me. He hardly sees me. I'm twenty years older than most of that lot, yet he's never once acknowledged it. That can't be down to my boyish good looks."

"Yeah, definitely not."

"Cheeky get," retorted Holmes with a withered smile. "He knows who I am but he doesn't want me to know that. The thing is he's overdoing it. His level of avoidance is ever so slightly too high."

"What's this thing about the shoes?" I asked.

"His feet are tiny. Size six maybe. Remember when we lay under those floorboards in Blakeston? The one thing I could see through the gaps in the floor was his feet. Such small feet. Then there was the other two lads…"

"What? Their feet?"

"No, their accents. They weren't from round here. They weren't from anywhere. They spoke in that strange hotchpotch of an accent that some university students adopt. The fickle ones. The ones easily manipulated. Pitch that against the age difference of the soldiers and their commandant and there's nowhere left to go but to the People's University of Teesside. I shoulda twigged it yonks ago."

"It all seems to fit, Sherlock."

"It looks like he's given up recruiting soldiers in Camp Bastion and moved his recruitment office a little closer to home. He now targets university students who he can make into soldiers. I expect he spins them some noble yarn of the greater good and a few months later bish bosh, trained assassins. He's like a fucking vampyre. Hypnotic. The students seem entranced by him. Do you know what the funny thing is?"

"I would struggle to find humour in any of this."

"Can you remember when we were investigating those cold cases? When we did that map thing to pinpoint the geographical centre of the crimes. Do you remember? The centre appeared to be Flat 1B, but then we figured it was the university. It wasn't just those two student clowns who came from there, it was their gaffer too, Professor Moriarty. It's disappointing we missed that. Sometimes it's just too bloody obvious."

I exhaled through rounded lips. "If we'd have taken one more step, we'd have made that connection from Grimesby and Roylott to the Professor. I never thought he'd actually be a professor, teaching in a university."

"Indeed," he said, "but it was a fair-sized step. He didn't teach them or anything. None of them even studied in his department. He must have met them in the union bar or something. The Southfield, maybe."

"When did it dawn on you?"

"Just after my reboot in the hospital. When I was coming round. I had this massive fight with him inside my mind, and in the struggle, I pulled the hood from his head. That's what woke me up."

"You never said."

"You never asked."

"This is all very concerning, Sherlock, this chap has always seemed to be much more of a criminal than you and I can take on. That's been obvious for a long time."

"Really?" remarked Holmes. "I haven't even got to the scary bit yet."

"Enlighten me," I replied, a dark cloud of growing awareness enveloping me.

He exhaled through his nostrils before continuing. "There's more to Professor Moriarty than a few cronies supplementing their grants with some contract killing. He's created this network that runs in the shadow of the internet."

"The Dark Web, you mean? I've read something about that."

"No, this is not dark, it's pitch black. It runs on its own protocol. I've never seen anything like it before. Well, there's perhaps one thing, but I built that."

"Its own protocol?"

"Yeah, a protocol is the set of rules which allows something like the internet to work. This network runs in the spaces the internet leaves unused."

"I'm still not getting you, Sherlock."

"Data moving across the internet is packaged up in packets. The data in this black web travels in the gaps between those packets."

My face told him this was a concept I was finding difficult to grasp.

"I tell you what," he continued, "think of it like a train. At the front we have the engine, leading the train to its destination. Then, we have carriages carrying the payload, the data, and last we have the guard's van bringing up the rear. The data I'm talking about travels between the engine, the carriages and the van. It's a bit like a hobo cadging a sly lift on the railroads in the wild west.

"Occasionally, the train travels through a tunnel, a private node or switch in the network, and the black data is either transferred to another train or it's harvested and used. These switches appear and disappear in a fraction of a second. They're virtual, delivered like a virus, but they live for only moments before deleting themselves. You could have one on your laptop now, your phone, your television, whatever. This whole thing is completely invisible. Well, invisible in that if you were to notice it, you would dismiss it as background noise, static maybe."

"Okay, I'm starting to understand what you mean, but what is it used for?"

"I don't know its exact purpose, but the clever money says this is what Moriarty and his merry men use to communicate. Safe in the knowledge that the police, the security services, the whole world is completely oblivious. He could communicate via the internal networks of the CIA and they wouldn't even notice."

"But what could it be used for? Can you speculate?"

"It could be used for anything, John, anything. It's a tool that could organise crime on a global scale."

"But if this 'black web' is so invisible how did you spot it?"

"While he was in those lectures, he kept sending messages. I grabbed hold of a few and found they were blank. When I replicated some blank messages, I discovered his were a lot noisier than mine. I filtered out the noise and found there was a rhythm and rhyme to it, and therefore probably a reason."

"So what's the reason? Can you decipher this noise, or whatever you do? See what it's actually being used for?"

"That's what I've been working on, but it's a difficult nut to crack. I'm gonna need a few more days."

"Right then. Let's get back to it. You do the deciphering and I'll make the tea and sandwiches."

"Okay, but there's something I want to do first."

"What's that?" I asked.

"Go and see the wanker. Tell him he's going down. Down, down to Dormanstown."

"Whoa there," I shrieked. "From what you've just told me, this chap is the evillest and most connected criminal on the planet. You want us to knock on his door and try to put the frighteners on?"

"Yup, pretty much."

"Why in heaven would you do that? We need help with this, Sherlock. We need to take this to the police."

"Nah, they're rubbish. What's the likes of Lestrade gonna do with this?"

"Lestrade's alright," I appealed. "He's at least a better detective than that Bradstreet character. I don't recall her ever solving a crime."

"That's not saying much," he replied. "He's also a faster runner than Stephen Hawking."

"Sherlock, why?"

"Data, data, data. I can't make bricks without clay. Come on!".

"Sherlock, stop!"

Holmes, who was now halfway to the exit on to the main road, skidded in his tracks and turned back.

"I'm not going," I said, hoping that my abstaining would prevent his continuation of this madness. "This is far too dangerous. We've had scrapes in the past, but this is another level. Another ten levels and you want to walk straight into it."

Holmes returned to the bench to retake his seat opposite me. "I need your help, Doc," he said, with hope pleading in his eyes.

"My help? I thought you were a big boy who can look after himself?"

"I am, but someone's gotta write it up. This is the last story. The swan song."

"Is that why we're here?"

"Where?"

"The Swan."

He looked around in bewilderment, clearly not assimilating the coincidence. Perhaps his choice of words took some subliminal influence.

"I assumed we were here because the whole of Middlesbrough is bugged," I explained.

"No, just your office, Marth's boutique and the Twisted Lip," he replied.

"And how do you know this?"

"I've intercepted their signals"

"Their signals. Who are they?"

"Moriarty maybe. Are we gonna go or what?"

"Go, where?"

"Up the bank. He has one of the big houses on the way up to Wolviston. It's only a few doors up from my place," he said, off once again to the exit.

"Sherlock, can't we just consider this for a minute? This chap makes Atilla the Hun look like Sooty. It's too dangerous."

Holmes stopped to look in my direction. "The danger is in the not knowing," he replied, his head moving side to side in a slow pendulum. "Right," he called. "Izzy whizzy, let's get busy."

"Wait, wait," I conceded. "If we're gonna go, we might as well drive."

"Drive?"

"Yeah, Martha lent me Hansom."

"Oooh, get you. She won't let me anywhere near it."

"It's not an 'it', it's a 'she'," I remarked, mirroring a scolding that Martha often administered.

I drove the taxi up to Wolviston and, on Holmes' instruction, passed both his and Moriarty's house to park up in the village, just opposite the post office. We ambled the hundred or so yards to Moriarty's place to turn casually into the drive.

"Look," said Holmes, skidding in his tracks on the gravel drive.

"It's a big house. What am I looking at?"

"The entrance. Those columns. Two either side of the door. If you think of those columns as number ones, you have eleven eleven."

"Or one-thousand, one-hundred and eleven, or three oblongs if you look at the spaces between them, or whatever you want to see really," I replied, not wanting him to dwell on a bizarre aspect of the trauma of a few months earlier.

"Not with the doors in the middle."

"Where else would you expect to find the doors?"

Holmes dismissed me with a sharp shake of the head and continued his journey up the drive. As we got closer, a brass plaque, screwed to one of the columns, came into sight. Etched into it were the words 'Copper Beeches'.

"What do you reckon that means?" asked Holmes.

"It's just the name of the house," I replied. "It probably has something to do with that clump of rusty-looking trees to the far side of the door."

Holmes screwed up his nose. "My house hasn't got a name. This gadgie's really starting to get on my tits. He's one of them, isn't he? 'I've been to Tenerife.' 'I've been to Elevenerife.' "

Our passage halted for the second time as we reached the large double doors. Holmes stood to consider for a couple of seconds and then banged on one of the doors with the heel of his clenched hand. If I'm honest with you, I was expecting a slightly more elegant approach.

"He's not in," said Holmes.

"How did you deduce that?" I asked, my nervousness at the undertaking getting the better of me.

"Never mind, I'll let myself in. There hasn't been a lock invented that I can't pick."

"That one old Davy Arrowsmith put on the door of the goldfish bowl had you stumped." Facetiousness was fast developing into a coping mechanism.

"I was having a bad day. All those ginger kids freaked me out a bit. The glare of their Persil white skin blind-spotted me. Besides, I didn't have one of these then," he said, pulling a metal, cylindrical gadget out of his pocket, slightly fatter and longer than a cigar tube.

"What's that?" I asked.

"A sonic screwdriver," he replied, flicking a switch to make it omit a sound very similar to that I'd heard on the television.

"Sonic screwdrivers don't exist. Not unless you're Doctor Who."

Holmes pointed me a look of disdain before spinning the tool in his hand and pressing a different button. A flat metal hook propelled from his 'screwdriver' as a blade would from a flick knife. Flashing me a cheesy smirk, he set to work on the lock. Within a moment, he had both the door unlocked and had gifted me a second helping of his grin. "Feel that," he said as he stood flat across the threshold.

"I can't feel anything but fear," I admitted.

"Feel it. Try. The energy. All that sparkling electromagnetism. Can you feel it? Can you feel it? Can you feel it?"

"Nope, not a thing."

Holmes stepped back and put his hand into his jacket pocket. He fished around in the coat's lining and pulled out his smartphone. Tapping it a few times, he handed it to me, the phone's camera activated and pointed into the room. Through the screen of the phone, I could see red beams of light crisscrossing the room in every direction, their preponderance so dense it was difficult to see through them to the other side of the room.

"That looks a bit state of the art, Sherlock," I remarked.

"Tomorrow's world," muttered Holmes, his mind chattering to a solution as his eyes searched every part of the room. "There's the answer. It's deactivated by that keypad in the far corner."

"That's a bit odd. You normally find them by the door."

"You do," he said. "See ya." With that, he shot across the room and through the beams, skidding to a halt on his knees in front of the small table upon which the keypad sat. Leaning over the device, which was now emitting a low volume beep, his head snaked around as he examined the keypad from every possible angle. He then stuck out his hand, his finger poised. He tapped in a six digit number and the beeping stopped.

Holmes worked his way up off his aging knees and stood to face me. "What you doing out there?" he asked with a clever smile.

I made my way over to him, across the very well-proportioned sitting room, scanning the surroundings as I went. Every single feature said money. Lots of money. Perhaps the most notable element being a large oil painting of Napoleon, hung to the side of a dark marble fireplace.

"I bet that's worth a few bob," I remarked, gesturing with a nod towards the artwork.

"Probably," said Holmes. "Can you smell that?"

"Chlorine?" I replied.

"Yeah," said Holmes, heading across the room towards an internal door. He threw open the door to be illuminated by the light reflecting off a large swimming pool. "The git's got a swimming pool. I bet you he's been throwing pool parties and not inviting me round."

"Sherlock, this is a house in Wolviston, not the Playboy Mansion."

"Still, that WI lot don't half get frisky after a few sherries."

As we walked into the pool room, the artefact of interest was the old style swimming pool safety notice posted to the wall. It was this vestige that was central to a series of cold cases we'd investigated months previously. Holmes stood to examine it for a moment, but offered no comment. Instead, he spun around and returned to the room we'd just left.

On re-entering the sitting room, Holmes took up a familiar stance. Standing with his feet together and his hands in his jacket pockets, his eyes scanned the room, occasional movements of the neck serving to extend the scope of his survey. Then after a shorter period than normal, strange given the size of the room, he stopped. He walked to the far side of the room before turning to pace out its length from wall to wall.

"Okay," he said, "let's go."

"Shall we not have a look upstairs?" I asked as he led me away.

"No, we've been here long enough."

"So was there any point in that? Did we learn anything?"

"Knowledge levels have definitely risen," he replied, enigmatically.

We made our way back up to the village, me none the wiser. As we approached the taxi, I stopped, pulling Holmes back by his elbow. "I didn't park the car with the front wheel angled like that."

"Right," said Holmes, pondering our predicament.

"What should we do?" I asked, frozen in my tracks.

"Option one, run. Option two, run faster."

We turned around and ran with all the speed we had, back down the road in the direction we'd just come from. After around a hundred yards, Holmes slid to a stop, panting heavily. A few yards later, I stopped too, in a similar state of distress. We both turned to look back up the road to where the taxi was still parked. Nothing. The taxi just sat there.

"We need to call the police. Get them to send the bomb squad," I said.

"They will take ages. What happens if old Ethel comes to get her pension and the wind gets up? Boom! Do you wanna leave poor Bert warming up his own shepherd's pie?"

"It might not even be a bomb. I might have caught the steering wheel as I got out."

"Did you?"

"I don't think so."

"I have an idea," he said, before leaving me to mooch around the grassed communal garden area adjacent to us. Shortly after, he returned carrying an array of large stones and half wall bricks.

"What are you going to do with those?" I asked.

"I'm gonna throw them at the wheel of the taxi. Hit and no explosion, probably no bomb. Explosion, probably bomb."

His first throw was hopelessly overcooked. It cleared the taxi, skidded off the roof of the car parked behind and landed on the bonnet of the car behind that.

"I'm just getting me eye in," said Holmes dismissively. His next shot fell hopelessly short, crashing through the windscreen of the car in front. Shot number three skewed wide and skidded along the road ineffectively.

"What are you doing?" called a woman from the door of the post office.

"Minding my own business," shouted Holmes. "Now, get back in the shop."

"There's a bomb under the car, now get back inside," I added. "And close your shutters."

"We don't have any shutters."

"Then get behind the counter," screamed Holmes.

"Sherlock, I've got a better idea," I said, just as the next missile, a half wall brick, left his hand.

Holmes didn't get a chance to respond. The brick hit its intended target and the taxi exploded. The blast knocked us both off our feet, various bits of metal and other debris showering down on us.

I propped myself up to sit there aghast. "Martha's going to kill me," I breathed. "What am I going to do?"

Holmes screwed his mouth to one side and sucked in a breath through his nostrils. As he made his consideration, I hoped with every sinew that he had a solution that would extract me from this fix. "You could try running it under a cold tap," he replied.

3

As we trundled our way back to Middlesbrough on the bus, I played over in my mind how I was going to inform Martha of the demise of her beloved Hansom. Not wanting to complicate matters further, we'd left the scene of the explosion ahead of the arrival of the emergency services. At that moment, I was more concerned with the retribution that Martha might serve up, than our potentially fatal entanglement with Professor Moriarty. Holmes seemed void of concern as he watched the Teesside scenery transit across the bus window, the identifying elements of Martha's taxi sequestered in a bag for life he'd recovered from a bush, on our journey to the bus stop opposite the Kings Arms pub.

"You weren't expecting to discover anything at Moriarty's place, were you?" I asked at low volume. "That was the first shot in the war, wasn't it?"

"Yeah, I wasn't expecting him to shoot back so quickly. I thought he'd spend a few days considering his options."

"Sherlock, you need to stop managing down my information."

"What d'you mean?"

"You should have told me we were breaking into that place to announce ourselves. Given me the chance to stay at home."

Holmes nodded. At least he appeared to. It may well have been the motion of the bus.

We alighted the bus at Middlesbrough Bus Station. My assumption was we would head back to 22 Baker Street, making as wide a berth as possible of Hud Couture and Martha, in order that Holmes could make a start on his decryption on the noise that travelled the black web. The evening was wearing on by this point, however I didn't want to run the risk, however slight, that Martha had stayed late to undertake a stocktake or the like.

To my relief, Holmes had another idea, instead directing us to my office. We approached to find the building lit up. Ms Hunter often worked late on a Thursday night to give herself a short day on the Friday. Her receptionist duties were generally light on a Friday due to Anstruther taking a half day and my proclivity for working flexibly.

"Sherlock," shrieked Ms Hunter as we entered, galloping around her desk to smother Holmes in an embrace. "When are you going to give me that call?" Her glee was somewhat out of character for my normally staid colleague. I had to check to see her feet were still on the floor.

"Hi, babe," said Holmes. "You couldn't get me a massive cup of really hot black coffee, could you? As hot as you can make it."

"For you, darling, anything." Running her hand across his chest, she left us to go to the kitchen.

"Sherlock?" I queried as she left earshot, an exclamation being the only expression my confusion would allow.

"V and me got friendly during those counselling sessions we did back when."

"I thought Violet was a confirmed spinster?"

"I'm not sure about spinning, but she can't 'arf rock 'n' roll. Oooh," said Holmes, "and she's got a bum like a drum."

Any further discussion of this revelation was curtailed by the return of Ms Hunter, who handed Holmes both a large mug of steaming black coffee and a long lingering look. Holmes smiled, took the coffee and led me to my office.

As we passed through the door, Holmes held his finger to his lip to signify we should be silent. He moved to my desk to place the mug in the centre of it, before indicating that I should take my seat. As quietly as I could, I complied.

Holmes then set off, stepping around the room, a lot of the time with his eyes closed. His head looped clockwise and occasionally his eyes opened for a while when he would glare at a particular item or aspect of the room. Sometimes he would stand perfectly still except for the movement of his hand massaging his left temple. At other times, his only movement would be the air drumming of the fingers of his right hand on the end of a semi-extended arm. After a period that must have been just shy of ten minutes, he stopped all activity and turned to smile at me. He then set off again, moving in a glide to one of my bookshelves. Pulling out a book, he let a small object, I assumed to be a bug, drop into the palm of his hand, before presenting it to me between the forefinger and thumb. He then threw it from some distance for it to land in the cup of coffee on my desk. The hot coffee splashed up and onto me, causing me to lurch backwards in my chair. In response, Holmes held up his hand in apology, before continuing his hunt. Five or six further bugs were identified in various locations. Some behind wall hangings, some in light fixings, some concealed within the various artefacts of bric-à-brac I used to decorate the place. Each device was dispatched with aplomb to land in the coffee cup. Finally, Holmes approached me at my desk, dropped to his knees and disappeared from my view. A few seconds later, his hand appeared from between my knees. He flicked his wrist and the bug he was holding in his fingers propelled upwards before plopping in the coffee. Holmes' head then followed his hand out from under my desk.

"This house is clean," he said in a squeaky, old lady voice.

"I can only assume those devices are the work of our friend Moriarty," I commented as Holmes returned to his feet.

"No," he replied, "that tech's a bit dated. It's government issue. MI5 I reckon."

"MI5? Why would they be interested in me?"

Holmes shrugged, before turning his attention to the business card of Spencer Munroe, which was still lying on my desk after his visit earlier.

"I meant to tell you about that," I said. "It completely slipped my mind. That chap came looking for you earlier. He said his company had won a large commission and wanted your help with some of it. He said he couldn't say exactly what it was."

"Really, that's interesting. Do you mind?" he said, holding the card up to confirm he could take it.

"It's yours," I nodded distractedly, my mind racing. How long had those bugs been there and what on earth might I have said that could incriminate me in one or other of Holmes' dalliances?

Ms Hunter had gone by the time we made our move to leave.

"Sherlock," I asked, "what exactly went on between you and Violet?"

"We've had this discussion before, Doc. A gentleman never tells. Besides, I would struggle to put it into words. She's a beast. I was frightened I was gonna need me hips replacing."

I had always thought Ms Hunter, Shrinking Violet as we called her, generous in mind and spirit. I never once entertained the fantasy she would also be so generous in body.

The next morning, I entered the Kitchen to see Holmes sucking on half an orange. I'm not sure I'd ever seen Holmes eat fruit before. He included onion bhajis and cider in his five a day quota. Occasionally a look of curiosity would strike and he would fish out a pip from his mouth to lay it carefully on the table in front of him. On the consumption of this second half of the fruit, there were five pips, neatly arranged in a perfect pentagon.

"I've ordered you a tea," he informed me.

As I sat, the waitress placed a cup and saucer before me.

"This gadgie from Westerways," said Holmes. "Five eight, skinny, dark blue suit, white shirt, thin black tie, thick rimmed glasses?"

"Yes," I replied, "that sounds like him. Spencer Munroe."

"I'm pretty sure I'm about to meet him," he said, flicking his eyes past me to glance out of the window. I looked across my shoulder to see Munroe entering the cafe.

"Mister Holmes," announced Munroe on reaching our table and offering his hand to Holmes. "Spencer, Spencer Munroe."

"Yes," replied Holmes, declining his handshake. "You've heard a lot about me. You'd better take a seat."

Munroe sat, nervously scrabbling in his pocket before pulling out a business card to present to Holmes. Holmes just looked at the card with an air of disinterest before re-fixing his stare on Munroe, who placed his card on the table in front of us.

"What can we do for you, Mister Munroe? What is so important that you feel you can interrupt our breakfast."

As Munroe stuttered to reply, Holmes dragged the fingertips of his right hand across the table, scooping up Munroe's business card. I actually found Munroe quite endearing in a nerdy type of way, however Holmes appeared to have formed an initial dislike.

"Erm, yes, Mister Holmes, I work for a company called the Westerway Agency. I would like to secure your services, on a sub-contract basis, to work with us on a large commission we have recently been engaged on."

Holmes made no response, but instead examined Munroe's business card edge on. "Can I see your shoe?"

"My shoe?" asked Munroe.

"Yes, your shoe. Either one. They're both very similar."

"Err, yes of course," said Munroe, handing his black brogue to Holmes.

Holmes took an oblong-shaped magnifying glass out of his pocket and started examining the shoe as he rotated it in his hand. "You don't work for a detective agency," he said. "At least not a private enterprise. This shoe has seen more carpet than pavement. You work in a large office, with long corridors, very few windows and lifts that you rarely need to use." Fixing his look on Munroe, he continued. "Private investigation is all about shoe leather. This is the first time you've seen sunlight in months. You're a back office boy. You sit behind a computer screen while others do the heavy lifting."

Munroe sat motionless, attempting no response.

"That suit," said Holmes, handing Munroe back his shoe. "That suit has been hanging in a cupboard somewhere. In your offices, perhaps. Not a wardrobe, but somewhere not designed to hang clothes in. Something not quite wide enough that rubs on the shoulders. You've had that suit on what, twice, three times maybe, and yet it's six months too big for you. You know if MI5 are going to buy their operatives suits, they really shouldn't be getting them from Montague's of Cheltenham. There are other places."

"Amazing," replied Munroe. "I didn't think I would have you fooled for long, but fancied myself to last a little longer than that. How do you know my suit's from Montague's?"

"The buttons on the cuff. Three buttons, each with three holes. There's only two places in the world that do that. Montague's of Cheltenham and Jephro Rucastle and Sons, Illinois."

"Very good, Mister Holmes, I probably need to feed that back to our procurement department."

"Call me Sherlock. Would you like a tea?"

"Oooh, thank you. I'd prefer a coffee."

"Coffee, black, two sugars," called Holmes to the counter.

With Munroe's nervousness diminishing slightly, he addressed Holmes. "Sherlock, could I speak to you privately about a matter of great significance?"

"Anything you can say in front of me, you can say in front of Doctor Watson."

Munroe paused to consider.

"Look," said Holmes, "he's a respected member of society, I'm a convicted criminal. Do the maths."

"It's just my orders say I should only speak to you."

"You don't get out in the field much, do you?"

"No, they picked me for my computing skills. They thought you would feel some type of affinity towards me."

"Really?" laughed Holmes.

Munroe sucked in a wide breath before continuing. "I've been asked by the agency to speak to you about an investigation we've been involved with for a number of years. It concerns a gentlemen called Professor James Moriarty. We've become aware that you may have had some dealing with him, and we're concerned that your, shall we say, interactions may become detrimental to the work we've been undertaking. There's no doubting your talents, Mister Holmes, the agency is well aware of your capabilities, but I need to ask you to leave it to us, the professionals if you will. I can assure you, we will get this chap. You're getting too close and there's a danger you will derail a very important project, and undo all of our hard work."

"Are you warning me off?"

"No, it's a request. We've spent a lot of man hours getting this close and would appreciate a clear road. We've watched you in aw,e Mister Holmes, but we're in the final stages of our operation and are afraid you might get caught in the crossfire. Will you pull back and leave it to us?"

Holmes stared back, providing no confirmation.

"Mister Holmes, Sherlock," said Munroe, "this is bigger than you could imagine. We can't even involve the local police. We're sure they have been infiltrated and Moriarty has at least one, probably more of them on the payroll."

Munroe rose from his chair. Offering Holmes his hand and

reaffirming. "Let us take it from here." He then shook my hand, pointing me a look that suggested he would appreciate any influence I could bring to bear on Holmes.

"So we stop?" I asked, as Munroe transited back across the window. "Leave it to the professionals?"

"You can," said Holmes. "I'm not pulling out of the tackle. This is what I live for."

"And die for?" I asserted, trying to stress the seriousness of the situation. "We need to step back."

"I'll keep you safe, and I won't get in the way of the spooks. In fact, the distraction we provide will help them more than they know."

I sat back in my chair, staring up at the ceiling as I considered the options. There weren't any. It's hard for me to articulate this to you. It felt like we were in the midst of a chain of events. Wherever this chain led, we could do nothing but follow. If we did anything else, the outcome could only get worse. Does that make any sense to you? At the time, it made little sense to me.

"Have you got your credit card?" asked Holmes.

"Yes, why?" I replied, suddenly concerned for my bank balance.

"We need some hardware," he said, reaching down to the pocket of his jacket, which was hanging from the back of his chair, to pass me a strip of paper. On it was scribbled the name and specification of a laptop computer.

"So how much will one of these cost me?

"About fifteen-hundred quid."

"Fifteen-hundred pounds! Wouldn't a cheaper one do?"

"We need six."

I just sighed.

"We also need some help," he added. "I can't crack the black web on my own. It reconfigures itself too quickly."

"Well, I'll help all I can, but my computing skills stretch little beyond sending emails and playing Solitaire."

"Okay, we need to get Munroe back. You get yourself to Teesside Park, I'll give Spence a ring and see you in the Lip in a couple of hours."

"Do you think he'd be happy working with us? That will likely be well outside his remit."

"Yeah, but what self-respecting computer nerd would give up the chance to work with the great Sherlock Holmes, creator of the organic attack? Besides, if not, he goes back from his trip in the sun empty-handed."

"Can we trust him? Do we even know he's really MI5?"

"He's MI5 alright. I hacked into their HR system last night."

"Don't tell me any more, Sherlock. I'll see you in a couple of hours."

I arrived at the Twisted Lip to find Holmes sitting alone. Alone except for three-quarters of a pint of Engineer's Thumb and two empty glasses. As I sat, he rose, moving to the bar to return with a pint for myself.

"Did you get the gear?" he asked.

"Yeah," I replied. "I've stuck it in the flat."

"Good lad. I'll square up later."

"It doesn't matter."

"I'll square up anyway."

Our mini squabble was interrupted by the arrival of Munroe.

"Would you like a beer?" asked Holmes.

"I tend to avoid alcohol," said Munroe.

"Me too," he replied to prompt a quizzical look from Munroe. "It struggles to avoid me," he appended. "Doc, can you get the lad a coffee?"

I returned to the table with the coffee to find Holmes and Munroe in deep conversation, the content of which I could hardly understand, never mind relay. From what I could gather, he was sketching out the concept of the "black web" he had explained to me earlier. There was also the mention of "organic attack", which Holmes dismissed as old hat in favour of something he had been developing called "dynamic threat optimisation". Besides, explained Holmes, there was no need to hack the black web as it sat in plain sight.

We finished our drinks and made our way to Flat 1B, where

Holmes and Munroe proceeded to unbox the laptops I had left there earlier.

"Would either of you like a sandwich?" I called out as I mooched around the kitchen, searching, in vain, for the required constituents. With no response forthcoming, I stuck my head around the door of the living room. "A cup of tea then?"

"Nope," said Holmes.

"Coffee, Spencer?"

"No, thank you."

"Okay then, my work here is done," I said, settling myself on to the most comfortable settee in Middlesbrough. I watched as Holmes and Munroe laid out the laptops and wired them together with a myriad of yellow cables and what looked like junction boxes. When they had finished, there was a circle of technology arranged with some obvious design on the living room floor.

"There is one thing that concerns me," said Munroe. "As soon as we put this online, it's going to lead a trail from Professor Moriarty right back to this flat."

"He's been in this flat six times already," remarked Holmes.

"Yes, but if we start harvesting his information, he'll likely be back for a seventh."

Holmes, who was sitting in the middle of the circle, hopped over the walls of his technology castle and left the room to return with his laptop. "We're going to use this as a hub," he said, presenting the laptop to Munroe.

"How does that help? We'll still need to connect to the internet. We'll still leave that machine's IP address on every switch between us and Moriarty."

Holmes' explanation was quite technical but I understood the concept. He seemed to go to lengths to explain it in a language I would understand. Our connection to the internet would be made via a computer in Lithuania. The question then was how do we get to Lithuania? This was achieved by a method of Holmes' devising. Pointing his exposition at me, he described how the only necessary condition for transmitting data was variation. Normally, in its most base form, this variation is achieved using binary, the ones and noughts, or ons and offs that computers speak in. The technique Holmes had developed didn't use these ones and noughts to communicate, but rather their cadence. He would fractionally delay the transmission of some of the bytes of information. A delay would represent a nought, and an unaffected transmission a one. To my understanding, this appeared genius. In the unlikely event that delays were noticed, they would be dismissed as the natural variance due to the background effects of traffic levels and variable cable quality, effects that Holmes filtered out with what he called "baseline packets", transmitted unfettered to determine the prevailing environmental conditions.

Munroe, whose knowledge of these things far exceeded mine, was as amazed as I was. "I congratulate you," he said. "You've created your own version of this, what did you call it in the pub, this 'black web'. You, working alone, have created what Moriarty required a team to create. A method of stealthy communication across a public network. I commend you, Mister Holmes, I'm impressed."

Holmes was untouched. "Shall we get on with it?" he said.

"Why not?" replied Munroe.

Holmes returned to the circle of technology, his bones creaking as he sat cross-legged within it. "Right," he said, "I'm going to go divining for some of this noise, the language of the black web, and ping it over to you, Spence, for you to turn into words."

"How do I do that? I don't recognise any of this software."

"Okay," said Holmes, jumping out of the circle to snatch back his laptop. "Use this. It's what MI5 will be using next year."

"I've seen earlier versions," he replied, shaking his head in dismay. "How did you get hold of it?"

"I built it. I'm Sherrinford Systems, the company you pay one point two million pounds a year to build these little toys for you." Holmes resumed his position in the circle to commence work. He tapped furiously on the keys of the first laptop, before shuffling around and hammering on the adjacent one. This continued until he'd done a full lap of all six machines. I didn't always appreciate what Holmes was up to, but he was always fascinating to watch.

"Oooh," he said, "your spooky mates would love a piece of kit like this, Spence. It must be the most complete surveillance network ever created. It's miles ahead of anything MI5 have got. There's even data on here concerning how many times the Doc has had sex with Mary. Ah, that's why you rush home early on a Tuesday. You filthy pup."

"Really," I exclaimed, having been drawn into the wonderment of it all.

"It looks like it's starting to tail off a bit."

"Surely not, Sherlock!"

"Doc, we haven't interpreted the data yet. I'm just collecting it," came Holmes' deadpan response, subsequently punctuated by Munroe's broad smile. "Right, Spence, see what you can do with that."

"Will do," replied Munroe.

As the work progressed, the freneticism of Holmes' gyrations increased to the point where he took the form of an aged body popper. He would rock forward on his stomach creating a kind of wave that allowed him to hop from one computer to another one, two positions around the circle. Perhaps his pièce de résistance was when he rolled onto his shoulder to run around with his legs and perform a two-hundred and seventy degree adjustment. What he had against anticlockwise I'm not sure. Then, without warning, he stopped.

"What have you got, Spence?" he said, before bouncing down between the pair of us on the settee.

Munroe pointed the laptop screen towards him and scrolled down the list of translated messages. All I saw was a list of random and unconnected sentences. The content of these sentences seemed unrelated and it was difficult, for me at least, to form a bigger picture.

"This is phenomenal," exuded Holmes. "All that kerfuffle about Spence and his mates snooping for the government and they've got nowt on these gadgies. And from what I saw in the message signatures, there's thousands of them. It's a social network for complete fucking psychopaths."

"With Moriarty at the head?" I added.

"He might have created it," replied Holmes, breathless in thought, "but this is bigger than one man. It's an organised crime syndicate that encircles the globe. There's all sorts going on here: cybercrime on a massive scale, contract killing, character assassination of leading politicians, you name it. They even appear to be crowd funding a government coup in Venezuela. It's like a marketplace for evil, with Moriarty skimming twenty percent off the top."

"What can we do about the likes of this?" I queried.

Holmes shook his head, his mouth turned down with bewilderment.

"I know what I have to do," said Munroe, rising from his seat. "I've got to call the office. This is a game changer. It's far bigger than we've uncovered. You really need to back off now, gentlemen."

As Munroe made his way down the stairs, I looked to Holmes for his response. There was something in his expression that I'd not seen before. My hope was that he could be realising this fight was beyond us.

"What are you thinking, Sherlock?" I asked.

"I'm thinking about this tech. I'm thinking how far things have moved on in the short time since we were kids playing with Ataris and ZX Spectrums. I'm wondering where it all ends. It's frightening," he gasped. "Technology moves on in leaps and bounds, and yet people have barely advanced an inch in the last hundred, two-hundred years. All of history really. It's still about the same self-serving lunatics looking to control and enslave. Moriarty is just Hitler with a different moustache, Caesar in more practical footwear, Simon Cowell with a slightly lower waistline."

We breakfasted in the Baker Street Kitchen the next morning, before heading along the road to Hud Couture. My hope was that

Martha would assume I'd parked up her taxi, and therefore not enquire after it. I still hadn't decided upon a way to break the news of Hansom's untimely end.

"Stick the kettle on, Martha," called Holmes, as we entered the boutique. "The Doc here is thirsty. No sugar and only a splash of milk. He's on a diet. Poor Mary's starting to get rolled out."

"Yeah, I've noticed her ankles are starting to swell up a bit," added Martha, much to my embarrassment.

As the three of us stood sharing a pot of tea, the door swung open and in walked a tall, well-presented gentleman, murine in features and perhaps ten or so years older than myself. Without introduction, and having not previously been in his direct presence, I knew it was Professor Moriarty who stood before us.

"Sherlock Holmes and Martha Hudson," he announced. "The star-crossed lovers."

Sherlock and Martha both turned to look at each other, each confirming their bewilderment at the reference.

"And Doctor John Watson, the faithful companion of the 'great detective'," he smiled. "You chaps are becoming quite the local celebrities, aren't you? Most of the time at my expense."

"Yeah," replied Holmes, nonchalantly sipping his tea, "we're in talks to get a range of perfumes named after us."

Moriarty just smiled. "I do envy you, Doctor, to be able to study this wonderful creature at such close quarters."

"Who is this dick?" interjected Martha.

"Missus Hudson, I do apologise. How remiss of me not to introduce myself. Professor James Moriarty at your service," he nodded. "In my mind, I feel I know you all so well. It's you I like the most. But then I am an incurable old romantic, and who could not be moved by the story of love unrequited."

"What the hell's he on about?" she sneered.

"The dilated pupils, the raised heart rate, the way you adjust your hair when he's around you, etcetera, etcetera. It's such a shame Sherlock here can't see beyond Irene Adler. What do you call her? 'The woman'. I tried to recruit her once, you know. One kiss more and I would have had her."

"Okay, Jeremy Kyle," interrupted Holmes, "is there a point to all this?"

"A point," pondered Moriarty, "a point? Ah, yes. You visited Copper Beeches the other night. While I was elsewhere. What exactly were you looking for?"

"A cup of sugar."

"I strongly recommend you knock next time. My people have been known to shoot intruders."

"I'll do more than knock," replied Holmes with calm certainty.

"Is that a threat?"

"No. A threat would imply uncertainty. What I have in mind is definite."

Moriarty flashed a confident smile. "You don't know who you are dealing with."

"Yes I do, Professor. I'm dealing with an international crime network which uses extortion, bribery and assassination to control both governments and industry. So basically, bad people."

"There's nothing either good or bad, but thinking makes it so," responded Moriarty. "Do you know much Shakespeare, Sherlock?"

"I know the Shakespeare pub. It was the first and last place I had Scampi-flavoured fries," retorted Holmes to garner a smile of acknowledgement from the Professor.

"Only Sherlock Holmes could be ignorant of the Bard."

"I've read his stuff," said Holmes. "It was written by at least three gadgies."

"That's one theory."

"It's not a theory. It's true. The writing style, the words used. There's definitely three hands in that game of brag. The only mystery is why pretentious little wank chops like you keep rolling it out."

"Ha. You know, you never cease to amaze me."

"That's what your wife said last night. But she added 'Bad Boy'."

The insinuation shot past Moriarty, who maintained his calm almost disinterested demeanour. "Always the wit. We should team up, Sherlock," he said. "Between us, we could run the world."

"For fuck's sake," remarked Holmes. "He's gonna tell me he's me dad next," he added before turning to me. "Watson, the needle."

"Sorry?" I replied.

"Can you carry on giving him some needle. I need to nip for a wee. That tea's gone right through me. Back in a bit."

As Holmes made his exit, Moriarty moved to the window. As calm as September, he screeched the finger of his leather gloved hand down the glass. "You know," he said, without facing us, "we did think of recruiting Holmes at one stage. But he failed all of our tests. In spite of his waywardness, it appears he's an honest man."

"Bollocks," remarked Martha, prompting Moriarty to spin round.

"So have you been in the crime business long?" I asked, breaking a silent standoff.

Moriarty straightened his lips with a knowing smile. "I just see it as business, Doctor. I do tend to work to my own rules, but then who doesn't? Yourself and Sherlock have ignored the lines that guide others on more than one occasion to my knowledge."

"Yeah, but we tend to draw a line at bombing and shooting at people."

"Indeed," he replied.

As I struggled to extend the conversation, Moriarty stood stone still, unperturbed by the din of silence. After a few minutes, Holmes lumbered back in, shaking water from his hands.

"Ah, the prodigal returns," announced Moriarty. "We're so alike you and I. Excepting I tend to make better use of the hand towels."

"We're nothing alike," responded Holmes. "You're a criminal, I'm a logician. Crime is common. Logic is rare."

"I'm not a criminal, I'm a philanthropist."

"What has stamp collecting got to do with anything?"

Moriarty sighed. "This is getting tedious now. I think it's time for me to bid you farewell. Suffice to say, stay away. Stay away from my home, stay away from my workplace, stay away from me. You can't win a war with me. I command an army. Why don't you think that over with that wonderful mind of yours?"

"I've thought it through already," replied Holmes, deadpan. "You're going to jail, or worse."

"Sherlock, this is your one chance to walk away from this. I found you very interesting at first, entertaining even, but you're becoming bad for business. I have a reputation to maintain. I can't afford to let you damage that. There's too much at stake. I've put too much hard work into this to have you cause any more disruption."

As Moriarty stepped to leave, Holmes called out, "How about we sort this out between just you and me? You know, we could meet somewhere, just me and you and a big lump of wood? You can have the wood."

"That's not my style, Sherlock. I don't get my hands dirty. Were you not listening? Your fight is not with me, it's with an army of thousands. Any mark you put on me will be redeemed a hundred fold by the members of my organisation. It's not one man that stands in front of you."

"Yeah, you are carrying a bit of timber, like. Don't worry, I'll get you a gym membership for Christmas. You can pick one up really cheap these days. Of course, I don't need the gym. I'm a natural athlete."

Moriarty shook his head in exasperation, Holmes' mockery starting to wear thin.

"I can kill you, Moriarty. I don't even need to touch you, I can hurt you with just a thought. It's a curse that's sometimes useful. It must be something to do with my gypsy blood."

"You can't harm me, Sherlock," laughed the Professor.

"I've got you worried though, haven't I?"

"No, not in the slightest. You know, you really are ungrateful. I got you what I thought was the perfect present and you threw it back in my face, thou marble-hearted fiend."

"Present? What present? I like presents."

"The bomb under Lestrade's car."

"Ah right, you should have asked first. I would have preferred Travel Scrabble."

Moriarty fixed a look on Holmes which he then flashed across Martha and myself before resuming his exit.

"Mister Moriarty," called Holmes, "you better be prepared to kill me, because I'm gonna kill you."

"I've tried to kill you, Sherlock. Three times."

"Oh yeah. I forgot about that."

"If I hadn't found you such an interesting subject, I'd have stepped up my efforts and completed the task. Fortunately for you, I'm an academic. I like to study and experiment on things of interest. Sometimes people support my research with their lives. It's just a consequence of me advancing science. The science of crime."

"Whatever, I'm still gonna fuck you three ways to Brighton," scowled Holmes. "Terms and conditions apply."

"Sherlock, profanity really doesn't suit you." With that, he held a look on us all and left.

"Wanker," mumbled Holmes, as the door clicked shut.

"Who was that?" remarked Martha.

"Professor James Moriarty," answered Holmes, in a pensive tone that approached a whisper as he moved across the shop.

"I meant you. You're not a killer, Sherley. What was all that about and why aren't the police dealing with this bloke? He's well scary."

"Yeah, I know," said Holmes, tracking Moriarty's departure through the window of the shop. "He reminds me of our English teacher."

5

After a threat to our lives by a criminal mastermind whose influence encircled the globe, we took the only course of action available to us. We went to the pub. Holmes was quiet. This wasn't unusual, but I assumed it a result of unresolved concerns. Even a man of his confidence couldn't escape the doubts generated by the size of the challenge we were facing. But he was steadfast. He would square up to Moriarty, no matter the consequences.

We were struck from our daze by the entry of Detective Inspectors Lestrade and Bradstreet.

Holmes flipped like a coin. "Are you two working together now? The criminal classes must be bricking it."

"We can do without your glib attempts at humour, Holmes," scowled Bradstreet.

"Oh, Annie," he cried, "don't be like that. I know you've still got that twinkle in your thighs for me. When are we gonna get round to sealing the deal?"

"Ooooh, I don't know. How about the week after never?"

"Park it, Sherlock," snapped Lestrade.

"That's what she's after, mate. Charges apply, except Sundays and Bank Holidays."

"Holmes!"

"...No return within two hours."

"Look," said Lestrade, frustrated by Holmes' diversionary tactics, "there was an explosion up in Wolviston yesterday. Do you know anything about that?"

"Nah, I've not seen the news. Gas leak, was it?"

"No, a taxi cab exploded. We believe the cause to be an explosive device."

"A car blows up and you suspect a bomb?" pondered Holmes. "That certainly makes sense. Well done, Detective. Grab yourself a biscuit."

Lestrade cast a look of disdain.

"Do you know what I think?" continued Holmes.

"What's that?"

"I think it was a car... bomb."

"Holmes, two men answering your descriptions were seen throwing rocks at the vehicle shortly before the explosion. That's enough for me to have you dragged down the station."

"Bomb? Bomb, bomb, bomb, bomb?" said Holmes. "It doesn't ring a bell. No, the only bomb that I remember was the one that went off out the front there. I ruined me donkey jacket saving the life of some ungrateful twat."

Lestrade conceded with a snort. It was more than likely that Holmes had indeed saved his life.

This, it appeared, cut him some concession from Lestrade's usual approach of jail now, question later. "So what's all this about the university?

"What's that?" asked Holmes.

"We've had a complaint from the dean that you've been gate-crashing lectures."

"I just went in out of the rain. Besides, since when has listening been a crime?"

"It's theft and probably trespass."

"No, it's not. It's only trespass if I interfere with something."

"The university could still bring a claim. What are you studying anyway? You're a bit old to be going back to school."

"Criminologists."

"You mean criminology."

"Do I?"

"What are you up to, Sherlock?"

"Reading level six. You'll really enjoy it when you get there."

"You're up to something," sneered Lestrade, frustrated at the lack of progress he was making with his questioning.

"Do you have any evidence?"

"No, just gut feel."

"Gut feel?" snapped Holmes. "What the fuck is gut feel? You should be relying on logic and reasoning. Not last night's vindaloo."

"Enlighten us then," chipped in Bradstreet.

"There's no point in enlightening stupid people," sighed Holmes, turning back to his beer.

"Come on, Detective," sniped Lestrade. "Let's go an' find a better way to waste our time."

"Don't forget to agree a safe word," called Holmes as they passed through the door.

"Sherlock," I remarked, as they crossed the window, "antagonising them is not going to help us much. Besides, Lestrade concerns me."

"Don't worry about Lestrade, I know how his brain works."

"How's that?"

"Really slowly," replied Holmes in elongated response.

"Yeah, but if we find ourselves in jail in the middle of all this, we'll be sitting ducks. You heard what Munroe said. MI5 think Moriarty has people working for him within Cleveland Constabulary."

"You're not wrong, Doc. There's too many variables here, too many moving parts, and Lestrade's one we could cancel out." Holmes sighed. "Let me have a think about that."

6

That evening, after a vain attempt at an afternoon siesta, I returned to the Twisted Lip to find Holmes standing on a bar stool. With him perfectly still, a noticeable feature of this bizarre circumstance was some odd-looking glasses, with yellow wrap-around lenses, adorning his face.

"He's been up there for forty minutes," called Mary from behind the bar.

"Sherlock," I enquired, "What are you doing and why are you wearing those ridiculous glasses?"

"They're vertigo glasses," he replied. "I got them off the shopping channel."

"But you're only a foot and a half off the floor?"

"You've gotta start somewhere."

"Do they work?"

"I'm not sure, it's early days yet. What you doing here, anyway? I thought you were gonna get your head down."

"I was. I did, but I wanted to talk to you about something."

"Okay, fire away."

"Not here," I said. "Let's go down the road."

We made our way the short distance to Sherlock's, an establishment named in honour of my companion, and I ordered two pints of Ragworth Blonde, before directing us to one of the more secluded tables. There was something I had been needing to tell Holmes for a while, but with him disappearing, and then all the activity concerning Moriarty, there hadn't been the opportunity.

"Sherlock," I started, "Mary and I went out for a meal last week."

"Parmo?"

"No, we went up market."

"Garlic sauce as well."

"Will you let me talk?" I remonstrated.

"Sorry, carry on," he replied, duly admonished.

"Okay, to cut a short story shorter, I asked her to marry me and she said, well, she would."

Holmes was struck still. It was perhaps the singular time I had managed to heap surprise on him. The effect was so acute I became swathed in trepidation. The overriding, if ridiculous, thought was that I should have perhaps sought Holmes' permission before popping the question to Mary.

"Look, Sherlock," I intervened. "I appreciate the concepts of marriage and love are abhorrent to you, but I really like Mary, I'm in love with her, and I'm delighted that she accepted my proposal."

After a long pause to process the data, signed by the narrowing of his eyes in consideration, he responded. "Mate, that's brilliant. I'm chuffed to bits, for you. For the both of you."

"Really?"

"Yeah. What does 'abhorrent' mean?"

"It means you are disgusted by it."

"Right," he replied. "Why didn't you just say that? You think love disgusts me? Okay."

"Well, maybe not disgusts, but it's not something you appear to take a particular interest in. Apart from perhaps, well, you know, her."

Holmes swayed back in his chair. The tips of his fingers pressed together in contemplation.

"Okay," he said, "tell me what you love about her?"

"Well," I stuttered, "she's nice, she makes me feel special. I feel a bond."

"A bond? What does that mean?"

"It means I love her."

"That's where we started."

"We like the same things."

"We like the same things: parmos, the Boro, Engineer's Thumb…"

"She likes things that aren't gonna kill me."

Holmes smiled, exposing his attack as a light-hearted challenge. "Remember, John, when we talked about the subconscious? How it sucks in all that information and processes it in the background? Even when you're asleep?"

"Yes, of course," I replied. "We've spoken about it on many occasions."

"The subconscious handles more information than the conscious waking mind ever could. It refines it, orders it, stores it away. It's quite amazing really. It's what defines you. That's why I'm alright at this detective lark. It's nothing that other people don't do. It's just I'm a bit more conscious of the subconscious. That's how Irene did me in. She picked the lock to my subconscious, waltzed on in there and made a right mess of the place. It took ages to clean up after her."

" 'Irene'," I remarked. "Not 'the woman'?"

"Yeah, Irene. That's her name. She got married, you know."

"Yes, I do know that."

Holmes locked a look of surprise onto me, in shock at the revelation. That was the second time I'd confounded him in under ten minutes.

"So are you saying you're over Irene now?" I asked.

"I've tidied up a bit," he replied, "but I'll always know she's been in there."

"But you're telling me love isn't real? It's just a trick of the mind?"

"No, it's very real. It's a consequence of the millions of calculations your subconscious makes. It couldn't be more real. More relevant than anything the waking mind tells you. Think of it as some sort of compatibility quotient, calculated in the depths of the brain. The heart's got nothing to do with it. That's just a pump. They talk about trusting your heart, but what they mean is your instinct. It's real, my mate, and I couldn't be happier for you and Mary. She completes you, John. She closes your open bracket. You'll make a great parenthesis."

"You're expecting us to have children?" I joked.

Holmes just smiled that knowing, enigmatic smile.

"Did Irene close your open bracket?"

"No, she was an open bracket to my closed one," he said pensively, "but we were never going to compile properly. She's object-oriented. My skills lie in the procedural paradigm," he laughed.

I wasn't quite sure what he meant but I got the gist. I picked up our glasses and returned them to the bar for replacements.

I returned to my chair, placing another pair of Ragworth Blondes in front of us both, and offered Holmes a proposition I'd been harbouring for a while. "Sherlock," I said, "you're my best friend. It would be a great honour to me if you would be my best man."

"Me? Speeches and stuff? I'm not sure about that, my mate. But thanks. No one has ever asked me that."

"Okay," I replied. "I understand. I'll ask Anstruther. He's a good man. He'll do a great job. Mary probably wouldn't be happy with a best man with hair like yours anyway."

"What's wrong with my hair?"

"It's scruffy."

"No, it's not. It's just variable."

"But you'll come to the wedding?"

"Yeah, of course. Nothing could keep me away. Make sure Mary picks some nice bridesmaids. No munters."

"That's very much Mary's domain, but I will make her aware of your requirements. I might not use those exact words, however."

Holmes smiled and stared back at me, poised.

"What?" I asked.

"You haven't finished yet. You have something else to say. The tone of your voice. You haven't returned to the key you started on yet. There's another verse to this song."

"Actually, Sherlock, there was something else I wanted to tell you. The thing is I'm going to have to step back from all this. I'm marrying Mary until death do us part. I'd prefer it if that wasn't a week on Tuesday."

"Why? What's happening on Tuesday?"

"Nothing, I was just using that as an example."

"I know, my mate, I was just trying to lighten the moment. You leave all this malarkey to me and Spence. You've found a good woman there. You're a very lucky man." He made to mouth something else, but couldn't.

"No, I'll see this through. Whatever the hell it is. But after this, I'm done."

Holmes just nodded, his eyes twitching as if he were shepherding a tear. "I will miss you, you know. It's been good."

"We can still keep in touch."

"Yeah."

"You can come over for dinner sometimes. I'll ask Mary to cook."

"I won't miss you enough to risk Mary's cooking," he laughed.

"I'll tell her that."

"Doc, I don't have many people around me. Not since my dad died. His death was a problem without a solution, and I struggled with that. I couldn't escape it. Even when I was distracted, I missed having that feeling. He wouldn't have wanted that. Nobody wants that. No one good. That's why I stopped attaching myself to people. For years, there was just me and Martha. You've shown me that was the wrong thing to do. Do you know what I'm trying to tell you?"

"Yes, Sherlock, I think I do. But let's look forward not backwards."

"Yeah, why not? Let's go and kick Moriarty in the arse. Give the twat a massive wedgie."

7

We crossed the street to Number 22 and made our way up the stairs to Flat 1B, where I slumped on the settee.

"What are you doing?" asked Holmes.

"Sitting down. I was gonna let you get on with it."

"Get on with what?

"Dealing with Moriarty. Do you not have a plan?"

"Yeah, seven. None of them brilliant enough."

"Maybe good is good enough."

"You die in all of them."

"Okay," I said, "let's have a think about this."

"See, that's the problem," continued Holmes with a sigh. "He's only really interested in me, but other people are going to get between us. You, Martha... I don't want you caught in the crossfire."

"Neither do I," I replied, jumping up to think better on my feet. "How do two people wage war on a man backed up by an army of thousands?"

It's not hyperbole to say we were squaring up to take on a legion. It was as close to a biblical struggle as I could imagine. On this remark, Holmes just smirked and suggested our adversaries probably needed to strengthen their squad.

"How do we fight something like this?" said Holmes. "A network that silently circles the earth."

"How do you build something like that?" I asked. "What one man can invent, another can destroy."

"Brilliant," said Holmes, with as much eulogy as I'd ever seen.

"Has that given you an idea?"

"Nope. At least, I don't think so. I tell you what. First things first. Let's stitch Lestrade up."

Holmes' removal of Lestrade from the field of play was quite brilliant. He found an unsolved crime in which unidentified DNA was found at the scene, took the digital signature of that DNA, and applied it to the record on Lestrade's personnel file.

Normally, this record was used to exclude any DNA inadvertently left by investigating officers at the crime scene. In this case, the reverse was true, and Lestrade was placed at the scene of a crime, the investigation of which he was not involved in. When the police ran their nightly DNA analysis, their computer program would turn up Detective Inspector Barry Lestrade as the number one suspect in the botched armed robbery of Hemlington Post Office.

Poor Lestrade. Holmes didn't even do him the honour of implicating him in a successful act. To further reinforce Lestrade's guilt, he also hacked into Lestrade's mobile phone records and edited them to make it appear that the inspector was in the vicinity of the post office at the time the crime took place. Clearly this would be a simple bind for Lestrade to escape. A re-profiling of his DNA would scotch the incriminating evidence, however it would take the lab a couple of days to undertake the analysis. The next morning, Lestrade was arrested and detained, dragged from his bed like a common criminal.

Watching Holmes was like watching an artist at work, Lestrade's liberty being removed in a matter of minutes. At the completion of his work, Holmes, in a matter-of-fact manner, muttered the words, "Job done."

"Is that it?" I asked. "You cast scandal on the man so coldly, Sherlock."

"To be honest, Doc, I don't. I don't feel good about this but it's for the best. I'm sure of that. You may not believe it but I actually have a lot of time for him. He's a good gadgie. We just need him out of the way for a while."

"What about Bradstreet?"

"She's an evil witch, with ice water running through her veins."

"I mean, don't we need her out of the picture as well?"

"I just did. It's a bit like shooting a shark and watching the rest of the shoal eat it. All her efforts will be directed towards making Lestrade's conviction stick."

"I don't think the collective noun for sharks is 'shoal'," I said. "It doesn't sound scary enough."

"Yeah, it's probably something like a 'diarrhoea of sharks'," he said, angling a look that was perplexed at the irrelevance of my remark.

"What now?" I asked, trying to recover focus.

"Moriarty and the black web."

"Do you have a plan yet?"

"No. What was it you said earlier?

"About what?"

"Something about a gadgie inventing something."

"What one man can invent, another can destroy."

"Yeah, that's it. How do we destroy the black web?" he said, his mind turning over. "That's quite hard. We'd need to break the internet."

"Sherlock, if you were going to create such a thing as the black web, where would you start?"

Holmes rattled his tongue inside his mouth, simultaneously inhaling to produce a tepid whistle. "Money. Everything starts and ends with money. Moriarty sits in the middle of the black web. He's the banker. You did hear that correctly. Anyway, if we take away the money, then the black web seizes up. At least for a short while."

"Why only for a short while?"

"If I can hack into banks and move money around, I'm sure he can. At the very least, he'll know someone with the skills. A few days and he'll have it up and running again."

"A few days doesn't give us much," I sighed.

"It does if we build on that mistrust and uncertainty. Create a crisis of confidence. Look what happens to the financial markets when all the lemmings hurl themselves off the same cliff."

"It sounds like we have something, Sherlock."

"We do, my mate. If we can intercept some of those black web messages and have a play around with them, maybe we can contaminate it with disinformation. A kind of viral panic that might just snowball. The herd mentality spreads like wildfire. It's at the heart of all man's ills. Crashing stock markets, the rise of Hitler, those daft big redneck beards."

"Let's do it. How did you put it earlier? 'Give Moriarty a massive wedgie'."

A long absent smile folded across his face. "I can do the first bit. Hide the money. But for phase two, I'll need help. If we hold on to the messages too long they'll be resent. If that happens too often we'll get rumbled."

"How long is too long?"

"Parts of a second."

"Munroe?"

"I reckon so. I wonder where he's got to?"

"Have you still got his card? We can give him a ring."

"Okay," said Holmes. "But not before I do the first bit. I don't want MI5 knowing all my secrets." He picked up his laptop from where he'd parked it on the floor and begun to tap at the keys. I sat beside him on the settee in a state of wonderment. There wasn't a barrier he couldn't breach. He moved freely across bank accounts and the internal systems of MI5, pausing only briefly to place a one pound bet on the three-thirty at Chepstow. "Oooh, he's got some money this Moriarty," he said. "Well, at least he did have."

"You've stolen it?"

"No," he protested, "I'm not a thief. I've just moved it a bit. There's now a fella called Arthur Murray who's worth ten quid more than the queen."

"Arthur Murray?"

"Yup, it's an anagram of Moriarty."

"No, it isn't."

"…but with different letters."

After just short of an hour, he returned the laptop to the floor, a broad smile across his face.

"What are you gonna do when this is all over, Sherlock?" I asked.

"I've not thought about it. Maybe I'll go travelling. See a bit of the world."

"What? Back to Sheffield? See if you can track down that late night Greggs," I joked.

"No," he defended, "I was gonna check the Panama Swiss out."

"Where? The bank?"

"No, the country."

"What country?"

"Panama Switzerland."

"That's two countries."

"Is it?"

"Yeah, Panama and Switzerland."

"Well, yeah, but they're neighbours, like Portugal and Spain."

"No, one's in Europe, the other's in Central America."

"Oh right, I'll go somewhere else then. Ibiza maybe. Where's that?"

"Sherlock, before you go anywhere, do me a favour. Buy yourself an atlas. Your grasp of geography is positively American."

Holmes handed me Munroe's card. "Here, you ring him. Tell him we need a word." He then stood and moved into the kitchen to boil the kettle. "Don't tell him too much," he called. "Remember you're ringing an MI5 phone. We don't want the Chinese knowing what we're up to."

I tried several times with no joy. The number he'd given didn't even drop to voicemail. It just went dead. This was a problem.

We'd set wheels in motion, but without Munroe we had no way to execute the rest of the plan. Holmes returned to the lounge with two steaming hot cups of tea. Although puzzled, his level of concern seemed less than mine. It was getting late. There was every chance he'd gone to bed and switched his phone off. Holmes reassured me that given Munroe's reliance on technology, he should be easy enough to find. He also allayed my worries concerning Munroe's willingness to get involved. Apparently, a 'techhead' like Munroe wouldn't be able to resist the challenge that we had cued up for him. Bringing down the black web would make us all the thing of legend, albeit a legend confined to the shadowy world of the secret services.

We finished our tea and Holmes headed to bed. With the night wearing on, and the potential of an early start the next morning, I crashed on my familiar bunk of Holmes' settee.

I woke the next morning to the outline of a figure sitting in the chair on the opposite side of the room. As I fought with my eyes to get them to acclimatise to the light, the shape spoke, "Good morning, Doctor." It was Moriarty. I was jolted into consciousness. Simultaneously, I heard Holmes moving around in his bedroom. Rather than join me, he slipped into the kitchen and clicked on the kettle. "Tea, Doc?" he called.

"Erm, yes please," I responded, wondering how to react to Moriarty.

"Professor, tea?" shouted Holmes.

"No, thank you," he replied. It was surreal, especially given the fact that Moriarty had a revolver in his hand. Holmes made his way into the living room and handed me my tea, dressed, as I was, in a tee shirt and boxer shorts.

"To what do we owe the displeasure?" Holmes asked Moriarty.

"You know the answer to that," he replied. "I seem to have had an issue with my bank accounts. All twenty-seven of them."

"You do know we're Holmes and Watson, and not Bradford and Bingley?"

"Sherlock, only you could have created this mess, and it's causing me a few customer service issues. I'll have it fixed in forty-eight hours. The short and the long of it is I can't allow you to do it again. It's bad for business."

"Is that why you've brought the gun? Are you gonna shoot me, Jim?" The concern created in Holmes by our armed intruder appeared no more than casual.

Moriarty didn't reply, instead flashing Holmes a black stare accompanied by a nasal snort.

"No, you're not, are you?" said Holmes. "I've seen what Five have got on you and it's nothing. You're as clean as a shark's arse. You're not gonna spoil that by putting a bullet in me. Their only option is to assassinate you, and apparently they don't do that anymore… shame."

Moriarty stood up and paced to the window to look out onto Baker Street. "That it should come to this, Sherlock. You know when I started building the network, the 'black web' as you call it, it was as a force for good. I wanted the leaders of industry and commerce to be able to communicate and share ideas, without the encumbrance of governments and faceless bureaucrats."

"How quick the step from altruism to world domination," I remarked.

"Indeed, Doctor, indeed."

"So what went wrong?" asked Holmes.

"It wasn't happening quickly enough. They treated my ideas with suspicion."

"Pfff," exclaimed Holmes. "How wrong could you be?"

"You know, the lack of imagination in our business leaders is stupefying."

"Good job we've got you then, hey."

"Be not afraid of greatness: some are born great, some achieve greatness and some have greatness thrust upon them."

"Ri-ght," replied Holmes, elongating the word.

"It's Shakespeare, Sherlock, Shakespeare!" shouted Moriarty.

"Which one?"

Moriarty sighed. "Holmes," he said, in a low-volume, deliberate tone. "You've stolen my money. I want it back."

"No I haven't... I've just moved it slightly."

"Either way, there's some quite high-ranking politicians and officials that won't be getting their bonuses this month."

"Oh, I'm gutted," said Holmes, prompting rage in the hitherto calm Moriarty. His arm snapped up to point the gun at Holmes' head, as he glared along the barrel at him.

In contrast, Holmes' mood was one of nonchalance. He stared back, doing nothing more but observe. This seemed to antagonise the Professor even more, who swung around his arm to aim the gun at me. We stood in that strange standoff for a matter of seconds. It seemed longer.

"You should give the devil his due, Sherlock," he snarled, from behind a cold stare. "You're nurture not nature, my friend. Without me, you would be nothing. You'd most likely be dead by now. Before this week is out, you might well be." He then swung his arm back round to point the gun in Holmes' direction and flicked back the switch on his persona. "Goodbye," he chirped, before exiting the room and making his way down the stairs and on to the street.

Holmes looked to me, his calmness fractured by concern he exhaled silently through rounded lips. We'd clearly touched a nerve.

"You better try Munroe again," said Holmes.

"What? We're carrying on?"

"Ye-ah," he replied in two syllables.

"Right. I was hoping we were just gonna give him back his money and go live at the north pole."

Holmes smiled, confidently. "Nah, the game's afoot. He's gonna make a mistake. He may have already made it. The code loops but nothing ever really changes. The same mistakes occur over and over. The same bugs are written and rewritten."

I tried to call Munroe several times with the same level of success I'd achieved the previous evening.

Each time I tried, the call failed.

After four or five attempts I gave up, deciding to try again after breakfast.

We entered the Baker Street Kitchen and Holmes made his usual order of two soft-boiled eggs, toast and tea. I was a way away from being able to eat and elected for just a pot of tea. Slumped back in the chair, Holmes engaged his recently acquired mannerism of pressing together his fingertips in contemplation. I don't think he noticed the arrival of his food. He certainly didn't acknowledge the waitress.

"Maybe we don't need Munroe to take on the black web," he said. "I could knock something up. Something that searches for patterns in the messages and automatically mutates the content. It wouldn't look as human, but that might just add to the confusion we're trying to create."

"It might be the only the option we have. Munroe seems to have gone AWOL."

"I'm gonna go to my other place in Wolviston. Get me head down and write some seriously cool code."

"I'll come too."

"It's alright. I won't be much in the way of company. I'll be in the zone. When I'm programming, you can hardly get a word out of me."

Generally, I struggled to get a word out of him when he was eating toast.

"I'll take our mam out for lunch as well," he continued.

"Okay," I conceded, not wanting to encroach on the quality time he spent with his mother. "I'll go and see Mary. Just give me a shout when you need me."

"Will do, my mate."

I spent most of that day on Mary's sofa watching mind-numbing television, with her head resting on my chest. It was exactly the medicine I needed. I was exhausted, mentally drained by the exchanges with Moriarty and the resulting chaos they scattered through my mind. Given the nature of the confrontation, there was little I could do but support Holmes in whatever way he required. I only just understood the black web and the strategy Holmes was developing to disrupt it.

By mid-afternoon, I was drifting in and out of consciousness, when my phone vibrated in my pocket. It was a text message from Holmes telling me that Munroe had been in touch and they had arranged to meet early the next morning. Munroe, he said, had "bottled it" and had holed up in a safe house "over the border", an area of Middlesbrough between the railway lines and the river, that sits in the shadow of the Transporter Bridge, and is correctly known as St Hilda's.

That Munroe had been worried was understandable. He appeared a nervous type and it was easy to see how the knowledge of the black web would have caused him concern. I was surprised he'd got in touch, but even more amazed to learn that MI5 had a safe house in Middlesbrough. My assumption was that Munroe had ducked for cover and called for the assistance of agents more accustomed to working in the field.

All in all, the unexpected return of Munroe was a welcome bonus. With him and his colleagues working alongside Holmes, the days of the black web could well be numbered, sooner rather than later, given their respective skillsets. The burgeoning thought however concerned the aftermath. If Holmes and Munroe did take down the black web, how would Moriarty respond, and who would be the target of his retribution? My guess was definitely Holmes and probably me.

I was wrong. In all my assumptions. Early the next morning, Holmes sent another text. It read thus, "Caught in a trap. Munroe rogue... in bed with Moriarty". I rapidly replied but received no response. The obvious scenario was that Holmes had retrieved his phone from its hiding place in the lining of his jacket and managed to send out his message before his captors, probably Moriarty's cohorts, had wrestled the device from him.

We'd been duped by Munroe. That odd nervous little character had led us up the garden path. No doubt he was MI5, Holmes had checked that on their internal systems, but we'd never considered that Moriarty might have got to him. He just wasn't the type. Rogue agents just didn't look like that. Perhaps this was the very reason that Moriarty had selected him.

Annoyingly, in hindsight, there was one fact we should have grasped upon. What was an agent with little field experience doing working alone? This point was especially prevalent given the stature of him. I was reminded of something Irene said. Something about inconsistencies adding to the lie. If a story is too perfect, it looks fabricated. Moriarty seemed to exhibit some genius in this respect.

I had to find Holmes, go to his aid, but the first thing was to get Mary safe. Despite her protestations, I convinced her to get Martha and travel up to her sister's place in Northumberland. Who knew the extent that Moriarty's wrath would run to? Mary probably wouldn't have gone if it were not for the protection her flight was also affording Martha. Martha, having met Moriarty, was more than happy to run for cover.

Clearly, I needed help, but I had nowhere to turn. Lestrade was the obvious choice, but with him holidaying in a prison cell, that wasn't an avenue I had available. The next thought was Detective Inspector Spaulding, however an earlier suggestion that the tentacles of Moriarty's influence extended into Middlesbrough Police Station, left me wary. I didn't seriously think Spaulding to be corruptible, but didn't want my fingers burned twice by the same flame.

Then an idea struck. It wasn't officialdom that was going to get us out of this bind. If the black web had shown us anything, it was that corruption was endemic in those who supposed to serve the public. The help I needed lurked not in the corridors of power, but in the doorways and on the street corners of Middlesbrough. If I was going to find Holmes, I needed the assistance of Bradley and his irregular army of street troops.

Bradley was easy enough to track down. He was a creature of habit and, in the time that I had known him, I had grown to learn his inclinations. After a short search, I tracked him down to McDonalds on Linthorpe Road, where he was enjoying a breakfast.

I explained the predicament, including the risks, and within minutes he was rousing an army. We congregated at the junction of Grange Road and Linthorpe Road, and shared mobile phone numbers before making our way on foot to St Hilda's, in groups of two and three, so as not to attract attention.

9

On reaching St Hilda's, Bradley and his irregulars dispersed, working their way up and down the numerous streets and alleyways. Wherever you stood and wherever you looked, you could see at least one, usually two or more, of them. They peered through windows, tried doors, questioned the occupants of the various offices and business premises. It was remarkable to see the regimentation of their approach, more so given the ad hoc nature of their assembly.

They filtered through the network of streets of Georgian style houses, that have since seen office conversions, new build office blocks and the boarded up and derelict structures. My focus was on the latter, as I figured a deserted building would provide better concealment. After an hour, maybe an hour and a half, we'd covered the whole area and found nothing. I stopped on a street corner to lean on a wall and gather my thoughts. We needed another approach, but I was unable to decide what that would be. It was then that I took a call from Bradley. Holmes had been found, sitting, plain as day on a bench in Exchange Square, a location dead on the periphery of our search area.

I rushed up Cleveland Street, under the railway bridge and onto Exchange Square. Holmes was sitting bolt upright on a metal bench.

"Holmes," I called, "where have you been? How did you manage to escape?"

He didn't reply. Oddly, he sat wearing the vertigo sunglasses he had been experimenting with in the Twisted Lip previously, and a headset comprising large over-the-ear headphones and a microphone. It was the kind of thing an airline pilot might wear.

Having not gained a response from Holmes, or even an acknowledgement that I was there, I went to grab the headset from him. As I did, Holmes' hand shot up and grabbed my wrist. Trapped in a hypnotic daze, he didn't look in my direction. I released his grip and stepped back to assess the situation. I could hear a faint voice emanating from his earpieces.

"Stand up, Sherlock," said the voice, in a deep synthetic timbre.

Holmes complied, rising in a robot-like manner. Although the voice was disguised, I was sure from the intonation it was that of Moriarty.

"Take off your jacket."

Again, Holmes followed the instruction, removing his jacket to reveal what appeared to be a suicide vest. The tube-shaped explosives ran in two rows around his chest, connected together with thin red wires. In the centre was a large round dial with a blue light rotating around its circumference. Below it sat a large padlock that appeared to prevent the jacket's removal.

I staggered back at the sight, just as Bradley skidded onto the scene.

"Shit. What the fuck?" he said.

"Bradley," I replied, "call the police. We need to get these buildings cleared."

As Holmes and I stood face to face in the square, the streets filled with police cars, fire engines and military vehicles of a multitude of forms and sizes. Both military personnel and members of the police armed response unit trained their weapons on us. The first voice I heard was that of DI Bradstreet over a loudhailer. "Doctor Watson, move away. Get yourself to a safe distance."

I remained, certain I could coax him out of his trance. As we stood there, people from the nearby offices, accompanied by armed police officers, filtered nervously away, pointing worried glances in our direction.

"Doctor Watson, please move to a safe distance," repeated Bradstreet.

"No," I screamed. "I'm not leaving him."

"Start walking, Sherlock," came the voice in his earphones.

Holmes began to move. Stiff and robotic in manner, he turned right and walked across the square, turning right again to head down Exchange Place.

"Sherlock, it's me, John, snap out of it," I said with no response.

As we walked, we were caught up by PC Hardwick. "Doctor Watson," he said. "This is very brave of you but you need to get to a safe distance."

"I'm staying with him. I can get through to him."

"Doc, no, we need to get you away. You're not helping. Let's get back and try to figure what the hell we do about this."

I reluctantly agreed. Hardwick shepherded me away to a pack of police officers, many of whom were armed. DI Bradstreet sat centre in the group, clearly agitated.

"Where the hell is he going?" she shouted.

"The bridge," I replied, "the big blue thing five-hundred yards in the direction he's heading. Moriarty wants to make a statement of Holmes' death."

"Who the hell is Moriarty?" screamed Bradstreet.

"It's a long story," I sighed.

"Okay," said one of the armed officers. "We need to relocate. Get closer to the bridge."

The police filed away, arcing in a wide loop through the adjacent streets to reach the Prince's Trust building on the corner of Durham Street and Vulcan Street. We made our way through the building and up to the roof. From our vantage point, we had an excellent view of both Holmes' lumbering progress towards us and his ultimate destination of the Transporter Bridge.

"Sir," said one of the female officers, who was working on a large backpack of a radio, "I have the signal. I can hear the messages being sent to Holmes."

"Okay, Stoper, put it on speaker," said the commanding officer.

"Sherlock," came the voice, "I need you to move faster."

"Can we speak to him?" asked the commander.

"Yes, sir, it's just short wave radio. It's two-way."

"So, who here is a trained negotiator?"

"I am," replied Stoper.

"That's not going to work," I interjected. "He's in some sort of hypnotic trance. He's tuned to the voice he's hearing in those earphones. What are you going to ask him to do anyway? He's locked into that bomb."

"What if you talk to him, Doctor?"

"What do I say?"

"I don't know!" snarled the commander, slamming his fist down onto the parapet that bordered the roof. "Does anyone have any ideas what the hell we do with this?"

"Yes," said Bradstreet. "We shoot him."

"Sorry?" he replied. "He's the victim."

"He's dead anyway. This is about limiting collateral damage."

"I'm not ordering someone to shoot an innocent man, Inspector."

"I'm giving the order. I out rank you. Take the shot."

"Not in the field, you don't. I am not shooting an innocent man."

Hardwick flashed me a look, astounded that this conversation was even taking place.

"Take the shot," affirmed Bradstreet.

"He's a local hero, for fuck's sake."

"Stand down, DI," came a voice from behind us. "I'll take over." It was Superintendent Spaulding. "We're not shooting anyone. Especially not a man who is walking to his death." He then moved to shake the hands of both myself and the unit commander. "What on earth are we going to do with this?" he sighed.

"Doc," said Hardwick, "Do you think he fears death?"

"That's an odd question, constable. But no, I don't. I've always thought he fears life. He sees so much that we don't and every sight scars him a little. Why do you ask?"

"I once heard that you can't hypnotise someone to do something they don't want to do. How can he be walking to his death against his will?"

"Holmes' mind doesn't work like anyone else's."

"It would benefit us to have him conscious," remarked the superintendent. "However, I expect any interference from us will just accelerate matters. Do we all share the working assumption that those explosives can be detonated remotely?"

"Yes, sir," replied the commander. "We need to have a closer look at what we're dealing with. Stevenson, can you set up the lens?"

"Aye, sir," said the officer, before unpacking a large telescope from one of the many equipment bags they had with them.

With the lens trained on Holmes and the images it was capturing relayed through the screen of a laptop computer, we had a perfect view of our predicament, as my friend made his way slowly towards us along the street below.

"I don't think we're gonna get much change out of that," remarked the commander, commenting on Holmes' vest. "I don't recognise this particular set up, but I suspect that disk on his chest contains some sort of transponder that will allow the device to be activated remotely."

"Could we somehow jam the signal?" asked the superintendent.

The commander puffed out his cheeks and exhaled an empty whistle. "It could probably be overridden, but not with the equipment we carry."

"Who would have that sort of stuff?" I asked.

"I'm not sure. Suicide bombers normally pull the trigger themselves. We usually just shoot them before they get the chance. The security services maybe. MI5?"

"Bradstreet, get onto MI5," ordered Spaulding. "Brief them and see if they can lend us any help. Tell them time is of the essence."

"We could shoot it," said Hardwick. "A gunshot wound to the chest would be more survivable than being blown to pieces by twenty pounds of jelly."

"No," replied the commander, "if the transponder goes offline, the device will be triggered. We would need to override it and provide a replacement signal."

"Bradstreet," shouted Spaulding. "Have you got anything from MI5 yet?"

"Not yet, sir. I'm getting bounced around various departments."

Moriarty appeared to have every angle covered. As Holmes passed by the street below us, the situation seemed perfectly hopeless.

I've always thought the Transporter Bridge to have an air of menace. The way it towers above the river, two legs planted in each riverbank, always made me think of some slumbering, headless metal dinosaur. It's been the companion of Teessiders for their whole lives, and is an icon looked on fondly by those of the region, but through different lenses it can appear quite frightening. As Holmes progressed towards it, that fear moved from an idle fantasy to a perilous reality.

Holmes reached the now deserted bridge and started to climb the stairs to the gangway that runs across the top of the bridge. As he ascended, the reason for him wearing his vertigo glasses struck me. Perhaps Holmes' fear of heights was enough to jolt him out of his hypnotic state. Moriarty must have made him wear the glasses to mitigate against that possibility. If we could somehow get him to take off the glasses may be it would provide us with an intervention. But still, any interference could be enough for Moriarty to trigger the bomb.

As Holmes reached the centre of the bridge, another message came across the radio. "Sherlock, it's time. You and I are past our dancing days."

"Shut the fuck up," growled Holmes. "Did you for one minute think that you could control my mind?"

"Very good. You're quite the actor. You had me fooled. But, I can still blow you to pieces."

"Go on then," shouted Holmes. "Go on."

I grabbed the handset from the radio operator. "Moriarty, we know it's you. If you explode that bomb, there'll be nowhere for you to hide."

"Don't listen to him, Jim. There'll be plenty of places to hide. Press the fucking button."

"Sherlock, what are you doing?" I cried.

At that moment, the blue glow rotating on the transponder on Holmes' chest stopped. In its place a red light lit the whole circumference. There was a deathly pause as we all stared at Holmes via the screen of the laptop.

Holmes smiled. He reached down into his sock and pulled out the screwdriver thing he'd used to break into Moriarty's place. He held out the gadget in front of him. "I win, Professor," he said. "I've hijacked your signal. I'm afraid your little toy won't work." A response from the radio was not forthcoming.

As we breathed a collective sigh of relief, the wind whipped up. Holmes, in his exposed position on the top of the bridge, was buffeted, this causing him to lose his purchase on the screwdriver. He juggled with it between his hands, trying to regain his grip, before watching the device bounce on the gangway between his feet and slip over the edge.

"Shit," he said, digging into the coin pocket of his jeans to pull out his lock pick. He worked frantically at the padlock on his chest as the bomb transponder cycled through a series of colours. As it flashed blue and then red, Holmes unlocked the padlock, tore off the vest and threw it out in front of him. It exploded in mid-air.

For a second time, we were bathed in relief. Myself and the various police officers turned around to face each other, shaking our heads at the narrowness of the escape.

We looked back to Holmes to see he had climbed over the handrail and off the walkway.

"What are you doing, Sherlock?" I asked using the radio. "Come on down now. It's over."

"Doc," he replied, "these glasses don't work."

"Then come down."

He grabbed an arm of the glasses and then paused for a couple of seconds before straightening his arm out sideways. In the same motion, he threw the glasses some distance to the side of him.

They rattled off the steelwork as they fell through the structure of the bridge.

"John," he called, "look after Martha. Take the bins out for her. She never mentions it, but she doesn't like the smell."

"You look after her. Stop messing around and come down. Look, wait there. I'll come and get you."

"I'm scared, John. Is this what it feels like? It's bloody horrible."

In my time with Sherlock Holmes, I must have seen a hundred of his faces and personas. The one I saw through that monitor was new. Different from every other. It was a face of sheer terror.

"Are you crying, Sherlock?"

"No, I just yawned," he said, with mock-dismissal before clicking into something else. Something dark. "Moriarty, are you still there you blood-soaked piece of shit? I have a network too. And I'm about to turn it on you. Everyone in this town. This small town in Europe," he smiled. "Everyone in this town will be looking for you now. You'd better run."

The next is difficult to relay. He stretched out both his arms and then stood perfectly still for what could not have been more than a second. It seemed longer. For that moment, the world paused.

"What time is it, John?"

I looked down at my watch.

"Eleven minutes past eleven," I replied.

It was difficult to see from that distance, but I'm sure he smiled, the briefest of knowing grins flicking across his face. Then there was the slightest movement, barely detectable. I realised what was happening at the precise moment that it was too late to intervene.

He fell. Without sound.

"Sherlock, No!" I shouted as he tumbled through the air for what seemed an eternity, his arms outstretched either side of him. The sickening cacophony as he crashed into the river drowned me in darkness. I will never escape the sight of my friend's demise. It runs on an unrelenting loop in my mind's eye. The way he tumbled, his body rigid in the shape of a crucifix. But it's the sound that haunts me the most. That sound as he hit the water. The noise of his life force being thrashed from him.

It felt like every positive aspect of my being had been wrenched from me and sucked down into the depths of the earth, causing the blood to run dark in my veins. I can't escape it. I'm not even sure I want to escape it. I want to remember every moment of him. Hence these words. I'm no author, but I couldn't leave these stories untold. I shared a fleeting but crazy time with Sherlock Holmes. These words are my monument to him.

A monument I share with you.

10

It was days before they recovered the body. I was asked by the police to undertake the formal identification. Both Mycroft and Martha were perhaps closer to him than I was, but in their own ways neither of them were in any state to do it. Mycroft disappeared into denial and Martha was utterly destroyed, souped into an absent angst.

As I entered the morgue, my every thought hung on to the hope that it wasn't him. He was a magician who could have somehow wound his way out of that scenario. Doctor Pondicherry trembled as she pulled back the sheet. Our eyes met across the still body of my friend, before I glanced down to confirm my most debilitating of fears.

There he lay, he was ravished by the effect of the Tees, but it was him. I'd recognise him anywhere, I just didn't want it to be there. As doubt expired, each sinew in my body tightened sending me wheeling away from the table. Much to my shame, I staggered out of the room with no goodbye to either Doctor Pondicherry or Sherlock Holmes.

For the remainder of that day, I sat alone in Central Gardens. The world bustled around me, but my perception was one of silence. It was young Bradley who shook me from my stupor.

"What you doing?" he asked.

"What is there to do?"

"Same as always." He looked so unaffected. "You can buy me a beer if you want."

"Are you even old enough to drink?"

"I won't say owt if you don't."

To this day, I don't know why Holmes did what he did. The irony being, it escaped logic. The people of Middlesbrough, the People's Republic, were never going to band as vigilantes and hunt down Moriarty. They had lives to lead, loved ones to consider and protect. Through my chronicling of his exploits, Holmes had developed some cult notoriety, but nothing approaching the fanaticism he seemed to expect his suicide would provoke. Given that his skill in reading people was so incredible, so singularly unique, like nothing I've seen or even heard of, it baffles me that he could have misjudged people so badly.

There's no way of knowing what was really going on in his mind, or for that matter what state of mind he was in. It wasn't long since that he'd been involved in a psychotic episode so acute it had taken him to the brink of death. The theory I favour is one I rounded upon sometime later. It was still one of sacrifice, but not one with the incredible justification Holmes offered. I think he ran the scenarios and concluded that the collateral damage caused by his struggle with Moriarty would include the fatalities of those around him. Surely the expense of his life was to the benefit of Martha's, mine and perhaps even those of Mary and Mycroft. We'll never know, however this hypothesis gives me some crumb of comfort. Every other thought seems such a godless waste.

So upon this carelessly scribbled prose, I deliver my valediction. I never set out to be a writer, it was something circumstance threw upon me. Fate is one curious master. There's nothing for me to do now. Nothing but to thank you for staying with me, until this point at which we now part. You couldn't possibly know how much I've appreciated every single moment of your company. Goodbye.

AN END